Allan Prior wrote his f
Since then he has pul
been translated into r
into television series. \
(over 250 at last coun
BBC's famous *Z Car*
prizes for his television

By the same author

A Flame in the Air
The Joy Ride
The One-Eyed Monster
One Away
The Interrogators
The Operators
Z Cars Again
The Loving Cup
The Contract
Paradiso
Affair
Never Been Kissed in the Same Place Twice
Theatre
The Big March
Her Majesty's Hit Man

ALLAN PRIOR

The Charmer

GRAFTON BOOKS
A Division of the Collins Publishing Group

LONDON GLASGOW
TORONTO SYDNEY AUCKLAND

Grafton Books
A Division of the Collins Publishing Group
8 Grafton Street, London W1X 3LA

A Grafton Paperback Original 1987

ISBN 0-586-20095-9

Printed and bound in Great Britain by
Collins, Glasgow

Set in Times

Author's Note

The Charmer is dedicated to the memory of Patrick Hamilton, who began the story of Ralph Gorse but never finished it. Since I first read *The West Pier* and *Mr Stimpson and Mr Gorse* – novels by Patrick Hamilton which dealt with Gorse's boyhood and early life – I have wondered how he would have ended the story, if he had lived. Sadly, Patrick Hamilton died some years ago, and it was not until last year that I took up my pen and finished the story of Ralph Gorse. Originally, I wrote it as a drama serial for London Weekend Television, but Patrick Hamilton was a novelist, he wrote about Gorse in prose, and somehow I did not feel that the story of Gorse was really ended, really *over*, until it was set up in print. I only hope that Patrick Hamilton would have liked what I have done, but I have no way of knowing! I have to leave the final judgement, as I am sure he would gladly have done, to the reader.

Allan Prior.

Chapter One

A London taxi chugged into the quiet suburban street in Maida Vale.

The moon shone down on the rows of slumbering villas; the curtains were drawn in every house save one. The occupants were all perfectly respectable, and at this hour of the night – it was almost two o'clock – sound asleep.

Ralph Ernest Gorse was not asleep.

He was looking for Number Thirteen.

Number Thirteen had red curtains, and chinks of light showed from behind them. From the house itself came the faint sound of a gramophone, playing the most popular song of that balmy summer of 1938, 'Red Sails In The Sunset'.

The taxi stopped and Gorse got out.

Ralph Ernest Gorse was a tall, golden-haired young man in his thirties.

He was dressed in an opera cloak, white tie, and tails, and he wore a white silk scarf thrown carelessly round his neck. He took from his pocket a gold cigarette case and popped a Turkish cigarette into his mouth.

'Got a light, old boy?' he asked a small, crumpled man of indeterminate age, Ronnie Shooter, his companion. Ronnie Shooter fumbled in his pocket and found a gold lighter. He was very drunk.

Gorse took the lighter, used it, and turned towards Ronnie, but Ronnie was searching in his pockets for the cab fare.

Gorse looked at him for a long moment.

Then he pocketed the gold lighter.

'Got . . . got some change somewhere . . .' gasped Ronnie, his face, like his clothes, a crumpled ruin.

'Here! Try this!' Gorse negligently held out a large white square of what looked like tissue paper.

It was a five-pound note.

The taxi-driver scratched his head. 'Blimey, guv, I ain't got change for that!'

Gorse waved his hand airily. 'Keep it.'

'D'yer mean it, sir?'

Gorse did not even look at him. There was something god-like about Gorse as he stood there, at the end of an evening on the town, in this year of our Lord 1938, his overcoat round his shoulders; and something devil-like too.

The taxi-driver fingered the banknote doubtfully. To him, it represented two weeks' wages.

'Too much! Here!' Ronnie snatched the flimsy fiver back from the outraged taxi-driver and presented him with a silver coin.

''Ere, guv, that's only half-a-crown! The fare's two bob!'

'Sixpence tip, my good man!' retorted Ronnie, swaying slightly and fumbling for a cigarette.

The taxi-driver snorted. 'Thank *you,* sir!' He drove off in the rattletrap taxi.

'Ralph! Here, old boy.' Ronnie tucked the flimsy in the top pocket of Gorse's dinner jacket. 'I told you, my dear chap, this evening's on *me*!' He peered at the house in front of them. 'I say, is this the place?'

Gorse smiled. Or rather, his lips moved. His eyes remained exactly the same. 'Indeed it is, Ronnie, old boy, indeed it is.'

Ronnie Shooter swayed a little. 'The best girls in London, did yer say?'

Gorse clapped him on the back. 'In the world, my dear Ronnie, in the world!'

Ronnie shook his head in wonderment and, unlit cigarette in mouth, followed Gorse up the path to the front door. It opened as they neared it. A maid, not dressed in very much, opened the door. A blast of music came with her.

Ronnie Shooter goggled at those parts of the maid that were open to view. 'I *say*!'

As they entered, Ronnie Shooter first, Gorse closed an eye at the maid; behind them the door closed on the dark night.

Gorse led the way into a rather over-furnished room full of people drinking and smoking. There were several girls in kimonos and very little else. Nobody looked round as they entered. The music was loud, the girls laughed even louder and occasionally a man and a girl paired off – and headed for the stairs. The Madam, a French-sounding cockney called Odette, moved to greet Gorse.

'Ralph . . . How nice to see you . . . It's been ages. Where have you been, you naughty boy?'

Gorse smiled politely. 'Here an' there, y'know, Odette. Here and there. Let me introduce an old friend of mine, Ronnie Shooter . . .'

'Mr Shooter, *enchanté*.'

'What? Oh. Yes. Quite.'

Ronnie Shooter swayed. Then he sat down abruptly on a sofa. Odette smiled at him. Then she looked questioningly at Gorse.

'I think a bottle of your best, Odette . . .? The vintage . . .?'

'*Naturellement* . . . and, what else?'

'And then we'll see, what?' replied Gorse.

'But of course, Ralph. Please sit down.' Odette half-nodded to two girls. They promptly sat on each side of Gorse and Ronnie. Both wore kimonos and black stockings and suspender belts. Gorse looked at them. 'I'll be fine. Look after Ronnie, will you?'

The girls looked at Odette. She nodded. They moved over and sat, one on each side of Ronnie Shooter. Ronnie Shooter beamed. The champagne arrived at that moment and a tough-looking waiter opened it, with a loud pop, at which the girls laughed in mutual appreciation. Odette lingered a moment, to catch Gorse's eye. 'I will be free later, Mr Gorse.' Gorse looked at her a long moment. Then he nodded. Odette smiled and moved about the room, greeting her clients, offering them cigarettes and cigars, now and again dropping her voice to give instruction or advice to one of her girls. None of them was over twenty-five years of age. Lazily, Gorse surveyed the scene. It was one he had seen many times before. He sipped his glass of champagne. It was the vintage. Odette knew him. She knew he would not accept less than the very best. Unless he had to. Well, often in the past he'd had to. 1938 was not an easy year in which to live. It absolutely bloody well was not. Not with four million unemployed breadwinners in the country. Not that Gorse thought of himself as a *bread* winner, exactly. He grimaced. Caviar, perhaps? A caviar winner? That was more his style. But lately things had been hard. Bumping into Ronnie Shooter at the Café Royal had been a godsend. A slice of luck the like of which he hadn't had for a long while.

The thing, as ever, was to make the situation work for you. Just exactly how, Gorse did not yet know. That would no doubt be revealed unto him. It had better be.

The five-pound note he had offered the taxi-driver was all the money, apart from a few shillings of loose change, that Ralph Ernest Gorse had in the whole wide world.

The voice of Ronnie Shooter broke into Gorse's reverie.

'I say, Ralph, you were absolutely right.' Ronnie Shooter beamed at the girls, one on each side of him. 'Best girls in the world, what?'

Gorse smiled.

The boat train to the Continent stood puffing impatiently on Platform One at Victoria Station. Gorse and Ronnie Shooter were saying good-bye.

'I must say, old fellow,' declared Ronnie. 'This is a sad sendoff, what? Sure you won't come?'

Gorse, who still had the five-pound flimsy in his pocket – just that between him and the poor threadbare man who, for a grateful threepenny bit, had staggered over with Ronnie's bags from Gorse's car, parked round the corner – smiled. 'Nothing against Cannes and Monte and all that, Ronnie, but I do have a rather important meeting today.'

Ronnie Shooter's face crinkled even more than usual. It had been a hard night at Odette's establishment in north London. It had been an exhausting one for Gorse, too, but he was getting rather tired of Odette. Her tricks were wearing thin. It was all so mechanical with her. Couldn't be anything else, obviously. The name of the game to Odette was money. Everything she did, she did for money.

Gorse sighed. Well, was he any different?

He had to admit he wasn't.

Without money, there was nothing. Not in the middle of the Depression. Without money you sank without trace, down amongst the Great Unwashed. Gorse shuddered, despite the warmth of the day.

Ronnie Shooter asked, 'You all right, old boy?'

'Bit hung over, that's all, old man.'

Ronnie looked solicitous. 'Jolly decent of you to see me off like this, I must say. Never have managed on my own. Look here. What are your plans now?'

Gorse had no plans.

But he did not say that.

'Have to find myself an hotel for a week or two, I'm afraid.'

'I thought you had this meeting?' Ronnie looked curious.

Gorse smiled, deliberately sheepish. 'Well, I do. But it's not exactly a business meeting, Ronnie. More . . . er . . . personal, do you see?'

Ronnie Shooter saw. Or thought he saw.

'A woman? You're meeting a woman! You dog!'

Gorse smiled, modestly.

Ronnie looked thoughtful. He delved in his pocket and produced a bunch of keys. He deftly detached one and handed it to Gorse. 'Use my place. It's in Reading. A bit inconvenient, I suppose, too far out of town?'

Gorse shook his head. For once he had no words.

'All right. It's yours, long as you want it.' A thought struck Ronnie Shooter. He took out his wallet and extracted a business card. 'This fellow's my property man. Give him a call. Tell him you're moving in.' Ronnie looked along the platform. 'Got to move myself, old boy. See you soonish, say a month or even two. I'll drop a card. Must go, toodle pip!'

Gorse stood there until the boat train pulled out.

Then he walked away, across the station concourse, ignoring the awful spectres of the out-of-work beggars wearing their war ribbons; he brushed past their outstretched palms, not seeing them, not wanting to see them. They were the Great Unwashed and he did not wish to join them, he never would join them, not if brains and cunning and looking after number one would prevent it, by God no!

His step lightened as he remembered that he still had the five-pound note. It wasn't much but it was something. Ronnie had taken care of the expenses of the night. As he reached his battered sports car, Gorse felt more cheerful. He glanced at the business card Ronnie Shooter had given him. It bore a name, *Donald Stimpson, Estate Agent*, and a telephone number.

Gorse decided he would telephone Mr Stimpson, somewhere on the road to Reading.

Things were looking better.

Not good.

But promising, certainly promising.

He started the battered little car and drove off westwards, out of the sunlit morning city.

Donald Stimpson stood amongst the garden gnomes at the front of Ronnie Shooter's detached brick-built house in Reading. Mr Stimpson was soberly dressed, despite the warm sunny weather of that June of 1938, in a suit of dark worsted, with a waistcoat and a stiff white collar. He wore a Macclesfield silk tie and his black leather shoes shone brightly. A dark homburg hat sat squarely upon his head and his eyes glinted behind his spectacles. Donald Stimpson looked at his watch again. He was never late for an appointment and he did not approve of people who were.

This fellow Gorse was twenty minutes late already and there was still no sign of him along the tree-lined suburban avenue. Mr Stimpson, who was by profession an estate agent, and a very successful one (for even in 1938, even in those Depression days, young people still married and needed houses to live in), looked at Byron Avenue and liked what he saw. A row of excellent detached or semi-detached houses, solidly built some twenty years before, each well maintained and freshly painted, with trim front garden to match, and in many cases dotted with the stone gnomes that were such a feature of Ronnie Shooter's own garden.

'Blast this fellow Gorse, whoever he is,' muttered Donald Stimpson. He had been disturbed by Ralph Gorse's call. The whole business was irregular, and Mr Stimpson did not like anything irregular.

The sound of a motorcar engine disturbed the calm of Byron Avenue. No ordinary car engine either. A sports car, a two-seater of battered and ancient vintage, chugged into view.

The driver, Mr Stimpson saw at once, was a young man, with long fair hair blowing about in the turbulence caused by the Railton's progress. Mr Stimpson, who knew little or nothing about motorcars, did not own one (he never had) and considered them a dirty and noisy nuisance, did not know that Gorse's car was a Railton but it was information that Gorse imparted to him in the first moment.

'Sorry I'm late, old boy,' Gorse greeted Mr Stimpson. 'The old bus pulls a bit. Lovely job, the old Railton, but she's seen her best days, this particular one, what?'

Mr Stimpson studied Gorse. He did not like what he saw, not one little bit. He did not like Gorse's camelhair travelling coat, which he wore despite the warm weather. He did not like the grey flannel suit that was revealed when Gorse threw off the camel coat. He did not like the battered and heavily stickered leather case that was propped in the back of Gorse's sports car. He did not like Gorse's voice, which sounded almost upper-class but somehow not quite. He did not like Gorse's smile, which most people, especially women, found quite charming.

In fact, before they had even shaken hands, Mr Stimpson disliked Ralph Gorse in every possible way.

He was not to know that Ralph Ernest Gorse felt exactly the same way about him.

'You said ten o'clock,' observed Mr Stimpson, refusing Gorse's apology.

Gorse seemed not to notice. He gazed at the house – the front door was ajar but revealed nothing. 'Terribly sorry, old boy. As I said, the old bus pulls a bit these days.'

He sounded as if he did not give a damn what Donald Stimpson thought about anything. Mr Stimpson began to like him even less.

'You have the keys, I believe?' he said coldly.

Gorse jingled them in his hand. 'Yes, actually . . . I do.'

Mr Stimpson felt he had to explain himself. 'As you know, my name's Donald Stimpson of Stimpson and Snell, Estate Agents. I act for Mr Shooter in all property matters.' Gorse received this news with a marked lack of enthusiasm. Mr Stimpson went on, 'There are dust sheets in most rooms but I take it you won't be staying long?'

Gorse shrugged. 'Not sure, but not terribly long, I wouldn't think.'

'Have you known Mr Shooter for some time?' persisted Mr Stimpson.

Again, Gorse shrugged. 'A while. Is that a garage?'

Mr Stimpson looked at the garage, which could not be anything but a garage. 'Yes, but Mr Shooter's Alvis is in there, I'm afraid.'

‘An Alvis?’ Gorse looked interested to hear that, anyway, Mr Stimpson noted.

‘I must say all this is a bit irregular, but Mr Shooter is a rather irregular man.’ When Gorse did not reply, ‘Will you need anybody to do for you?’

‘What?’

Mr Stimpson hated that upper-class ‘What?’

‘A maid or anything?’

‘No, no. I’ll just pig along on my own. I expect I’ll eat out a bit.’

Again, Mr Stimpson wondered. ‘What line are you in, Mr Gorse, if I may ask?’

The reply surprised him. ‘Private means,’ said Gorse briefly, taking the battered leather case from the back of the equally battered sports car.

Mr Stimpson looked at Gorse’s shirt, which was frayed at the collar. Gorse looked back at him steadily. ‘Private means? I see,’ said Mr Stimpson, who did not see at all.

Gorse made his way up the path towards the house. At the door he turned. ‘Isn’t there some place called the Friar I should pop into? Ronnie said something about it.’

‘It’s at the end of the road, turn right, can’t miss it.’

‘Jolly good. Thanks very much for your help.’

Mr Stimpson made an offer. ‘I can show you round inside, if you like?’

Gorse refused it. ‘Absolutely not, old boy, I’ll be fine.’

Mr Stimpson hated to be addressed as ‘old boy’. It smacked of public school, which Mr Stimpson had never attended. The local grammar school had had to do, and it had done very well. Just the same, there was something about the public school manner. Gorse had it. Mr Stimpson respected it. But he didn’t like it. ‘Well. If that’s all . . . Mr Gorse?’

‘Yes. I think so. Thank you, Mr Stimpson.’

'You'll let me have the key when you go? Whenever that is?'

'Of course.'

'Then I'll say good morning.'

Gorse dumped the leather case inside the hall of Ronnie Shooter's house. 'Cheerio, old boy,' he said.

Mr Stimpson stared at Gorse for a long suspicious moment. Then he walked back down the path to the gate. At the gate he turned back for a last look at Gorse. Gorse, still at the door, smiled. Mr Stimpson did not smile. He walked off down the road.

Ralph Ernest Gorse watched him go, all the way along the sunny suburban street.

After Gorse had closed the door on Mr Stimpson, he turned to see what kind of place Ronnie Shooter had lent him. It was fine, as far as it went, but a quick perambulation through the rooms of the house told him the sad story. There was nothing whatever, saleable or pawnable, in the place. Dust covers draped the furniture that was left. The rest, the ornaments and trinkets, all the small, valuable things that make up a house – clocks, cutlery, silver ashtrays, glassware, even the sheets and blankets – all gone, obviously, into store. Ronnie Shooter had given him a roof over his head but nothing else. It was a blow, a savage blow, but Gorse was used to savage blows. He lit a Player's Perfecto, taken from his gold cigarette case, which he had stolen he could not remember where, and drew in a lungful of smoke. He could always pawn the case; and yet he couldn't. The case was *him*. How many people, in the Depression, had a gold cigarette case? That was the last thing to go, that and the little sports car. If they went, he really was down amongst the Great Unwashed.

Gorse opened his suitcase. It was full of dirty washing: soiled shirts, rumpled pyjamas, odd socks. He selected a pair of socks and pushed his fingers into one of them. His finger poked through. Gorse sighed and took out his wallet from his jacket. He laid the 'flimsy' fiver on the hall stand and combed his pockets very thoroughly, finding odd coins. He added them up, looking at his own reflection in the mirror on the hallstand. Ralph Ernest Gorse spoke softly to his mirror image. 'Five pounds, six shillings and threepence halfpenny . . . Something, old boy, will have to be done . . .'

The Friar Roadhouse was bad taste baronial. But as Gorse parked the Railton in the car park, he had a sense of familiarity. This was the kind of place he felt at home in, better class than a pub, but not quite a club. He straightened his striped tie and walked briskly towards the door.

In the Nook, off the main bar, sat Joan Plumleigh-Bruce. Joan smoked a cigarette in a holder, and listened idly to Donald Stimpson. Joan was fortyish, good-looking, blonde, plumpish, well-dressed, ever-so-slightly discontented; and she was a snob. In front of her, on the bar, was a *Daily Telegraph*, open at the racing page. She only half takes in what Mr Stimpson is saying. A Pekinese dog circles around her stool. This is Chinklywinkles.

Mr Stimpson is talking, and he is, for a change, somewhat animated. 'I tell you, Joan, there's something very odd about this Gorse fellow. Something very odd indeed, yes.' He blinked through his spectacles at Joan. 'Are you ready for another, dear?' Joan's reply sounded rude but it wasn't really. It is her class manner to sound rude, except to her equals. She does not, strictly speaking, consider Mr Stimpson her equal; but she would not tell him that, ever. 'Another *what*?'

'Another libation, dear.'

Joan relented. The dear man. 'Oh well, why not?'

Mr Stimpson, in his turn, spoke loftily to the barman, Albert. Albert was Mr Stimpson's inferior. 'For Mrs Plumleigh-Bruce!' He turned back to Joan. 'Ronnie Shooter let him have his place, so *he* says, for as long as he likes. Fortunately, there's nothing valuable, it's all in store.'

Joan Plumleigh-Bruce looked interested. 'Didn't he have a letter, this Gorse fellow?'

'He had a *card*, from Ronnie Shooter, that's all.' Joan felt Donald Stimpson needed another lesson in how things were done. 'Donald, *gentlemen* trust each other. My late husband would have done that. Sent a card. It's very Army, that, the card.'

Mr Stimpson grimaced. 'Is it? Well, I wouldn't know about that, but I do know there's something odd about our young Mr Gorse . . . Very odd indeed.' Mr Stimpson felt a touch on his arm, turned round, and there, in close-up, was the face of Ralph Gorse. 'Oh my God . . . !' said Mr Stimpson. In turn, he touched Joan's arm, and it jogged her drink. Joan reacted.

'Donald! You've made me spill my drink!' She saw Gorse. 'Oh?'

Gorse smiled his most charming smile. Joan Plumleigh-Bruce found it very charming indeed. 'All my fault, dear lady,' said Gorse, easily. 'Always creeping up on people. Awful habit, learned it in the Army . . .'

Joan smiled at once, as Gorse somehow knew she would.

'The Army? *Really?*'

Gorse called across to Albert. 'Barman, same again for

these two good people, and I'll have a brandy and soda.' He smiled at Joan.

'Yes, I was in the Frontier Scouts. Too young for the Big Show, so I had to be content with the Frontier, I'm afraid.' He turned to Donald Stimpson. 'Mr Stimpson, how are you?'

Mr Stimpson had hardly recovered but he rallied well. 'May I introduce Mr Ralph Gorse . . . Mrs Joan Plumleigh-Bruce.'

Joan looked surprised. 'Gorse? Really? We were only just . . .'

Mr Stimpson interrupted. 'Yes. Quite . . . Quite.' There was a silence. Gorse broke it, with an apologetic note. 'I say, buying you that drink, a bit off really, I'm sorry. But one can't go by rules and regs all the time, eh, Mrs Plumleigh-Bruce?'

Joan Plumleigh-Bruce looked at Ralph Ernest Gorse for a very long moment and saw all she wanted to see. 'Joan, please. We don't stand on ceremony in The Friar. Do we, Donald?'

'No, I suppose not,' said Mr Stimpson shortly. The barman served Joan with her gin and It, Mr Stimpson with his bitter, and Gorse with his brandy and a soda syphon. Gorse flashed his last fiver very obviously, holding it up for all to see. 'Barman, I say, can you *do* this? I've no change, I'm afraid.'

Joan Plumleigh-Bruce looked at the note with warm approval, Mr Stimpson with deep suspicion. 'I'll just see, sir . . .' As the barman inspected his till and Gorse kept the fiver in full view, Joan felt the need to be friendly. 'I believe you're living in Ronnie Shooter's house, Mr Gorse?'

'For the time being, yes.'

'Looking around for a place of your own?' asked Mr Stimpson meaningly.

Gorse shook his head. 'Oh, I have a place of my own. Trouble is, my mother's in it. Family home.' He went on before Mr Stimpson could ask where. 'In Ireland. Dreadful place, so terribly big . . .' He turned to the barman. 'Get yourself something, will you?'

'A half of bitter, thank you, sir.' The barman accepted the 'flimsy' with deep respect.

'Will you be all right?' asked Joan. 'All on your own, in Ronnie Shooter's huge old place?'

Gorse nodded. 'I expect so. I don't mind my own company. Do you live round here yourself?' Joan hung her head in mock shame. 'Yes. Dreadful, isn't it? The suburbs! I hate them really. Don't know what I'm doing here. When my dear husband was alive, I lived in town, Kensington mostly. Now I just have a little house out here.'

'I see.' Gorse touched the *Daily Telegraph*, lying open on the bar. 'Do I see a racing paper? Don't tell me you have a flutter occasionally?'

Joan smilingly confessed, 'I have to do something or I'd die of boredom in this place. All on my own, you see.'

'No?' Gorse looked surprised. 'Really? You aren't married then? I rather thought you and er . . .' He turned towards Mr Stimpson with a half-salute, holding up his glass in Mr Stimpson's direction.

Joan laughed, a tinkling note in it. 'Donald? No, no. We're "just good friends", aren't we, Donald?'

Gorse persisted. 'But tying the knot one day, eh?' Joan looked down into her gin and It.

'Stranger things have happened, Mr Gorse,' said Donald Stimpson, heavily. 'Stranger things have happened.'

Gorse looked quickly from one to the other. 'Oh, I'm sure . . . Well, cheerio, everybody.' He downed his brandy and soda in one swift swallow and carelessly gathered up his change. 'Well, I must love you and leave you, just popped in for the quick one, y'know.'

Joan looked disappointed. 'Oh, going so soon?'

''Fraid I must, but . . . terribly nice meeting you . . . er . . . Joan. Mr Stimpson.'

Joan smiled, still disappointed. Mr Stimpson looked anything but. Gorse nodded and left the bar. The door closed and he was gone. Joan looked at Mr Stimpson. When she spoke she sounded annoyed. 'Well, that was short and sweet, I must say. Not surprised though, you just standing there glowering like an old bear. Why didn't you get him to stay a bit longer, Donald? You could have offered him a drink or something!'

Mr Stimpson looked at Joan sharply, but he sighed and said nothing.

Joan, Mr Stimpson and Chinklywinkles made their way along the suburban street as they did most evenings after their visit to The Friar. As they approached the gate, Mr Stimpson stepped forward, and opened it with a gallant gesture, as he always did. Joan, however, did not do more than thank him somewhat frostily. Mr Stimpson, put out, followed her and the small dog which, privately, he hated, up the garden path to the door of the neat semi-detached house. Joan's garden contained no gnomes and the curtains were of velour and not linen. Even in suburbia, Joan Plumleigh-Bruce tried to keep up her standards.

At the door, Mr Stimpson hesitated. Normally, he did not hesitate. But tonight was not normal. Tonight had Gorse in it. 'Shall I . . . come in . . . for our usual coffee?'

'Not tonight, Donald,' replied Joan firmly.

'What's the matter?' asked Mr Stimpson, more put out than ever.

'Nothing's the matter. I'm rather fatigued, that's all.' Joan opened the door with her latchkey. 'Nighty'night, Donald.'

But Mr Stimpson was not so easily put off. 'What about my good-night kiss?' Mr Stimpson lunged forward but found himself fended off at once, quite abruptly. 'Donald . . . Really! . . . On the doorstep? Have you quite lost your manners, what do you think I am, a *shopgirl*?'

The door slammed behind her and Mr Stimpson found himself staring blankly at it. No, indeed, this was certainly not a night like any other. Mr Stimpson walked thoughtfully home to his solitary bed. He had been a widower for almost five years now and, to be frank, he was more than a little fed up with that state of affairs. He had, of course, high hopes. Joan Plumleigh-Bruce was the target of those hopes. Mr Stimpson was not an impetuous estate agent and he was not an impetuous lover. But he began to wonder, as he walked through the silent surburban streets, if a little impetuosity was not now more the ticket. Brooding on this, and finding no obvious conclusion, Mr Stimpson heated and drank his Ovaltine and went to bed.

Joan Plumleigh-Bruce's bedroom was a poem in pink. Plump pink eiderdown, pink curtains, pink lampshade at the side of the bed, pink silk nightdress case, pink silk nightdress covering the ever-so-slightly plump form of Joan herself. Now it was ten o'clock and Joan was waking from a rather puzzling dream in which, for some reason, Ralph Ernest Gorse figured. She could not recall details of the dream, except that it had been warm and exciting.

Joan was brought to the present by the appearance of a tray, prepared by Mary, her young, downtrodden Irish 'slavey'. Mary crossed the room to draw the curtains. The light offended Joan, as did the girl's cheerfulness. 'Mornin', mam! It's a nice mornin'. . . !'

Joan replied crossly, 'Don't be after pulling the curtains like that, we aren't in Bally-Go-Been, are we? How many times have I told you – *gently*! Do everything gently in the morning. What time is it?'

'Ten o'clock, mam.'

'My bedjacket!'

'Here y'are, mam!' Mary slipped the bedjacket round Joan's shoulders.

'The pillows, girl! The pillows!'

Mary plumped the pillows behind Joan. 'Not like *that* . . . ! Another!' Mary complied. 'Hmm . . . What's for breakfast?'

'What you said, mam. Poached eggs. Toast . . .'

'Yes, yes. Any letters?'

Mary by now was pouring coffee for Joan. 'Nothing in the post, mam. But there is a letter by hand, mam . . .' She indicated a letter lying on Joan's tray, hidden behind the toast.

'By hand? Who brought it?'

Mary pursed her lips. 'I didn't see him properly, mam, but it was a young man come in a motorcar. He put it through the letter box, mam . . .'

Joan was intrigued. 'Oh? Who? I wonder who would do that?' She opened the envelope and read the contents. 'Well . . . the *nerve* . . .' But she smiled.

Mary hovered. 'Good news is it, mam?'

'None of your business, girl!'

'No, mam. Sorry, mam.'

Joan was still smiling. 'Mary, we have a visitor for coffee, put out the best set! And grind some beans. The best ones. And use the lace doilies . . . All right, get on with it, girl!'

At the door Mary paused, greatly daring. 'Is it Mr Stimpson coming for coffee, mam?'

Joan frowned and her reply was sharp. 'No, it is not, and don't ask so many questions, silly girl. I despair of you sometimes, Mary, I really do! Ten shillings a week and all found, really . . . I don't know if I can afford you sometimes!' Mary was suitably terrified. 'No, mam.'

'It's my good heart. That's my trouble. Well, get *on*, girl!' Mary exited, flustered and not a trifle afraid. If she ever lost this job, what would she do? She thrust the thought from her mind.

Joan sipped her coffee, read the letter through again, and smiled, secretly. The strange dream, perhaps, had been an omen.

One hour later Gorse's Railton drove up to Joan Plumleigh-Bruce's gate. Gorse, carrying a bunch of roses, got out, and looked at the awful semi, for so he regarded it, and grimaced, but only inside. Gorse knew that to show such disappointment would never do. He straightened his striped regimental tie and walked up the path. He rang the bell, and it was answered very promptly by Mary. With a bob, she ushered him into The Presence.

Joan sat, like a Queen of Suburbia, prepared to receive supplicants. Her hair was neatly in place (she always had a 'perm') and her morning frock was worthy of a better setting than Wilton Avenue, Reading. There had been better times, before dear, dear Geoffrey died, and it was nice to remember them. Gorse, like Geoffrey, had plainly been Army. And that put him in a different category from, say, Donald Stimpson. Yes, indeed, a very different category, she thought, noting Gorse's striped tie once more, his elegant, bright brown leather brogues, and his excellent haircut. Obviously, Gorse was not one of the short-back-and-sides brigade but had his hair cut by scissors only, at a decent hairdresser's. Somewhere like Trumper's, no doubt, like dear Geoffrey. Joan sighed for happier days.

Then she remembered her manners. 'Good morning, Mr Gorse. How nice of you to call. And I do appreciate the warning.' Her eyes twinkled as she indicated that Gorse take a seat.

Confident in her make-up, hair, lipstick, powder, full warpaint really, Joan said, 'However, I must say I was surprised, Mr Gorse. I mean, it's not exactly done, is it? So soon?' There was no rebuke, however, in her tone, just an amused curiosity, she hoped. Gorse took the coffee cup, and his eyes met Joan's. Behind her, he saw the silver-framed photograph of the deceased Major Plumleigh-Bruce. He was unable to make out his regiment. He only hoped that Plumleigh-Bruce had never served in India. Mary returned to the room carrying the roses, now prominent in a Waterford vase.

Gorse looked rueful and apologetic. 'I agree. Absolutely. But as we said last night, there are times to be regimental and times when one feels it isn't necessary. This is one of the times.'

Joan looked intrigued. 'Is it? Why?'

'Well . . .' Gorse looked at the hovering Mary.

'Mary, you can go. I'll ring if I need anything,' said Joan.

'Yes, mam.' Mary bobbed and exited.

'Silly girl,' said Joan, 'but you simply can't get good servants these days. With four million out of work you'd think you could, but no. I sometimes think this Hitler has some very good ideas. He makes people work.'

'Yes, I'm sure. I'm not very political myself.'

'Nor I,' said Joan. 'But you were saying . . . Why?'

Gorse looked even more rueful. 'I have to confess, I wanted an excuse to see you again.'

Joan felt she had to be cool to *that*. 'Oh? Really?'

Gorse hurried on. 'Not just for the . . . obvious reasons. But because you showed yourself to be a student of form. Of the Turf. The sport of kings.'

Joan gave a little ground. 'Well, I only have the occasional flutter, you know. Just for fun, as it were.'

Gorse leaned forward. He really was very good-looking, Joan thought. 'Of course, I know that. But you see, when I got back to my place – Ronnie Shooter's place, that is – I was just lying in bed and I thought . . . I wonder if Joan would be interested in coming on a little expedition with me?'

'An expedition? Today?' Joan must have sounded cooler than she intended, for Gorse was instantly apologetic. 'Well, I expect you have a full engagement book and all that but I do have to pop in to see a fellow I know, at a stable, and I thought you might like to come along for a spin?' He smiled. 'I'm sure you can't manage it at such short notice but well, no harm done, nothing ventured and all that sort of thing?'

Joan was, for once, at a loss. 'Now? Do you mean we go *now*?' Gorse consulted his wristwatch. ''Fraid so. It's about an hour or something like that.'

'Well, I really shouldn't, should I? I mean, we hardly know each other, do we?'

Ralph Ernest Gorse moved a little closer, to the very edge of his chair. 'Sometimes, I find, people just get on. I don't mean two hearts that beat as one or any of that, but sometimes, well . . . Do you ever find that, yourself?'

For some reason, Joan found that she was ever so

slightly breathless. 'Yes. I find that . . . sometimes.' There was what seemed to Joan like a very long silence indeed. Gorse broke it.

'And of course, there's always the chance we'll come away with a couple of very good tips! I mean, that's the whole purpose of the exercise, isn't it?'

Joan felt suddenly deflated. '*Is* it?' Gorse smiled, enigmatically. 'Well . . . almost.'

Joan brightened. 'Then . . . then . . . I suppose I must say, yes please, mustn't I?'

Mary stood at the gate and watched Mrs Plumleigh-Bruce and young Mr Gorse drive off in the Railton. Joan had changed into a tweed suit, and there had been a lot of fuss about that, finding matching accessories like stout brown shoes and a suitable scarf and all that. Mary was more than glad to see the back of them, although she liked young Mr Gorse, whom she already regarded as a proper gentleman. Mr Gorse said thank you and he had remembered her name. Mrs Plumleigh-Bruce rarely thanked her for anything but that was the way she was. There were plenty of worse employers, Mary knew. Still, she wished she were back in Dublin, even if there were ten of them to the three rooms. There had been warmth there, and love. There was precious little of that commodity in Wilton Avenue. She looked up from her reverie to see Mr Stimpson staring at her. 'Was that your mistress just gone off in that car?'

'Oh . . . Yes, sir. Indeed it was, Mr Stimpson.'

'Who was the man with her?'

'Why, sir . . . That was Mr Gorse, sir.'

Donald Stimpson looked anything but pleased.

* * *

Joan Plumleigh-Bruce sat in Gorse's Railton and rather impatiently watched Gorse talking to a stable lad. The lad was fifty, small and weatherbeaten. Behind him a couple of horses were being led around the stable yard. Joan saw Gorse put his hand in his pocket and a coin changed hands. She had no idea why. If she had known she might have been surprised.

Gorse was saying, 'Thanks, anyway.'

'What for, sir?' grinned the lad. 'I never told you anythin'.'

Gorse looked alarmed. 'Just pretend you did!'

'What, sir?'

Gorse clapped him on the back, jocularly. 'Come over and say hello to the lady. Oh, and call me Captain Gorse. All right?'

The stable lad grinned again. 'For half-a-crown, sir, I'll call you anythin' you like, sir.'

Joan watched the two men as they walked back towards the car.

Gorse made a gesture of disappointment. ''Fraid we can't do an inspection of stables today, Joan. They've got the vets in. Have to be another time.'

Joan was downcast. 'Oh dear, and I was so looking forward . . .'

Gorse climbed into the sports car and started the engine. 'Never mind; Paddy here's been very helpful, eh Paddy?'

'I reckon so, Captain Gorse,' said that worthy, stoically.

'Very helpful indeed, I must say . . . Well, thank you Paddy . . . And see you next time.'

'Yes, *Captain* Gorse, and thank *you*, sir.' Paddy's face was very straight. Gorse merely nodded. 'Good-bye,' said Joan, ever gracious to the lower orders, anyway in company.

The stable lad touched his cap with a forefinger. 'Ma'am.'

'Wasn't it all a waste of time?' asked Joan, as Gorse drove the Railton back towards the main road. 'Tell you after lunch, my dear,' replied Gorse, placing his free hand on hers. Joan was thrilled. It was the only word. Thrilled.

Two and a half hours later Joan and Gorse were at the end of a splendid late lunch. They had drunk the bottle of champagne Gorse had insisted on buying on the way back and now they were on brandies. Gorse selected a cigar, offered by Joan, who was slightly tiddly. She was also somewhat loquacious. 'Well, it's not very often I finish lunch at four o'clock, Ralph, I must say. But I got so hungry, that long drive back! The champagne made it worthwhile, though.' Gorse lit the cigar correctly, allowing the tobacco to catch alight first from the match's flame then, and only then, drawing on it. 'Well, once in a while, no harm done. Least I could do.'

Joan leaned forward and patted his hand. 'You are awful, you know, Ralph, you spoil a girl.' Gorse drew on the Corona. 'Capital cigar, I must say, Joan.' Joan inhaled the aroma of the cigar. 'My late husband used to smoke them. I always keep a few in. But nobody around here smokes them. They're all so dreadfully surburban.' She laughed. 'Not even Donald, and he'll try anything – y'know, I shouldn't say this – but he'll try anything if it's free!'

Gorse laughed tolerantly. 'Well, why not?'

Joan persisted. 'No, but really, he isn't *poor*, he has an excellent business. I mean, I don't know anything about business, but everybody says so. He's a widower, you know . . .'

Gorse waved the cigar. 'No, I didn't know, actually.'

Joan grimaced. 'Married a bit of money, just trade, the lady of course . . . Wouldn't mind doing it again, I rather fancy.'

Gorse looked surprised. 'Who? Old Stimpson? And *you*?' he laughed. 'I don't believe it!'

'Well, yesterday in The Friar, you *thought* we were . . .' she twinkled.

Gorse pressed her hand in return. 'I didn't know you then, did I?'

'And you do now?'

'Oh yes. I do now.' Their eyes locked. Gorse broke away and offered Joan a cigarette from his gold case. He lit it with his lighter – or rather Ronnie Shooter's lighter – after she had put her Abdullah in her cigarette holder. Joan inhaled the exotic Turkish tobacco. 'I don't know . . . Today reminded me so very much of the old days. My husband, the Major, he loved his horses, y'know . . . It took me back, really it did.'

'Oh, was he cavalry?' asked Gorse.

'No, Service Corps actually, but he loved horses.'

Gorse resisted the impulse to smile. Instead, his voice solicitous, he asked, 'He passed on . . . your husband . . . suddenly?'

Joan sighed. 'Well . . . the heart, you know.'

Gorse was tentative, probing. 'Ah? And only an Army pension . . . I suppose? That's too bad.'

Joan demurred. 'No, he had . . . a little *other* money. I'm not exactly poor, you know. Even if I'm not exactly rich.'

Gorse drew on his cigar. 'Oh, I know all about *that*. There's family money in my crowd, but one has to wait one's turn. Knowing it's there helps, though.'

Joan was, again, intrigued. 'Is your family money in *trade*?'

Gorse emphatically denied that slur. 'Good Lord, no. It's City money. Broking house. That kind of thing.'

Joan was impressed. 'The City? Then you'd know about investments?'

There was a long silence while Gorse looked suitably serious. 'Well, my cousins do. They're at Lloyds and all that. They put me in the way of a good thing from time to time. But I find talk of money boring, don't you?'

Joan did not but she said, 'Yes . . . Yes . . . Of course. But I would be interested . . . If you ever heard about anything special?'

'Well, naturally . . . one shares these things with friends . . .' said Gorse. Again their eyes met. Joan, this time, broke the spell. 'Well, what did you learn? I mean, did that stable boy give you anything?'

Gorse looked startled, then recovered. 'Good Lord. Yes, he did actually, a horse running later this week.'

'No! What's its name?'

Gorse looked mysterious. 'I'm going to put five pounds on in your name. As well as my own investment. And if it wins, you win.'

'But that's not fair!' exclaimed Joan.

'I insist,' said Gorse firmly. 'I brought the information to you. If the horse lost, I'd be . . . devastated.'

Joan was mock-reluctant. 'Well, I don't know . . . really.'

Gorse held up his hand. 'Allow me my little whim . . . in payment for a wonderful day . . . which I hope will never end . . . but which must, of course . . .'

Joan cried, 'You're not *going*? Not already?'

Gorse relented. 'Well . . . not until I've finished this splendid cigar, anyway!' He held it up for inspection. It looked extremely phallic.

Joan responded. 'Oh, you are a naughty boy, Ralph Gorse.' She could not remember when she had been so happy.

It is early morning. Nothing is astir in the suburban street as Gorse comes, very quietly, out of Ronnie Shooter's front door. He is fully dressed, in his grey flannel suit. Gorse looks up and down the slumbering suburban street. Nothing, not a light anywhere. Gorse walks quietly towards the garage, stumbling over a lurking gnome. He curses, but under his breath. We now see he has a poker in his hand. With a wrench – and some small noise – he breaks the padlock on the garage door. Gorse is still, and listens. But there is only silence. Gently, he opens the garage doors. There, in a shaft of light, stands the splendid Alvis. Gorse quickly searches for, and finds, the starting handle. He swings. After a moment the engine starts. Gorse gets into the Alvis and backs it down the drive. Then he gets out and swiftly closes the garage door, again very quietly. Then, back in the Alvis again, he drives – without lights – away down the suburban street.

An hour later, we find Gorse in the yard of a secondhand-car dealer in north London. It is still only six-thirty and the car dealer is a very surprised man. He is forty years old and his face is unshaven and sleepy. He has an overcoat thrown over his pyjamas as he walks into the yard. His accent is London lowlife, as he complains to Gorse, 'It had better be a good machine, wakin' me up at this time o' the mornin'.'

'Oh, it is! There!' Gorse indicates the Alvis, in all its glory. The car dealer looks at it, thoughtfully.

'How hot is it?'

'It needs a coat of paint and new plates, that's all.'

The car dealer is amused. 'Thass all, he sez. Who gave yer my name?'

Gorse replied, 'I heard it somewhere, I forget.'

This pleases the car dealer. He does not care for people who name names. 'Hmm. I don't want it, matey. Too good. Too new. Too risky. Sorry.'

Gorse is unperturbed. 'You'd make yourself a nice profit. I'm giving it away.'

The car dealer relents. 'What kind of money are we talkin' about then?'

'A hundred.'

'Fifty.'

'Seventy-five.'

'Sixty. And thass it.'

Gorse debates. 'All right, sixty. But one condition.'

'Oh, and wass that?'

'I want you to drive me back where I came from. In your own car. Take you an hour.'

'What, now?'

Gorse smiles. 'Not quite to the door, naturally.'

The car dealer looks at Gorse again, this time with grudging respect. ''Ere! You goin' back where you nicked it from? Dear oh dear! You're a cool closet, incher?' He shakes his head and counts out six ten-pound notes from a roll in his grimy hand. 'Sixty sheets, right!'

Gorse takes the roll of flimsies and smiles.

In The Friar Roadhouse, Albert the barman is calling, 'Time, ladies and gentlemen! Your last orders, please!'

Joan Plumleigh-Bruce and Mr Stimpson are at the bar. Their 'usual' is in front of them. Joan has her spectacles on and is perusing the *Telegraph* racing page. Mr Stimpson is somewhat aggrieved, and is showing it. 'Joan, I must ask you again. Where did you go with young Gorse yesterday?'

Joan looks up at him, rather irritably. 'I told you, Donald. We went to see some racing people Ralph knows.'

'Oh, it's Ralph now, is it?' asks Mr Stimpson.

Joan replies mildly, 'Well, why not, he's a friend, isn't he?'

'Not of mine, he isn't. We don't know the first thing about him!'

Joan pouts. 'Yes, we do. He's a pal of Ronnie Shooter's. He was in the Army – which is more than can be said of some people.'

'It is well known,' says Mr Stimpson, 'that I have flat feet – that's why I was never called up.'

Joan does not seem to hear that. '*And* he has City connections, too. Ralph, I mean.'

'I'll bet,' replies Mr Stimpson rather dourly. This nettles Joan. 'Now what does that remark mean, Donald?'

'Nothing. Nothing at all.'

Joan persists. 'You snipe so at Ralph, and I can't think why.'

'No, I don't suppose you can.'

'Honestly, I do believe you're jealous, Donald.'

Mr Stimpson reacts. 'What, of Gorse?' But, as Mr Stimpson says that, Gorse comes into the Nook. He walks towards Joan Plumleigh-Bruce and Donald Stimpson as if he has known them all his life. 'Evening, everybody. The usual, Albert. For all three of us, what?' Gorse indicates to Albert that he means drinks for Joan and Mr Stimpson, too.

Joan responds. 'Oh, how sweet of you, Ralph.'

'Right away, Mr Gorse!' says Albert.

'Captain Gorse, Albert,' says Joan.

'Eh? Oh, sorry, Mrs Plumleigh-Bruce.'

Mr Stimpson is not impressed. 'Captain? Of what, I wonder?' he mutters.

Joan hisses, 'Donald. Try to be a gentleman, do!'

Gorse turns back from the bar and smiles at Mr Stimpson. Mr Stimpson nods at Gorse, reluctantly. After all, the fellow is buying the drinks. 'I hear you had a day out? With Joan?' he ventures.

Gorse is enthusiastic. 'Oh, rather! We have made a profit, too!' Gorse pulls three fivers from his wallet and places them on the counter in front of Joan 'One, two, three! A fiver invested at three to one!'

Joan goggles at the money. 'You mean this is *mine*?'

'Nobody else's.'

'But what was the *horse*?' asks Joan.

'Soldier's Story in the Third at Windsor,' replies Gorse promptly.

At this, Joan looks at Gorse with shining eyes. 'Well . . . I must say! That's wonderful, Ralph!'

Gorse puts a finger along his nose. 'Just inside information, that's all.'

Mr Stimpson is meanwhile trying to make sense of all this. He first addresses Joan. 'Do you mean that you didn't *know* the name of the horse?'

'Well, of course I didn't, hasn't Ralph just said so?'

Mr Stimpson then turns to Gorse. 'That's a bit of a risk, isn't it? Putting somebody's money on a horse without telling them you're doing it?'

But Joan is ecstatic. 'Oh shush, Donald, you don't understand these things! Ralph got the information and he acted on it. He'd hardly give me his own money, would he? Is that what you're saying?'

Even Mr Stimpson is not saying *that*. 'Well . . . no . . . I suppose not.' But he glowers into his beer.

Joan will not be denied. 'Well, then! I rather think this calls for a celebration, you know. Let's book a table for supper tomorrow evening – it's too late for tonight . . .' Joan glances at her watch. 'I say . . . is *that* the time?'

''Fraid so. Must go soon, myself,' says Gorse.

Joan takes his arm, fondly. 'You're always in a rush aren't you, Ralph? You should slow down a bit. Coming in here at the last moment, with all this money, well, I don't know what we'll have to do with you! Eh, Donald?'

Mr Stimpson merely grunts.

Gorse pats Joan's hand. 'Never mind, there's always tomorrow.'

Joan is by now, whether by excitement or alcohol or both, somewhat tiddly. 'Yes . . . so there is, isn't there?' Joan's tiddly look is noted by Mr Stimpson. 'I'll walk you home, dear,' he offers.

But Joan, recognizing the smallest hint of criticism in his voice, declares, 'Indeed you will not, Donald. I'll take a taxi. Albert, is there a taxi outside?'

'Yes, Mrs Plumleigh-Bruce,' says Albert.

'Go out and get it for me, will you, Albert, there's a good boy.'

'At once, madam,' replies Albert, and goes from the bar.

Mr Stimpson is petulant. 'But I always walk you home, dear.'

'Well, this will make a nice change. And it's raining.'

'Then I'll come with you in the taxi.'

Joan gathers up her winnings – all that money! – and crams them into her crocodile handbag. 'No, I will go home, to my chaste bed, by myself. Won't I, Ralph?'

Gorse nods, deadpan. 'I'm sure . . . Goodnight, Joan.'

'Goo'night, Ralph. Goo'night . . . Donald . . . Toodle-oo!' and she shakes off Mr Stimpson's guiding hand, and goes out of the Nook, pulling at Chinklywinkles, as Albert holds open the door.

Mr Stimpson is upset. 'Well! She's never done that before. I always walk her home.'

'Expect she was a bit excited, that's all,' said Gorse.

'Yes, I suppose that was it.'

Gorse looks long at Mr Stimpson, then he asks, 'I say, will you have the other half, while there's time?'

Mr Stimpson hesitates, then remembers it's free. 'Well . . . the other half *would* be acceptable, thank you.'

Gorse turns to the barman. 'I know you're closing, but a large whisky for Mr Stimpson and I'm all right.'

'Certainly, Captain Gorse.'

Mr Stimpson has by now sat down in the Inglenook. The other regulars are drinking up their last orders. Gorse carries his drink across and sits down. Mr Stimpson accepts his drink with a nod. 'Captain?. . . It's useful that. Rank. Sounds good.'

'Well, I don't know. Can't say it helps much really,' replies Gorse.

'In India, were you? In the Army?'

'That's right.'

Mr Stimpson is sad for the things he has missed. 'Led a fairly . . . wild life out there, I s'pose?'

'The usual. Too much drinking. Too many adventures with . . . the fair sex. The usual thing. You know how it is, old boy.'

'Really?' says Mr Stimpson, who most emphatically does not know how it is, and this Gorse realizes. Now begins his seduction of Mr Stimpson. 'Not much else to do out there, you see.'

Mr Stimpson downs his large whisky. 'No. I don't suppose so.'

Gorse leaned forward. 'Er, Donald . . . look, may I call you Donald?'

'Well, I suppose so.' Mr Stimpson lights a cigarette with just a little bit of difficulty. This Gorse notices. 'Donald, I know you think I'm being a bit, well, forward, with Mrs Plumleigh-Bruce.'

Mr Stimpson considers. 'Yes. You could say I think that, yes.'

'Well . . . I might as well tell you the truth . . . I am somewhat smitten with her.'

Mr Stimpson focuses on Gorse's face, with no little difficulty. 'Are you?'

'Yes . . . Yes, I am . . . But I realize she isn't for me.'

Mr Stimpson is pleasantly surprised. 'You do?'

Gorse shrugs. 'Well, of course . . . I mean, I'm just, as it were, passing through this place . . . I'll be gone in a week or two. Pastures new and all that. It's the way I live, I'm afraid. Footloose and fancy free.'

Mr Stimpson struggles to grasp the point. 'You mean you're leaving soon?'

'Have to. Other commitments.'

'Ah. Commitments. I see.'

'The family firm have a job fixed up for me. Abroad somewhere, for a bit, anyway. Paris, probably.'

'Paris?' echoes Mr Stimpson.

Gorse shows regret. ''Fraid so. Of course Paris has its compensations. If you follow me.' Gorse picks up Mr Stimpson's glass and crosses to the bar. 'Albert, can you break the law for once, and put a large scotch in that for Mr Stimpson?'

'I say, not another, Gorse, really!' protests Donald Stimpson.

But the barman is saying, 'I think I might just manage that for you, Captain Gorse,' and Gorse is answering,

'Awfully good of you, Albert.' He pays, gestures for the barman to keep the change and takes the glass over to Mr Stimpson. 'There you are, old boy, one for the road, what?'

Mr Stimpson stares up at him, somewhat blearily. 'Well. I must say . . . Jolly decent of you, Gorse.'

'*Ralph*, please.'

'Ralph.' Mr Stimpson drinks, looks a trifle more blearily at Gorse. 'Y'know. I love Joan. Really.'

Gorse is interested to hear that. 'Well, she's a lovely lady.'

Mr Stimpson looks at his empty glass. 'I worship her. That's more the word. She's a *real* lady, Joan. Much above me. Not that I don't have hopes of . . . that one day . . . I do. But it's the waiting.' Mr Stimpson sighs. 'I've been a widower too long, Ralph. Too long. One gets lonely. One gets to miss the feminine comforts, yes . . .'

'Hard cheese, old chap,' whispers Gorse.

Mr Stimpson agrees. 'It is, it *is* . . . and yet . . . you know . . . I'm not exactly without some . . . comfort . . . Joan and I . . . we're very good friends.'

'Really? I'm glad.'

'But . . . of course . . . she's a lady. And ladies won't go the Whole Hog.'

'The Whole Hog?'

Mr Stimpson holds up a warning finger. 'Mind you, she certainly kisses. She goes the limit there all right! She goes the Whole Hog when it comes to kisses. And she might go the Whole Hog altogether if she's handled in the right way. Y'follow?'

Gorse follows only too well. But he simply nods. Mr Stimpson on the other hand, feeling he has possibly said too much, asks, 'But where were we?'

'Paris,' replies Gorse promptly.

'Paris! I envy you. All the fun of the fair sex, as it were!'

Gorse is a long time answering. When he does he is careful to sound extremely casual. 'Of course, one doesn't need to go all the way to Paris . . .'

'No?'

'London,' says Gorse.

'London?' echoes Mr Stimpson.

Gorse lowers his voice. 'Matter of fact, just between you and I, old man, I'm going up there tonight. Going to walk out of here, get into my little bus and drive sedately for one hour to a very special place I know.'

Mr Stimpson is astounded. 'You *are*?'

'Absolutely French. The Genuine Thing. One Hundred Per Cent.'

'*Is* it?'

'And those girls! Well, I needn't tell *you*, man of the world as you are.'

'French girls are we talking about?' asks Mr Stimpson longingly.

Gorse looks at his watch. 'Naturally . . . I don't suppose you'd like to join me? I mean, simply as an observer, as it were. I mean, simply to keep me company. It gets a bit lonely on the drive back.'

Mr Stimpson can hardly believe this. 'You mean . . . you're going up there tonight? And you'll be back tomorrow morning?'

Gorse is reassuring. 'Back at the crack of dawn, dear boy. Couldn't persuade you, I don't suppose?' He lowers his voice even more. 'Nobody to know. Nice little car trip. Bit of fun. Back at the old desk tomorrow morning first thing. Nobody the wiser. What d'you say? Are you game?'

Mr Stimpson is adamant. He shakes his head. 'No. No.

I couldn't. Not possibly. No, no. Thank you. But really I absolutely couldn't. No.'

Gorse says nothing to any of that.

It is one hour later and Gorse's Railton is parked outside the house in Maida Vale. Mr Stimpson holds Gorse's silver flask, from which he has been imbibing. Gorse gets out and gestures to Mr Stimpson to do the same. Mr Stimpson peers at the house – and its red curtains – doubtfully.

'Is *this* it?'

'Indeed it is, Donald, old boy.'

Mr Stimpson is unimpressed. 'It doesn't *look* very French to me.' He follows Gorse up the path. As they reach the door, it opens. Mr Stimpson goggles at the maid. She wears very little and looks very French indeed. Gorse stands back and ushers Mr Stimpson inside. As they walk into the parlour, the scene is much as it was when he had been there with Ronnie Shooter a week before. There are scantily clad girls, and prosperous-looking clients. There is jazz music. And there is Odette. She greets Gorse with a smile. 'Why, Mr Gorse, this is a nice surprise, *mon cher*.'

'I hope so, Odette . . . I have brought a very special friend with me . . . Odette, this is Mr Stimpson.'

'Welcome, Mr Stimpson.'

'Er . . . just er . . . Donald. Please,' asks Mr Stimpson uneasily. He is feeling, if truth be told, very uneasy about the whole thing.

Odette smiles. '*Naturellement*, Donald. That is a lovely name, I always think. Donald, please to sit 'ere next to me . . .' Mr Stimpson does as he is bid. Odette addresses Gorse.

'Did you 'ave anything special in mind tonight?'

Gorse debates, then: 'Well, Donald rather thought . . . something French?'

Odette looks at Mr Stimpson. 'Oh, he is a very naughty boy, Donald, I can see that!'

Mr Stimpson smiles weakly. 'No. Really. I . . . well . . . perhaps. Sometimes. On occasion, as they say.'

Gorse looks at Odette. She laughs throatily. Mr Stimpson accepts a glass of champagne from Odette, taken from a passing tray. The bubbles get up his nose and he has a coughing fit. When it has passed, Odette has moved away and is talking to Gorse, and in her place is a much younger girl, whose name, she confesses, is Fifi. Mr Stimpson looks at her through his thick spectacles, and likes what he sees. He likes it very much indeed.

It was four o'clock in the morning and Ralph Ernest Gorse was out to the world.

He lay stretched out on the sofa in Odette's now deserted parlour, and snored gently. He still wore his white evening shirt and black trousers, but his dinner jacket hung on the back of a chair and his patent leather shoes had been kicked carelessly to the floor.

The lights were low and the scene looked cosy, almost domestic.

All this the girl saw as she tiptoed into the room.

The light from a table-lamp glinted on the golden hair of the sleeping man, who was very handsome.

The girl stood, quite still, watching him for a long moment.

Then she shivered.

It was odd to do that, she thought. The room was warm. It was a soft and balmy summer night. Just the same, for a moment she felt very cold, as if a chill breeze had somehow filtered through the room.

The man moved in his sleep.

Then he wakened.

His eyes looked at her.

The girl shivered again. She did not move.

The man spoke. 'What time is it?'

He might have been talking to a servant.

'Four o'clock,' the girl said.

The man raised himself on one elbow. 'Do I know you?'

'I don't think so.'

'New, are you?' He grunted and tasted the coffee in the pot. It was cold. He grimaced. 'Well-spoken, for this place.'

The girl said, 'Yes, I suppose I am.'

He looked at her afresh. 'Helps, I suppose.'

'Yes, rather.' She shivered again.

'What's your name?'

'Clarice.'

The man laughed. 'Odd name for a tart, Clarice?'

'Yes, I suppose it is.' The girl did not move.

The man said, 'Aren't you busy tonight?'

'No.' The girl added, 'You?'

'I have special tastes.'

The girl caught her breath. 'Really?'

'Yes . . . what about you?'

'Oh . . . I'm adaptable.'

Gorse said, 'Couldn't get a job, had to go on the game, I suppose that's your story?'

'No, I just like it.'

'You do?'

'Yes, normally I do.'

Gorse sat up, very lazily. 'Why don't you come over here and sit down? I'm not going to bite you.'

Slowly, the girl did as she was told.

Sitting next to him, she saw his eyes were blue and cold, like the sky on a clear winter day.

'Now you know all about me,' she said, 'what about you?'

Gorse did not reply, except to say, 'Expensive dress?'

'A present.'

'Of course.' Gorse grimaced. 'Nice haircut, close to your head, suits you.' He looked slightly perplexed. 'You know, you really do look like a lady.'

'Do I?'

Gorse looked at the dark close-cropped hair, the jewellery, the dress, the large cool eyes. He shook his head and grimaced. 'Must be the light. You couldn't very well be a lady, in this place, could you?'

'No, I couldn't, could I? Why are you here? I mean . . . *asleep*?'

'I'm with somebody currently engaged upstairs.'

'Snap!'

'What?'

'So, aren't you interested in girls?'

Gorse looked at her a long moment. 'Sometimes I am. If they're the right type.'

Clarice steps forward and her legs show in the light. Gorse looks at them. Clarice stands up. Slowly her dress falls to the floor. 'Do you think I might be the right type?'

'Perhaps.'

Clarice sits beside Gorse on the sofa, clad only in her dark blue slip and her sheer silk stockings, with the suspenders at the top. 'What,' she asks, 'do you do?'

'Well, I had a job selling second-hand cars on commission, in Brighton, which I lost two weeks ago.'

'And what do you do *now*?' Clarice starts to undo his tie.

'Well, I can tell you one thing. I don't mean to starve . . . whoever else does!'

'I suppose there's always the dole?' Clarice unbuttons his shirt.

Gorse does nothing. He watches her. 'Seventeen shillings a week for a single man. Just about buy you a decent shirt.'

Clarice laughs gently as they start to kiss. She whispers, 'Shame!'

'Yes, isn't it?' Gorse, by now, is tying Clarice's wrists with his necktie – her hands have just finished pulling his shirt open. Clarice looks at Gorse wide-eyed but she is not afraid.

'I expect you'll survive.'

'Yes. I expect I will . . . somehow.' Gorse kisses her on the mouth and at the same time stretches her arms over her head, hooking her tied hands onto the corner of the sofa. '*Now*,' says Ralph Ernest Gorse with satisfaction. 'Now, let us see, shall we?'

Three hours later, at seven o'clock in the morning to be exact, Mr Stimpson wakes up, yawns, and realizes where he is. In an upstairs room at the sporting house in Maida Vale, and alone. A scent of cheap perfume hangs in the air and Mr Stimpson grimaces, repelled. He finds and puts on his woollen longjohns. Slowly, he gets out of bed and at that moment realizes his head is on fire. He gropes for his trousers and pulls them on, followed by his shirt, collar and tie. He reaches in his jacket and realizes his wallet is gone. Slowly, Mr Stimpson sits on the edge of the bed. His head is now a thumping, fiery ball of pain. His mouth tastes gritty and Mr Stimpson would do a great deal to cancel out the events of the night. He knows he cannot do that, so he emits a very long painful sigh which, to his shame, turns into a sob. Mr Stimpson sits there a very long time.

In Odette's parlour, Gorse is lying on the sofa. He is asleep. The room is still dark, but now the maid comes in and opens the curtains. Gorse stirs. He is attired only in his shirt and trousers. The rest of his clothes are scattered about the room. The maid picks them up, expertly, and lays them on a chair.

'G'morning, sir.'

Gorse feels his head. He has no headache. In fact, he feels surprisingly well. 'What's the time?'

'Seven o'clock, sir.'

'Oh, my God . . . Is it? What . . .?' Gorse looks at the maid and, very softly, laughs. 'Quite a night!'

'I imagine it was, sir.'

Gorse stands up and slowly puts on his jacket. 'Quite a girl, that one, Clarice.'

'Well. Not the usual, anyways,' says the maid, enigmatically.

Gorse remembers the proprieties. 'Is she around? I don't think I paid her.'

The maid sniggered. 'I don't think that's necessary, sir.'

Gorse stared at her. 'Why not?'

'She doesn't work here, sir. She came here to get her brother. He's a bit wild – *you'll* know how some men are, sir – and she came to take him home.'

Gorse, for once, is astounded. 'You mean she really *is* a lady?'

'Oh yes, sir . . . I disremember her name, though.'

Gorse unblinkingly holds out a half-crown. 'No, you don't, do you?'

The maid snaps up the coin. 'Miss Clarice Mannors, I

just remembered.' She makes her way out of the room. 'I'll just get you some hot coffee, sir.'

Slowly, thoughtfully, Gorse begins to put on his tie. At that moment Mr Stimpson bursts into the room. He is unshaven and in his shirtsleeves, and looks very distraught. 'I say, Gorse, a terrible thing, my wallet's gone!'

Gorse is still thinking about the girl. 'No. Here. I kept it for you.' Gorse hands it over, his mind still working.

Mr Stimpson grasps the wallet like a lifeline. 'You are a very decent fellow, y'know that, Gorse?' He grimaces. 'Oh, my head! How did you go on, old boy?'

'I'm not absolutely sure . . .' says Gorse, who isn't.

Mr Stimpson holds his head, and Gorse passes him a bottle of the morning-after 'pick-up' (ingredients: brandy, tomato juice, peppermint) that always graces the breakfast tables at Odette's establishment. 'Here, try this!'

Mr Stimpson did and grimaced even more. After a moment he said, 'Y'know, I rather enjoyed myself, Ralph.'

'That's the general idea, Donald old boy.' Gorse was still not entirely awake. The events of the night were still in his head.

Mr Stimpson sighed. 'Yes, I suppose so . . . How did you really go on, old boy?'

Gorse shook his head. 'Not sure.'

'Doesn't sound like you,' Mr Stimpson grunted.

'Well . . . It was all rather special,' said Gorse. And that was all he did say.

The Railton, containing Gorse and Mr Stimpson, turned into the quiet suburban road and came to a stop in front of Ronnie Shooter's home. It was still only eight o'clock and the road was quiet. Most male householders worked locally in white-collar jobs and left home as late as possible. Mr Stimpson looked blearily at his pocket-watch. Thank God he lived alone, and it was not one of his cleaning woman's days to call. He must get a wash and shave and change into another shirt before going to his office. He began to regret coming to this place first. He said as much. 'I say, it's awfully nice of you to offer me a snifter, but really I'd better get home and get washed and brushed up.'

But Gorse has already gone ahead of him and opened the garage doors. What he sees makes him stand stock-still. So much so that Mr Stimpson asks, 'What *is* the matter, old boy?'

'Hold on a minute! It's *gone*!' cries Gorse. It is an excellent performance. 'What?' asks Mr Stimpson. 'What's gone?'

Gorse looks at him, as if shocked. 'The Alvis! Ronnie Shooter's car! It's gone! Somebody's broken the garage lock and taken it!'

Mr Stimpson stares at Gorse and then at the empty garage. 'I'm really not up to this,' he says hollowly. 'Let's go inside and talk about it.'

Gorse opens the front door and they go through to the kitchen, Gorse saying, 'I can't believe it, it's impossible!' and Mr Stimpson saying nothing at all, he is so shocked and shaken. So much so, he sits down, his head in his hands.

Finally, Gorse reaches a conclusion. 'Somebody must have taken it last night!'

'Last night? Yes I suppose so,' says Mr Stimpson. 'Oh, my God! What will Ronnie say?'

'That's hardly the point, is it?' asks Gorse. 'It's what the police will say. We *have* to tell the police, I suppose?'

Mr Stimpson is alarmed. 'If we do that, do we have to tell them where we've been all night?'

Gorse is pensive. 'I don't see how we can avoid it, old boy.'

Mr Stimpson is desperately remorseful and shows it. 'What a mess! What a bloody awful mess! . . . What can we *say* to the police?'

Gorse studies the man. This, he reflects, is the tricky bit. 'It is a bit difficult, I agree. I mean, they don't know me, you're a local bigwig, I'd need you for an alibi, I'm afraid. Wish I didn't, but there it is. We'll just have to own up and tell the truth.' Mr Stimpson is more shattered than ever. 'If I do that it would get out and I'd be ruined in this town! Absolutely ruined! Finished!'

Gorse shakes his head. 'And I don't suppose we could keep it from Joan, either . . .'

This is too much, too much altogether for Mr Stimpson. 'Joan? Oh, yes! My God! Joan! It doesn't bear thinking about . . . Why did we go? It was madness! I'm ruined, finished, Gorse, absolutely finished.' He lapses into silence, contemplating nothing except ruin.

Gorse muses. 'How long had Ronnie Shooter *had* that car?'

'I don't know. About a year,' answers Mr Stimpson, apathetically.

Gorse looks at Mr Stimpson a long moment. Then: 'Look, it's only an idea and I'm not sure if I can do anything about it, but . . . well . . .'

Stimpson responds eagerly. 'What, *what*?'

'Well,' says Gorse, 'I know some people in the motor trade. We might find a replacement – an exact replacement, same year, same colour . . .'

'Are you serious? *Could* it be done?'

Gorse looks dubious. 'I don't know until I talk to people but I daresay it could. I mean, there's no point in just lying down and dying, is there?'

'What about numberplates, even if you got the exact model? Do you *know* the exact model?'

Gorse is prompt to reply. 'It's an Alvis dropped-head coupé, white, 1935.'

'You *do* know?'

'Trouble is,' says Gorse, 'we'd have to pay full retail price . . . Three hundred or so.'

Mr Stimpson winces, then, 'Well . . . Do it! If you can. Anything!'

Gorse hesitates. 'Only if you're sure?'

'I'm sure, I'm sure. Ring this friend, try it, for God's sake, Ralph!'

Gorse raises his hands, palms outwards. 'All right. Keep your hair on, old boy. I'll ring him now. I expect people will still be in bed, but desperate remedies, what?'

Gorse goes into the hall and picks up the telephone and asks for a number. Mr Stimpson listens, from the kitchen.

'Mayfair, 7070 . . .' (a long wait as it burrs) 'Oh . . . hello . . . I'm making an enquiry about a car, an Alvis 1935, dropped-head coupé. White . . . Sorry to trouble you . . . You *do*? Look here, I'll be coming to see you later today. The name's Gorse.'

Meanwhile, Mr Stimpson, in a terrible state of nerves, has run the tap, splashed his face with water, wiped it on a greasy tea towel . . . struck a match for tea. He fumbles . . . forgets the match, burns his fingers . . . He looks up, pathetically hopeful, as Gorse comes back into the kitchen. Gorse smiles at him. 'Expensive. But I think it's going to be all right. He has the exact model. He's a dealer I know.'

'Will this man take a cheque?' asks Mr Stimpson, trying to cope.

Gorse doubts that, with a shake of his head. 'We can get cash from the bank when it opens.'

Mr Stimpson is relieved, and at the same time shattered. It had been a long and terrible night, laced with fleshly delights, and there had been a price to pay. It could not, he reflected, have been otherwise. From now on, he swore to himself, he would behave as befitted the senior partner of Stimpson and Snell, estate agents of good renown. If, that is, Gorse rescued him from the awful predicament he was now in. He thanked God for Gorse and almost said as much. 'Ralph. Will you get me out of this?' he asks, plaintively.

Gorse nodded. 'Of course I will, dear boy. What are friends for?'

The Alvis stood sparkling in the dealer's yard, where Gorse had left it. The dealer is regarding Gorse, debonair as ever in his flannel suit, with admiration and puzzlement. 'You sell me this hot car for sixty quid and come back and buy it for a hundred. Can somebody please tell me what's happening?'

Gorse replied idly, 'You've made forty quid profit, why complain?'

'I'm not complaining, mate. All I did was change the plates. You want the old ones back on?'

Gorse shook his head. 'Throw them in the back.'

'All right!' The car dealer did as he was bid.

Gorse climbed into the Alvis. The dealer regarded him with a grin. 'You're the funniest bugger I ever met, you are.'

Gorse merely smiled and drove out of the yard.

The dealer watched him admiringly, then looked at the money in his grimy hand, and shook his head.

Ralph Ernest Gorse was indeed the funniest bugger he had ever met. But, at that point, he did not know exactly how funny, or in what way.

* * *

The Alvis now stands, spanking and shiny, back home in Ronnie Shooter's garage. Gorse regards it with sardonic pleasure. He closes the garage doors and goes into the house. Once inside, Gorse picks up the London telephone directory. His finger moves down a list of names with ink circles round them, under 'M'. He asks for a Speedwell number. 'Can I speak to Miss Clarice Mannors . . .? Oh . . . No Clarice Mannors at your place? I'm so sorry.' He puts the telephone down and tries the next number. 'Operator? Mayfair 729, please.' He waits and a woman's voice answers. 'Hello, yes?'

'May I speak to Miss Clarice Mannors, please?'

'I'm afraid she's not in. Who's speaking?'

Very softly, Gorse replaces the receiver. He stands in thought for a very long moment.

Mr Stimpson is ill in bed. He is sitting up, in his flannel pyjamas. By the side of the bed is a bottle of bismuth mixture. Gorse stands in the background. Joan Plumleigh-Bruce is sitting at the bedside. The grapes she has brought are on the side table.

Joan is asking a peremptory question. 'Now, what's all this about an upset tummy?'

Mr Stimpson shakes his head. 'I don't know. I *never* have an upset stomach. And I have a terrible head, too!'

Joan can think of no obvious explanation. 'Is your business all right? Have you been worrying about your business?'

'The business is fine! But I have been worrying, certainly. I've had one or two things on my mind, Joan. One or two very worrying things.'

Joan sniffs. 'Well, I'm sure I can't think what they might be. I think you and Ralph here were two very bad boys, going on that night out, and now you're paying the price.'

Says Mr Stimpson miserably, 'Something like that, I suppose – I mean, *what* night out?'

Joan looks very disapproving. 'It's all right. Ralph has told me everything.'

'Everything?' echoes Mr Stimpson, alarmed.

'Well. I *hope* everything.'

Mr Stimpson looks at Gorse, who is impassive. 'Surely not?'

'He *said* you went to the Café Royal and ate too much and drank too much. I hope that's all you did, Donald!'

Mr Stimpson hastily affirms to that. 'Yes. Of course! Of course it was!'

'Good! Well, I'm going now.' Joan stands up. 'Coming, Ralph?'

'In one moment. I have to have a word with Donald.' Gorse adds, 'Business, you know.'

Joan smiles, a bright smile that Mr Stimpson notes miserably. 'Oh, you men, it's always business. I'll be in the car. 'Byee, Donald.'

'Good-bye, my dear,' answers Mr Stimpson gloomily.

As the door closes on Joan, Mr Stimpson too closes his eyes, then makes an effort, and opens them again, and addresses Gorse. 'Is the new car in the garage?'

Gorse nods to that truth. 'Indeed it is, with exactly the same numberplates and everything in apple-pie order. There's nothing at all to worry about, old man.'

Mr Stimpson cannot believe it. 'Really? It's all sorted out? Ronnie – ?'

'Ronnie Shooter won't know that car from the original.'

'Well I hope so!' Mr Stimpson reaches out and takes Gorse's hand. 'You've been a brick, old man. A real brick. I shan't forget it.'

'It's nothing at all.'

'Oh, but it is! A good friend in this world is worth a very great deal. You have been a good friend to me. I am in your debt, Ralph.'

'My dear chap,' says Gorse, 'not at all.'

Mr Stimpson adds, 'Take care of Joan for me. I'm not up to snuff today . . .'

'I will. Don't worry. I will. Must go now,' says Gorse.

'Yes. Thank you anyway, old man.' As Mr Stimpson moves, his head hurts. He hardly sees Gorse go. He picks up his bedside portrait of Joan Plumleigh-Bruce. Gently, he kisses it.

We are in Joan Plumleigh-Bruce's living room, and lunch is over. Gorse is smoking a cigar. Joan is sipping her coffee. Mary, the slavey, is noisily clearing the dishes away.

This activity annoys Joan. 'Leave all that, Mary. Later.'

'Yes, mam.'

'All right, girl, you can go! I'll ring if I want you.'

Mary sneaks an admiring glance at Gorse and goes. Joan leans back in the armchair and exclaims, 'Two large drinks at The Friar . . . and all that wine . . . Really, I *am* going it!'

Gorse regards her tolerantly. 'About time, what?'

But Joan is suddenly reflective. 'Wasn't that odd, Donald taking a turn like that?'

Gorse nods. 'It was, rather.'

'I don't suppose you're going to tell me exactly what you were up to in London the other night?' asks Joan archly.

'No, I don't suppose I am,' replies Gorse, po-faced.

'I don't think I can make you out, Ralph Gorse. I never know what you're thinking.'

'Well, I sincerely hope not!'

'Why, would it shock me?'

'D'you know, I rather think it would.'

'Oh Ralph, you really are incorrigible!'

Gorse nods to that. It is the truth, anyway. 'Oh, by the way, my cousin rang.'

'What?'

'My cousin. In the City. I told you.'

'Oh . . . Yes. *Did* he?'

Gorse nods. 'He was talking about some new company stock that's being floated. Said it was a good idea to get in on the ground floor, make a nice little killing. Of course, these City chaps exaggerate sometimes.'

'Oh. I don't know. What company is it?'

'Can't say. He's sending me details. Of course you may not want in.'

'Well, my money is tied up really,' says Joan. 'I mean, I have almost all of it on deposit at the bank, apart from a few blue chip investments Donald's been advising me on. He'd be very upset if I did anything . . . drastic.'

Gorse considers. 'On deposit at the bank? Well, that's as good as anything. Leave it there . . . I would.'

'It's all right saying that, Ralph, but it's only three per cent, you know. One doesn't exactly get fat on that. What am I saying, do you think I'm fat?'

Gorse is mock-shocked. 'You? *Fat?*'

'Well, just a trifle?'

'Never! Absolutely just right, I'd say. Not an ounce too much anywhere. Just right.' Gorse lights Joan's cigarette. She regards him a long silent moment.

'Ralph . . . Do you really *like* me?'

'Well, of course I do, Joan. You know that.'

Joan is pushy. 'No, but I mean, *really* like?'

Gorse reaches out and presses her hand. 'Really and truly. I promise.'

Joan persists. 'You know, Ralph, sometimes . . . I think you feel . . . that Donald and I . . . that he and I have an understanding. And that makes you – '

Gorse cuts in hastily. 'Well, yes, that's it exactly! I mean, Donald's a very good friend. Well, I know I've only known him a very short time, but well, he's such a splendid character, so honest and upright, and all that . . .'

'He can be an old stick-in-the-mud sometimes,' protests Joan.

'Yes, he can rather. But I think he likes you. In fact, I know he does.'

'Has he been talking about me?' asks Joan suspiciously.

'Well, not exactly – but he did let a few things slip . . .' answers Gorse, innocently.

'What things? What did he say?' demands Joan, troubled.

'Well, just he was hoping that you'd . . . well, he was a bit sick of waiting, that's all, really . . .'

'Sick of waiting for *what*?'

'Well, the usual thing. I suppose . . .'

'The usual *thing*? What *else* did he say?' asks Joan, terribly.

Gorse protests. 'I really can't remember . . . Oh yes, he did say something else . . .'

'What was that, pray?'

Gorse is a long moment before he replies. 'He said that if you were properly handled you'd do something – now what *was* it? It was a funny phrase – he'd been drinking – it meant to go to extremes – go to the limit? Go the whole way or something – what on earth *was* it?'

'Hog?'

'Hog! That was the word. Go the Whole Hog?'

Joan looks very white, suddenly. 'Donald Stimpson said . . . *that*? About *me*?'

Gorse is immediately repentant. 'Look here, old girl, I've said too much – terribly sorry! I'm sure Donald didn't mean anything at all by it.' He stands up, suddenly. 'May I just use the Little Boy's Room?'

'Of course . . . I can't believe he really said *that* . . .'

But Gorse has gone and does not hear.

Gorse does not hear because he has gone upstairs and is now in Joan's bedroom. The curtains are almost drawn and the room is shadowy. Gorse is in the room, now, and is looking in the drawers, opening and shutting them silently and quickly – looking for what? Jewellery, money, some clue as to what Joan *has*?. . . And something *else* . . . His hands touch lingerie . . . linger . . . Ahh . . . the *feel* of it! Strange sensations come over Gorse. But he represses them, as Joan calls up to him. 'Ralph . . . Did you *find* it?' In the dark and shadowy room Gorse has a silk stocking in his hand. He knots it into a loop. It is as well Joan Plumleigh-Bruce cannot see him now. But Gorse calls down to her, in a natural enough voice, 'Yes . . . Down in a tick!'

Downstairs, a moment later, Joan looks up as Gorse comes in. Behind him a toilet flushes, faintly. Gorse has his raincoat over his arm.

Joan cries, 'You're not going? You're *always* going!'

'Not by choice, I must say.' Gorse kisses her hand. 'Oh, by the way, I promised my cousin I'd call him if I wanted to get in on the City thing . . . Will you be interested at all?'

Joan hesitates, but only for a moment. 'I don't know what Donald will say, but *yes*!'

Gorse frowns. 'Look here, I wouldn't want old Stimpson to be upset.'

'Well, I would,' answers Joan.

'Well, whatever you say,' murmurs Gorse.

'Come to tea tomorrow. *Promise?*' Joan comes very close to Gorse. Gorse kisses her on the nose. Not the lips. Not yet. Possibly not ever. 'Promise,' says Gorse.

Back in Ronnie Shooter's house a little later, Gorse is on the telephone. 'Hello . . .? Is that Mayfair 729? Is Miss Clarice Mannors there, please?'

'Clarice Mannors speaking. Who's that?'

'We met in Maida Vale.'

'Good God, it's *you*!'

'How about the Ritz for tea, on Friday? Four o'clock?'

There is a delicious chuckle. 'Can you afford it?'

'I've come into a little money . . . and I'm hoping to come into a lot more . . .'

Again, the disbelieving chuckle. 'And how on earth are you going to do that?'

Gorse speaks slowly and means it. 'By doing whatever I have to, darling. *Whatever* it is . . .'

Clarice's rather mocking laughter goes on and on, as Gorse replaces the receiver on the hook.

Chapter Two

An unemployed man was playing a mouth organ, moving slowly along in the gutter, outside the Ritz Hotel in Piccadilly. The man was thin, wore a cap and scarf, had no teeth and his clothes were dirty, stained and worn. He had three medals pinned to his ragged jacket. He was one of the vast army of the unemployed, at that moment four million strong. All men. All breadwinners. Unemployed women were not counted in the statistics.

A taxi draws up, and Ralph Gorse gets out. He is dressed in his one good suit, the grey flannel, worn with the striped regimental tie. Gorse pays the taxi-driver. The doorman takes his tip and salutes him, as Gorse goes quickly into the hotel.

The Tea Room at the Ritz is one of the most gracious sights in London, abutting as it does onto Green Park, at the side of the hotel. Ladies – and a few gentlemen – of the leisured classes chatter, as the three-piece orchestra plays subdued music, loud enough to disguise the chatter but not loud enough to drown it. The talk anyway was mostly gossip, about Wallis Simpson and the Duke of Windsor or whether one should order one's next frock from Molyneaux as normal, or try this new designer, Hardy Amies. And dear Cecil Beaton of course would be doing the photos to Joanne's Coming Out . . .

Amidst all this, in a discreet corner of the Tea Room, sits Clarice Mannors. She is beautiful and moneyed and her clothes reflect that. She smiles as she sees Ralph

Gorse arrive, pause, look around and be pointed discreetly in her direction.

Tea is in front of her: cucumber sandwiches and cakes on a silver stand. Gorse walks towards her and smiles. Clarice does not rise. Gorse sits down.

'Hello . . . I ordered tea.'

'Fine.'

Clarice feels nervous with Gorse. That is something she rarely feels. 'I knew you'd be on time. Not like my other men friends.' Gorse raises an eyebrow. 'Why? Do you have many?'

'Yes, actually I do, rather.'

'Congratulations,' says Gorse drily. 'Is all this paid for?'

Clarice nods. Their eyes are still locked. 'I never thought I'd see you again.'

'No?'

'I'm very naughty really, meeting you like this.'

'I don't think you had any choice. Not if you feel like I do.' For once in his life, Gorse is telling the truth.

'No. I don't think I had. How do *you* feel?'

Gorse grins. 'Mad. Absolutely mad.'

'So do I.'

Gorse breaks the spell. 'Don't you think you'd better pour the tea?'

'How do you like it?'

'Strong. With milk.'

Clarice pours the tea, then puts milk in. Gorse watches her. She hands him a cup. 'There.'

'Thank you.'

Clarice takes her own tea and looks at him over the cup. 'What's your full name? You never told me.'

'Ralph Gorse.'

'Where do you live?'

'Do you really want to know?'

'No. Not really. Cake?'

'Couldn't eat it. Lost my appetite.'

Clarice laughs. 'Me too . . . You look very smart. Nobody would guess you're on the dole.'

Gorse grimaces. 'I'm not on the dole. Not yet, anyway.'

'I'm sorry. That was thoughtless of me.'

Gorse demurs. 'It's possible I might be. One day. Four million people are.'

Clarice shakes her head. 'Hard to think of all those people. Sitting around, or whatever they do.'

Gorse's voice is suddenly harsh. 'Starving is what they do. Or damn near it. If they ate any of those cakes they'd probably be sick.'

'What?' asks Clarice, startled at his tone.

In answer, Gorse points to the cakes. 'Too rich, cream, butter, all that, you see? Not used to it. More used to bread and marge.'

Clarice is silent for a moment. 'Are you . . . used to bread and marge?'

'I've tried it.'

'Tell me about it.'

'No. You'd be bored. Or disgusted. Or both.'

'Try me.'

Gorse looks around the Tea Room, at the rich bored women, the money, the safety of it all. 'All right. If you're interested . . . I've had a lot of rotten jobs since I left school. Quite a decent school, but my people had no money. My first job was in an office but I couldn't stick being cooped up all day. So I sold stuff door-to-door. Encyclopedias. Beauty creams. Breakfast food. You say it, I've sold it.' He grimaced. 'Or rather, tried to sell it.'

'What sort of money did that pay?' Clarice wonders.

'Thirty bob a week. That might just about buy us supper here tonight.'

Clarice is still. 'Who said we were having supper here tonight?'

'I did,' replies Gorse.

Clarice looks at him a long moment. She isn't sure whether all this is serious or not. But the pull is there, very much so. She can feel it, as she has never felt it before: the danger. She tries to keep her voice level. 'What was your last job?'

Gorse shrugs. 'Selling cars. I lost it two weeks ago. My money ran out. All I had left were a couple of decent suits, and my old sports car. When I sell her I'm finished, I'm down among the Great Unwashed.' Gorse offers her a cigarette from his gold case and she takes it. He lights it for her, with Ronnie Shooter's gold Ronson.

'What about . . . the bread and marge?' asks Clarice.

'I lived on it for a week. In a cheap room, no fire.'

'My God!' says Clarice, softly.

But Gorse is suddenly jocular. 'Fear not, I have great expectations. With money in my pocket, I hope to see you in future . . . on equal terms?' There is a pause, as the trio plays Ketelby's 'Bells Across the Meadow'. Clarice breaks it with an apologetic grin. 'I'm going to have a cake! All this talk of bread and marge has made me quite hungry!' She helps herself to a rich, gooey cake, and eats some with a fork. Gorse watches her. Her every movement speaks one word to him: Class. Money, too, of course. But most of all, that strange indefinable English thing: Class.

'Why do you tell me all this? About yourself?' asks Clarice.

'I don't know.' He doesn't. 'I don't usually tell anybody anything.' That, anyway, was God's truth.

'No. I can believe that.'

Gorse grins. 'I think I will have a cake, too.' He helps

himself to a vanilla slice and, turning it on its side, slices off a section. It is quite delicious. To live like this every day: that had to be the ultimate aim. Not just now and again. Every single day. Clarice is looking at him quizzically. 'Sometime . . . when you want to . . . you must tell me where all this money you talk about is going to come from?'

Gorse smiles, very slightly, but says nothing. He eats his cake. For once in this awful world, he thinks, I can have my cake. And eat it.

In The Friar Roadhouse that evening, Mr Stimpson is raising a half of bitter to his lips as Joan Plumleigh-Bruce makes an entrance, Chinklywinkles trotting behind on his lead. Joan is even more well-dressed than normal, which is to say that she is overdressed. Mr Stimpson does not notice that. 'My dear, good evening. I called at the house but your maid said you were resting.'

Joan replies, 'So I was. But I decided to stop. So here I am.'

Mr Stimpson calls to the barman. 'The usual for Mrs Plumleigh-Bruce, Albert.'

'Gin and It coming up, sir.'

Joan sits on her bar stool with a bit of an effort and, rather grumpily, she plumps her handbag down on the counter. Chinklywinkles settles at her feet. Mr Stimpson knows the signs. 'Something wrong, my dear?'

'Not really. I just expected to hear from Ralph today, and he hasn't telephoned or anything.'

Mr Stimpson is perturbed at this news. 'Was it business? Or was it personal?'

'Why do you ask *that*, Donald?'

Mr Stimpson retracts hastily. 'No reason, my dear.' He turns to the barman. 'Here you are, Albert, I think that's correct.' He puts some coins on the bar counter, and Albert picks them up. They are, indeed, exactly correct. 'I just wondered if . . . er . . . young Gorse had been annoying you?'

Joan stares hard at Mr Stimpson. 'Why should Ralph Gorse annoy me? He gets me tips on horses, ones that win, which is more than anybody else does!'

'I know nothing of the Turf.'

'Or of much else, I sometimes think!' Joan sips her gin and It. 'And it was business, if you must know.'

Mr Stimpson says 'Ah' in a long, relieved hiss of breath. It is not lost on Joan.

'To do with my investments, actually.'

Mr Stimpson sets down his glass. 'In what way your investments?'

'Well, you heard Ralph say he had City connections?'

'I heard him *say* he had City connections, certainly.'

Joan is beginning to get rather annoyed with Mr Stimpson. 'There you go again. You don't believe anything anybody says, do you?'

Mr Stimpson does not reply to that. 'You said he was talking to you about your investments?'

Joan takes a deep breath. 'Ralph said he'd call in for tea today, to talk a little more, but he never turned up. I must say I'm very disappointed in him, I am really. I don't know why, nobody seems to care about me or my affairs now poor, dear Geoffrey has gone, but there it is, I'm disappointed in Ralph.' She drains her gin and It. 'I think I'd like another of these . . .'

'Albert, same again!' calls Mr Stimpson.

Joan is a trifle mollified by that. 'I said I had some investments, but that most of my money was on deposit in the bank.'

'You told him *that*?'

'Why not, it's not a secret, is it?'

'And what did he say?'

Joan shrugs. 'That I couldn't do better. Even if it's only three per cent interest.'

Mr Stimpson is vastly relieved. 'Well, I must say I agree with Gorse. This time, anyway.'

'This time anyway?' retorts Joan. 'You sound as if you don't like him, after all! You go up to the West End with him and behave quite disgracefully, far too much to drink!'

'That was only the once . . . And I must say Gorse behaved very well.'

'How do you mean?' demands Joan.

Mr Stimpson retreats. 'Well, he got me home safely, all that . . . Yes, he's all right, Gorse, only . . . only things seem to happen . . . odd things . . . when he's around . . . He's what I'd call a sort of . . . disturbing influence . . .'

Joan's mouth turns down at the corners. 'I think we could do with a disturbing influence, now and again! Look at you, standing in this place every night, drinking *beer*, talking about nothing in particular, never *doing* anything!'

Mr Stimpson is stung by this remark. 'You haven't grumbled before.'

'No. Perhaps I should have.'

Mr Stimpson feels it is time to strike back. 'He'll be moving on soon, apparently.'

This has an electric effect on Joan. She puts down her drink and stares Mr Stimpson in the face directly, something she has not done since she came into the bar. 'Ralph? Moving on? Where?'

Mr Stimpson shakes his head. 'Paris, seemingly. Some job in the family firm, or so he *said*.'

Joan's voice is icy. 'You don't believe *anything* anybody ever says, do you, Donald?'

'In the estate business,' declares Mr Stimpson, 'it pays not to, my dear.'

Joan drinks her gin and It in one. Mr Stimpson watches her. He sees she is upset, but is at a loss to imagine why. Surely she cannot be all that fond of young Gorse, can she? A cold feeling starts at the pit of Mr Stimpson's stomach, a feeling that even the warm bitter or the whisky to follow it will not drive away. Mr Stimpson indicates Joan's empty glass. 'A fresh regalement, my dear?'

'No, thank you!' She collects her handbag and Chinklywinkles' lead. Mr Stimpson is surprised. 'Where are you going?'

'Home!' declares Joan emphatically. 'There may be a telephone call. Or something. Anything to break the bloody monotony!' And with that she vacates the Nook of The Friar Roadhouse, leaving a very thoughtful and perplexed Mr Stimpson staring after her.

In a bedroom, in the Ritz Hotel, the lighting is dim, but a dead champagne bottle upside down in an ice-bucket sets the scene. A small table where lie the plates, glasses and dishes of a luxury supper is next, and then follow items of clothing, male and female – lingerie, stockings, a tie – which litter the floor, leading towards the bed. In the bed sit Clarice Mannors and Ralph Ernest Gorse, smoking cigarettes. They are both naked. Gorse has another bottle of champagne and is emptying the last of it into tall glasses held by Clarice and himself. 'The last dregs, I'm afraid . . . Shall we send for some more?'

Clarice laughs. 'Hardly. Look at the place.'

Gorse stares around the room. 'It does rather look . . . like a motor accident.'

Clarice sips her champagne. 'Well it is a bit, isn't it?' They stare at each other a long moment and then they kiss, but without passion. They've used all that up.

Clarice touches his face with her finger. 'I thought I knew something . . . about all this . . . I don't know how I'll ever go back to the Reggies and Ronnies of my usual set.'

'Why go back to them at all?' asks Gorse, his eyes on hers.

Clarice is womanlike, evasive. 'Well. How often am I going to see you, darling?'

'Pretty often, I'd say.'

Clarice laughs again. 'You mean, when you get your money?'

Gorse's expression changes. 'That's right. Then I can do anything and everything with you, can't I?'

Clarice does not see the danger signs. 'Hunting with the Quorn? Ascot? Henley? Shooting in Scotland in August? Can you really see yourself doing all *that*? It costs an awful lot of money, darling, to live that way. I don't notice it because I don't need to. The money's always been there.'

Gorse's voice is harsh. 'Lucky you.'

Clarice leans back. Her breasts are very shapely but Gorse is not looking at them. 'Yes, I suppose so. But I couldn't live any other way . . . I just couldn't. You see, darling, I'm too used to it by now.'

'You mean I'm just a fling?' asks Gorse. His face has no expression at all. He might be a doctor asking about a patient's symptoms.

'No . . . No . . . But Ralph, listen . . . in a way my life is all set out for me. I can play around a bit now, but sooner or later I'm expected to marry somebody of my own type . . .'

'Somebody rich?' asks Gorse, sullenly.

Clarice smokes on, unseeing. 'Yes, well. But it'll be a sort of arranged marriage . . . Money and land marry money and land in my world. So I would be able to lead my own life, in a sort of way . . . I might even be able to see you like this from time to time?'

Gorse's voice is level, untroubled. 'As your gigolo, you mean?'

'Hardly, darling! I don't suppose you'd ever let me *pay* you, would you?'

In reply, Gorse grips her shoulders, tightly, ferociously. They are face to face. Gorse just stares and stares at her. Clarice waits, frozen, for Gorse to speak. '. . . Don't you ever talk to me like that again. Ever.'

Impassioned, Clarice shrugs him off. 'And don't you do *that*, ever again! Or I go! Out of the door! For good!'

'Then go!'

Clarice is still furiously angry but she doesn't take Gorse up on his offer. She looks at him as if seeing him for the first time. The truth is, Clarice is scared but intrigued. After a long moment she touches him softly on the cheek. 'I'm sorry, darling. I keep forgetting. You aren't a gentleman, are you, Ralph? You want to be one, God knows why, they're all so utterly bloody boring, but you just aren't one, are you?'

Gorse says nothing. He is still coldly angry.

'You frighten me sometimes, Ralph . . . and I've never been frightened by any man before . . .'

Still Gorse does not trust himself to reply. Clarice moves to him and gently puts her arm around his neck. 'I'm going to a crowd of people, in France, in two weeks. If you have your money by then, why not come with me? It would be lovely if you could, really.'

'Don't worry . . . I'll have the money.' Gorse is staring

straight ahead. He ignores her arms around his neck, and lights another cigarette, with Ronnie Shooter's lighter.

A laundry van chugs up to Ronnie Shooter's house. The laundry man, in a cap and overalls, walks up the path to the door, carrying a bundle of laundry. He rings the bell and waits. Then rings again. The door opens and Gorse stands there, in a dressing gown. Under it are silk pyjamas.

'Sorry if I got you up, sir.'

'Oh. It's you.'

The laundry man replies pointedly. 'Sixteen shillings and ninepence, sir.'

'That much?' queries Gorse.

The laundry man consults the bill. 'Yessir. You had a lot of laundry done, sir. Plus the socks and repairs to the shirt collars, and suit cleaned, and so on.'

'Yes, yes . . . all right, there you are.' Gorse gives the laundry man a note from his dressing-gown pocket. 'Keep it!' Gorse takes the parcel from the laundry man, who looks surprised at the amount of the tip. Sixpence is more usual. 'That's *very* good of you, sir . . . Er, Mr Shooter's away, is he, sir?'

'Yes. I'm staying here for a while.'

'Shall I call weekly, sir? Anything to go this time?'

'No. I shan't be here much longer.'

The laundry man touches his cap. 'I see, sir. Well, thank you again, sir.' The laundry man walks back to his van, gets in and drives away. Gorse looks up and down the sunny suburban avenue, grunts with dissatisfaction at the very look of it and goes back into the house. Gorse is not a domestic animal. The kitchen, where he basically lives, is untidy. A loaf of bread and a milk bottle stand on the table. It is a bit squalorish, Gorse decides, as he lays down the laundry and puts a kettle on the cooker for tea.

He takes his wallet from his jacket, which lies over the back of a chair. From it he takes a number of large white banknotes. In front of Gorse on the kitchen table lies a copy of the *Financial Times*, plus various sheets of his own calculations. An item in the share-price index is ringed heavily in ink. Gorse counts the banknotes. 'Seventy-six quid!' He sighs. 'Seventy-six quid in the world!' It is certainly not enough to gain admittance to Clarice Mannors' world, although to the laundry man it would represent a fortune. Gorse ponders, musing. Somehow he will have to play it up, until he has enough to enter Clarice Mannors' world. Gorse makes his tea and drinks it slowly, the germ of an idea taking full shape in his mind.

An hour later, Gorse is knocking at Joan Plumleigh-Bruce's door, a bunch of red roses in his hand.

In the sitting room Joan is reading the *Daily Telegraph*. The radiogram plays music by Ambrose and his Orchestra, and she is reading how an unemployed man and his family can live on thirty shillings a week. She looks up as Mary, the maid, comes in.

'Ma'am . . . We got a visitor . . . It's Mr Gorse, ma'am.'

Joan is surprised and a little annoyed, and of course, as always, intrigued. 'Oh. Well. I don't know.'

Mary presses. 'He 'as a bunch of roses agen, mam.'

'So I should hope,' declares Joan. 'All right. Ask him in.'

'Yes, mam.'

Joan checks her appearance in a mirror, and finds it satisfactory. She turns to see Gorse there in his grey flannel suit, with a bunch of roses in his hand.

Mary says, 'Mr Gorse, ma'am.'

'Yes, well, thank you, Mary,' replies Joan in dismissal.

Gorse's mannor is apologetic. 'Hello, Joan.'

'Better late than never, I suppose,' sniffs Joan.

'Terribly sorry about yesterday. I can explain – '

Joan notices that Mary is still hovering. 'That will be all, Mary. I'll ring if I want you.'

'Yes, ma'am. Don't you want water for the flowers, ma'am?'

'No, *thank* you!' says Joan, icily.

Defeated, Mary goes with her usual sidelong, admiring glance at Gorse, who notices but does not acknowledge it. Gorse is nice to servants but he does not see them as human beings. 'These are for you,' he tells Joan. 'What shall I do with them?'

Joan is frosty. 'I expected you yesterday. No telephone call, nothing!'

'I had to go to London, urgently,' Gorse lies, quickly. 'To see my cousin in the City. I'm terribly sorry but it was all such a rush . . . I couldn't get to a telephone. I was on the Floor with him, you see . . .'

'The Floor?' echoes Joan.

'The Exchange . . .'

'Oh. I see.' Joan is being won over, but it isn't easy, thinks Gorse, but he manages more contrition. 'I would have thought you'd have tried later,' adds Joan.

'Yes, of course,' agrees Gorse. 'But I didn't get back till quite late and although I wanted to talk to you, I thought I'd better leave it until this morning. Can't talk business in the evenings, myself.'

Joan is mystified. 'Business?'

Gorse holds up the roses. 'I say, what about *these*?' He offers the flowers to Joan. She takes them, sniffs them. She rings a small bell. Finally, she smiles. 'They're quite lovely. But you aren't entirely forgiven, Ralph Gorse. I was quite worried I wasn't going to hear from you ever again.'

Gorse affects to find this very funny. 'What? Absolutely not! Whatever gave you that idea?' Joan rings her tiny silver bell again to summon the maid. 'It was something Mr Stimpson said. About your going to a new job?' questions Joan.

'Oh, that? Well, it's not entirely fixed, as yet. I'll be here, boring you, for a while yet, I fear.'

Joan is very relieved to hear this news. 'Ralph, you are a lot of things but never boring.' Mary comes in. 'Mary, put these in water and bring us coffee and toast.'

Mary bobs and goes out, sneaking another look at Gorse who is, after all, she reflects, nearer her age than madam's, the silly old cow.

Joan, meantime, is smiling at Gorse. 'I don't know why I should forgive you, Ralph, but I do . . .'

Gorse takes her hand. 'You look very lovely today, Joan.'

Joan smiles and preens a bit. 'Do I? Do I really?'

'Absolutely stunning,' declares Gorse, and lets go of her hand. He does not want that side of things to go too far or too fast. Joan sits and fixes him with an eager gaze. 'Well, Ralph . . . what *was* it you said about the Stock Exchange?'

Gorse is extremely careful now. A false word, a wrong inflexion could ruin it all. He unfastens the button of his double-breasted jacket (the bottom button is always correctly left undone), and casually, oh so very casually, declares, 'Don't know if you'd want to be involved or anything like that . . . Just felt I should mention it.'

Joan leans forward. 'Go on, go on. I'm quite excited!'

'It's a good tip on a flotation. These are the details . . .'

He hands her the copy of the *Financial Times*, with the 'flotation' ringed around in red ink.

Joan hardly looks at it. 'Oh. I can't understand all *that* . . . Just *tell* me.'

Gorse is now very reluctant. 'My cousin says, if we . . . Are you *sure* you're interested?'

'Yes, of course, go on!'

Gorse finally comes out with it. 'If we were to buy today I think we'd show a fifty per cent profit in two days.'

Joan's eyes are round with greed. 'Are *you* investing?'

Gorse nods. 'Only fifty pounds, I'm afraid. I'd like it to be more but I'm a bit, well, I've rather overspent the old allowance . . . so that's my limit.'

Joan is now quite transformed. Her face is pink, her eyes are round, she trembles a little. 'Well, if you're putting fifty in, I'll do the same!' she says, in a breathless rush.

Gorse relaxes. The first bite of the hook is the most important. After that it still isn't easy, but it is easier, the first hurdle has been cleared. When he speaks he makes sure his voice sounds noncommittal and, above all, businesslike. 'Really? Well, if you like . . . The thing is, we've got to have a joint bank account. You and I. Share and share alike. You put in fifty. So do I. Just a sort of little flutter. We don't want it to get out of hand.'

Joan is impatient for action. 'All right. Shall we go to my bank?'

Gorse looks as if he is debating that course of action. He isn't. 'I think not, Joan. Or mine, either. Somewhere new. And we don't tell the bank manager anything except it's a . . . business arrangement between us. No point in letting all our little secrets out, is there?'

Joan agrees. 'Of course not. Ralph, you think of everything . . . Oh, isn't this all so exciting?'

Gorse takes the *Financial Times*, folds it and puts it in his pocket. 'Yes, isn't it?' he replies.

The Southern Counties Bank loomed up as Gorse drove his Railton to the kerb and parked the car. He reflected that this was a wise decision. Joan had no account at the Southern Counties. Nor did he. He had no bank account anywhere.

He held the door of the Railton open and Joan, still looking excited, got out and together they walked into the bank.

Gorse would have been glad, had he known, that Mr Stimpson had come out of his office, higher up the street, but missed catching sight of them. The sign 'Stimpson & Snell, Estate Agents' hangs above Mr Stimpson's head as he puts on his hat and walks down the main street, in the opposite direction.

The manager's office in the Southern Counties Bank is somewhat fusty and old-fashioned and so is the manager, Mr Norris. He wears a dark jacket, pinstripe trousers, wing collar and a regimental tie, of the Sussex Regiment. He greets Gorse and Joan Plumleigh-Bruce with geniality. It is not every hour of the day that new business finds its way into the bank, not in the middle of the Depression. 'Ah, Mr Gorse and ah . . . Mrs Plumleigh-Bruce?. . . I believe we *have* met, Mrs Plumleigh-Bruce?'

Joan is vague. 'Oh, have we?'

Mr Norris presses. 'I *think* so. The Friar? With Mr Stimpson?'

Joan is less than enthusiastic. 'Oh, really?. . . Mr Norris, yours is not my *usual* bank . . .'

Mr Norris knows this very well. 'No indeed, dear lady.'

Joan goes on, 'But Mr Gorse and I have a little business partnership started, and we thought of . . . somewhere . . . *new*?'

Mr Norris is delighted and says so. 'Delighted to be of assistance! Let me recapitulate, if I may? You are opening a joint account in the sum of one hundred pounds? The passbook to reside with . . .?' Mr Norris waits expectantly, looking at Joan. She, in turn, looks at Gorse.

'Well . . . With . . . you, Ralph? You should keep it, you're the *man*.'

'Oh . . . Very well,' says Gorse, as if it does not matter at all.

'Both to sign? Or either to sign?' asks Mr Norris.

'I'm sorry?' says Joan.

Mr Norris looks over his spectacles. 'Both to sign cheques? Or withdrawals, or whatever? Or either one to sign?'

'Oh. I see . . .' Joan looks at Gorse again, smiles fondly. 'Either, of course.'

Mr Norris smiles professionally and makes a note.

Mr Stimpson, who has been out of his office for a cup of coffee at the ABC Dairy Shop (an excellent cup – much better than anything the office staff can make) returns from his ruminant 'break' too soon to see Gorse and Joan come out of the Southern Counties Bank; he is already back in his office, at his desk, wondering whether to invest in a new housing estate soon to be built on the outskirts of the town. Mr Stimpson intends to study the prospect carefully, as he always does any business proposition . . . But something stirs. He feels constrained. He puts on his hat and goes out again.

Gorse too is pleading business to Joan, as he leaves her

in front of the Southern Counties Bank. 'I have a bit of business, Joan . . . Could you possibly see yourself home?'

Joan is put out, a little. 'Oh *you*! It's always business. But, yes, of course. When do I see you?'

'Tomorrow . . . Evening?'

'That would be lovely. Let's have supper – sevenish?'

Gorse signals to a taxi on a rank opposite. 'Lovely!'

Joan is asking, 'Are you all right, dear? You look worried.'

Gorse shakes his head. 'It's nothing . . . I'd just hate you to lose any money.'

'Don't worry. Fifty pounds won't bankrupt me!'

The taxi wheels round. Gorse directs the driver. '27 Wilton Avenue. Here's the fare.' Gorse gives the driver a silver coin.

Joan exclaims, 'Ralph, really you shouldn't . . . !' She kisses Ralph on the cheek and gets in the cab, waving her hand as it drives off. Gorse turns away with a sigh of relief and finds himself looking directly into the face of Mr Stimpson. Mr Stimpson is curious and not best pleased at what he has seen.

'Was that Joan?'

Gorse is annoyed and abrupt. 'Yes it was. I just put her in a cab. Did you want to talk to her or something?'

Mr Stimpson wilts a trifle under the attack. 'No, no. It'll wait.' Mr Stimpson gropes in his pocket and finds a letter there. 'I had this from Ronnie Shooter today. He's fed up with Cannes and he's coming home this weekend. It looks as if I'll have to ask you to vacate his house by Saturday at the latest.'

'Oh, I see,' says Gorse as if it is a matter of complete indifference to him.

But Mr Stimpson is watching Gorse with unrelenting interest. 'Terribly sorry, old man.'

'That's perfectly all right. Thank you, Donald.' Gorse walks to the Railton, gets in and drives away. Mr Stimpson watches him go. Suddenly he realizes where he is standing. He looks up thoughtfully at the portals of the Southern Counties Bank.

Gorse had business to transact, but not of the kind he had hinted to Joan. For now, Gorse is on the telephone, which is just in the hall, outside the kitchen door. The kitchen still is a lived-in mess, but enlivened by a bottle of Scotch. Gorse is drinking a large one, which he feels he has earned. Now, he is talking to Clarice Mannors, and she has told him some news that he finds annoying and, more than that, upsetting.

'What? I thought it wasn't till the following weekend.'

Clarice explains, airily. 'No, we're all so *bored*, so we're going early. Look, shall I meet you at the Ritz on Friday at three?'

Gorse rubs his face, tries to think. 'Let me see . . .'

Clarice sounds impatient. 'Oh, Ralph, you *are* coming, aren't you? Or is is still the wretched money?'

If only you knew, Gorse thinks. 'No, no, it's not that . . . it's just . . . I don't know if I can get away by then.'

'Well, darling, you can always get a ticket at the last minute, can't you?'

Gorse protests. 'Clarice, I *want* to come but I'm not exactly my own boss – '

Clarice cuts in, even more impatiently. 'You certainly don't sound as if you want to come, darling!' She hesitates. 'But look – *is* it the money? If it is, I suppose I could chip in. But I don't have much spare, I'm always broke, and – '

'No, it isn't the money . . . Well, it is in a way. What kind of money will I need?'

'Oh, I don't know, six or eight hundred pounds.' She could have said thousands, as far as it went. 'Hello, darling . . . Are you still there? . . . Look darling, just don't come if the money's a problem.'

But Gorse has made his decision. 'I'll see you at the Ritz on Friday at three . . .'Bye.'

Gorse looks very grim, as he puts down the telephone. He thinks for a moment, then takes out his wallet and counts out fifty pounds from the banknotes, leaving himself only three fivers. He looks at these banknotes for what seems a very long time.

An hour later the Railton drives up to the Southern Counties Bank and Gorse gets out. This time Mr Stimpson sees him. He is feeling unusually jumpy that day, Mr Stimpson. It is *most* unusual for him and remarked on by his staff. 'Up and down like a jack-in-the-box,' his office boy mutters to the typist who mutters it to old Mr Snell who is deaf and past it. Mr Stimpson puts on his hat (in the style of the time, he never goes outdoors without wearing it) and stands at the door of his office, surveying the length and breadth of Reading High Street. He could not tell anybody why he is doing that. He doesn't know. What he does know is that he stands and watches Ralph Ernest Gorse go through the front door of the Southern Counties Bank and that for some reason, he is disturbed by the sight. He would be even more disturbed if he could see the transaction taking place that very minute in the bank manager's office.

For Gorse is putting a number of banknotes down on Mr Norris's desk. 'Fifty pounds, Mr Norris.'

'You're putting some more *in*?'

In reply Gorse produces the bank passbook. 'You'll need the passbook.'

'I'll get it written up at once.'

'I'll wait.'

Mr Norris is anxious to help. 'I can do it myself then.' He carefully writes in the sum. 'You and Mrs Plumleigh-Bruce . . . You've known each other some time?'

Gorse is equal to this clumsy overture. 'I wouldn't be surprised if I couldn't persuade her to do all her banking here. In due course.'

Mr Norris carefully blots the passbook and gives it respectfully back to Gorse. 'That would be most gratifying, I must say.'

'Myself, too, possibly,' adds Gorse.

'Even more so, Mr Gorse.'

'Captain Gorse, actually.'

'Captain Gorse?. . . I'm so sorry. If I may ask, which Regiment? I was West Sussex myself . . .'

But Gorse, by now, knows how to evade further questions. He picks up the passbook and looks at his watch. 'I must rush . . . Business appointment.'

'Of course. If I can be of any further assistance, please call on me, Captain Gorse.'

Gorse permits himself a reply to that. 'Don't worry. I certainly will.'

Mr Norris opens the door. Gorse goes out with a nod, no more.

'Good-day, sir.' The bank manager closes the door and picks up the money lying on the desk. He nods his head. He is very satisfied with the little transaction, very satisfied indeed.

In her living room, Joan is half-listening to the radio, gin and It to hand. It is the BBC News, and a commentator is intoning the momentous news of the day . . .

'Since Mr Neville Chamberlain returned from Munich

yesterday, observers from all over the country are convinced that the British people approve of his actions in coming to an accommodation with the German Chancellor, Herr Hitler. The British people do not want war any more than the Germans do, said a prominent Government official today . . .'

The telephone rings, suddenly. Joan turns down the wireless and answers it. Her manner changes as she hears Gorse's voice. 'Joan? I have to see you . . . but it'll have to be late, I'm afraid . . . Say, ten o'clockish, is that all right?'

'That's a little late, isn't it?' asks Joan, dubiously.

Gorse sounds testy. 'Well, if you've got something on?'

Joan retracts hastily. 'No. No. That'll be fine.'

In Ronnie Shooter's hallway Gorse puts down the telephone and smiles at himself in the mirror.

In her living room Joan rings her bell. Joan is thinking hard as she tastes her gin and It, thinking very hard indeed.

Mary puts her head round the door. 'You rang, mam?'

Joan is brisk. 'Mary. Supper will be cold. I'll do it. You can have the rest of the evening off.'

'Oh, mam! I thought you were going out, mam?'

Joan ignores that. 'Haven't you got a sister in Paddington or somewhere?'

Mary is hesitant. 'Well . . . Yes, mam, I do, but – '

Joan cuts in. 'Well, go there, spend the night with her . . . You do really need a rest. I have been working you terribly hard lately . . . And it's all right, I'll pay your train fares and a few shillings over. You can come back tomorrow morning, not too early. Now, off with you!'

Mary is astonished. 'Yes, mam. Thank you, mam.'

Joan nods and sips her gin and It and lights herself a cigarette. She exhales . . . expectant . . . then suddenly catches sight of herself in the mirror. She smiles happily, and runs upstairs to prepare herself for the arrival of Ralph Gorse.

Meanwhile, in The Friar, Mr Stimpson is holding his customary half of bitter, and consulting his watch. He turns to the barman. 'Albert? No sign of Mrs Plumleigh-Bruce?'

'No, Mr Stimpson. Not like her, is it? Usually in like clockwork – '

'Yes, thank you, Albert!'

Mr Stimpson looks up as Mr Norris, the bank manager, enters. He greets Mr Stimpson. 'Evening, Donald.'

'Oh. Evening, Norman.'

Mr Norris calls, 'My usual, Albert.'

'One scotch coming up, Mr Norris.'

'"Coming up!" Where do they get these Americanisms?' asks Mr Norris.

Mr Stimpson cannot imagine. 'The pictures, I should think . . . Oh, let me get that for you, Norman.'

'Oh. Thank you. Very kind of you, Donald.'

Mr Stimpson counts out his change. 'Here you are, Albert. That's correct, I think.'

'Yessir, *exactly* correct, sir,' says Albert, drily.

Mr Norris and Mr Stimpson drink, silently saluting one another. After a decent moment, Mr Norris asks, 'Building that new estate yet, Donald?'

'We have high hopes,' replies Mr Stimpson.

Mr Norris's mind is never far from business. 'You won't forget we're your bankers, will you? Anything we can do, naturally. Yours is a very valued account, Donald.'

Mr Stimpson nods to that. Mr Norris looks around the bar. 'Mrs Plumleigh-Bruce not in tonight, I see?'

'No.'

'She usually seems to be in with, er, your good self, Donald.'

'She is, usually, yes.'

'Indisposed? I hope not.'

'No, no. Nothing like that. She'll probably be in later.'

'Yes. Of course.' There is a silence. Then Mr Stimpson, greatly daring, asks, 'She called in to see you today, I hear?'

But Mr Norris is wary. 'Matter of fact she did call in, yes.'

'Young Gorse, too. Bright chap, young Gorse.'

Norris answers unhappily, 'Yes, indeed.'

'Bank with you, does he, young Gorse?'

Mr Norris is hesitant but feels he can say this much. 'Well. Now he does.'

'Yes. Of course. That's what I thought. Yes. Ready for another?'

'Well, not quite . . . It's my shout.'

'No, no. Please. Allow *me*. Albert!'

Albert cannot recall when Mr Stimpson had bought a drink out of order. The old bastard must have something on his mind tonight, Albert tells himself.

He is right.

In Joan Plumleigh-Bruce's bedroom that evening there is a scene of some chaos. Joan's bed is covered in rejected gowns from her plundered wardrobe. She is in her 'undies' now, and at her wits' end what to wear for the impending visit of Ralph Gorse. Then . . . she pulls out a kimono and, slowly, tries it on. Joan smiles at herself in the mirror. She twists and turns and makes her decision. The kimono, of course. That is what she will wear.

* * *

Back at the Nook, in The Friar Roadhouse, Mr Stimpson is consulting his watch yet again. Mr Norris is looking at him looking at it.

'You'll wear that watch out, Donald,' he remarks.

'What?' asks Mr Stimpson.

'The watch!'

Mr Stimpson nods, worried. 'Ah, yes . . . Indeed.'

Mr Norris thinks he knows why. 'Mrs Plumleigh-Bruce still expected?'

'Er . . . possibly, possibly.'

Norris sighs. 'I *think* it's my shout. Two scotches, please, Albert.'

Mr Stimpson shakes his head, mystified. This is not like Joan, not like Joan at all.

If he had known how Joan was greeting Gorse at that very moment, Mr Stimpson would have been very upset.

Joan is in her kimono. It covers most of her plump, but to many, alluring figure, but suggests more than it reveals. Gorse is inspecting it with evident, but not necessarily sincere, attention.

'Joan! What a vision of loveliness!'

'Do you think so? Really?'

'Oh, I do!'

'Thank you, Ralph. Do sit down . . . Will you have a drink?'

Gorse sits on the sofa and relaxes. 'Well, a scotch would be nice. Shall *I* get it?'

'Oh, please *do*! . . . My usual, please . . .'

Gorse gets up again and crosses to the drinks cabinet. He fixes a scotch and a gin and It. As he does so, he throws a remark over his shoulder. It sounds casual. In reality it is anything but. 'I come the bearer of very good news, Joan.'

'Oh, what? Do tell!'

Gorse keeps his back to her and his voice level. 'Our one hundred pounds investment is now worth one hundred and fifty pounds.'

Joan is astonished. 'What, in a day?'

'Stock Market's a funny place. We got in early. It was a very good tip.' Now Gorse feels safe enough to turn around and give Joan her drink.

'You mean we're both twenty-five pounds better off? In one day?' Joan cannot believe it.

Gorse fishes the passbook out of his pocket. 'There it is, entered in the passbook. I took the cheque straight down to the bank myself.'

Joan protests, 'But we only put it in today?'

Gorse sits opposite and sips his whisky. 'I told you a little untruth, Joan. I had already invested the one hundred pounds. I did that yesterday. I didn't know if you'd want in. But when you did, what the hell, I just cut my own investment in half and gave you the other half!'

'I say, that's terribly nice of you, Ralph.'

Gorse raises his glass. 'What are friends for, my dear?'

Joan feels the need for a small correction. 'Not just friends, Ralph . . . I mean, we're not *just* friends, are we?'

Gorse swallows and then bravely bites the bullet. 'No, Joan. Of course we're not. You know we're not.'

Joan is much affected by this and says in a low and trembly voice, 'Ralph. You're *so* sweet. Really.' Gorse responds by quickly opening the passbook for her to inspect. This means Joan has to use her spectacles, which she *hates* to do, fumbling them from her handbag. Gorse sits next to her but is all business. 'Actually, I asked my cousin for a cheque rather than putting it on the old monthly account, because I thought you might want to take a profit. Sell your shares.'

Joan pouts. 'What are you going to do?'

'I'm going to hang on. I only wish I had some more spare cash to put in.'

Joan waves the passbook. 'Couldn't *I* put in some more, if it's as good an investment as this?'

Gorse is doubtful. 'You could, but I'd insist you took out the winnings in proportion to what you put in.'

Joan begins to calculate. 'Let's see . . . Fifty pounds has won us twenty-five pounds . . . A hundred pounds could win us fifty pounds . . . Three hundred pounds – a hundred and fifty pounds!'

'That's an awful lot of money, Joan,' warns Gorse, the good friend. Joan replies simply, 'I feel lucky. You make me feel lucky, Ralph.'

Gorse smiles at her.

In The Friar it is closing time and Albert the barman is shouting, albeit genteelly, 'Closing time, ladies and gents . . . If you please!' Mr Stimpson and Mr Norris are drinking up. Mr Stimpson is by now – he has had several more drinks than usual – slightly tipsy and looking very disappointed. 'Well, I must go, Donald,' says Mr Norris, 'or Mrs Norris will never forgive me.'

Mr Stimpson sighs. 'Yes, indeed . . . I must toddle, myself.'

Norris asks meaningly, 'A little lady waiting, too, I have no doubt?'

Mr Stimpson grimaces, but in a sickly fashion. 'I should have 'phoned her, really . . . but didn't. There you are. Take potluck, what?'

They part at the door of The Friar with a cheery

'Goodnight, old boy!' Mr Stimpson walks off, disconsolately, into the dark night.

By now they are in Joan's bedroom. Gorse wishes that this had not happened, but of course, he reflects, it was bound to happen, absolutely no avoiding it, really. In all situations of this sort, Gorse reflects, the time comes when the woman demands to be loved. That moment is at hand. Gorse has been in similar situations before and has always carried them off with bravado, or with seeming bravado. This must be no different. Joan Plumleigh-Bruce must not suspect, not for one moment, what Ralph Ernest Gorse's real feelings are.

Joan is sitting in front of the dressing table. She is wearing her kimono. It falls open ominously, displaying Joan's full, mature charms, which hold no charm for Gorse. But this is no time to say so, no indeed.

'Darling . . .' breathes Joan.

Gorse stares at the door as if ready to leave. He has a full glass in his hand. He feels a little bit out of control, as if he's been drinking too much, which indeed he has.

'Come in, darling. Don't be afraid.'

Gorse tries a gambit. 'Well, I am, rather. Joan, is this wise? The neighbours?'

Joan shrugs, suddenly angry. 'To hell with the neighbours! I don't care what they think! They're only silly suburban clerks and such, anyway, I can't run my life by their stupid prejudices . . . And anyway, you can go early, before it's light . . . Can't you?' She turns and stares at Gorse intently.

Gorse sighs. 'Well, yes, I suppose so. But Joan, it's you I'm thinking about, it's your reputation – I mean, if it gets about that I – ' Joan stands up. The kimono falls totally open. Beneath it, Joan is nude. 'Shush. No more talk.'

Joan holds out her arms. Gorse steps forward and embraces her. She cannot see the expression of hatred on his face, for he buries it in the silk of the kimono. 'Just one minute, darling!' Joan breaks away, and goes and pulls the curtains together.

Outside a figure stands under a tree on the other side of this suburban street. He gazes up at the front bedroom window to see Joan, nude but for the kimono, drawing the curtains.

It is Mr Stimpson.

Mr Stimpson steadies himself by putting his hand on Gorse's Railton sports car, plainly recognizable to him in the light of a streetlamp. Mr Stimpson's face, in the pool of light, is impassive; but he sways very slightly as he looks up at the darkened window.

Gorse and Joan lie on the bed: Joan nude, Gorse in shirt and trousers. His fingers are toying with a silk scarf, which he playfully loops around her neck. Joan looks startled but Gorse makes a reassuring movement with his lips, and she relaxes even more. Slowly, even more playfully, Gorse tightens the scarf, until Joan cries out suddenly in frightened protest, and then, and then only, does he relax the pressure . . . and bend his head down and kiss her on the lips . . . Gratefully, greedily, but shaking from the sudden fear, Joan Plumleigh-Bruce clings to him, and gives herself to him . . .

But she cannot see Gorse's eyes. It is as well she cannot.

It is lunch time at The Friar the next day, and the Nook is a little busier than usual, with one or two commercial travellers eating ham or beef sandwiches. Joan is not looking best pleased to be sitting with Mr Stimpson at a table and not in her usual place at the bar. Mr Stimpson is putting two drinks on the table.

Joan complains. 'I do so hate this place at lunch time. Full of commercial travellers.'

Mr Stimpson is reassuring. 'It seemed the handiest place to meet, my dear. We can go for a lunch in the restaurant later, if you like.'

Joan demurs. 'Well, let's see . . . What *is* it that is so important that you telephone me at home and drag me out here in such a hurry?'

Mr Stimpson sips his bitter, and controls his voice. 'I saw you come out of the Southern Counties Bank with young Gorse yesterday.'

Joan begins to get very angry indeed. 'Donald, are you spying on me now?'

'No, no. Of course not. Certainly not spying, no.' Mr Stimpson looks around and lowers his voice. 'I remembered what you'd said about Gorse advising you on your investments, and I thought perhaps – '

Joan interrupts. 'Well, you thought too much! I'm not asking for your thoughts.' Mr Stimpson persists. 'Then you *have* come to some kind of . . . arrangement with Gorse?'

'I don't see how you can know that.'

'But you have?'

'Well, what if I have, it's my money.'

'How much?'

'What?'

Mr Stimpson asks patiently, 'How much have you invested . . . in whatever it is?'

'What possible business is that of yours, may I ask?' Joan demands. One or two commercial travellers look round. Joan decides she does not care. She is extremely annoyed by this line of questioning. For one thing, she is far from being at her best this morning. There had been, first, the events of the night (or rather of the early part of the night, for Gorse had not stayed long) and those events she wishes to put out of her mind – well, some of those events. Certainly her dear husband, the Major (the only other man with whom Joan had had sexual relations) had never done some of the things Ralph Gorse had done the previous night. The Major had been clumsy and fumbling, but respectful. Ralph Gorse had been anything but respectful. He had treated her (despite his honeyed words) as if she had been . . . well, a whore. Some of the things he had said . . . and done . . . *Well* . . . ! They were outside her experience.

On the other hand, despite the pain and strangeness, she could not wait to see him again.

But Mr Stimpson is answering her question. 'Strictly speaking, Joan, it isn't my business . . . But I have given you very good financial advice up to now, have I not?'

'All you say is keep my money on deposit. Three per cent. Don't take risks . . . Well, sometimes I feel like taking risks!'

'This is a very hard world, Joan. If one is without money.'

Joan is enraged now. 'Who said anything about being without money?'

Mr Stimpson lectures her: 'Shares can be very dicey, you know, especially if you don't know the market.'

Joan speaks harshly. 'Ralph knows the market, it's only a few pounds. For God's sake, Donald, stop going on as if you're my father!'

Mr Stimpson is shocked by this outburst. 'Well . . . Perhaps I've been over-concerned.'

'Yes, you have!' She drinks, and he drinks. There is a

small silence. Then, greatly daring, Mr Stimpson returns to the attack. 'Er . . . There is another thing I wanted to say, Joan.'

'Oh yes, and what's that?'

'. . . This is a very small town, Joan.'

'Small and small-minded!'

Mr Stimpson persists. 'I was just wondering, as a friend . . . Purely as a very . . . close . . . friend . . . if it's really wise to be seen around quite so much with Gorse.'

'Explain that a little more, please, Donald?'

Mr Stimpson does not see his danger. 'This business you have with him, Stock Exchange, horses, whatever it is . . . There's not a lot of harm in it, is there, unless it gets . . . well, out of hand . . . But . . .'

'But *what*, Donald?'

'Perhaps I shouldn't say any more.'

'Perhaps you shouldn't, but you're going to! Because I want to hear what it is you are trying to say!'

Mr Stimpson drops his voice, looks round, then: 'I . . . er . . . I happened to pass your house on my way home from The Friar last evening . . . and I . . . saw Gorse's car parked outside. He's a strange young man, Joan, and we don't really know anything about him, do we . . .? I must say . . . I was a little shocked, Joan . . . Yes, I must use the word, shocked!'

This is altogether too much for Joan, and for the first time in her life she creates a 'scene' in public. She leans forward towards Mr Stimpson and does not trouble to lower her voice at all. 'Use any word you damn well please, you silly old fool! What I do, Donald Stimpson, is my business, whether it's to do with my money or my personal affairs – and I know you have been talking about me, Donald, so don't deny it. And stop *spying* on me!' With that Joan gets to her feet, grabs her handbag and departs from The Friar. Mr Stimpson – uncomfortably aware of the curious eyes of the commercial travellers – sips his half of bitter miserably. It has been a disastrous meeting.

In Mr Norris's office in the Southern Counties Bank sits Joan Plumleigh-Bruce with her crocodile bag on her knees, an embattled and angry look about her. Gorse sits on another chair, looking anxious and concerned. For the moment, they are alone in the room.

'What's all the hurry, Joan?' asks Gorse. 'You don't have to do anything today.'

Joan snaps, 'Oh yes I do!'

Gorse shakes his head. 'I'm sorry, I don't understand.'

Joan tries to explain, in innocent terms. 'I just made my mind up to put the money into our account today, that's all, and I wanted you to be here.'

Gorse is, in truth, somewhat anxious at this turn of events but does not show it. 'Yes, well, that's fine . . . Is this the three hundred pounds you were talking about?. . . I wouldn't put in more than that . . .'

But before he can say more the door opens and Mr Norris comes in, washing his hands in invisible soap.

'So sorry to keep you waiting, Mrs Plumleigh-Bruce, Captain Gorse . . . How can I help you?'

Gorse looks at Joan. She comes, at once, to the point. 'I know I could have put this money into the account over the counter, but it's rather a large amount, so I felt – '

'But of course,' interrupts Mr Norris. 'What kind of sum are we talking about, Mrs Plumleigh-Bruce?'

In reply, Joan opens her handbag and takes out a very large bundle of white banknotes. She puts them on the desk. Both Gorse and Norris stare at them. Their reactions are, in a way, similar.

Joan breaks the silence. 'I think you'll find there's a thousand pounds there.'

A little later, Joan and Gorse arrive back at Joan's house. The maid is taking their coats out, and Joan is giving Gorse a glass of sherry. She is flushed and happy.

'I think this demands a small celebration, Ralph. We are going to get quite rich. I can feel it!'

'We will if the shares go up,' Gorse adds hastily, 'which they will, of course.'

Joan holds up her glass. 'Of course . . . You're lucky for me! Here's to us!'

Gorse does the same. 'And to Maitland Securities.'

Joan laughs. 'And to Maitland Securities . . .'

After that, Gorse looks at her somewhat pensively. 'Joan, I do wish you hadn't put the whole thousand in. You don't want to change your mind, do you?'

'Certainly not! Unless there's any reason why I should?'

'. . . No . . . None at all. It's just . . . I'd hate . . .'

'What?'

'. . . Nothing, really.'

'*Do* sit down, Ralph.'

Gorse sits. 'Just for a moment. I have to ring my cousin, the broker chap, and buy those shares, or we'll none of us be rich, will we?'

'You can telephone from here . . .' offers Joan.

Gorse demurs. 'I have all the papers and things at my place . . . I mean Ronnie Shooter's place . . .'

'Donald Stimpson said something about your having to leave the house, is that right?' asks Joan.

'Ronnie's coming back this weekend,' replies Gorse.

Joan calculates. 'It's Friday tomorrow . . . You mean you have to find somewhere to live by *Saturday*?'

'I'll be all right, don't worry.'

Joan looks at him a long moment. 'Ralph. Are you really going to take that job with your family firm? Will you really *have* to go away?'

Gorse smiles, uncomfortably. 'For a while, until I get settled in. Then I'll come back and see you, I expect.'

'I won't be seeing very *much* of you, will I? If you *do* go, that is?'

'Can't see what choice I have. I could have hung on a bit, but Ronnie coming back has rather dished that.'

Joan, greatly daring, and after a long moment's thought, suggests, 'You could always . . . stay here.'

Gorse has been expecting a lot of things but not that. In fact, he can find no ready answer. So he waits.

Joan goes on, 'I don't know what the neighbours would say but *I* don't care if *you* don't!' She laughs. 'Officially, you could always stay in the spare room.'

Gorse is cagey. 'Well. I don't know . . .'

'Don't be too enthusiastic whatever you do!' declares Joan, in what Gorse thinks of as her huffy voice. He is quick to reassure her. 'Joan, I'm thinking about *you*, really. The neighbours? As you say – '

'Really, Ralph, you sound just like Donald Stimpson! He read me the same Riot Act in The Friar at lunch time today!'

'. . . *Did* he?'

Joan's annoyance returns to her face in the form of an unusually pink flush. 'I'll ruin my reputation if I have you in for a drink after ten o'clock at night, would you believe it?' Joan's mouth sets. 'I shan't be seeing anything like so much of Donald Stimpson from now on, I can tell you!'

Gorse wonders, 'Did you tell him all about our arrangement?'

'Of course not, but you know how he is. If you talk to him long enough he'll know your date of birth!'

Gorse replies, slowly, 'I suppose in his place I'd feel annoyed.'

Joan confirms that. 'Annoyed, my dear! He was absolutely blazing! Didn't show it, of course, never does. I wouldn't put it past him to ferret around. He won't rest until he knows all our business.'

Gorse feels alarm bells ringing. 'How would he do that?'

Joan refills their sherry glasses. 'Well, he banks at Southern Counties himself. Never mind about Donald Stimpson, let's talk about us! Look, why not forget that stupid job, I can tell you don't want it! Move in here, and any profit we make from our investments we go fifty-fifty! How's that?'

Gorse protests, 'I can't let you do that. You've put in all the money!'

Joan crosses and sits on the sofa, puts down her glass and puts her arms around Gorse. Her voice is soft in his ear. 'Ralph . . . I don't care about that. It's *you* I care about. I've been so bloody miserable in this place, for so long. You're the best thing that's happened to me for a very long time. If I lost you I'd be . . . desolate.'

Gorse knows he must retreat from all this emotion. He is thinking hard. He disengages Joan's arms, gently, taking care not to offend her by seeming to repulse her embrace. 'Let me think,' he says.

But Joan presses his hand, firmly. 'Promise you'll stay, Ralph. Pack your things and bring them over tonight!'

Gorse looks for a way out – and finds one. 'Look . . . first things first. I do have to ring the brokers . . . Then there are one or two other things I must do . . . Call my people in . . . er . . . Paris . . . And . . . then . . .'

Joan stands up quickly, delighted. '*Tomorrow* then? You'll come over tomorrow?'

Gorse nods, and stands too. 'All right . . . Tomorrow afternoon sometime.'

'Oh, Ralph . . . I'm *so* glad.'

Joan reaches up, kisses him passionately on the mouth. Gorse holds her. The door opens and Mary, the slavey, enters. Her eyes pop, as Joan disengages herself from the embrace.

'Oh, sorry, mam! *Very* sorry, mam!' Mary turns round and disappears the way she has come.

Gorse takes the opportunity to move. 'I'll get on. I'll see you . . .'

'Tomorrow afternoon,' prompts Joan. 'Come for tea.'

Gorse kisses her on the cheek. 'Yes. Of course. Tea.'

'Until then, darling.'

Joan squeezes Gorse's hand. Gorse has a sudden attack of curiosity. 'Joan . . . You *are* all right? . . . I mean, that thousand wasn't your *last* penny or anything, was it?'

'Stop worrying. I feel alive again! Living dangerously suits me!'

'See you tomorrow,' promises Gorse.

Joan sees him to the front door, watches as he gets into the Railton and drives away, waving, up the street. She goes back into the living room and finishes her drink. Then she rings the tiny silver bell.

Mary appears round the door as if by magic, agog for news. 'Yes, mam?'

Joan is to the point. 'Mary, I want you to get the spare room ready. Captain Gorse will be staying with us for a while.'

'Yes, mam, how long, mam?'

Joan pours herself yet another glass of sherry. 'Quite some time, I should think . . .'

* * *

That same evening Mr Stimpson is standing at the bar of the Nook in The Friar, his usual half of bitter in his hand. He is paying for a scotch for Mr Norris, the bank manager. This is so rare an occurrence that Mr Norris feels he must comment on it. 'Rather pushing the boat out these days, aren't you, old chap? Second scotch you've bought me tonight.'

Mr Stimpson agrees, drily. 'I have ulterior motives, Norman.'

Mr Norris laughs. 'What *can* they be?'

Mr Stimpson drops his voice. 'I want you to break a professional confidence.'

Mr Norris is frosty at once. 'You'd better have your scotch back, Donald.'

Mr Stimpson shakes his head. 'Let me put it another way. I am, or rather I always have been, a financial adviser to Mrs Joan Plumleigh-Bruce . . .'

'Oh, really? That wasn't my impression.'

'Why do you say that?' asks Mr Stimpson.

Mr Norris explains. 'Because you were not with her when she came into my office today, and she made no mention of you in the course of our . . . er . . . discussions.'

'Today? She's been in your office *again*?'

Norris is alarmed by the tone of Mr Stimpson's voice. 'I don't think I should say any more about this matter.' He takes out his pocket-watch, hastily. 'Good Lord, is that the time? Now, you'll have to excuse me, I really must go – Mrs Norris is expecting me.'

'Norman,' declares Mr Stimpson, 'if you don't help me in this little matter, I shall have to seriously consider removing my account from your bank. And you know your bank auditors don't like to lose accounts of my size.'

Mr Norris drinks the whisky, miserably. 'I can't say

anything about another client! Donald, be reasonable!'

Mr Stimpson persists. 'In this matter I'm not reasonable. Did Mrs Joan Plumleigh-Bruce put more money into her joint account with Ralph Gorse *this afternoon*?'

But Mr Norris will not be drawn further. 'Donald, I really *must* go . . . Goodnight, Donald . . .' And he makes his exit in so determined a fashion that Mr Stimpson cannot raise a voice or a hand to prevent him except to call out, 'You'll regret not having helped me, Norman. I promise you!'

But Mr Norris is gone.

It is one o'clock in the afternoon of the following day. In a side street just opposite the Southern Counties Bank, Gorse sits in his Railton. In the back is his battered and stickered case. He has a good view of the bank but cannot easily be seen from it. He has been there for almost twenty minutes. He looks up as a couple of customers come out, middle-class, middle-aged, female. Gorse looks anxiously at his watch and, for once, feels a prickle of anxiety. Then the anxiety is suddenly dissipated. For Mr Norris comes out of the door of the Southern Counties Bank, wearing a hat and carrying a newspaper. He walks off up the street, obviously on his way to lunch at a nearby café, where Gorse has, by observation three days running, ascertained that he spends at least forty-five minutes.

Gorse sits in the car for a long moment. Then he gets out and crosses the street and goes into the Southern Counties Bank. What Gorse does not know is that his action has been observed by Mr Stimpson, who stands at the door of his estate agent's office. It is pure chance, but Mr Stimpson believes in Providence, and here is a situation, he reasons, that merits investigation. But it is not reason only, more what is sometimes called a hunch, really. Mr Stimpson could not have said why he behaved exactly as he did. He really did not have very much to go on. But he behaved with decision and despatch. He forgot lunch, went back into his office and called to his office boy, 'Get me Mr Norris at the Southern Counties Bank. Now! Quick, lad!'

'Yes, Mr Stimpson. Right away, sir!' The boy – no more than fourteen at best but already brisk in the ways of business – looks up the telephone number of the Southern Counties Bank, which takes him half a minute, and then asks for that number and waits for the bank's operator to reply, which, since it is the lunch hour and she is alone, takes some little time. Mr Stimpson uses up this period by going out again and standing outside his office, staring at the door of the bank.

Gorse does not come out. Nobody comes out. The office boy comes out. 'Mr Stimpson . . . Mr Norris has gone to lunch, sir . . . You can talk to the senior clerk on duty, sir?'

Mr Stimpson casts one last look at the bank. 'Oh . . . All right . . .' He goes inside.

Not half a minute after he has done so, out of the door of the bank comes Gorse. He crosses the road to the Railton, stuffing an envelope into his pocket as he does so.

Mr Stimpson, by now, is talking – or rather shouting – into his telephone. 'I'm not asking you to *do* anything! I'm asking you *not* to! If anybody is drawing any money out of that account . . . All you have to do is make an excuse and – *What?* Oh never mind!' Mr Stimpson slams down the receiver and hurries from the office, putting on his hat as he goes. He is just in time to see Gorse pulling away in the Railton. Gorse drives fast, past Mr Stimpson, who has to jump from the car's path. Mr Stimpson, puffing, perplexed and angry, watches Gorse drive impassively on. He cannot be sure Gorse has seen him. By now extremely apprehensive, Mr Stimpson crosses the busy street towards the Southern Counties Bank.

Gorse has not gone back to Ronnie Shooter's house. He has not gone, as promised, to take tea with Joan Plumleigh-Bruce. Gorse, in the Railton, is driving very fast out of Reading, towards London. He is taking back roads for safety's sake, and back roads in the late 'Thirties were dirty and quiet. That suited Gorse as he sang to himself a popular ditty of the day; as he drove, beating time with his gloved hand on the steering wheel, a feeling of freedom took him over, something he has not felt for many, many months now, a feeling that nobody owned him, that his destiny is in his own hands. 'South of the Border,' sang Gorse, 'Down Mexico Way . . .'

Gorse has an appointment with Clarice Mannors at the Ritz Hotel at three o'clock that afternoon. He knows that he is in good time. No hurry, old son, Gorse tells himself, no hurry at all.

Mr Norris has just returned from his lunch, and it sits very heavily on his stomach at that moment. For Mr Norris is very annoyed, and very shaken. Mr Stimpson – who looks equally grim and angry – faces him across his desk.

Mr Norris is trying to remain calm. 'These allegations are very serious indeed, Mr Stimpson. I don't know on what you base them.'

Mr Stimpson is prompt to reply. 'Human gullibility! Including yours!'

Mr Norris is aghast. 'Mine? I don't know how you can say that. I have done nothing.'

'Then tell me exactly how much Ralph Gorse drew out of that account!'

'Indeed I will not!'

'You'll have to when Mrs Plumleigh-Bruce gets here!'

Mr Norris stands on his dignity at the narrow confines of his duty. 'I shall tell Mrs Plumleigh-Bruce what I shall tell her because she has every right to know. As a co-signatory of the account.'

Mr Stimpson is bitter but admiring. 'Co-signatory! So *that's* how he did it!'

Mr Norris becomes prim. 'I can discuss this no more until Mrs Plumleigh-Bruce gets here. The bank will close soon, anyway. We shut at three, you know.'

Mr Stimpson closes his eyes. 'Norman, you are a complete idiot, did anybody ever tell you that?'

Mr Norris looks shocked and very angry indeed.

Gorse has halted the Railton in a cloud of dust at a country crossroads. At these crossroads there is a sign: 'Little Waring 1½ miles. Sudleigh 2 miles'. Gorse takes out a map-case and pulls out a large road map. He curses, as he fails to find any reference that will help him. For in taking the back routes, Gorse has managed to get himself thoroughly lost. He shakes his head irritably, revs the Railton and makes a choice to the right. Suddenly, the car develops a stutter. Gorse looks at the petrol gauge and curses. He has remembered everything except the bloody petrol! The car stops with a shudder. Gorse leaps out, grabs the spare petrol can and with a silent curse walks off, looking for a garage, down the dusty, silent country road.

It is now exactly two o'clock.

* * *

Joan Plumleigh-Bruce is standing in the doorway of Mr Norris's office, ushered in by Mr Saxby, a male clerk, fortyish, in glasses. Mr Norris gets up from behind his desk. 'Ah . . . Mrs Plumleigh-Bruce. Come in. Do sit down.'

But Joan has seen Mr Stimpson standing there. She looks at both men in turn. 'What is all this about, pray?'

'Tell her,' Mr Stimpson advises Mr Norris.

Mr Norris protests. 'I think perhaps you should go, Mr Stimpson. This is banking business between Mrs Plumleigh-Bruce and myself.'

Joan has a feeling of disaster. 'What *is* all this about? A taxi is sent for me, to bring me here on urgent business . . . *What* urgent business?'

Mr Norris commands, 'Saxby, don't go!' Mr Saxby waits, deferentially.

'Saxby,' says the bank manager, 'tell Mrs Plumleigh-Bruce how much you paid out to Mr Ralph Gorse at one o'clock today.'

'Exactly one thousand pounds, sir.'

Joan feels the earth is spinning all around her. She sits down, quite abruptly.

'Thank you, Saxby,' says Mr Norris.

But Mr Saxby feels he must explain. 'It was all in order, sir, one signature only. Mr Gorse's or Mrs Plumleigh-Bruce, sir. I had a job finding a thousand in large denominations, sir – '

'Quite, quite,' interrupts Mr Norris. 'That will be all, Saxby.' Mr Saxby nods, and leaves, closing the door quietly behind him.

Joan Plumleigh-Bruce sits there. She is saying nothing, just looking at her hands. She is avoiding the eye of Mr Stimpson.

Mr Norris is justifying himself. 'Nothing that I or my

staff did was anything but correct! Either Mrs Plumleigh-Bruce signed or Mr Gorse signed for withdrawals. I asked her on two occasions if the arrangement was to be in both names to sign, or one, and on each occasion she said *either* name . . . Am I correct, Mrs Plumleigh-Bruce?'

Joan looks up at them both. She is like stone. 'He's gone. Let him go.'

Mr Stimpson remarks, as if idly, 'I can get the police on to him.'

'No. Let him go,' says Joan.

'I'll talk to the Inspector. I know him.'

Mr Norris feels he must speak on the legal position. 'Gorse has done nothing illegal! He has drawn money from a joint account, arranged so that he could draw money on his signature alone! For all we know he may be investing the money elsewhere!'

'Oh, he's doing that all right,' says Mr Stimpson bitterly.

Slowly, Joan asks, 'Do you think that's possible . . . Mr Norris?'

Mr Norris answers without hope. '*Anything* is possible, dear lady.'

'He means no,' clarifies Mr Stimpson.

Joan looks at Mr Stimpson and shakes her head slowly, from side to side, like a child. 'Why? I simply don't understand . . . I don't *understand.*'

Mr Norris remarks, 'He at least left one hundred and fifty pounds in the account.'

'He did that to make it look right,' says Mr Stimpson, curtly.

'Perhaps,' agrees Mr Norris. 'He even left the Pass-book, to be collected by Mrs Plumleigh-Bruce.'

'He's very sly, our Mr Gorse,' agreed Mr Stimpson.

'Very smart and very sly. As, I think, some of us have found out to our cost.' Mr Stimpson is looking at Joan. She refuses to meet his eye.

At the crossroads, carrying a heavy can of petrol, Gorse staggers back to the Railton. He has walked forty minutes each way to and from the country garage, and he is shaking with exhaustion. Slowly, cursing, he pours the petrol into the tank. He glances at his watch. It is almost three o'clock.

In the Tea Room at the Ritz Hotel Clarice Mannors is sitting, afternoon tea in front of her. She consults her watch. Clarice is becoming rather irritable. She lights a cigarette and sighs. She is waiting for Ralph Gorse. He is late.

Gorse is driving the Railton like a maniac, along narrow streets, heading for the West End. He is trying to make up lost time but he knows that now it is only a matter of how late he is going to be. Clarice will wait for him, surely, he tells himself as he is held up in a traffic snarl at Hammersmith. Somewhere in front, a horse has fallen, and blocked all kinds of traffic. Horses are still allowed in the Metropolis, it is unbelievable. Gorse drums on the steering-wheel in impatient anger. Clarice will wait, he repeats aloud. Of course she will.

At that very moment Clarice Mannors walks into the Ritz Hotel reception area and asks to use a telephone. She is directed to a booth and asks for a Mayfair number. A man's voice answers. 'Hello . . . yes?'

Clarice gets straight to the point. 'Look, Archie, it's Clarice Mannors . . . I was going to Cannes with a friend

– you know, to join the Cavendish lot – but it looks as if I've been stood up. Aren't *you* going?'

'Where *are* you?' asks the man.

'The Ritz, actually.'

'Pick you up in fifteen minutes, all right?'

'Lovely!' answers Clarice. Sadly, she replaces the telephone.

It is now late afternoon in Mr Norris's office in the Southern Counties Bank. Mr Stimpson is leaning across the desk and his eyes are cold. Mr Norris is holding his head in his hands. Joan is still just sitting, somewhat shellshocked, in the same position she has occupied for the last hour.

'What I want to hear from you, Norman,' says Mr Stimpson in a loud clear voice, 'and I don't care how long it takes or what strings you have to pull to get it, I don't care *what* you have to do . . . But when Ralph Ernest Gorse opens a bank account *anywhere* . . . I want to know about it!'

Mr Norris looks up. 'I'm not sure I can do that, Donald! It isn't ethical!'

But Mr Stimpson is remorseless. 'Or I put in a complaint to your Head Office, about all *this*! The crass way you've allowed it to happen! Oh, they'll stand by you. Until the enquiry's over. But it wouldn't do you any good, would it, Norman? Not an enquiry!'

Mr Norris closes his eyes to the truth of that. 'Donald . . . I'll see what I can do.'

Mr Stimpson looks at him and nods, grimly. Then he turns to Joan. 'Come along, Joan.' He helps her out of the chair and out of the office.

* * *

The unemployed man still plays his mouth organ in the gutter outside the Ritz Hotel. Gorse, driving up in his Railton, does not even see him, this time. The doorman approaches the car but Gorse anticipates him. 'Look here, I have to park this car, can I leave it here? I'm in a terrible hurry, I'm desperately late.'

The doorman looks at the Railton and then at Gorse. 'Are *you* Mr Gorse, sir?'

'Yes.'

'Young lady left a message for you, sir. Sorry, but she's gone, sir.'

'Is that *all*?'

'Said she'd see you in August, sir. For the shooting, sir.'

Gorse grimaces at that. He turns the Railton round in a very sharp, fast-turning circle and drives away.

Now Gorse is at the open door of a town house in Mayfair, the Railton standing in the road. A butler is at the open door.

'I'm afraid Miss Mannors is out, sir,' the butler tells Gorse.

'Where is she, do you know?'

'Miss Mannors has gone away, sir. To the South of France, sir.'

'Which boat is she getting?'

'I cannot assist you, sir, I'm sorry.'

'Look here, what's your name?' asks Gorse.

'Blundell, sir.'

'Look, Blundell, I have to see her.' Gorse takes out a pound note. The butler's eyes are on it at once.

'Miss Clarice is taking the Dover ferry for France, sir. The boat train leaves Victoria at four-thirty, sir . . . Is your name Gorse, sir?'

'Yes, why?'

'Miss Clarice left a message, sir. See you in August – '

'For the shooting! I *know*!' Gorse gives Blundell the pound note and runs back to the Railton. Blundell watches him go. He pockets the pound note, which will buy his drinks (he consumes three bottles of Guinness Stout each evening, never more, never less) for a week. The ways of the rich never cease to surprise him, even after thirty-five years of ministering to them.

At Victoria Station the boat train is about to pull out. Steam, smoke, whistles, excitement, well-dressed people waving to those about to leave – all the ingredients of leave-taking are there, but Gorse sees none of this as he pushes through the people towards the iron barrier. The barrier clangs shut just as he reaches it.

'Sorry, sir!' apologizes the porter.

'Open it, there's a fiver in it!'

'Sorry, sir, I'd lose me job.'

Gorse just stands there, soaked in sweat, his shirt clinging to his back, and as his eyes clear, suddenly he sees at the far end of the train two figures: Clarice and a tall, dark man boarding the train. They are laughing and have their arms round each other . . . As Gorse watches, speechless, Clarice and the man board the boat train. A porter slams the door, shrill whistles blow; the steam is thicker than ever. Slowly, the boat train for the Continent pulls out.

'Bitch,' hisses Gorse under his breath, 'bloody, bloody bitch.'

Nobody hears him.

At Joan Plumleigh-Bruce's house, Mr Stimpson pays the taxi-driver. As the taxi wheels away, he turns to Joan, who is walking slowly, in a convalescent fashion, up the path to her front door. She turns as Mr Stimpson hurries after her. 'I'll be all right, Donald, please.'

But Mr Stimpson is taking charge. 'I'll come in. We'll have a drink. I need one if you don't.'

Joan submissively hands him the key and he opens the front door.

'Donald. In that bank . . . you sounded as if you wanted to murder Ralph Gorse.'

Mr Stimpson savours the words. 'Not murder him . . . No. *Destroy* him . . .'

Joan decides that Donald Stimpson looks quite mad.

But she says nothing.

There is nothing, absolutely nothing, to say.

Chapter Three

The Hotel Royal, on the seafront at Brighton, was a huge and imposing monument to Victorian values. Here, Edward VII had slept with his mistress, Mrs Keppel, and here with wives and mistresses (but mostly mistresses, for the Royal was the most expensive hotel in the town) had slept many, many men since the Prince of Wales had personally given the Royal its royal warrant of approval. Most of those men had been rich, or at least well-off, or had, anyway, lived a life devoted to expensive habits; habits of food, clothing, sex. Besides royalty, the Hotel Royal was frequented by City men, oil magnates, Rajahs of the various Indian royal families, lower gentry, as well as bookmakers, racehorse owners and professional gamblers. And, naturally, since they follow the money, by con men of some style. For the important thing at the Royal was to look like a gentleman. The lady with you need not be (in fact, rarely was!) a lady. That was perfectly acceptable. But the man must look a gentleman. The other requirement was that a gentleman paid his (usually very pricey!) bill when presented. On the day he left the hotel. Not before. To ask for payment on account would have reduced the place to the status of a boarding house. For the Royal was not called the Royal for nothing.

In the late summer of 1938, the hotel is full. The weather has been good and many well-to-do people are staying there, who found the heat of Monte or Cannes far too excessive at this time of year. Also, there was the dreadful, oily French food to contend with. The Royal served English food, often under a French name. These people had said to one another: 'A few days, a weekend maybe, down at the coast? Why not the dear old Royal? That would be the ticket, what?'

So here they all were, the men in silk pyjamas from Turnbull and Asser, and the women in crepe-de-Chine nightgowns from, possibly Harrods, if one was in a hurry. Mostly asleep, many drunk on whisky, wine, port, and sea air.

In Room 313 sleeps Ralph Ernest Gorse. As the dawn light filters in, this opulent room is in something of a mess. Items of men's and women's clothing are strewn about the furniture. There are full ashtrays and many empty bottles and glasses. Two people lie in the large bed. Gorse is sound asleep, wearing only one half of his silk pyjamas. His partner is a blonde young woman of twenty-five and nobody we know. She is nude, or near enough. Her name is Bunty.

At this very moment Bunty wakens, very gently, and she sits up just as gently. She takes in the scene and for a long moment she is still, only her wide blue eyes moving. Bunty gets out of the bed, very slowly and still very gently, casting a glance every now and then at the sleeping Gorse. She tiptoes across the room, to the bottom of the bed, where Gorse's jacket lies carelessly thrown. Bunty is still for a very long time, then she slips her hand into the inner pocket of the jacket.

As she does so, Bunty glances back at Gorse. He is still asleep. Bunty feels in the pocket and takes out a white flimsy five-pound note. She looks intently at it, then quickly back at Gorse. Then she puts her fingers in and tries for another. What happens next is so fast that she is unable to remember it afterwards. For Gorse is out of the bed and has slapped her very hard – twice! – across the face. As the girl falls violently backwards across the bed, shocked, she finds herself staring up into the maddened face of Ralph Ernest Gorse . . .

The one thing she is always to remember, all her life, is that she was quite, quite sure that he was going to kill her.

Some two hours later, that very same day, Mr Stimpson, dressed for the office, is waiting impatiently outside the Southern Counties Bank in Reading High Street. He holds a letter which he re-reads while he waits. The contents appear to bring him some satisfaction. He looks up as Mr Norris comes along the street. Mr Norris, as manager, must open the bank to allow his staff access. As he approaches and sees Mr Stimpson standing there, he does not show any marked enthusiasm for the encounter. Mr Stimpson, undeterred, accosts him, and shows him the letter he holds in his hand. Mr Norris is impatient, but he reads it, under duress. He is impressed, even resigned, as he hands it back to Mr Stimpson, who puts it back into his pocket. Then Mr Norris unlocks the front door of the bank, and his staff troop inside. He looks at Mr Stimpson, sighs, and then nods.

Together, they go into the bank.

In the bedroom at the Royal Hotel (now cleaned up by the chambermaids) Bunty is gazing petulantly into the dressing-table mirror. There is a bruise on her face and she has an incipient black eye. She is doing running repairs, using powder, rouge and mascara, without enthusiasm.

'You're a bastard, Ralph Gorse . . . I thought you were going to kill me for a minute!'

'If you do it again I might,' replies Gorse calmly. Gorse is eating breakfast. He is in his shirtsleeves and looks rested.

'I would have only taken a fiver! Honestly! You keep me so short of money!'

Gorse looks over the top of his *Sporting Life*. 'You can always make some your usual way.'

Bunty is nettled. 'Oh, and how is that?'

'On your back,' replies Gorse, equably.

Bunty grimaces at him in the mirror. 'You say such lovely things. If I had the train fare I'd go back to London.' Suddenly, she wheedles. 'You wouldn't let me have it, would you Ralph, and call it a day, darling?'

Gorse shakes his head. 'If you check out of this hotel, they'll present a bill for quite a lot of money.'

Bunty stops work on her face. 'Oh God, don't say you can't pay them!'

'So you can't go. Any more than I can,' says Gorse with an air of finality.

'But I thought you were rolling in it?'

'I was.'

Bunty is suddenly very sober. 'So what now?'

Gorse permits himself a small, wry smile. 'We will have to put on our thinking caps, won't we, dear . . . that, or take off our unmentionables . . . whatever the situation calls for, what?'

Bunty looks at Gorse in some consternation as he lights a Player's Perfecto from his gold cigarette case, with his gold lighter which, a long time ago, he stole from Ronnie Shooter. One thing is certain. Bunty is hurt, and more than a little afraid of this man.

Which is the way Gorse likes it.

* * *

Mr Stimpson hurried towards Joan Plumleigh-Bruce's house, fresh from his interview with Mr Norris. Mr Stimpson rarely hurried but today was a day different from all others. Today, he had information that would bring him a step nearer to the sweet sickening revenge that he felt he must, surely, sooner or later inflict upon Ralph Gorse. He had thought of little else these last weeks and months. He had thought of Gorse, the swindler, the debaucher, through the long days of summer. Quite simply, Mr Stimpson could contain himself no longer. His partner, old Mr Snell, had even remarked upon it. 'Not feeling yourself, these days, Donald?' he'd asked once, catching Mr Stimpson in a reverie of revenge, just sitting at his desk, smiling at the thought of Gorse brought to justice. These reveries fed upon his fevered imagination, as he pictured Gorse, who had posed as his friend – *friend, that* was a joke! – finally standing in some court, accused of . . . *what*? At this point Mr Stimpson's imagination failed him. For as Norris had wearily repeated to him, only that very morning, Ralph Gorse had done nothing wrong. Nothing legally wrong, that was . . .

Mr Norris though had news for him; and it was this news he now imparted excitedly to Joan Plumleigh-Bruce, as she admitted him to her living room. 'A cheque for one hundred pounds has been presented to a branch of Barclay's Bank in Brighton and "Referred to Drawer"!'

Joan showed only a cursory interest. She had been withdrawn during these long months, but that was only to be expected. 'What does that *mean*, Donald?'

'No funds! The drawer – the person who signed the cheque – was one *Ralph Ernest Gorse*! He has had the account only four weeks and he has overdrawn sixty-three pounds in that time!'

Still, Joan did not seem to take it in. 'But . . . if his cheques are being refused, what can it mean, except – ?'

Mr Stimpson felt slightly deflated, and more than slightly irritated. 'What it means, my dear silly woman, is that *Ralph Gorse* has now spent all of your thousand pounds and is getting into the red at his bank, bouncing rubber cheques!'

Joan sat down on the sofa. She did not want to hear any of this. She wished it would all go away. On some days she could almost believe that it had never happened. Except of course that it had. 'Donald, I wish you would try not to speak to me that way. It's extremely rude and I will not stand for it!'

'No?' asked Mr Stimpson, nastily. He looked at her a long moment. She looked away. There had been many moments like this in that long hot summer. Many moments when Mr Stimpson had wanted to speak his mind in full about his suspicions as to what, exactly, had happened between her and Gorse, to ask questions, but of course he didn't ask because he did not want to know, not exactly. But the worm was in the bud. And it was eating away at Mr Stimpson's very sanity, he often thought.

Joan was moving adroitly away from this dangerous area of thought and discussion.

'So Ralph's in Brighton, is he?' she asked, mildly.

Mr Stimpson nodded. 'So it seems. I shall find out more when I get there.'

Joan asked wearily, 'Donald . . . what good will it do? Chasing down there? Even if you find him, what will it accomplish?'

'It will give me great satisfaction.'

Joan tries once more. 'It's been months since Ralph . . .'

Mr Stimpson does not spare her. '. . . Since Gorse deceived you and ran off with your money!'

'Donald, you don't have to say it in that awful way. Don't you think I'm as upset as you are?'

Mr Stimpson looks at her. Nobody is as upset as he is. Nobody in the whole world. But his day will come. He knows it will.

'. . . You won't . . . attack him . . . I mean . . . Or anything silly like that . . . will you, Donald?'

'Can you see me throwing him off Brighton Pier?' asks Mr Stimpson, sarcastically.

'Not really – he's very fit and strong!'

Mr Stimpson cannot resist the thrust. 'Well, I suppose you would know all about that!' Mr Stimpson picks up his hat and turns to go. He had been a fool to come. She still cared for the rotter Gorse, had feelings for him, deny it if she dared.

'You will ring, Donald?' Joan asks, tentatively.

'At some point.'

'I don't suppose it's any good saying . . . don't go?'

'None whatever. I'm catching the early evening train . . . Good-bye.'

'Good-bye, Donald.' Joan offers her cheek to be kissed. Mr Stimpson kisses it duly, pulsing with rage. Then he goes out briskly, and slams the door behind him.

Joan pours herself a gin and It and sits on the sofa. She cannot think why Donald should want to pursue Ralph Gorse, to open up the dreadful wounds that, for her, are just beginning to close. For she knows that what Ralph did was not exactly what Donald Stimpson says he did. It was not all as cruel and unfeeling, as unloving as Donald Stimpson insists it was; it was not as premeditated and calculating as that. This, Joan in her heart knows. Ralph Gorse would never be so unkind. Somewhere, if she could but know them, there are extenuating circumstances. There had to be.

Or life would, indeed, not be worth living. Joan drank her gin and It and poured herself another. She had consumed a lot of lonely gin and Its that long, hot summer.

Around ten o'clock that very same evening, in a rather sleazy night club in Brighton, Gorse and Bunty are sitting at a corner alcove. With them is Harold Bennett, Gorse's ex-employer, fiftyish, sharply dressed, a local business-man; a seller of new and used cars, to be precise. He is on a night out, and already rather drunk, also somewhat nervous. This is a bit near home for him, but Bunty's charms, which can easily be seen, as she is half-falling out of her dress, are very attractive indeed to Harold Bennett. He is looking at Bunty as he talks to Gorse.

'Must say, last thing I expected . . . Hearing your voice on the 'phone today, Gorse.'

'*Ralph*, please! I'm not working for you these days, Harold,' says Gorse ironically.

Bennett addresses Bunty. 'That's Ralph. Always there with the sharp answer.'

Bunty's smile is all for him. 'Oh, I don't know, I think you're pretty sharp y'self, Mr Bennett . . . Good card player, I bet?'

'Not bad,' admits Bennett, turning to Gorse. 'I hear there's a good School going tonight?'

Gorse nods. 'You and me and Vinny the bookie, and a friend of his. The four of us.'

Bennett frowns. 'That *is* sharp company. Vinny knows his poker.'

Gorse reaches over and fills Bennett's glass. 'Well, if

you want to cry off, if it's a bit strong for you, Harold, just say so, no offence taken.'

But Bennett is aware of Bunty's eyes. 'Not at all. I know my poker as well as the next man. Just surprised to hear you were staying at the Royal, that's all. Things must be looking up, what?'

Gorse smiles, lying through his teeth, 'I'm doing all right, Harold.'

Bennett does not believe a word of it. 'Glad to hear it.' He smiles at Bunty. 'How do *you* know this fellow, eh, young lady?'

'Bunty, call me Bunty, please, *Harold* . . .'

'Delighted . . . Bunty.'

As Harold Bennett turns to pour the last of the wine, Gorse and Bunty exchange an ironic glance. Now Bennett is asking Bunty, 'Haven't I seen you in here before?'

'I was hostessing for a bit, then I met Ralph, and . . . you know how it is.' Bunty leans closer, and so does he.

Bennett asks throatily, 'You'll be going back to the hotel with us?'

'Of course.'

Harold Bennett is smiling, in sexual anticipation, when there is a sudden flash. A club photographer stands there, young, thin, in a poor-grade dinner jacket, smiling, and holding the camera pointed at Bennett . . . and Bunty.

'Lovely one that, sir!' calls the photographer.

Bennett is tipsy, but now very annoyed. 'Here! I say, I didn't ask for that!'

Gorse is quick to intervene. 'That's all right, Harold, I'll look after it!' Gorse gets up from the table and shepherds the photographer away towards the bar. Once there, he explains with a smile. 'My friend's having a *quiet* night on the town, away from the pressures of business, and doesn't want any publicity.' Gorse then winks and palms the photographer a note. 'Give me your card and I'll collect the photos in the morning. Just a precaution. We don't want them falling into the wrong hands, do we?'

The photographer is all ears. 'Got it, sir. Be ready first thing in the morning.' He finds a grubby business card for Gorse. Gorse takes it. 'Thanks, old boy . . .' He turns to find Bennett and Bunty coming towards him, Bunty's arm in Bennett's, proprietorially. 'We're ready to go,' says Bennett, thickly.

Gorse looks at Bunty. On the blind side, Bunty closes one eye.

In the hall of 'Briny View', a most ordinary boarding house on Brighton seafront, Mr Stimpson is on the telephone to Joan. 'Joan, I'm calling to let you know where I am . . . It's a boarding house . . . Briny View . . . No need to write it down . . . I'll be home in a couple of days, I expect . . .'

'Have – have you found him?' Joan's voice sounds oddly tremulous.

'Not yet, but I'm going to his bank in the morning and, as one of his creditors, I will demand his address, on your behalf.'

'Will they give it to you? His address?'

'I think so. I've got Norris's backing.'

'But if Ralph has no money, what can you expect to get from him? Donald, I really think . . .'

Mr Stimpson has had enough. It has been a long day. The train to Brighton was a 'stopper'. He is tired. 'I know what you think, Joan! You think I should come home and forget it. I think I should find out just exactly where Ralph Gorse *is* and put the police on to him, for false pretences. Goodnight.'

'But Donald . . .'

Mr Stimpson puts the telephone down sharply, cutting off the sound of her voice. It was an action he would never have dreamt of three months before. But things had changed. Joan Plumleigh-Bruce was no longer rich. She no longer held the whip hand in their relationship. In fact, sometimes he wondered if it was a relationship he wished to maintain. But it was. For Joan Plumleigh-Bruce had been his. Or almost his. Joan Plumleigh-Bruce had sat on a pedestal. Not now, Mr Stimpson thought, the pain of it going through him like a knife. Not now.

It is now very late and, in Gorse's room at the Hotel Royal, looks it. There is hard liquor in evidence, for nobody here drinks beer or wine. Playing poker at a table are four people: Gorse, Harold Bennett, Vinson, a dark, tough-looking but well-dressed local bookie, and Mr Jackson, a well-dressed resident of the hotel. Bennett is now the worse for drink, and his mind is only half on his cards. The other half is on Bunty, who is showing a lot of front as she stands watching the game. Gorse himself is in shirtsleeves, but wears a discontented sneer. Now, as Vinson turns up a running flush and pulls in the very large 'pot', he is plainly out of the money. Gorse is good at many things but not cards, or any kind of gambling, where the golden rule is to pull in when losing and step up the ante when winning. It is a rule Gorse has never learned.

Gorse throws his cards down. 'Never had a decent hand all night!'

'You never did know how to play poker!' observes Harold Bennett.

'I suppose you'd know, would you?' asks Gorse, nastily.

Bennett shrugs. 'I know nobody can afford to lose twenty quid on one hand, even if he is living – for the moment – in the Hotel Royal.' He turns blearily to

Vinson. 'This young fella used to work for me, y'know?'

Vinson is putting his winnings in his pocket. 'Doing what?'

'Selling cars. Or rather, *not* selling 'em. That's why I had to sack him.'

Bunty is hastily going round freshening drinks, hoping to avoid conflict. 'I never knew you sold motorcars, Ralph?'

'Shut up!' replies Gorse.

'Oh, charming!' says Bunty. Bennett puts a proprietorial arm around her bare shoulders. 'Love's Young Dream over is it, Bunty?'

Bunty smiles into his face. 'Looks like it doesn't it, Mr Bennett?'

'I've told you – Harold. Bennett's Motors! You can see my name all over this part of the world, right Vinny?'

Vinson grunted, 'It's a good job you know something about motorcars, Harold. You play poker about as well as young Ralph here.'

Harold Bennett is offended. 'I don't need any advice from a bookie on how to play a hand of cards. You fellas aren't even legal!'

By now, Vinson is standing up, refusing Bunty's offer of whisky. Mr Jackson stands up with him. He yawns. It's been a long night. Vinson says, 'Getting a bit late. Let's call it a day.' He slips into his jacket. 'Give us a call, Ralph, any time. You an' all, Mr Bennett. It's been a pleasure taking your money.' And he is gone, patting Bunty's bum as he goes, Mr Jackson with him.

'That's it, then . . .' Gorse rises to his feet.

'Not quite! You owe *me* twenty-six pounds!' corrects Harold Bennett.

Gorse sways. 'Do I? Do I really? Oh, well . . .' He reaches in his pocket.

'No cheques, Ralph. Sorry.' Bennett smiles at Bunty. She, hesitant, smiles back.

Gorse says, 'Well I'm sorry, Harold, but you'll have to wait. No can do.'

Harold Bennett laughs out loud. 'So you're broke, are you?' He looks at Bunty, revelling in the moment. 'Ralph Gorse. The gentleman of leisure. Good school. Well, he did go to one but I believe they expelled him. What was *that* for, Ralph? Sleeping with the Matron, was it?'

Gorse is suddenly very white and still. 'Shut your bloody mouth, you turd!'

Bennett is taken aback and, looking at Gorse's face, has reason to be, for it is a cold mask of hate. 'No offence meant, Ralph . . . Just a joke, eh . . . Nothing intended,' stammers Harold Bennett.

Gorse does not reply. He slips on his jacket. 'Ralph . . . Where are you going?' asks Bunty.

'For some fresh air. I need it.' At the door he stops and looks at Bunty. 'I'll be a while.'

'It would serve you right if I was gone when you came back,' says Bunty, boldly.

Gorse looks at her. 'Darling, it would be a relief.' He goes out of the room.

Bunty's face shows hurt, turned away from Bennett. When she turns back to him she wears a smile, on her lips anyway. But Harold Bennett is stumbling to his feet. 'I think I'd . . . better be going . . . it's very late.'

'It's only one o'clock . . .' whispers Bunty.

'Ralph's in an ugly mood . . .' Harold Bennett feels unsafe. 'He has a very black side to him . . . Looking at your face, I'd say you know that.'

Bunty touches her face. 'I'm fine . . . Tell you what, let's go to your room and have a last drink, shall we?'

'My room?' echoes Bennett. 'I haven't booked a room.'

'I booked it for you. In case,' whispers Bunty. 'It's just along the corridor.'

'Well . . . I don't know . . . I shouldn't really . . .' But Bunty is already steering him towards the door. And he is not resisting. Well, not very much anyway.

At that moment, in a corner of the reception office are Gorse and the night porter, a man of about fifty. Gorse slips him a pound note. 'Mr Bennett would like to change his room to a double . . . Mrs Bennett has joined him. I'll adjust the register, shall I?' Gorse promptly writes in 'and Mrs' beside Harold Bennett's name.

'Very good, Mr Gorse.'

'Thank you. Goodnight.'

'Goodnight to you, sir.'

Bunty and Bennett reach the bedroom and stagger in, arm in arm. Bunty steels herself for what is to come, but before she can get her dress off, Harold Bennett has decided to be sick. The stuff he's poured into himself, it was not surprising, she thought. Bunty took off her dress and hung it up in the wardrobe, hoping she'd get a night's sleep. God, it was awful, the things a girl had to do to get along. It was all the bloody Depression, everybody said so. The Depression was to blame for everything, including her present predicament. This turned out to be even worse than she expected, for Harold Bennett recovered from his sickness after half an hour, woke her peremptorily from a deep sleep, and instantly pressed his sexual attention on her. Half asleep, rocking to and fro, feeling nothing whatever, Bunty cursed Harold Bennett, Ralph Gorse, and the bloody, bloody, Depression.

Very early the next morning, six o'clock to be exact, down the fire escape at the rear of the Hotel Royal comes Ralph Ernest Gorse, carrying his battered suitcase. He looks around him as he reaches ground level. Nobody. He walks briskly on. Then suddenly he is accosted by a young kitchen hand, on early-breakfast duty, who has come outside for a quick smoke. 'Morning, sir. Looking for somebody?'

Gorse whips round. 'Oh. Morning . . . No, no . . .' As he goes on, the young kitchen hand looks after him. 'Hey! Mate!'

Gorse half-turns. 'Yes?'

'You a hotel thief or just jumping your bill?'

'What?'

'You heard!'

'Neither. I came with a woman. I'm leaving without her.'

'Go on! I believe you, thousands wouldn't!'

'It's true. I swear.'

'Well . . . *I* ain't seen yer, have I?'

'No. Really . . . It's true . . .'

'What's it to me, mate? On yer way! Be lucky!'

Gorse needs no second bidding. He goes. Fast.

When Bunty Burrows returned to Ralph Gorse's room from her night with Harold Bennett she was surprised to see no sign of Ralph Gorse. The bed, however, had been slept in, and that meant Gorse was around the place somewhere, she supposed. Bunty lit a cigarette and surveyed the ruin of the room: empty glasses, ashtrays overflowing, she wondered how Gorse could have slept in the place. She debated asking for breakfast to be sent up to the room, but decided to put it off until Gorse came back from his early morning walk or wherever the hell he was. Bunty decided she would have a hot bath, and drew the water. She soaped herself thoroughly and decided to forget the events of the night, as she had forgotten so many similar nights. Harold Bennett had been a vigorous but unskilled lover, and had soon fallen into a deep alcoholic sleep, only waking when she shook him awake at seven o'clock on the dot. Wise in the ways of businessmen (a lot of her one-night lovers had been businessmen) Bunty had surmised that Harold Bennett would want to be out of the hotel before most of the residents were up and doing. So he had, and he had gone, just as he was, after a cursory wash and shave and putting on a clean shirt. Obviously, he had expected to spend the night with her and had made some kind of explanation to his wife. Such men always had wives, in Bunty's experience. Just as obviously he had made some financial accommodation with Gorse, or would do so, for he had not left her anything, not even a fiver. No, Harold Bennett had behaved as if she didn't exist, that morning, and now she had to reckon with Ralph Gorse.

Bunty hoped Gorse had got some decent money out of Harold Bennett. She had certainly earned it. Men like Harold Bennett, as far as Bunty was concerned, were not real gentlemen, they were pigs.

Bunty was not a common tart. She would have been affronted if anybody had called her that. A tart would have asked Harold Bennett for money *before* she went to bed with him. That, Bunty could not conceive herself doing. Just the same, lying in the hot tub and acutely conscious that she only had a few copper coins in her expensive purse, Bunty Burrows began to feel anxious. She reached a wet hand out of the water and looked at her wristwatch. Twenty minutes to eight.

Where the hell was Ralph Gorse?

Suddenly, Bunty Burrows felt afraid.

* * *

Two and a half hours later, at ten past ten precisely, Mr Stimpson came out of the Brighton branch of the Southern Counties Bank. In his hand he carried a slip of paper. Mr Stimpson looked very pleased with himself, as he imperiously hailed a taxi. 'The Hotel Royal, if you please!'

The taxi rolled off along the Front, past the young holidaymakers in their blazers and sweaters and their bright silken dresses, now to the calf in the fashion of the day. Mr Stimpson did not normally like holidays or holidaymakers; such things were frivolous and a waste of good money. But today he looked upon the young people with something approaching approval. Today, Mr Stimpson felt good. Today, he would confront Ralph Gorse.

At that precise moment, had Mr Stimpson known it, Ralph Gorse was paying a call upon the young photographer at his somewhat sleazy lock-up shop, just off Brighton seafront. For the photographer worked by day on the promenade, carrying a large 'chopper' or old-fashioned, wooden-based tripod camera, which produced photographs (of neat or blowsy holidaymakers) that looked all right for a day or a week even, but afterwards soon faded into a blur. Only in the evenings did the thin young photographer frequent the night club at which he had taken the picture of Bunty Burrows and Harold Bennett. So he was surprised to see Gorse up so early to collect those very pictures, give them a quick glance, and pop them back into the envelope, departing without a word of thanks. A curious bugger, thought the thin young photographer who, like most people, was living as best he could in the Depression. He noticed also that Gorse carried a large, much-stickered leather travelling-case. That meant no car. That meant, to the thin young photographer, that

Gorse was probably, like himself, living on his wits.

The thin young photographer shrugged. Who wasn't, for God's sake?

When Mr Stimpson walked into the Hotel Royal and asked for Mr Ralph Ernest Gorse, he had not bargained for the reaction that that simple request provoked. For at once, the hotel manager – portly, fifty, coldly angry – was in front of him, asking how well he knew Mr Gorse, did he know Mr Gorse's present whereabouts, did he have any permanent address for Mr Gorse?

Mr Stimpson felt the hope run out of his boots. 'You mean he isn't here? My information was he was living in this hotel,' said Mr Stimpson.

'Where did you obtain that information?' asked the hotel manager, stiffly.

'From the Southern Counties Bank,' replied Mr Stimpson, feeling cold and lost, and very, very angry.

'That information was correct until last evening,' said the hotel manager. 'Now it is not. He has gone. He scarpered. Without paying his bill. You are not a friend of his, I take it?'

'Anything but,' declared Mr Stimpson fervently.

The hotel manager sighed, and lowered his voice. 'He had a girl with him.' He pointed. 'That girl there.'

Mr Stimpson stared at the downcast form of Bunty Burrows. Her face was pinched. She was looking at nobody, as she pushed her way irritably out of the swingdoors to the street.

'She was with him?'

'We couldn't keep her. She has nothing of value. We could report her to the police but the scandal – '

But Mr Stimpson had gone, after Bunty.

Mr Stimpson introduced himself to Bunty as a friend of

Ralph Gorse. Bunty looked unimpressed. 'That's more than I am, dear,' she said.

'And you've no idea where he can be?' Mr Stimpson asked, in despair, as they stood outside the Hotel Royal in the warm sunshine, the holidaymakers pushing past them.

'Wish I did, the rotten bastard, leaving me to face all *that*!'

'Yes, it looked rather nasty in there.'

Bunty was indignant. 'They took my address, but they can't get blood from a stone! . . . When I think what I did for him. *He* didn't even leave me the cab fare!'

'Gorse never . . . mentioned anybody he might go to . . . If things were bad?'

Bunty shook her head, bitterly. 'Ralph Gorse never tells anybody anything.'

Mr Stimpson feels there is no more he can say. '. . . Well, good luck,' he manages.

'I'm going to need it,' declares Bunty. A thought strikes her. 'I say . . . *You* haven't a quid to spare, have you? I've got to get to London, somehow . . .'

Stimpson studies her. 'I can manage five shillings. If you will help me.'

'. . . How?'

Mr Stimpson gives her his card. 'If you *ever* hear from Gorse, or anything of his whereabouts, telephone that number!'

'Don't you worry. I will!'

Mr Stimpson hands her the two coins. Then, gloomily, he touches his hat and walks off down the promenade.

'Thanks Mr . . . er . . . Thanks!' Bunty watches Mr Stimpson retreating. She looks at the card, then puts it in her handbag and walks off in the opposite direction, towards the railway station.

* * *

Bennett's Motors was what was then called a 'Splendid Emporium', with a couple of excellent 1938 models on outside view. The showroom itself was glass-fronted and contained even more, equally expensive, models. An 'office' bearing the legend 'Bennett's Motors' stands along the concourse. Gorse, carrying his much-stickered case, sighs as it all comes into view. He has been here before. He has worked here before. And he has hated every minute of it. Then he sees Pamela. She is twenty-four, plain and plumpish, and wears glasses. She works in the office, and is coming out of it when she sees Gorse. Her reaction is one of surprise and pleasure. Gorse is not so enthusiastic but, Gorse-like, feigns it. After all, she *is* Harold Bennett's daughter.

'Ralph!' exclaims Pamela, 'What are *you* doing here?'

Gorse permits himself a wry smile. 'Looking for my old job back, actually.'

'You're *not*!'

''Fraid so. Times are bad.'

Pamela looks round, then drops her voice. 'But I heard . . . Well, Daddy said you were staying at the Royal.'

Gorse sets down his case. 'I was, but please don't talk about that, Pam. I left under a bit of a cloud, actually.'

'Money?' asks Pamela.

'Nothing important like that. Just a lady. Bit of trouble, so . . .'

Pamela stifles a nervous laugh. 'I *had* heard you'd got some girl with you!'

'Please don't *you* be angry with me, Pam!' replies Gorse.

Pamela is petulant but not really. 'It's none of my business what you do, Ralph, is it?'

Gorse sighs. 'Sometimes . . . I wish it was . . . D'you know that?'

'You don't mean that, do you?' asks Pamela, in a low, intense voice.

Gorse changes the subject. He looks at one of the motorcars on display, an SS Drop-head Coupé. 'Lovely bus.'

'I say, you're walking! Where's yours?'

'In the garage. Twenty quid to get it out,' replies Gorse, flatly.

Pamela is shaken. 'You're broke?. . . For twenty *pounds*?'

Gorse feels in his pocket, produces three silver coins. 'Three half-crowns, my dear.'

'In the world?' gasps Pamela, thrilled and shocked.

'In the world.'

Pamela looks at him with large, luminous eyes. 'Ralph . . . Whatever am I to do with you?' Then she smiles. Gorse smiles back. At this moment a cab arrives and Harold Bennett gets out, looking somewhat the worse for wear, and with cotton wool sticking to a shaving cut on his cheek. He catches sight of Gorse and is anything but pleasantly surprised. Before he can say anything, Pamela speaks. 'Daddy! You look *terrible.* Where've you been?'

'I . . . er . . . had some important business . . . out of town . . . went on rather late.'

'You remember Ralph, Daddy?'

Bennett grunts. He does not trust himself to speak to anybody. His head is killing him.

Pamela adds, 'He's looking for his old job back.'

Harold Bennett looked closely at Gorse. He saw the case at Gorse's feet and he thought he understood the situation.

'I'm not looking for any salesmen,' he said, and moved to go into his office.

'I think,' interposed Gorse gently, 'we should talk.' He

smiled and added, 'I refer to some unfinished business between us.'

Harold Bennett, again, thought he understood. Gorse was broke, and talking about money for services rendered. He was talking about Bunty.

Harold Bennett grunted. 'All right. Come into the office.'

Gorse smiled at Pamela and followed her father into the building.

Pamela watched him go, with the eyes of love.

Harold Bennett's office had a large desk, with a large leather chair behind it. Rows of catalogues and framed portraits of racing drivers hung on the walls. Bennett sat behind his desk and looked at Ralph Gorse without enthusiasm. 'You want money, I suppose?' he grunted. 'Ten quid's the best I can do.'

'I don't want money, I want a job,' said Gorse.

'I sacked you, remember?' replied Harold Bennett.

'Yes,' nodded Gorse, 'and I want five quid weekly, basic, with sales commission on top.' Bennett laughed. 'You're mad! You were on commission only when you did work here.' Gorse helped himself to a cigarette from the silver box on Harold Bennett's desk, and lit it. 'This is different. Very, very different, isn't it?'

Harold Bennett was getting very angry by now. 'How is it different?'

Gorse blew out smoke. 'I need this job and if I have to be unpleasant, believe me, I will be. Very.'

'Oh? . . . In what way, may I ask?'

Gorse took a brown envelope from his pocket. 'You spent last night in the Royal with "your wife". It's in the hotel register. "Mr and Mrs." Oh, and I've got some very nice snaps of "Mrs Bennett" too.' Gorse taps the brown envelope. 'I'm sure she'd love to see them.'

Bennett just stared at him. At that moment he would gladly have killed Gorse.

'I told you,' explained Gorse, 'I need the job.'

Mr Stimpson is again on the telephone, in the Briny View boarding house in Brighton, and again he is talking to Joan Plumleigh-Bruce. Joan is upset and alarmed.

'Donald! I've had your office on *again*! You really must come *home*!'

Mr Stimpson brusquely asks why.

'Because,' explains Joan, 'your partner, Mr Snell, is very angry with you. He says that if your signature is not on that new estate deal tomorrow, the firm could lose the contract . . . Donald, do you hear me?. . . Donald?'

Mr Stimpson speaks as one in a trance. 'I'm very close to Gorse, Joan. I know I am.'

This makes Joan even more agitated. 'What does it *matter*? He'll have no money even if you *do* find him! You said he got out of that hotel without paying his bill.'

'He has to be in this district *somewhere*,' says Mr Stimpson, implacably.

'Why? He may have left, gone to London, anything.'

'No, I don't think so.'

Joan gives up. 'Well, I don't know what to say. Are you going to stay there for ever? On the off chance you'll bump into poor Ralph in the street?'

Mr Stimpson stirs at that. 'Oh? It's poor Ralph now, is it? Well, I suppose that's all I can expect, from *you*.'

Joan feels the earth turn, in her drawing room, but swallows bravely. 'What does that remark mean, Donald, may I ask?'

'You know very well what it means. Tell Mr Snell I'll be back tonight. Good-bye.' Mr Stimpson puts the telephone down. He is bitterly disappointed and angry. It has all been for nothing. Gorse has eluded him. Again.

It is nine o'clock in the morning at Bennett's Motors. Pamela Bennett is walking down a passageway to her office when she is suddenly grabbed from behind by a pair of male hands. She is shocked for a moment, until her 'attacker' spins her round and kisses her on the mouth. It is Ralph Gorse.

'Oh Ralph! You scared me to death . . . You know I don't like silly games!'

Gorse pulls her closer. 'Don't you?'

Pamela softens a little but is still shaken. 'Not here. Daddy will see us.'

'He's with a client.' Gorse's hand toys with the top of her blouse. 'Ralph! No!' And she hurries off into her office. As for Gorse, he simply smiles tolerantly, and walks out into the concourse. In reality, unless there was an interested customer in tow, a salesman had little to do. It was a boring job but it suited Gorse, who did not like anything that made too physical a demand on him. Outside, he is surprised to see a large, prosperous middle-aged man come out of the showroom with Harold Bennett. Obviously, an Important Customer, judging by Harold Bennett's obsequiousness. '*Do* call by, Sir Robert . . . any time. We try to be of help.'

The large, prosperous man nodded. 'Well, I stick to my Daimler, y'know, Harold.'

'For business, naturally,' agreed Harold Bennett. Gorse edges his way across to the SS Jaguar. Sir Robert sees the motorcar and stops in admiration. 'I say, what's *this*?'

Harold Bennett promptly tells him. 'Newest model. First on this coast.'

'Really?' Sir Robert inspects it with interest. This gives

Gorse, who is now next to the SS, a chance to interpose. 'Good morning, sir . . . The ultimate in sports cars, the Jaguar, I think. A wonderful machine. Capable of ninety mph in the right conditions.'

Sir Robert nods, still looking at the machine. 'A young man's car . . . But I agree, she looks very good.'

Gorse ignores Bennett's frown and presses on. 'A young man might *like* to drive her, sir. But only a mature man *could* drive her.'

Sir Robert laughs at this, turning to Bennett. 'Very persuasive salesman you have here, Harold.'

'Yes. Very,' says Harold Bennett, bleakly.

Sir Robert nods to Gorse. 'If I were fifteen years younger, Mr . . . er?'

'Gorse, sir. Ralph Gorse.'

'Lovely motorcar, Gorse. You should sell her soon, I hope.'

'Whoever has the first model would be a bit of a celebrity. No doubt about that.'

Sir Robert is suddenly thoughtful. 'You think so?'

'No doubt about it, sir . . . A talking point, you could say. Whoever owns it. All eyes would be on him.' Sir Robert scrutinizes Gorse for the first time. 'Is that tie the Frontier Scouts?'

'Er . . . matter of fact, it is.'

'Hmm . . .' Sir Robert has a last lingering look at the car, like a man looking at a woman who is far too young for him. 'Well, Harold, I must go. Business.'

'Of course. Good-day, Sir Robert.'

Sir Robert nods to Gorse and goes off towards his Daimler. Harold Bennett has a word for Ralph Gorse. 'Gorse, you are not only an unprincipled rotter, you are an idiot to boot.'

'If *you* say so, Mr Bennett,' replies Gorse, unfazed.

In reply Harold Bennett points at the SS sports car. 'Sir Robert Simms would never buy a car like that! I can't think who *will*. I don't know why I stocked the bloody thing in the first place! We'll never shift it. Never!' He glares at Gorse, who does not reply. Then he turns and goes into the office. Gorse looks after him with some amusement. Then he looks back at the SS and pats it as if it is a woman. An idea has occurred to Ralph Ernest Gorse.

The following morning finds Gorse driving along the promenade at Hove in the SS sports car. Seated next to him, in the passenger seat, is Pamela Bennett. Gorse drives fast and well and Pamela is in an ecstasy of happiness. Gorse guns the sports car towards a man in a trilby hat, a young woman and an untidy man holding a camera. Gorse brakes the car to a sudden stop. The man in the trilby hat, the representative of the local newspaper, *The Argus*, calls out, 'Stay just like that, Mr Gorse! For the photograph!'

Pamela corrects him. 'It's Captain Gorse, you know.' The pressman notes that in his book. 'Sorry. Army, sir?'

Gorse nods. 'I was, for a bit, yes.' Pamela again puts the record straight. 'He was on the North West Frontier. With the Scouts. He was ever so brave.'

The pressgirl has her notebook open. 'You are . . .?'

'Pamela Bennett. Bennett Motors.'

The pressgirl notes that in *her* book. 'Oh, I see, and Mr . . . I mean, *Captain* Gorse works for your father, is that right?' Then, as Pamela nods, 'In what capacity?'

Gorse replies with a smile. 'Manager, actually.'

The man in the trilby cuts in. 'All right, Margie, it's the car we're here for, dear, not the woman's page! Charley, get some pictures, will you?' Charley, the doom-laden photographer, nods, his unlit cigarette tight between his lips. He lines up his shots gloomily and the pressman asks Gorse, '*This* is the very first model of its kind on the coast, is that the case, Captain Gorse?'

Gorse nods. 'Only a dozen in the country, yet. It's going to be at the Motor Show, of course.'

'Can I have the price again?'

'The list price is seven hundred and fifty guineas. And worth every penny.'

The doom-laden photographer speaks. 'I'll have two. Look *this way*, folks!' and takes a photograph as Pamela smiles and Gorse looks serious.

The pressman closes his note book. 'Lovely! . . . Got enough, Charley?' Charley nods, lugubriously.

But the pressgirl insists. 'Well *I* haven't . . . Miss Bennett?. . . Are you and Captain Gorse . . . friendly?'

'Well . . . yes, of course we are . . .' replies Pamela.

'May we expect an announcement?' the girl asks. But Pamela looks at Gorse. 'Not really . . . No.'

'But possibly . . . One day? Captain Gorse?'

'Who knows?' Gorse smiles at Pamela, who looks shocked. 'Who knows!'

'Congratulations to you both!' cries the pressgirl.

Pamela protests. 'No, really! . . .' But Gorse starts the engine, with a roar. The pressgirl calls reassuringly, 'I'll put Not Yet Official, it's all right!'

The pressman in the trilby looks at the photographer and sighs. 'Get one of him going, Charley!' Charley nods and his camera explodes as Gorse and Pamela drive away in great style down the promenade.

In Reading, that very evening, Joan and Mr Stimpson are at the end of supper. Mary is clearing the dishes. Mr

Stimpson is gloomy and silent, Joan apprehensive, Mary terrified and clumsy.

Joan breaks the silence. 'I'm so glad your firm has the contract for the new estate.'

'I'm glad you're glad, Joan,' replies Mr Stimpson, ironically.

'Well, you've worked so hard on it,' says Joan, placatingly.

Mr Stimpson snorts derisively. Joan reacts. 'Donald, don't sit there like a bear with a sore head, please!' Too late she remembers her reduced status. '. . . Mary! Give Mr Stimpson some more coffee, girl!' Mary pours too much coffee into Mr Stimpson's cup. Mr Stimpson erupts. 'I don't *want* any more coffee! I can't sleep if I drink the stuff . . . I said no, girl!'

'Oh, sorry sir, I'm sure, sir!'

Joan's voice is sharp. 'Mary, take the dishes into the kitchen. I'll ring if I need you.'

'Yes, mam.' Mary collects the tray and crashes out.

Joan sighs. 'Really. That girl. If she . . .'

'. . . wasn't so cheap you'd fire her?'

Joan debates the point, seriously. 'Well, I would. But as you know, I'm in somewhat reduced circumstances since – '

'Since you let Ralph Gorse have his way with you.'

Now it has actually been said, Joan goes cold. And angry. 'Donald! What a thing to *say*!'

'Why not? It's true.'

Joan takes a deep breath and lies. 'It is *not* true, Donald Stimpson, and you know it isn't! I would never do a thing like that! Why, Ralph's years and years younger than me! Well, maybe not years and years, but – '

But Mr Stimpson, too, has had enough. 'Joan. You are a silly woman. I don't know whatever I saw in you.'

'Donald! Not so *loud*! The maid – '

'It's all right if I say it in a low voice, is it? That stops it being true, does it?'

'It *isn't* true! You know it isn't true! I *swear* it!'

Mr Stimpson is stopped in his tracks for a moment. 'You do?'

'Yes, I do!'

Stimpson would like to believe it, oh he would, but . . . 'Mmmm . . .' is all he can find to say.

'Let me get you a brandy,' cajoles Joan, and pours, watching him. Mr Stimpson accepts it and sips. 'Thank you, it helps me to sleep . . . I'm not like some people, who have no conscience.'

Joan finds a semblance of sympathy from somewhere. 'Then what's keeping you awake, dear?'

Mr Stimpson is a long moment before he replies. 'The thought of having Ralph Ernest Gorse at my mercy.' Mr Stimpson extends his hand, open, the brandy glass in it. 'In the palm of my hand . . . like *that*.' Mr Stimpson closes his fist. The frail glass breaks.

Joan is aghast. 'Donald, don't . . . Donald, you've cut yourself!'

Mr Stimpson looks unsurprised at his hand. A trickle of blood oozes from it. 'So I have, so I have, haven't I?' He smiles. Joan looks at him, alarmed, upset, repelled, all at once. One thing is certain. She is going to have to be very careful with Donald Stimpson. Why, she asks herself and answers in the next unspoken breath: because he is all she has.

Gorse's 'combined room' in a lodging house at the back of the town is a cosy scene. The gas fire is noisily on. Pamela is in her best frock, lounging on a couple of cushions on the single bed. Gorse is pouring two glasses of red wine. A 'dead' bottle stands on a small table. So do the remains of a sandwich meal.

Gorse is apologizing. 'It's not much of a place to ask a girl to, but it's all I have, I'm afraid, Pam.'

Pamela shakes her head. 'I don't mind, really.'

Gorse gives her the glass of wine. 'I know, but I'd like us to have something a bit . . . nicer.'

Pamela sips the wine. She looks flushed. 'Really, I don't *mind*! The only thing that worries me is the landlady. I have a feeling she knows who I am. I have been here pretty often.'

Gorse sits and kisses her gently on the cheek. 'Would that be a big worry? If she talked?'

Pamela nods. 'It would be if Daddy found out.'

Gorse drains his glass in one gulp. 'Well, he's not going to, is he? I won't tell him if you don't.'

Pamela puts down her glass, untouched. 'Oh, Ralph . . . you scare me sometimes. You don't seem to care . . . about anything . . . Or anybody . . .'

Gorse grunts, looking at nothing. 'Maybe I don't.'

Pamela asks, shyly, 'Not even me?' And as Gorse doesn't reply, 'Sometimes . . . when we're . . . making love, I feel . . . you're very violent, Ralph . . . sometimes . . .'

'Am I?' Gorse then kisses her, very softly, and Pamela struggles with her feelings. '. . . I love you Ralph. I always have. Ever since the first day I saw you. I died when you left. I never thought I'd see you again.'

Gorse is suddenly brusque. 'Well, here I am, so stop worrying.'

Pamela shakes her head. Her dark hair, her best feature, cascades over her face. 'Daddy might sack you over that car business.'

'He won't.'

'How can you be so sure?' Gorse kisses her. 'Ralph. How are you for money?' Gorse stops kissing her. 'How d'you think?' he asks.

'Here.' Pamela puts an envelope, taken from her handbag, on to the table. 'You can at least get your car out of the garage.'

Gorse pockets it unblinkingly. 'I'll pay you back, Pam.' Pamela leans forward. 'I don't care . . . I'd do anything for you, Ralph . . .' She puts her arm round Gorse's neck, and clings to him. As Gorse methodically undresses her he shows no passion, but Pamela doesn't see this. Her eyes are tightly closed. For her, sex with Ralph is ecstasy – and fear, for it is frightening and strange at times, a thing of bonds and restraints, in the form of neckties or silk stockings. And there is hurt in it. Pamela keeps her eyes closed through it all. That way she can pretend to herself that some of the things Ralph Gorse does are not happening to her.

Phyllis Bennett looks up from her book (*South Riding*, a bestseller of the time) in her somewhat over-furnished drawing room, as her daughter Pamela comes into the room. Phyllis has a cigarette in a holder. She has social pretensions but she's nobody's fool. Her problem, she reminds herself, is this plain daughter of hers.

Pamela is surprised to see her still up, for it is late. 'Oh hello, Mummy . . . I thought you'd be in bed.'

'Well, it *is* eleven-thirty . . . Sit down a moment, dear.' But Pamela doesn't sit down. 'I rather wanted a word, Pammy . . .'

'Oh, what about?' asks Pamela, abruptly.

'I think you know,' replies Phyllis Bennett. Pamela does and evades it. 'I'm a bit tired – can't it wait? And I expect Daddy will come bursting in any time now.'

Phyllis lays down her book. 'No he won't, he's at the Club, and it's poker night tonight. He'll be two o'clockish, if I know him, and with a bad head in the morning. Do sit down, girl . . . Please.'

'Oh, well. All right.' Pamela sits defiantly on the edge of the overstuffed couch. She is indeed very tired. It has been a long and exhausting evening.

Mrs Bennett tries again. 'Have a cigarette?. . . A drink?'

'No thanks, I'm fine.'

Mrs Bennett sighs, looks at her, then . . . 'Ralph Gorse. You're seeing him, aren't you?'

'That's my business, Mummy.'

Phyllis keeps her voice reasonable. 'I'm not criticizing you – well, not exactly. He's very attractive, even *I* can see that.'

'So what's the trouble, then?'

Phyllis Bennett feels it is time to speak plainly. 'The trouble, darling, is that he has no money, no probability of ever having any, and you are the daughter of a comparatively rich man.'

Pamela protests, 'I don't want Daddy's money!'

'You won't get it, darling, if you tie yourself up, in *any* way, with Ralph Gorse.'

'Mummy, I'd rather you didn't say any more!'

But Phyllis does. 'You've seen Ralph Gorse tonight?'

Pamela accuses her, 'You've been spying on me!'

'Anybody who has eyes in their head can see that your lipstick is fresh. Your clothes are a little . . . crumpled . . . Need I go on? My dear, I was a girl myself once.'

'I'm not a girl, I'm twenty-four!'

'Yes, I know how old you are. The point is, whether you know it or not, your father dislikes Ralph very much indeed. Sooner or later, for one reason or another, he'll sack him. Take my word for it.'

Pamela stands up, near to tears. 'I don't know why Daddy dislikes Ralph so much! He works so hard. He sells cars – well, anyway, as often as anybody else does. Including Daddy.'

'Yes, well, *that* might not endear him to your father.'

'I don't see why not.'

Mrs Bennett looks at this stubborn girl in sudden exasperation. 'Darling, don't you know *anything* about men!'

But Pamela decides to cut loose. 'I know when I meet somebody I like and who likes me – and I haven't met many who do, have I? I'm going to do nothing to drive him away! Not for you. Not for Daddy. And particularly not for Daddy's money!'

Mrs Bennett sighs. 'Bravely said. But I have a feeling Ralph Gorse might not be interested in you if you had absolutely no money at all!'

Pamela is now very agitated. 'That's a *foul* thing to say, absolutely foul!'

'Darling, it's *fact.*' Phyllis leans forward and touches Pamela's hand. 'When I married your father he had a lot of ideas and no capital. I lent him that capital.'

'Perhaps I should lend Ralph some money, if I had it, which I don't.'

'Darling, Ralph Gorse isn't exactly your father, is he? Your father is hard-working, gives total attention to business and worked twenty-four hours a day to get where he is – '

'I don't think Ralph wants to be a motor dealer in a boring old place like this all his life!' declares Pamela, heatedly.

Her mother hesitates, then . . . 'What I'm saying is, if

you can't . . . resist Ralph Gorse . . . at least don't go into deep water with him . . . Are you following what I'm saying?'

Pamela shakes her head defiantly. 'No, and I'm not trying either! I don't want to talk about this subject any more, Mummy, so don't – '

'Your father will find out. Sooner or later.'

'He won't if you don't tell him.' At the door she turns. 'One thing I do know. Ralph loves me. Nobody else ever has. Not you. Or Daddy. Nobody.'

'Just think! That's all I'm saying. Think, girl!'

'About what? Ralph loves me. I trust him and he trusts me. There's no more to say. Goodnight, Mummy!' As she goes, Phyllis Bennett closes her eyes in exasperation. It had gone even worse than she had expected it would. Of course, Ralph Gorse was attractive. Too attractive for her plain daughter. Why would he want to sleep with her? Phyllis Bennett did not need two guesses.

Harold Bennett is extremely angry. The local *Argus* lies open on his desk and he is reading from it, a note of amazement in his voice. On the other side of the desk sits his wife, looking somewhat alarmed.

'"Captain Gorse said modestly that he'd be willing to return to the Colours in the event of an emergency . . ." Captain Gorse? What was *he* ever a Captain of?'

'That doesn't matter, Harold. What does is the last paragraph.'

Bennett looks up at her. 'What are you talking about, woman? The bloody man's taken my car from the show-room, without my permission!'

'I know all that, Harold, and it *isn't* important.'

'You may not think so. I *do*!'

'The publicity might even be useful, Harold. That *isn't* the point . . .'

But Harold Bennett is in a full flood of anger. 'What the hell was Pamela thinking about, to go off with him in that car, that's what I want to know. Have you talked to her about this?'

'Not yet and I'm not going to. You are, if anybody is.'

'Me?'

'You employ her here. Presumably she went in office hours?'

Harold Bennett peers at the newspaper. 'It says Wednesday here. I was in London at the Motor Show.' His anger rises. 'Gorse is going, he's going, and that's that!'

'I never knew why you gave him the job in the first place.'

'Well,' replies Harold Bennett warily, 'he's a good salesman. But he might have crashed that car. Anything. It isn't even insured.'

But Phyllis holds up her hand. 'Harold, read the last paragraph, will you, dear?'

'What?' asked her husband. 'Is there more?' There is. He reads out aloud. '"The handsome, gallant Captain Gorse did not deny that there was a . . ." I can't believe this! . . . "a romantic association between himself and his charming companion, Miss Pamela Bennett, daughter of local businessman Mr Harold W. Bennett, proprietor of Bennett's Motors, where the Captain is manager." Manager? Romantic association! Am I going mad?'

Phyllis now delivers the final blow. 'I think she's been seeing him, Harold.'

'Seeing him, seeing him!' shouts her husband. 'What does that mean, for God's sake?' He pauses, horrified.

'You don't mean she's been going to bed with him, or anything like that?'

Of course Phyllis Bennett does, but she doesn't say so. 'No, no, of course not, Harold. But he is attractive and she . . . well, she doesn't have a lot of luck in that department, does she?'

'For God's sake, woman, you sound as if you like the fellow!'

'I don't like or dislike him, Harold,' says Phyllis, patiently, 'I simply want to know what we do about that newspaper report. What do we say to our friends?'

'Deny it, naturally. Say the paper got it wrong.'

'Well, I suppose we'll have to . . .'

Harold Bennett sits a moment in deep thought. 'Just go out into the other office and ask Pamela to come in.'

Phyllis is alarmed. 'Harold! Be careful!'

'Just do as I *say*!'

Phyllis would like to say a lot more. But she bites her tongue and goes out. Bennett stares at the *Argus*. 'Handsome and gallant, my Aunt Fanny!'

After Phyllis had put her head around the office door and told her daughter that her father wanted her, she felt she had done as much as she could, and went out into the open air with some relief. Harold would lose his temper and she did not want to be there to see it. Hardly had she started to walk across the forecourt, however, when she heard the voice of Ralph Gorse. She turned to see him standing there, dapper in a blue blazer and striped tie, as if he had not a care in the world.

'It's not very often we have the pleasure of seeing you down here, Mrs Bennett.' Gorse made the 'Mrs Bennett' sound like a private joke.

Phyllis said, 'Ralph! My husband is absolutely blazing mad about that car business.'

Gorse shrugs. 'Oh, that? Nice little publicity stunt, that's all.'

'Have you seen the article in the paper?'

'Matter of fact, no. Do you have it with you?' replies Gorse, coolly.

'The only copy I know of,' said Phyllis, 'is in my husband's office.'

'Oh, I see,' said Gorse. 'How do I look in the photograph?'

Phyllis half-laughs. 'Ralph,' she said. 'You are the limit. But this time you've overdone it.'

But Gorse has raised his hand for silence. From inside the office they can hear Harold Bennett's voice . . . 'Pamela, that motorcar is an extremely expensive machine and it isn't insured for the *road*! Whatever possessed you to agree to go out in it with Gorse? I have to tell you I'm displeased, very displeased, my girl!'

In reply Pamela sounded almost tearful. 'But Daddy, it got some good publicity for the car, everybody knows about it now!'

'Rubbish!' roared Harold Bennett. 'I don't think we'll ever sell the damned thing, it's too expensive for my usual trade here.'

'Well then I'm sorry – '

'Yes, and so you damn well should be. And what's all this nonsense about you and Gorse?' At that point Harold Bennett must have closed his office door, because they could hear no more. Phyllis said, 'Ralph – you heard all that?' Gorse nods. 'You are in the doghouse. Pamela, too, I'm afraid.'

'I'm sorry to hear that,' said Gorse, not looking at all sorry. 'You're looking very pretty today, Phyllis. All this excitement must agree with you.'

Phyllis Bennett laughs again, then lowers her voice. 'Ralph! Don't try it on with *me*!'

'All I'm saying is, how lovely you look. Is that a crime?'

'No. But – '

Gorse, too, lowers his voice. 'I think you can cool your husband down, Phyllis. Of course, that isn't the effect you have on *other* men.'

Phyllis looks at Gorse, not knowing if he is serious or joking. 'Ralph, you really are the *end*! Really! . . .' For a moment their eyes are locked. Gorse is – almost playfully – trying his usual ploy with women, outrageous flattery, and, as usual, it half-works. Then Phyllis Bennett's eyes widen. She is staring past Gorse. 'Oh . . . Good afternoon, Sir Robert!' trills Phyllis.

Gorse turns round. Sir Robert Simms stands there, an *Argus* in his hand. He is admiring the Jaguar SS sports car that Gorse had so jauntily driven down the promenade at Hove the previous day.

Gorse crosses to him airily. 'Sir Robert? Can I be of help?'

Sir Robert holds up the newspaper. 'I just read that bit in the *Argus*, and I've come right over to buy it! Now, accept my cheque and let me drive it away before I change my mind!'

Gorse looks at Phyllis and winks on Sir Robert's blind side. 'Delighted, Sir Robert.'

Harold Bennett, at that moment, emerges from his office. He takes in the scene, with some amazement. Pamela, wiping her eyes, comes out after him. She runs across the forecourt into the main building, towards the refuge of the ladies' washroom.

Meantime, Gorse, who has seen all of this, is watching Sir Robert write a cheque for the full retail price of the

SS Jaguar, on the bonnet of the car. As he does so, Gorse turns round and smiles trimphantly at them all.

In Joan Plumleigh-Bruce's living room Mary is serving coffee to Joan and Mr Stimpson. They are sitting each side of the fire. Mr Stimpson is reading the local evening paper, Joan is sipping her coffee. Mary leaves the tray next to her. 'Will that be all, mam?'

'Yes. I'll call you if I need you.'

'Yes, mam. I'll do the dishes now, mam.' Mary bobs and makes her way out, glancing fearfully at that silent monster, Mr Stimpson.

'Anything in the paper, dear?'

'Property prices are going up.' Mr Stimpson looks at her over the paper. 'If you sold this place you'd get a good price for it.'

Joan is alarmed but coy. 'Where would I live, dear, if I did that?'

'With me.'

'Is that a proposal?'

'Perhaps it is,' says Mr Stimpson. 'Perhaps it isn't.'

'If it is, why not come and live here? Your gloomy old place would depress me unutterably, Donald.'

Mr Stimpson says, 'So your answer is not exactly yes, is it?'

'Not exactly no, dear,' says Joan.

'What you have to realize is that your only real liquid asset *is* this house.' He adds, heavily, 'Since your capital was stolen by Gorse.'

Joan, in defence, picks up the Major's near-to-hand photograph. 'Not all of it! I have a few hundred. And the poor dear Major's pension!'

'That will be worth less and less as time goes by. If there's a war.'

Joan replies, very brightly, 'Donald, why don't we go down to The Friar and have a few drinks to cheer ourselves up? All we ever seem to do these days is sit in the house and listen to the gloomy old wireless!'

'In case young Gorse or somebody like him comes in?' asks Mr Stimpson. 'You'd like that, wouldn't you?'

Joan loses her patience at last. 'Donald, you are unutterably tiresome . . .'

'Am I? Am I really? And should I tell you what *you* are?' This is the most verbally violent Mr Stimpson has been yet.

Joan's instinct, and it is very sound, is to smokescreen. She stands up and gives him a kiss on the cheek. 'Oh, come on, old silly-boots, let's go down to The Friar – forget all about Mr Chamberlain and Hitler and Mussolini . . .'

'You go if you must . . . I think I'll go home and have an early night.' He gets to his feet.

'Oh, well, then . . .'

Stimpson looks at her a long moment. 'Goodnight.'

'Goodnight, dear.'

And Mr Stimpson goes, without a further word. Joan shakes her head and sighs. Really, Donald Stimpson is getting worse. All he ever seems to think about is Ralph Gorse. Joan decides she'll have to wait the situation out. Sooner or later, the memory of what Ralph has done to them both will surely fade, and things will go back to being the way they were before. Will that ever happen? Joan wishes she knew.

Back at home, Mr Stimpson is preparing for bed. He is in his flannel pyjamas and is winding his alarm clock. His Ovaltine stands at the side of the bed. Suddenly, the telephone rings. Stimpson looks surprised, then answers it. A woman's voice speaks. Mr Stimpson listens closely and makes an appointment for the next day. He puts the telephone down. He is so excited by what he has heard that he allows his Ovaltine to grow cold.

The following day, at exactly noon, Mr Stimpson keeps his appointment, in the Green Man public house on St Martin's Lane, in the West End of London. Bunty Burrows is only five minutes late. Mr Stimpson rises and raises his hat, for she is, however dubiously, a lady. 'Good afternoon, Miss Burrows.'

'Wasn't sure you'd come!' declares Bunty, sitting next to him in the busy room.

'May I ask, what is your tipple?'

Bunty, unused to such politeness, stares at him, then, 'Oh? Er, gin and orange, please.'

Mr Stimpson signals to the barman. He waits a moment then asks, gently, 'You have some news for me?'

Bunty nods. 'Sent to me by a friend at the Club. She thought I'd be interested. It's going to cost you a fiver, sight unseen, dear.'

Mr Stimpson hesitates. 'Oh . . . very well.' He takes a white flimsy five-pound note out of his wallet and hands it to her. In reply she gives him a newspaper. It is the Brighton *Argus* and has a photograph, heavily ringed round in ink, of Ralph Gorse and Pamela sitting in the SS Jaguar on Hove Promenade. Mr Stimpson stares at it, and cannot think when he has felt so happy.

Twenty-fours later, Joan Plumleigh-Bruce is sitting comfortably in her corner seat on the fast Brighton train as Mr Stimpson brings two cups of tea into the compartment. Joan is pleased but protests. 'I don't know why you troubled.'

'. . . Cheaper to go to the Buffet. Those attendant fellows always expect a tip for nothing.'

Joan takes her tea. 'Thank you.' She looks at him a long moment. 'Donald, I hope you know just what you are doing?'

Mr Stimpson settles comfortably and sips his tea. 'Oh, I do, my dear, believe me, I do.'

The train roars on and Mr Stimpson looks content. Joan is anything but. In fact, she is seriously disturbed by it all. It is only the possibility of seeing Ralph Gorse that has got her on the train at all. Seeing him, and hearing the truth from his own lips. That, anyway, is what she tells herself.

In a small but select Mayfair flat that very same afternoon, Ralph Gorse lies on a long settee, his feet up, and a glass of wine in his hand. His shirt is open, his jacket and shoes are off, and he looks somewhat tousled, in a very cool way. 'This,' declares Gorse, 'Is. Most. Certainly. The. Life.'

Clarice Mannors, who is sitting on a stool putting *on* her stockings, smiles at him. She wears fashionable lingerie of the period, made of filmy silk and lace. 'Thank my friend Viv. It's her flat.'

Gorse raises his glass. 'Here's to Viv, whoever she is!'

Clarice fastens a suspender. 'You'd have met her if you'd come to France. Or up to Scotland for the shootin'.'

'Sorry I missed all that,' says Gorse, ironically.

'I *was* expecting to hear from you, you know,' replies Clarice.

'I believe you.'

'What happened? Didn't your money come through?'

'Yes, it did actually.'

'What happened to it?'

'What usually happens to money, darling. It got spent.'

Clarice pouts. 'It was a pity about France. But I had no address for you. No telephone number. You'd stood me up. I was furious. *And* upset.'

'Not for long though.'

Clarice looks up from her second suspender. 'What?'

'How was he,' asks Gorse, 'the tall handsome *friend*? The one you went to France with?'

'Who? Oh, Archie you mean?'

'Is that his name? Well yes, I suppose it would be.'

'Archie's just an old chum. Wants to marry me, though, actually.'

Gorse is amused. 'Does he now?'

Clarice straightens her stocking-seams. 'Don't worry, whoever I marry it won't be him. He's too . . . unenterprising.'

'Unlike me, are you saying?' muses Gorse.

Clarice laughs out loud. 'Yes I am, rather.'

Gorse laughs, too. 'Then the trip wasn't exactly wasted, was it?'

'No, not exactly . . .'

Gorse probes. 'You like it, don't you . . . enterprise?'

Clarice looks up. Something sexual clicks between them. 'Yes. I do, rather.'

'That's what I gathered.'

Clarice looks at him, almost decides not to ask the question, then does. 'Ralph . . . You've never . . . gone too far, have you?'

Gorse looks at her, stonily. 'I can't imagine what you can mean.'

'Yes, you can.'

Gorse keeps looking at her for a while. Then he gets to his feet yawning, and stretches his arms. He looks at his watch. 'God, four o'clock, is that the time?'

'Ralph, you're not going, are you?'

''Fraid so,' declares Gorse.

Clarice wails, 'But I thought we'd have an evening out. Dinner or a show or something? Blast and bugger it!'

'I agree, but there it is.' Gorse begins to dress. He slowly puts on his tie and shoes. Clarice watches him. A sudden thought strikes her. 'Ralph . . . You're not married or something absolutely stupid like that, are you?'

'No,' replies Gorse, for once truthfully.

'If you are, say so. It probably won't make any difference but I'd rather like to know.'

Gorse is still. 'I could marry you, if you like?'

Clarice doesn't take this seriously. She laughs. 'And what would we live on? I told you, I'm broke until my father fixes some kind of marriage settlement with some eminently suitable chap.'

Gorse is offended but Clarice does not see that. 'Which I'm not?'

Clarice kisses him. 'Which, however much I wish you were, you're not, darling.'

Gorse does not return the kiss. 'Thank you kindly.'

'Well, *are* you, darling? No money. On the dole, for all I know.'

'Not quite. Not quite yet,' says Gorse quietly.

Clarice catches his irritation and pleads, 'Darling, can't we just leave things exactly as they are? Of course, I'll have to go out with other people or there'll be problems with my mother – '

Gorse shrugs. 'Of course. No strings. I fully understand.'

Clarice puts her hands on his shoulders and faces him. 'Ralph, darling. We're two of a kind. I don't think I'll ever meet anybody else like you. Anybody I'd want to do all *this* with . . . ' Her eyes indicate the room. 'As much as I want to do it with you . . . Anybody who . . . is just right for me – in this way.'

'You mean for an afternoon quickie?' asks Gorse.

Clarice answers, very coolly. 'Yes, that, but not just that. Whatever it is, it isn't the stuff marriages are made of, anyway the marriages I've seen . . . So can't we leave it, just as it is, and enjoy it? For what it is?'

Gorse says, very deliberately, 'Of course we can. It's my fault I'm broke and you're rich. It's my fault it's 1938 and there's a Depression. It's all the fault of Ralph Ernest Gorse. Anybody can see that!'

In reply, Clarice stands up and puts her arms quickly around his neck. 'Ralph. Make love to me again. Now. Please.'

But Gorse is almost dressed and he completes the exercise. His movements brush her off. He picks up his jacket and saunters to the door, conscious of her eyes on his back. 'I'll call you. Perhaps.' And the door closes and he is gone.

Clarice feels all this is too much, too bloody much altogether. '*Merde!*' she declares.

As for Gorse, he drives back to Brighton in a morose frame of mind. Normally, he enjoys the very act of driving but not this evening. He feels tired, out of sorts and ill-at-ease with the world. The difference between Clarice Mannors and all the other women he's ever been to bed with, or robbed, or both, is that she is rich and beautiful, and it is just possible (however unlikely it may seem) that he is in love with her. Gorse has never ever been in love with anybody before, and so he finds it hard to understand. It could of course be just her money and her class and the expensive, desirable person she is. It could be the fact that sexually she is surprised by nothing, indeed wills him on, in his escalating excesses of small violences and bondages . . . It could be all or any of those things. The fact remains that the feeling is new, and robs him ever so slightly of his power over her. Gorse does not like that. He does not like it at all. So when he gets back to his combined room and finds Pamela Bennett sitting alone in the place he is not pleased. Pamela is made-up and wears a dress he has not seen before but her mouth is turned down at the corners, and she looks pointedly at her watch. She is playing a broken-down old gramophone. The song is a popular one of the time, 'Stormy Weather'. Her eyes look, to Gorse, a practised observer of this kind of thing, as if she has been crying.

'. . . Oh. Hello,' he says in greeting. 'What are *you* doing here?'

'Waiting for you,' answers Pamela. 'Remember? Where have you been?'

Gorse is instantly repentant. 'Oh Lord, yes! My fault! I had a prospect of a sale.' He flops in a chair but doesn't kiss her. 'Turned out NBG!'

But Pamela is hardly listening. 'Your landlady let me in. She wasn't very pleased about it.'

'Shame. Oh . . . I could use a drink.'

Pamela pours him a scotch and hands it to him. 'Don't get too comfortable, darling. Mummy's waiting for us. She wants to talk.'

'What about?' asks Gorse.

'I don't know.'

'No idea at all?'

'None. Except . . . She knows about Us.'

'Yes,' sighs Gorse. 'I suppose so.'

'We'd better get home soon,' presses Pamela.

'All right, I suppose we should go and charm the old

girl . . . In a minute . . .' Gorse drains the whisky. 'But what on earth *is* it about?'

'You and me.' Before Gorse can say more . . . 'It might be about money or something.'

'Money?' asks Gorse.

Somewhat to her dismay, this seems to cheer him up. It could of course be just money but Pamela is sure, for some reason, that it isn't. She looks fondly at Ralph Gorse and she wonders how it is that she can love him as much as she does and understand so little about him.

Pamela and Gorse drive up in the Railton to the Bennett house. It is, Gorse notes, a splendid place, with a large lawn at the front. Gorse gets out of the car and holds the door for Pamela. At the front door to greet them stands Phyllis Bennett, looking anything but charmed. 'Come along in, you two! Pamela! Your father will be home in thirty minutes!'

They look at each other, Gorse and Pamela. 'Coming, Mummy, what's it all about anyway?' asks Pamela. But Phyllis Bennett only repeats, 'Come along, do!' and she ushers them inside the house.

Gorse does not know what awaits him on the other side of the drawing-room door or it is very likely he would never have gone in. For, as the door opens, the first thing he sees is Mr Stimpson, sitting on an upright chair and, next to him, Joan Plumleigh-Bruce. Pamela looks at them both without recognition, and with some puzzlement. Phyllis Bennett moves to the centre of the room and takes the floor. Ralph Ernest Gorse stands stock-still, feeling the earth move under his feet.

Joan speaks first. 'Ralph . . .'

Gorse finds his voice from somewhere. 'Hello, Joan . . . Donald.'

Mr Stimpson nods but does not reply. He is enjoying this.

Phyllis Bennett smiles but her eyes are stone. 'Well, I see you *do* know one another. This is my daughter Pamela. Mr Stimpson. Mrs Bruce.'

Joan corrects her. 'Plumleigh-Bruce, in fact.'

Phyllis replies, icily, 'I'm so sorry. Sit down, you two. May I offer anyone a drink?'

Joan sees Mr Stimpson's eye. '. . . Not for me. Thank you.'

'Mr Stimpson?' asks Phyllis.

'I thank you, no.'

'Well, I'm having a very large sherry and I suggest you have one too, Pamela, because I think you are going to need it,' declares Phyllis.

Pamela looks at her mother, then at Gorse, who is drifting over to the drinks cabinet. 'Mother, who are these people, and how do they concern Ralph and me?'

Phyllis considers this. 'They concern Ralph. They do not concern you, unless you want that.'

'I don't understand.' Pamela turns to Gorse. 'Ralph? What *is* all this?'

Gorse turns to her, seemingly self-possessed. In this last moment or two he has poured and swallowed a very large whisky, without the benefit of water. He squares his shoulders. He makes a face that suggests sympathy and contrition. 'Mrs Bennett . . . Pamela . . . This is all a terrible misunderstanding . . . These people used to be my friends. One of them . . .' He looks at Joan, and she looks back mistily, '. . . if she will allow me to say it, a very, very dear friend . . . The other . . . a, let me say, willing accomplice on at least one occasion that we both of us enjoyed but over which I will draw a veil.' Gorse's eye rests on Mr Stimpson, who does not react at all.

Joan suddenly demands, 'What *are* you talking about, Ralph? Really!'

Phyllis asks, 'Mr Stimpson, do you know what Mr Gorse is talking about?'

Mr Stimpson answers, 'Yes, I do, but it isn't relevant, Mrs Bennett.'

Gorse interrupts, 'Oh, but I would have thought it was, Donald.'

'No. And my name is Stimpson, *and* you cannot blackmail me. Not any longer.'

Phyllis Bennett is shocked. 'Do you really mean to use *that* word, Mr Stimpson? I mean seriously?'

'Unfortunately, madam, I do.'

Joan interposes, with a quick look at Gorse, 'Donald. Please. There isn't any need for unpleasantness.'

Mr Stimpson demurs. 'Oh yes there is, my dear. There is a very great need for it.'

Pamela, who has been listening in some bewilderment, asks, 'Will you please get to the point! If there *is* one!'

In reply, Mr Stimpson delves into his briefcase. 'Oh there *is* one, my dear young lady. Very much so. Allow me to give to you this passbook. It is issued by the bank – '

'I know what a passbook *is*!'

Mr Stimpson is unperturbed. 'Please look at the signature. In the withdrawal column against a sum of one thousand pounds. Do you recognize the signature?' Pamela takes the passbook. She looks at it, and then looks up. 'It's Ralph's . . .'

Gorse interrupts now. 'I can explain it, darling. Total misunderstanding.'

Mr Stimpson replies, slowly. 'Total fraud, would be my description of it.' He raises a hand before Pamela can interrupt. 'Look at the names on the front of the passbook.'

Pamela looks and repeats, 'Mrs Joan Plumleigh-Bruce and Mr Ralph Ernest Gorse.'

Mr Stimpson explains. 'A joint account. In both names. Either to sign. You understand?'

Pamela is now looking at him closely, beginning to understand. 'Go on.'

'Gorse took that thousand pounds and ran away with it. Simple as that. Mrs Plumleigh-Bruce's money. That was six months ago. We haven't seen him from that day to this. Have we, Joan?'

Joan looks away, then at Gorse. '. . . Oh, Ralph, *why*?'

Gorse is ready with an answer. 'I had an opportunity to double it. It went wrong. I couldn't face you . . . Terribly . . . sorry.' Joan yearns to believe it. 'Was *that* it? Was it, *really*?'

But Mr Stimpson will have none of it. 'He's spent your money and since it went, he's been bouncing cheques all over the coast. Without information being laid as to his whereabouts, we'd still be looking for him!' Gorse looks into the glinting eyes of Mr Stimpson and sees no hope there. 'A lot of creditors will be coming after you. We just happen to be the first.'

Gorse appeals to Joan. 'Joan . . . there was no intent to deceive . . . You *do* believe that, don't you?'

'Ralph, I'd *like* to, but . . . my dear, you see how it looks?' Pamela looks from Gorse to Joan and back again. The whole thing is clear now. It is terrible, yes, but it could be worse.

Mr Stimpson turns to Phyllis. 'Well, Mrs Bennett?' Phyllis is cool, almost insulting. 'I fail to see how any of this concerns my family?'

Mr Stimpson holds up his copy of the *Argus*. 'I understand from the local newspaper that your daughter is engaged to Gorse?'

'Then you understand wrong,' answers Phyllis coldly.

'Ah,' says Mr Stimpson. 'Then I must talk to your husband about this matter. I thought you wished to avoid that?'

'I did not know the amount involved then.'

Joan tries for peace at any price. 'Is there no . . . accommodation possible, Mrs Bennett?'

Phyllis turns on her, cold and merciless. 'If some people are . . . *silly* with their money, for whatever reason, it's no business of ours, is it?' Joan recoils as if struck. 'And, as far as I can see, Mr Gorse is free of prosecution. Legal prosecution.'

Mr Stimpson's reply is prompt. 'Not when his creditors find out where he *is*. You *can* go to prison for debt, Mrs Bennett.'

'Thank you for telling me, but shouldn't you be telling Mr Gorse? He'll be leaving Mr Bennett's employ anyway, I imagine – '

But Pamela brings the whole discussion to a stop with words that are almost a scream. 'Stop it! Stop it! *Stop it!*'

'Pamela!' gasps Phyllis. 'My dear girl, please, no hysterics.'

'I'm pregnant,' declares Pamela, flatly. 'To Ralph. Two months.'

'Oh, my God!' says Phyllis, and sits down abruptly, blinking hard. The faces in the room all stare at Pamela – Phyllis shocked but resilient, Mr Stimpson not surprised, but bitter, Joan Plumleigh-Bruce deeply hurt.

Joan whispers. 'Oh. Ralph. Ralph.'

It is Gorse's moment, and he knows it. 'Naturally, I will stand by her.'

Mr Stimpson remarks, drily, 'Naturally.' But he feels

the sharp sword of defeat. He has, almost, achieved his object. But Gorse has again escaped, if only to a marriage he surely didn't want. He ought to feel satisfied, but he doesn't. Mr Stimpson sits and stares at nothing.

Two minutes later, in the hall, with the drawing-room door closed, Gorse and Phyllis face each other. Gorse has his words ready. 'Phyllis, I'll marry her, but I'm afraid I'll have to ask a price . . . First, you pay those people in there.' Phyllis nods tightly and makes to move back. Gorse restrains her gently, with a hand on her arm. 'And all my debts? I'd have to insist on that, I'm sorry. That would be at least another thousand. You wouldn't want me in prison for debt, would you? Not as your new son-in-law?'

Phyllis shakes her head. She asks, 'Did you know about Pamela?'

Gorse is adamant. 'Absolutely not . . . she must have let it happen.'

Phyllis looks at Gorse a long moment, then goes back into the drawing room. Gorse, after a moment, follows her. Things could certainly have turned out a hell of a lot better, he thinks. But they could have turned out a hell of a sight worse.

Back in the drawing room, Phyllis goes across to her writing desk. She takes her cheque book out of a drawer. Mr Stimpson, Joan and Pamela watch her every movement. 'How do I make out the cheque?' Phyllis asks Joan Plumleigh-Bruce.

'To Joan Plumleigh-Bruce. That's l-e-i-g-h.'

'Thank you,' says Phyllis icily, as she writes. Joan stares at her, still very unhappy. On the couch Pamela is silent, dry-eyed. Gorse pats her hand, and looks up, mildly triumphant, at Mr Stimpson. Phyllis offers, and Joan takes the cheque, silently. Joan looks at Mr Stimpson. He nods. 'I'll say good evening,' says Mr Stimpson, ever the stickler for niceties. Nobody replies as Mr Stimpson and Joan walk out.

As Joan and Mr Stimpson make to walk down the drive, Gorse follows to the front door. Mr Stimpson turns. He retraces his steps. Joan watches helplessly. Mr Stimpson comes eye to eye with Gorse. Mr Stimpson speaks gently but inexorably. 'You think you're oh so bloody clever! But one of these days you'll go too far. And when you do . . . I'll be there . . . Waiting . . .'

Gorse does not reply. He just watches, as Mr Stimpson and Joan Plumleigh-Bruce walk away down the drive.

Saved, Gorse says to himself, by the Dear Old Bell. God, it had been a near thing.

Chapter Four

A young couple stand on the steps of a Church of England church, in a semi-rural setting. This church has a green graveyard with many headstones, and a lych-gate. We are gathered together for the marriage of Ralph Ernest Gorse and Pamela Bennett. The ceremony is over and now it is time for the photographs.

Gorse smiles at Pamela and she smiles back and hugs his arm. Gorse looks well satisfied with the situation. He feels, at this moment, that he is in command of it all. So they stand, Gorse and Pamela, for the group photograph, Gorse in grey morning coat, grey topper in hand, Pamela in traditional bridal dress, looking very radiant, and showing, as yet, no sign of her pregnancy. Ranged on the steps around them are close family – but only on the Bennett side. Gorse has no living relatives. Or none he would care to invite.

Harold Bennett, who is paying for all this, is there too, looking anything but happy. So is his wife, Phyllis, looking very grand, and relieved, if anything, to see it all over. A photographer – the very same one from the *Argus* – is using a stand camera with a cowl. He peers out from under it. 'All right! Everybody! Look straight at the camera! And all together when *I* say cheese, you say cheese, wait for it, wait for it, *cheese*!'

The group all smile together, even Harold Bennett who is hurting badly as he reckons up all the expenses. Gorse is calm. Pamela is looking at him adoringly.

The photographer cries . . . 'And *again*! Just one more

. . . Captain Gorse sir, a nice big smile . . . if you *please* . . . This *is* your wedding day, sir! . . . A really *big* one, sir!' Gorse manages a very superior smile.

'That's it!' calls the photographer. 'Thank you, everybody!' Everybody relaxes, and laughs and chatters. Pamela's eyes are huge. 'Oh Ralph, I'm so happy . . . aren't you?'

'Yes, of course. Of course I am.'

'I'm going to make you glad we did this. I mean it, Ralph.'

'Yes, I know you do . . .' he adds, 'darling.'

Pamela smiles. 'I know it isn't as big a wedding as Mummy would have liked, but – '

' – I think it's fine. Fine.'

Harold Bennett takes Gorse's hand extremely briefly, and turns to Pamela. 'The best of luck, my love!' Pamela, tears in her eyes, embraces him. 'Oh thank you, Daddy! . . . for everything.'

Phyllis Bennett kisses Gorse coolly on the cheek. 'Ralph . . . you're one of the family now.'

'That'll be nice.'

Phyllis laughs: Gorse's charm works on her, too. At that moment she is prepared to forgive him anything. 'Come along, Ralph, you're in the first car!'

Gorse and Pamela go down the church steps to a shower of confetti and 'Hoorays!' from Phyllis and Harold Bennett and the others, and then down the path, quite quickly, towards the lych-gate and the waiting limousine. At the limousine the driver holds the door open for the bridal pair, and they half-collapse into the back of the car.

Pamela tucks her bridal dress around her. 'Oh . . . I'm so glad it's all over . . . I was *so* nervous. You weren't at all, were you?'

'Nothing to be nervous about, really . . .' Gorse says no more. For he has seen, standing in the churchyard alone, away from the celebrations, the figure of Donald Stimpson. For a long moment, Gorse stares at Mr Stimpson, as if he cannot believe what he sees..

Pamela sees the expression on Gorse's face, and asks, 'Ralph . . . Are you all right?'

'Yes . . . perfectly all right.'

'Are you sure? You don't look it. You look as if you've seen a ghost.'

'Not exactly . . . Driver, can we *go*?'

The driver closes the door and gets into the limousine. Gorse does not look out again. He stares straight in front of him. The limousine moves off, to the cheers of the well-wishers. Behind them, Mr Stimpson, in the green churchyard, looks on.

The Bennett drawing room is rather a crush of people, including Pamela, Phyllis and Harold Bennett, the vicar, and the many guests. Everybody has a drink in their hands. Ralph Gorse, who is standing silently, a little apart, looks very thoughtful. The encounter with Mr Stimpson – even at long range – has shaken him.

Pamela glances across at him rather anxiously as she talks to her mother. 'Mummy, go and chat to Ralph, will you?' Phyllis looks towards Gorse. 'Why, he seems all right.'

'No, he isn't, he's a bit upset.'

'What? First night nerves? Now really, Pamela!'

'Oh, never mind then!' says Pamela and turns away. The vicar instantly detains her.

Phyllis Bennett looks after her, then moves across to Gorse.

'Well . . . it's all over, Ralph.'

'I would have thought it was just beginning, Phyllis.'

'I'm not sure you should call me Phyllis, should you?'

'It's your name, isn't it?' asks Gorse. 'And I don't intend to call your husband *Mister* Bennett, I can assure you of that.'

'Ralph . . . go slow with Harold. He's not too happy about any of this, you know.'

'Yes, I can imagine. This wedding must have cost him a few bob.'

'Not just that,' answers Phyllis. 'He does care about Pamela. And so do I . . . Be nice to her, won't you?'

Gorse is smiling, he is – again – in command of events. 'Whatever gives you the idea I won't be?'

Phyllis Bennett looks at him, seriously. '. . . Oh . . . Quite a few things, actually.'

At that moment, Harold Bennett arrives. He has been imbibing, just a bit, as he feels he has every right to do, all things considered. 'Oh, *there* you are, Gorse!'

'Ralph, please. As I was just saying, it will have to be Harold and Ralph from now on, won't it?'

Bennett stares at him, pop-eyed. 'Indeed it will not. At my office I'm *Mister* Bennett to everybody on my staff. And that includes you.'

Gorse sees Phyllis's warning eye on him. 'On parade, off parade, as it were? Just like the Army?'

'Exactly. Excuse me, I must see to these culinary arrangements.' Bennett nods and bustles off.

'What did I tell you, Ralph? . . . Really!' says Phyllis Bennett, scandalized but amused.

Gorse is instantly mock-contrite. 'Well, actually, if he'd given me the chance, I wanted to thank him . . . for buying the house for Pamela.'

'Least we could do. Can't have our daughter starting

married life in some scruffy little combined-room, can we?'

Gorse looks at her steadily. 'Just thank your lucky stars, Phyllis, you've never had to do that.' The intensity of Gorse's expression unnerves Phyllis. 'I'm sorry, Ralph . . . I didn't mean anything.'

'Yes, you did.'

'Don't be *so* thin-skinned. It's so boring.'

Gorse looks at her, po-faced. 'Stimpson was here.'

'What?'

'In the churchyard.'

'He wasn't! The awful old thing! *Why?*'

Gorse shakes his head, ruefully. 'I think he's quite mad.' Phyllis looks at him a long moment, curiously. Then she asks a question that has long been troubling her. 'That awful Plumleigh-Bruce woman. *Was* she anything to you? Honestly?'

But Gorse does not have to answer because Pamela has come to claim him, flushed and radiant. 'Come along Ralph! It's about time you paid some attention to your wife.' She drags him off into the crowd. Phyllis Bennett looks very thoughtfully after them both. She just hopes that she has done the right thing. Not, of course, that she had much choice.

It is six weeks later and the moon shines down on a suburban street in a reasonably select quarter of the town. On, in fact, a small, detached suburban house. A light burns brightly in a downstairs window and Gorse's Railton stands in the drive. This is the lovenest, if such it can be called, of Ralph and Pamela Gorse. It is a decent little space as far as it goes, but to Gorse it is a prison. Now, bored and a little drunk, he sits in the kitchen, while Pamela, wearing an apron, serves up his supper, which is a shepherd's pie and a bit of a burnt offering at that. Gorse looks at it with distaste and more than a little blearily. Behind them, a wireless plays the music of Jack Payne and his Orchestra.

'What do you call *this*?' asks Gorse.

Pamela is almost tearful. 'Well, it *was* a shepherd's pie, but you *are* an hour and a half later than you said you'd be, darling . . . If I made some gravy, perhaps?'

Gorse shakes his head. 'Take it away! Give me some bread and cheese or something!' Pamela is even nearer to tears. But she takes it away. Gorse gets to his feet and finds himself a pint bottle of beer from a cupboard. 'No whisky left, I don't suppose?'

Pamela, quickly sensing the atmosphere, switches off the radio. 'You drank the last yesterday, darling.'

Gorse pours the beer. 'Why didn't you get another bottle if you knew that? . . . A gentleman only drinks beer when he's thirsty.'

Pamela, greatly daring, replies, 'I should say you've had enough to drink already, darling.'

'And I'll be the sole judge of *that*! Darling!' snarls Gorse.

Pamela says no more, but arranges cheese and bread on the table. Gorse ignores it and drinks his beer, with no particular enthusiasm. Pamela says, low, 'Ralph. Eat *something*!'

'No appetite, my love. Lost it somewhere down at bloody old Bennett's Motors, when your silly old fool of a father talked to me as if I was a grease monkey!'

Pamela shows her anguish. 'Please . . . Don't talk like that about him . . . he's helped us . . . he *did* pay all your creditors! He means well, really . . .'

'No, he doesn't.'

Pamela sits at the table and sighs. 'Darling, I know

things are difficult for you . . . My fault. I got pregnant . . . my fault . . . But, darling, Daddy *gave* us this house and everything in it . . . the furniture . . . everything. We have to be grateful, Ralph.'

Gorse's reply is violent. 'No, *we* do not have to be grateful. *You* have to be grateful. He did it all for *you*. What did he do for me, tell me that?'

'As I just said, darling, he gave us the house.'

'No, he did not, *darling*, he gave *you* the house.'

'I don't see the difference,' whispers Pamela.

'Ah, but I do,' says Gorse. 'I see the difference, and shall I tell you what it is, *darling*?'

Pamela flinches. She hates rows and she's been having a lot of them. 'Ralph, please. No more rows. If it wasn't for the child coming, I'd say, let's leave this place and take our chance somewhere else . . .'

But Gorse is in full flood. 'A man likes to feel he's the master in his own house. I don't feel that. I feel as if I'm a lodger . . . Or as your dear Daddy so charmingly put it, a poor relation.'

Pamela is aghast. 'I'm sure Daddy never said *that*? He wouldn't!'

'He would, and he did. Ask him.' It is not quite true, but Gorse does not care about that.

'Oh, I don't know what you want, Ralph. I do everything I can for you – '

'Considering this house is yours, yes.'

'It's *ours*, darling!'

'It's in your name.'

'That's only Daddy being – '

Gorse sneers. 'That's dear Daddy being himself. He hates me. He loses no opportunity to insult and belittle me, and you aid and abet him.'

Pamela is on her feet at the injustice of that. 'I don't! I

don't! I love you, Ralphie, all I want is for us both to be happy! Oh, I don't know what's gone wrong, I do my best, I gave up my job in the office because you didn't want me walking about looking pregnant – '

' – No, I didn't! A man should keep his wife, and he should own his own home. Or he gets no respect from anybody.'

Pamela looks at him a long time: Then: very gently, she wonders, 'I don't know if Daddy would agree to my transferring the house into your name.'

Gorse drinks. 'Then don't. Or do. And don't tell him. What business is it of his? It's *your* house!'

'Yes, but he gave it to me!'

Gorse shrugs. 'Then don't bother. To hell with it!' Gorse sits and pours himself more beer. Some of it slops on to the table. Pamela gets a cloth to mop it up and comes back. 'Leave it!' cries Gorse.

Pamela leaves it and sits next to him. 'Darling . . . You know what Daddy's thinking?'

'No, I don't know what Daddy's thinking.'

Pamela talks very delicately, unaware of the risks she's taking. 'Well . . . he's thinking that . . . it's him I'm talking about, not *me* . . . but *he's* thinking that since you got into such trouble with *people*, owing them money and everything . . . and not paying them . . . All those dud cheques and everything . . . Well, you have to see it from his point of view, darling, he wonders if you've really turned over a new leaf? . . . I mean, you do *see*, don't you, Ralphie?' She falters to a halt.

Gorse looks at her. There is no expression in his eyes. 'Thank you.'

'What?'

'I can see just how much you love me.'

'But I *do* . . . Oh . . . I can't show it . . . being like I am . . . But I *will*, Ralphie . . . I will!'

Gorse looks at her so coldly that she flinches.

'Two things,' says Gorse.

'Yes . . . Ralphie?'

'One. Never call me Ralphie again.' Pamela is petrified by this coldness. 'I'm sorry, darling. I didn't know . . . you . . . didn't like it.'

Gorse puts his face very close to hers. 'Two. If you ever talk to me like that ever again, I will probably kill you.' And without another word Gorse gets to his feet and goes out of the room. As for Pamela, she is shattered. It is all going wrong. It is all her fault it is going wrong. She knows it is. She would do anything for Ralph Gorse. Anything at all. Only she cannot think what it is he wants. But she knows it is all her fault.

It is the following day, as Gorse comes quietly into Harold Bennett's office and closes the door gently behind him. He picks up the telephone on Bennett's desk and, cupping his mouth, asks the operator for a long-distance number. 'Mayfair 729, please . . . Brighton 1071.' Gorse waits impatiently and in some apprehension in case Bennett should come in.

In the Mayfair flat, Clarice, dressed by Molyneaux in a tweed suit, answers the telephone. 'Hello, Clarice Mannors.'

Gorse hisses, 'It's you.'

'And it's *you*. Well, hello stranger.'

'How are you?' asks Gorse.

'Do you really want to know?' asks Clarice, coolly.

'Why d'you ask that?'

'Because I haven't heard from you for simply ages.'

'Well, you're hearing from me now,' answers Gorse, rudely.

'Obviously. Why?'

'Because I want to see you, what else?'

Clarice debates. 'But I'm not sure I want to see you, Ralph.'

'Of course you do. Look, Sunday afternoon? At the Ritz? Tea at four o'clock?'

'Well . . . I am supposed to be busy.'

Gorse's voice is grating. 'All right. Don't.'

Clarice recants hastily. 'No . . . I can do it. See you then. But I shouldn't. Ralph – what on earth's been going on, are you all right?'

But Gorse cuts the conversation short. 'Must go now . . .'Bye.' He puts the telephone down as Harold Bennett enters.

Bennett glances at him, annoyed. 'What are you doing in my office?'

'Using your telephone to call your daughter. Telling her I'll be late. I have a prospect for the Morris,' says Gorse, easily.

But Harold Bennett is still annoyed. 'This is a place of business, not a domestic agency. And I hope your prospect's a good one. If you were as good at selling motor cars as you are at putting girls in the club, we'd all be rich!' Bennett crosses to his desk and picks up some papers. Those who know Gorse would know from his eyes that Gorse could – really *could* – murder him then and there. But Gorse merely smiles, and goes out.

That very same evening Pamela is alone in the suburban house. She has eaten – her appetite is the only thing that seems all right these days – and she is restless with Gorse not there. He is out on a possible 'sale'. In the 'Thirties a possible sale was never neglected, a sale of anything.

Nobody worked set, trade-union hours. Pamela tries to believe that Ralph is trying hard to make enough money for her and the baby. She tries so hard she almost does believe it. Perhaps, if Ralph could get a job elsewhere, things might be different. But what job? In the 'Thirties, jobs were simply not to be had. They were well-off, compared to most people. They have a house. A car. Enough to eat. Pamela told herself they were lucky.

Suddenly the 'phone rings. Pamela lets it ring a few times before lifting the receiver, thinking it might be Ralph and paying him back for leaving her, alone and miserable, in the lonely kitchen. 'Hello,' she says, at last.

Mr Stimpson is using the public 'phone at The Friar. He has been drinking and his manner is very deliberate. There is no Joan Plumleigh-Bruce in the bar behind him. 'Hello . . . Is that the Gorse residence? Is that Mrs Pamela Gorse?'

Pamela answers, in her mild, pleasant voice. 'Yes, it is. Who is that, please?'

Mr Stimpson speaks very softly, for him. 'This will be a little bit of a surprise, Pamela, but I don't want you to be alarmed . . . This is Donald Stimpson.'

'Donald . . . who? . . . Oh. I remember . . . Yes . . . ?'

'*Do* you remember me?'

'What . . . ? Do you want to speak to Ralph? He isn't here,' gabbles Pamela, nervously.

'No, I want to speak to you,' insists Mr Stimpson.

'To me? Why?'

'Because I care what happens to you, Pamela . . . Are you all right?'

'How do you mean, all right?'

'Well . . . it's been six weeks now, since the wedding. Is Gorse . . . Is Ralph behaving himself?'

Pamela is a long time replying, 'I'm afraid . . . I don't know what you mean, Mr Stimpson.'

'I think you do.'

'No. I don't.'

Mr Stimpson speaks very slowly and clearly. 'Then, sooner or later, you will, my dear. Now, I'll say good-bye, but please remember that I'm your friend . . . If Ralph becomes a problem . . . and you feel you can't talk to anybody, your father or your mother, about it . . . Will you ring me? Reading 4073? You can talk to me. You can tell me anything . . . Reading 4073. Anything at all.' Mr Stimpson's voice is suddenly cut off, for, trembling, the pregnant Pamela has put down the telephone. But in The Friar Roadhouse Mr Stimpson has replaced the telephone with some satisfaction. One step at a time, Mr Stimpson tells himself. One step at a time.

In the Mayfair flat, Clarice and Gorse are drinking coffee. Clarice is looking at Gorse with profound interest and curiosity, not to say amazement. '. . . You're *married*? I don't *believe* it! But *why*?'

Gorse shrugs. 'All sorts of reasons. None of them good ones.'

Clarice is pensive. 'So . . . You don't love her?'

'Love her, I hardly know her! I haven't a single bloody thing in common with her!'

'Then why on earth did you *do* it?' demands Clarice.

'Oh. Circumstances. People. Money.'

'Money?' asks Clarice. 'I could have always found you some money, Ralph. A hundred or so anyway.'

'It took a lot more than that, darling.'

'Let me get this straight. You got into this marriage because of money?' She decides to be angry. 'Ralph, I'm a bit speechless.'

'I'm more than speechless! I'm absolutely devastated by it . . . I have to get *out* of it!'

'What, just go! Can you do that?'

Gorse considers his fingernails. 'I think . . . I really do think . . . that I have to.'

'What does that mean, exactly?' asks Clarice.

Gorse is very agitated for once. 'What I say, no more and no less. I *have* to get out of it, I *must*!'

Clarice decides to remain angry. 'Well, I *can* see it being boring and all that, and if you don't love her?'

'I don't feel anything for her. I hate what she stands for, a lot of damn tuppenny snobbery. Oh, it isn't her fault, she's not so bad in her way, she just shouldn't be married to me!'

'That does sound pretty final,' says Clarice.

Gorse is on his feet and walking around the room. 'The thing is, I need some money . . . Before . . . before I leave her. For her . . . And for me . . . I can't leave her penniless . . . Or myself . . . When we split up.'

'And how do you propose to get that? Some sort of business deal, or something?' asks Clarice.

'Well, that's all the marriage has ever been, a business deal,' replies Gorse, but Clarice had decided to be decisive about the whole business. 'Don't *tell* me about it, Ralph! You know where to find me when you want me. Whether you're free or not free isn't anything to do with Us. Come and see me when you've sorted everything out . . . including the money, yes?' It is a kind of aristocratic semi-brush-off, and Gorse reacts stonily. 'The money? Of course. Naturally.'

Clarice ignores that. 'One rather complicating thing. There's a lot of war talk, you know. If the Germans go into Poland, my father says it'll be war for sure.'

'War?' Gorse laughs. '*Then* we'd all have something to

worry about, wouldn't we?' He is still smiling as Clarice, despite her coolness, moves close to him. He gently takes the silk scarf she wears around her neck in his hand and very, very slowly, he tightens it. Clarice's eyes widen in shock . . . Then suddenly Gorse lets the scarf go, and takes her in his arms. Clarice is shaking. ' . . . Oh, Ralph . . . Oh, Ralph . . . '

Joan and Mr Stimpson are ensconced in the Nook at The Friar. Joan is in a bored, distracted mood as Mr Stimpson, oblivious to that as to so many other things, talks on: 'Joan, I've bought that land over by Marsh's Farm, for building a small engineering factory.'

'To make what, for goodness' sake?' enquires Joan.

'Small parts for aircraft. A war's coming, Joan, whatever Mr Chamberlain says.'

'You don't usually tell me your business . . . Why now?'

Mr Stimpson speaks with sudden emphasis, for this isn't just a business suggestion, it has deep emotional undertones for Mr Stimpson. 'If you put the thousand pounds you got back from Gorse into the project, you could almost certainly double it, if not treble it, in a year or two.'

'You're asking me to gamble my money on there being a war?' asks Joan.

Mr Stimpson reacts frostily. 'I am offering to let you in on the ground floor . . . with me.'

'That's very good of you,' retorts Joan. 'But no thank you! I had all that with Ralph Gorse. My money is back in the bank, drawing its three per cent and there it stays!'

'It didn't stay there for Gorse, did it?' remarks Mr Stimpson.

'Well, possibly I've learned something since then.'

‘Yes,’ says Mr Stimpson, ‘and possibly so have I.’

They stare at each other. Joan gives a little ground. ‘Maybe . . . I could put a hundred pounds in?’

‘No, thank you. I don’t need your money. Snell and I are quite well enough britched to handle it. I simply thought you’d want to take my advice, and get in on a genuinely good thing. But no.’

‘Donald, you know all this talk of money upsets me!’ says Joan, much put out.

‘Then we won’t talk about it any more.’ Mr Stimpson finishes his drink. ‘In fact, I’d better be off home. I’ve got an early start in the morning. Are you coming?’

Joan thinks about it, then, ‘Very well.’ She wiggles off her stool and tugs at Chinklywinkle’s lead. ‘Where are you going that’s so important anyway?’

‘Oh . . . just business.’ Joan reflects that Mr Stimpson tells her very little nowadays. Of course, it was thoughtful of him to give her the opportunity of getting in on the ground floor, in his new business. But there would be No War. This Year or Any Other Year. The *Daily Express* said so.

Joan follows Mr Stimpson out of The Friar.

Mr Stimpson’s ‘business’ takes him back to Brighton the following day, alone. To an appointment in a small, somewhat genteel tearoom, just off the Promenade. As Mr Stimpson enters the tearoom, he sees Pamela Gorse sitting at a table in the corner. He smiles and sits down. ‘I’m so pleased you telephoned, my dear,’ he tells her.

‘I shouldn’t have, really. Ralph would be . . . very upset if he knew.’ Pamela looks very nervous and is trembling slightly.

Mr Stimpson nods. ‘Then we’ll have to see he doesn’t know, won’t we?’ As a waitress comes up, ‘Another cup, please.' He waits, then, 'Now first of all, how are *you*?'

Pamela smiles wanly. 'I'm all right . . . I mean . . . I'm healthy enough.'

'But . . . not happy?' probes Mr Stimpson.

Pamela looks down at the tablecloth. 'No. Not really . . . I suppose.'

Mr Stimpson's voice is very, very gentle as he asks, 'And . . . why is that, my dear?'

'Oh, I don't know . . . A lot of things . . .' She falls silent as the waitress returns with a cup and saucer for Mr Stimpson. Mr Stimpson pours her a cup of tea. He adds milk. She is sitting quite still.

'Like what, for instance?' presses Mr Stimpson, softly.

But Pamela says, 'You said you had something important to tell me. About Ralph. What is it? Please?'

Stimpson shakes his head. 'First, *you* must tell *me* how he has been behaving? It may not be necessary for me to tell you anything, if he's treating you as a good husband should. Is he doing that?'

Pamela is silent a long moment. 'No . . . Not exactly.'

Mr Stimpson moves forward, almost imperceptibly. 'In what way is he being . . . difficult?'

'You're very prejudiced against him, aren't you?' asks Pamela. Mr Stimpson denies this. 'No, I'm not. I'm hoping you'll tell me all is well, that all that's wrong is a little tiff? A lovers' quarrel?'

'I can't talk to Daddy. Or to my mother,' says Pamela.

Stimpson says very, very softly, 'You can talk to me.'

Pamela is silent for so long that Mr Stimpson is afraid she isn't going to say anything at all, that his journey has been in vain and that his long, painful plan of revenge is about to be denied him. But then it all pours out, all the words he has been waiting to hear, everything confirmed, everything exactly as he expected it to be, all there in the broken, confused words of this poor young girl. For Pamela says in a low voice, '. . . We've been having a lot of rows . . . Ralph's been out a lot at night, all night sometimes. He spends all our money, gambling, drinking, I don't know what. I've found lipstick on his shirts, I think there's another woman . . .' She almost breaks down, but recovers. Mr Stimpson waits. '. . . But worse even than that . . . He . . . he got very upset when I refused to put the house in our joint names . . . He kept on about it . . . So I did it . . .' Mr Stimpson expels his breath. '. . . He really frightened me over that . . . We had a row, and he said . . . he said . . .' Pamela falters to a stop. Mr Stimpson leans forward. 'Yes, what did he say, Pamela?'

Pamela is still as stone. Then: 'That he'd kill me! And you know, Mr Stimpson, the awful thing is, I felt, at that moment, he . . . he meant it . . .'

Mr Stimpson leans back and nods very slightly; he is almost not breathing at all.

In Joan's living room that evening there is something of a confrontation going on. Mr Stimpson is sitting morosely in front of the fireplace but Joan is putting on her coat, preparatory to going out. She has what she would call her warpaint on; that is, a heavy coat of powder on her face and a film of vivid lipstick on her lips. 'Well . . . *I'm* going out for a drinkie down at The Friar, even if you're not, Donald! I must say, you've become a dreadful old grouch these days! With all this war talk I'd have thought you'd want to get out and forget it all for a while!'

Mr Stimpson interposes, 'What's the point of forgetting it? It's *there*. In my opinion we'll be at war this week.'

'Well, don't sound so pleased about it!'

'If you'd put your money into my factory you'd be a richer woman today.'

'Not until the war starts,' replies Joan. 'If it ever does. Are you coming?'

'No. I'll stay in, I think. Listen to the News.'

Joan stands, pondering. 'You won't ring that poor girl again, will you?'

'That is my business, Joan.'

'I'd say it was very much *my* business. This is still my house, Donald.'

Mr Stimpson gets to his feet. 'Very well, I'll make the call from my own house.'

'So you *are* making a call to her! Donald, really!'

'I will not trouble you. I will go back to my place.'

Joan sits down and speaks more softly. 'Donald, don't be stupid! You'll make yourself ill, chasing after Ralph Gorse. All I'm concerned about is you! He's gone. He's out of our lives! He's married to that poor girl, Pamela, or whatever her name is! Can't you put him out of your mind?'

Mr Stimpson's reply is curt. 'No. And I don't want to.'

Joan gives up. 'There you are, you see! Look, Donald . . . if the marriage isn't going too well, what's new about that? A lot of marriages don't, at first.'

'When Gorse is in the situation, *that* makes it different,' says Mr Stimpson with an air of finality. 'You'd better get off to The Friar, if you're going.'

Joan cajoles. '*You* come? Come on!'

'No. Really.'

'Oh, all right then.' At the door Joan turns, thoughtfully. 'Y'know, I'm not sure we'd ever be suited for marriage, you and I.'

Mr Stimpson regards her with a steely gaze. 'One thing

for sure. I'll never marry you while Ralph Gorse is still alive.'

Joan is very hurt by this remark but doesn't show it. 'How very charming! Enjoy your bad news on the radio!' And she is gone, out of the door and on her way to The Friar Roadhouse. Mr Stimpson waits until he hears the door close. Then he rises to his feet. He picks up the telephone. 'Operator . . . This is Reading 4073 . . . I want Brighton 1063 . . . Thank you . . .' He waits. A male voice answers. 'Hello? . . . Is that Mr Bennett? Mr Harold Bennett? You don't know me, Mr Bennett, but your lady wife does. My name is Stimpson, Donald Stimpson. I am calling you because I am somewhat concerned about your daughter . . . to be precise it is in regard, actually, to her husband, Ralph Gorse . . .' Mr Stimpson takes a deep breath. This is – almost – the moment of truth. For himself and for Ralph Ernest Gorse.

Gorse, naturally, knows nothing of all this but sits in his kitchen finishing his supper, looking at the now obviously pregnant Pamela, and . . . thinking. Pamela starts to take the dishes away. Gorse has left most of his meal. Gorse is, as usual, well-dressed, but he has taken off his jacket and has been eating in his shirtsleeves. It is, almost, a domestic scene, except that no scene could be domestic with Gorse in it.

'Have you finished, darling?' asks Pamela, fondly. She wears a print dress and an apron, and her manner around Gorse is more hesitant and uncertain than ever.

Gorse makes an effort. 'Not hungry. Sorry. It was very nice.'

'Are you all right?'

'How d'you mean?'

Pamela half-smiles, nervously. 'You're being very nice

to me, that's all. I'm not sure how to . . . behave . . . It's such a long time since we . . .'

'I know. I'm sorry. It's all my fault. Here, let me!' Gorse gets up, takes the plates from her and puts them in the water at the sink. 'I'll do these. You sit down.'

Pamela is surprised. 'If you're sure? . . . Thanks. I do get a bit weary.' Gorse keeps his back to her as he talks. 'Pamela . . . One thing I've been meaning to ask you.'

'Yes?' Pamela lights a cigarette nervously, puffs amateurishly at it, and coughs. Gorse waits until she has stopped coughing but he does not turn round. 'If . . . anything happened to me . . . Where would you go . . . what would you do?'

Pamela is alarmed. 'Why? What could happen to you?'

'Haven't you noticed? We look like getting into a war,' says Gorse, gently.

'Oh . . . that . . . you mean if you went away in the Army or something like that?'

'Something like that.'

Pamela debates. 'Well, I don't know . . . I suppose I'd try to keep this place on . . . I'm not sure Daddy would make me too welcome . . . with an infant . . . Or Mummy, for that matter . . . No, I'd stay on here.'

'But what if . . . if something *happened* to this place . . . ?' asks Gorse, still preoccupied with the domestic chores.

'What, this house?' asks Pamela.

'Well, yes.'

'How do you mean? In a bombing raid or something?'

'One has to think of all possibilities, Pamela,' says Gorse, still gently.

Pamela puzzles. 'Do you think it could happen? Out here? I mean, it's not as if we're in London or anything?'

'It's always possible. They're even issuing gas masks for

children . . . *Anything* is possible, I'd say,' says Gorse, the dutiful husband.

Pamela is pleased – and surprised – that he is thinking about her like this. 'Well . . . I suppose, in a crisis, I could always go to live with my folks. I'd hate it, but . . .'

Gorse is silent for a moment, then, still not turning to her, '. . . And if I went away and didn't come back?'

Pamela puts down the cigarette. 'Ralph, please . . . Don't talk like that, it frightens me.'

Gorse persists. 'But if I did?'

'Oh? In the war . . . you mean?' Gorse says nothing. 'I suppose I'd do what everybody else does, I'd live through it somehow. But Ralph, please don't go on about such awful things . . .' She gets up and puts her arms around Gorse's waist from behind. 'Oh, I do love you, Ralph.'

Gorse ignores that and talks on: 'You see, now that the house is in our joint names you'd get half and I'd get half . . . You'd be all right . . .'

Pamela hugs him. 'Oh, I know things haven't been very good between us lately, darling, but I still love you more than anything in the world . . . All this talk about going away . . . I know it *could* happen – the war and everything – but I'll face it when it does!'

Gorse still has his back to her. 'Just so long as I know you'll be all right,' he adds.

Pamela feels she must say it. '. . . Ralph, it's not like you to . . . well, think ahead like this. Some people – who don't know you as I do – wouldn't believe how nice you can be.'

'Which people?' asks Gorse sharply. 'What are you talking about?'

'I think it's wonderful of you to worry about *us* so,' replies Pamela quickly, putting Mr Stimpson hastily out of her mind.

Gorse turns to her and puts his arms around her, and they kiss. But his eyes do not change. Gorse is still thinking hard. 'Darling . . . I have to go up to London for a couple of days . . . I have a good sales prospect up there . . .'

Pamela is disappointed. 'Oh, it gets so lonely all on my own in this place, when you're away . . .'

Gorse is now the considerate husband. 'Well, why not go to your parents? Just for the weekend? My prospect may say yes to half a dozen company cars . . . I may even be able to impress darling Daddy with that!' But he smiles, and Pamela smiles, too.

'Well, I don't know . . .' says Pamela.

'I don't like the idea of your being miserable all weekend. If you don't go to your folks, then I won't chase the order up.' Gorse hangs up the tea towel, miserably. 'I might not get it anyway.'

But Pamela is guilty, at once. 'No, Ralph. You must try for it!'

'Well . . . But don't say anything to your father. It could all fall through. Promise?'

'Promise. You know, some people really do have the wrong idea about you, Ralph.'

Gorse is very still. '*Which* people? Your father?'

But Pamela is thinking of Mr Stimpson again. 'Oh . . . Well . . . Yes, I suppose so.'

Gorse is reassured. 'Well, not a word to your folks. Just say I'm in London.' Pamela waits, Gorse smiles. He thinks of Clarice and of her wonderful breasts. 'Visiting a close friend, who's in bed with a chest complaint.'

Pamela laughs out loud. 'What a curious thing to say, Ralph, you *are* funny!'

Gorse says, 'Yes, aren't I?' but he does not smile.

* * *

The following afternoon finds Gorse doing one of the things he likes best in life: driving his sports car fast, along a double carriageway towards London, the bright lights and Clarice Mannors. He is singing 'South of the Border, down Mexico Way!' and beating time with his gloved hand on the wheel. No other vehicle passes him.

At last he turns into the drive leading to the exclusive Hurlingham Club. Gorse has not been here before, but it is a meeting place of Clarice's choice, and it could be made for Gorse. He parks his car and strolls out into the grounds to watch the last stages of a polo match. The players are well-to-do, if not rich, or they wouldn't own polo ponies. The watchers are mainly dressed in old tweeds (both sexes) and felt hats (the women) or caps (the men). Gorse speaks to nobody, but one or two people – mostly young women – glance at him curiously. Gorse is used to this. Women are always interested in him because he normally isn't interested in them. Clarice Mannors, of course, is an exception: Clarice joins in. Clarice is ready to do things in private that these worthy people would be shocked by, if only they knew. Gorse smiles to himself and goes into the Club.

A flunkey is at the door to keep out intruders. Gorse, perfectly correctly dressed in a tweed sports jacket and good-quality flannels, perhaps a mite too *new*, tells the man, 'Captain Gorse. Miss Mannors is expecting me.'

'Are you a member, sir?' asks the flunkey.

'No, I'm not, but I understand I'm signed in?'

The flunkey looks at his book, which is obviously his bible. 'Ah. Yes. So you are, sir. By Mr Archibald, sir.'

Gorse is surprised. 'Archibald *who*?'

'Mr Jonathan Archibald, sir.'

Gorse recovers. 'Oh . . . *Archie*? Of course.' The

flunkey points. 'He's in the bar, sir. Through that door, sir.' Gorse nods and goes through the door.

The first thing Gorse sees in the bar, which is crowded with people drinking and shouting at each other, is Clarice accepting a glass of champagne from a sweating and cheerful young man with dark curly hair, in polo kit. He pushes his way over, then stops as he hears Clarice say, 'Archie – you were dreadfully unlucky, I thought.'

Archie shakes his curly head. 'Not really. They were too bloody good.'

'You're being too modest, darling. As usual.'

But Archie has seen Gorse looking. 'I say . . . I think your friend's turned up.'

Clarice turns her eyes to meet Gorse's, and the usual chemistry happens between them. Gorse only hopes the man called Archie hasn't noticed it.

'. . . Or am I wrong?' asks Archie, drily. He has noticed. Too bad, thinks Gorse.

But Clarice is gesturing. 'Ralph! . . . Over here!' To Archie, she says, 'No, he's an old friend. Be nice to him. He doesn't know many people. He's been abroad.'

'Oh. I see,' says Archie, noncommittally.

As Gorse joins them, Clarice kisses him, but ritually, just like an old friend, thinks Gorse. 'Ralph, how nice of you to come! This is Archie . . . Archie, Ralph Gorse.'

'Hello,' says Archie. 'Let me get you a drink.'

'Thank you. A gin and tonic,' replies Gorse, then, 'Pleasant place.'

'Yes, isn't it?' replies Clarice. Gorse's eyes are on Clarice's but she will not meet them again. Archie hands Gorse his drink. 'Here you are, old chap.'

'Thank you.' Gorse's eyes are still on Clarice. Archie sees this, there is really no way he can avoid seeing it.

Archie ventures, 'I hear you're a colonial?'

'I'm sorry?'

'Been abroad. Colonial service, was it?'

'Oh . . . er, not exactly.'

'No? I thought Clarice said . . .'

'I was abroad . . . Now . . . I'm in business, I'm afraid.'

Archie nods cheerfully. 'Well, somebody has to be, don't they? I mean, Mr Chamberlain will soon have a government composed entirely of 'em, won't he?'

Gorse nods. 'Well, I hope so. I can't see them doing any worse than all those Old Etonians, can you?'

It is obvious that Archie is just that. But, as such, he is well-mannered. 'What? . . . Oh . . . Absolutely not. No. Well, I'm all sweaty. If you'll excuse me, I'll go and have a tub.' He smiles at Clarice. 'See you later . . . Er . . . old chap?' Gorse nods, but does not smile. Archie looks from one to the other, nods almost to himself, and goes, carrying some of his kit. Archie is exactly the sort of man Gorse despises; and exactly the sort of man he would like to be.

'What do you want to do, Ralph?' asks Clarice, coolly.

Gorse answers without hesitation, 'Get out of here.' Clarice smiles, a private, knowing smile. Gorse finishes his gin and tonic. They go. Some girls, who are obviously Clarice's friends, stare curiously after them.

It is after dinner in the drawing room at the Bennetts' house, and Phyllis is serving coffee. Pamela is sitting contentedly in an armchair. But Phyllis is looking anxiously at Harold Bennett, who looks awkward, as he lights his cigar.

'Enjoy your supper, darling?' Phyllis asks Pamela. 'Scrumptious, Mummy. I get so hungry,' Pamela looks self-consciously at her swelling body. 'That's only natural, darling,' says Phyllis fondly.

Pamela smiles. 'It's so nice to be home. I didn't know how much I missed it.'

Bennett says, bluntly, 'Always room for you here, you know that.'

Pamela laughs. 'Daddy, what a funny thing to say! I'm married to Ralph now, I have a home of my own, why should I come back here?'

'Exactly,' says Phyllis sharply. 'Harold, please.'

But Bennett persists. 'You know what I mean . . . if things were ever . . . difficult between you and Gorse . . . er . . . Ralph . . . Well . . .' He falls silent.

'Harold – don't go on, darling,' says Phyllis lightly, glancing anxiously at Pamela.

But Bennett will not be denied. 'No. I have to say it. No need for the girl to stay a minute longer with Gorse if she's unhappy.'

Phyllis says, trying, still, to keep it pleasant, 'She hasn't said anything about being unhappy.' Then to Pamela, 'You're not unhappy, are you, darling?'

Pamela, suddenly serious, asks, 'No . . . what makes you think I might be?'

'Nothing . . . It's just your father worrying, as usual.'

'No. It isn't,' says Harold Bennett. 'It's more than that. I understand . . . from a person who might know . . . that Ralph Gorse has threatened you . . .'

Pamela says, in a very different voice, 'This person . . . Is it Mr Stimpson?'

'Harold. Please. Leave it,' pleads his wife.

But Harold Bennett has started, and he will finish. 'Indeed I will not . . . it has to be said and I intend to say it. Stimpson says you told him Gorse threatened to kill you!'

Pamela turns pale, and stammers as she replies. 'It was a row, that's all, people say things they don't mean – '

'That's true,' says Phyllis, with a forced laugh. 'I've *said* I could kill you, Harold.'

But Harold Bennett ignores her. 'Gorse has been in trouble before, according to Stimpson. Some scandal over a boy drowning.'

'You didn't say anything about that!' says Phyllis, shocked.

'That's what Stimpson *says*,' declares Harold Bennett. 'It seems he's been sort of . . . well, investigating Gorse's background, to the year dot . . . like . . . Well, Gorse has never been in the Army . . . And his father was just a clerk in an office and Gorse won a scholarship to his public school . . . And they expelled him, after the drowning incident.'

Phyllis Bennett has been listening to all this with mounting irritation. 'Is that *all*? . . . A lot of nasty, unproven conjecture and rumour? Put together by a man who hates Ralph Gorse! Harold, really, I despair!'

Harold Bennett is suddenly very angry. 'You can despair all you like. Pamela, I don't think you're safe with Gorse. I think he's a rotter. I want you to stay at home with us. Don't go back there tomorrow. We'll look after you.'

'Oh, Harold, really,' says his wife.

Pamela gets to her feet. 'It's all right, Mummy.' To Harold Bennett she says, 'Daddy, I can't believe you hate Ralph so much. He can be so sweet and tender – I think you're simply awful to talk about him that way – I'm not listening to any more of it. Mummy, I'm sorry but I'm going back home this minute.' And she sweeps out of the room.

Phyllis Bennett looks at her husband. '*Now* are you satisfied?'

Harold Bennett shakes his head in total and bitter confusion. Then he pours himself another drink.

Fifteen minutes later, Pamela lets herself into her house, using her latchkey. She has refused a lift from her mother and has taken a taxi home. She feels awful about her row with her father, whom she really loves very much – Pamela naturally loves most people and things – dogs, horses, cats, ponies, her parents and, of course, Ralph Gorse. Ralph Gorse more than anybody or anything. The problem is they do not love her, not the dogs or cats or ponies, or even her mother and father, not really. She has learned not to love them. She will love Ralph Gorse, her husband, and the expected baby. That will be enough.

As Pamela comes into the hall, taking off her hat and coat, the telephone rings. She is instantly galvanized, and picks it up. 'Hello . . . *Ralph*?' She is disappointed by the reply, 'Oh, hello, Mummy . . . No, I'm all right . . . I'm sorry about all *that*, but I think Daddy was most unfair . . . Yes, I'm going straight up to bed now . . . I feel . . . so tired . . . Yes. 'Night, Mummy . . .' Pamela puts the telephone down and slowly walks up the stairs.

Two hours after Pamela has gone to bed, Gorse turns the Railton into their road. He parks the machine, but not immediately outside his own door. Then he gets out of the car, and looks quickly around. Nothing stirs in the suburban street. All the lights are out. It is two o'clock in the morning. Nobody sees him, as Gorse walks rapidly towards his house.

Gorse silently lets himself in, putting on no lights. He does not notice Pamela's Tam O'Shanter and coat on the hall stand. Very quietly, Gorse goes down the hall and into the kitchen.

Gorse is very soon engaged in a task which he has long thought about and rehearsed. He opens the stove, which is of a type with an open grill, and burns coke. He puts some twisted magazines and newspapers in a trail leading to a bundle of firelighters in the grate. Gorse checks to see that he's done everything correctly. He waits a full minute. Then he lights the trail of newspapers with a match, looks at them a moment to see they are burning well, then quickly leaves the kitchen.

A moment later Gorse steps out of his house. He closes the door very quietly. Slowly, in the moonlit, suburban street, Gorse walks to where he has parked the Railton. He gets in and drives away, through the quiet, slumbering town.

In the kitchen of Gorse's house the rope of paper is alight now, and the flickering flames are almost reaching the firelighters. When they do, they ignite with a 'pop'. Before long, the flames are high and getting higher. There is a lot of smoke. Almost as if by magic, the smoke is very thick and billowing and it fills the stairwell, and begins to infiltrate under the door of the upstairs bedroom. Thicker and thicker it grows, and higher and higher grow the flames, until they fill the entire stairwell and begin to consume the wooden bannisters.

And still there is no cry or call.

The following morning at nine o'clock Gorse drives up to the Bennett house in the Railton to collect (as has been arranged) his wife. He gets out and goes into the house. The front door is open, which is unusual, but Gorse reflects and decides that, of course, the family know all about the fire by now. He squares his shoulders, and enters.

The Bennetts' uniformed maid stands there with wet eyes, holding the door open for him.

'Morning, Milly . . .' says Gorse. 'How are you this lovely morning?' But the maid sobs, and runs past him. Gorse frowns and goes into the drawing room. As he enters, the first thing he notices is that the curtains are drawn and the room is quiet, except for a woman's sobs. The woman is Phyllis and she sits in a chair, her back to the door. Harold Bennett, however, sits facing Gorse, as if he has been waiting for him. His face is drawn and has something beast-like about it.

'And where the bloody hell have you been?' asks Harold Bennett.

Gorse looks from Bennett to Phyllis and to the drawn curtains. The awful realization comes to him, like a clap of dark thunder. He sits and closes his eyes but says nothing. He is waiting to find out what he feels. But when his senses return, which they do after a minute or so, there is one overriding emotion that blocks out pity, remorse, sorrow, regret.

That feeling is one of relief.

Very slowly, four black motorcars return from the cemetery to the Bennett house. As the first car nears the house we see that Gorse, Harold Bennett and his wife, Phyllis, sit in it, dressed in black and not looking at each other. In many ways the scene resembles that of the wedding a few months earlier, in the Bennetts' living room. The same people are present, dressed this time in black ties and dark clothes. Drink is still on hand; some people are eating. Gorse is standing alone, as if shunned. He certainly looks shocked, some people think. Phyllis Bennett is putting a brave face on it all, moving around, talking to people in a low voice, accepting their condolences. The vicar, a veteran of these occasions, moves to Gorse. 'Such a trial for you, Ralph . . . God give you strength.' Gorse nods. 'If you feel the need . . . for help, or just to talk, you know where to find me,' adds the vicar.

'Thank you,' says Gorse, the bereaved young husband to the life.

'On such a day as this, too,' murmurs the vicar. 'Sunshine and death . . . and for all we know, worse to come.'

Gorse simply nods. The vicar – at a signal from a silent Harold Bennett – takes the floor and the whole company turns, as he clears his throat to speak.

'Our hearts go out,' says the vicar, who has often said words like this. 'Each and every one of us, to Harold and Phyllis in their great loss . . . and to the unhappy young husband . . . Ralph . . . Most of you have read the report of the Coroner's Court. His verdict, of death by misadventure, is a sad summary of a young life, snuffed out . . . The poor, dear girl.'

There are muted 'hear, hears' from some male guests, at this. Gorse's expression, however, does not change. He is stony-faced. He is also conscious that Harold Bennett is looking at him bleakly from across the room, and that Phyllis is looking at him equally sadly, not knowing what to think.

The vicar pauses, then: 'It is a mark of the good citizen and patriot that Harold Bennett is, that he has asked me to say to you that, despite the occasion . . . we must also live in our own day . . . A most grave day indeed since we are all of us soon to be called on to face who knows what perils and dangers. Poor dear Pamela has been spared all that . . . We, for our part, have to endure whatever is to come, as we are all now . . . a nation at war.'

There is a reaction from the mourners, a low hum of talk. War has been declared the previous day and nobody is used to the idea of it yet. Like the death of Pamela Gorse, it seems unreal. The people in the room are sober, silent and absolutely still. Gorse hardly seems to have heard the vicar's words. Like the others, he does not move. For he had earlier seen something that none of the other mourners had noticed: the spectral form of Mr Stimpson, all too real in dark homburg hat and black overcoat, standing some distance away from the flower-heaped grave, a lone and menacing figure amongst the tombstones.

In the corner of the tearoom where he last talked to Pamela, Mr Stimpson now sits, still dressed in the homburg hat, overcoat, gloves, and black tie, drinking his tea and listening to the hubbub of voices in the place. Opposite him sits Joan, wearing her best black out of respect. But she has not been to the funeral, as Mr Stimpson has. She devoutly wishes, as her demeanour shows, that she had never come. She speaks in a low voice. 'What a terrible, terrible day . . . That poor girl . . . and now . . . war.'

Stimpson nods, absently. 'You know . . . I had almost forgotten about the war.'

'Well . . . It's here and we have to get on with it,' says Joan, 'though I'm damned if I'll be joining those blessed women's committees. I never could abide them when I was married to the Major.'

Stimpson nods again, as if surprised. 'Yes . . . I had almost forgotten the War.'

Joan says, 'You'll have plenty on your plate, anyway, won't you? Now, we'll see whether your little investment makes money or not. Buying that land! . . . Preparing for war, *that* was!'

But Mr Stimpson is hardly listening. 'I expect it will all work out, Joan.'

'Well, you'll have something else to think about, apart from Ralph Gorse, for one thing! All that nonsense must be over and done with now, put away and forgotten.'

But Mr Stimpson whispers after a moment's reflection, 'Not quite.'

'What?' Joan lowers her voice even more. 'It's *over*, Donald! Ralph's widowed! He's lost his wife and his unborn child . . . There's nothing else that can happen to him. Even *you* must see that?'

Mr Stimpson shakes his head. 'There are still some ends to tie up.'

Joan tries again. She wonders if Mr Stimpson is entirely sane. 'Donald, I have my money. You have had . . . in some kind of way . . . your revenge. Surely you aren't going to go on and on with this ridiculous vendetta?'

Mr Stimpson looks at her coldly. 'Is that what you think I am? Ridiculous?'

Joan puts her hand on his, across the chequered tablecloth. 'Donald . . . we may all be dead in a month! A week, if those gas attacks start! Let's go home. If anything is going to happen to us, let it happen at home.'

'I told you, my business here is not quite finished.'

Joan declares, 'Then mine is! I don't know why I came, although I can guess why you did. You wanted to see Ralph broken, and now you have. What that poor boy must be feeling at this moment.'

'Nothing.'

'What?'

'That poor boy is feeling . . . nothing whatever.'

Joan is scandalized. 'Donald . . . what a wicked thing to say! I know Ralph has behaved very badly . . . All right . . . He's . . . he deceived me.'

'Robbed you . . . and more.' They stare at each other a long moment. Then Joan gathers her handbag. 'Well . . . I'm catching the next train home. If you want to stay here, that's your business.'

'Yes, it is, isn't it?'

'Yes, and pretty nasty business as well! I'll see you when I see you, Donald.'

Mr Stimpson watches her go out of the tearoom, then slowly pours himself another cup of tea.

At the Bennett house, Harold Bennett is seeing out the last mourners and the vicar. 'Thank you both once again . . . Vicar . . . for coming. I'll see you out.'

Milly, the uniformed maid, is clearing away glasses on a tray. Phyllis is sitting numbly in a chair, smoking. She has been drinking but seems sober. Gorse stands where we last saw him, alone, near the window. Phyllis turns to him and in a low, desperate voice, asks, 'Well, Ralph . . . what will you do now?'

'No idea.'

'Haven't you thought about it at all?'

'No.'

'I expect you'll be going into the Army? Won't you?'

'Won't most people?'

Harold Bennett comes back in. He looks as if he has not slept for a long time and his voice is hoarse with grief. 'You were with a woman in that hotel room, weren't you?'

Phyllis sighs. 'Does it matter?'

Gorse answers her. 'All that matters is that the hotel clerk testified I was there that night. The Coroner accepted his evidence.'

But Harold Bennett is not satisfied with that. 'There's something bloody fishy about all this, and I wish I knew what it was!' He finds himself a glass, and pours a large drink. 'That . . . lovely girl . . . all we had . . . gone . . . if she'd never met you, you young bastard!' He chokes, he can say no more.

'Harold. Please,' says Phyllis, 'it's no good. The Coroner was satisfied with Ralph's explanation.'

'He might have been, but I wasn't, by God I wasn't!' Bennett leans drunkenly on a table, peers up into Gorse's face. 'I'm satisfied with nothing about this young man, nothing!'

'Harold,' says Phyllis, 'for God's sake stop talking like this! You can't bring Pamela back!'

Harold Bennett turns away, his glass in his hand, and talks as if to himself. 'D'you know, I was hoping the child would be a boy? Take over the business. Hah! Probably turn out like you, Gorse . . . So . . . I'm selling Bennett's Motors, taking whatever I can get. And leaving this town.'

Phyllis nods, bitterly. 'First sensible thing you've said today, Harold.'

Bennett turns to Gorse. 'So, you're out of a job, Gorse. That, at least, I can do.'

Gorse looks at Harold Bennett and at Phyllis. Then he speaks, very low and deadly. 'What *I* can't understand is . . . why was Pamela back at the house? I thought she was staying here over the weekend? Why did she *go* back?' Gorse looks at them both, in turn. Harold Bennett looks at Phyllis. She looks down. Gorse sees it all. '*Very* strange, that,' adds Gorse. With that he turns and goes out, picking up his coat on the way. Harold and Phyllis sit, not looking at each other.

On the forecourt of Bennett's Motors early the following morning Mr Stimpson, carrying a briefcase, walks towards the office. A couple of garage hands are putting up blackout panels on the windows. Mr Stimpson addresses one of them. 'I have an appointment with Mr Bennett.'

The garage hand indicates the office door. 'Straight inside, guv'nor.'

Mr Stimpson goes in.

Ten minutes later, two insurance assessors, the first, Mr Smith, a quiet thirty-year-old, the other his deadly and much older boss, Mr Sawyer, both dark-suited undertaker-like figures, walk towards the office, exactly as Mr Stimpson has done.

The garage hands still work at the blackouts. Mr Sawyer stops and looks around the place, thoughtfully. Mr Smith consults his watch. 'We're late, Mr Sawyer.'

'I'm thinking, Mr Smith.'

'Sir?'

'What is our objective here?'

'To pay out as little as possible, sir.'

Sawyer nods. 'Exactly. And I don't like this one at all, Smith. Not at all.'

They go in, Mr Sawyer leading. The two garage hands go on working at the blackout.

Exactly five minutes after that, Gorse drives up in his Railton, and parks it at the kerb. He gets out, and walks up to the office. He is well-dressed and almost jaunty. The garage hand calls, 'Mr Gorse!'

'Yes, Albert?'

'Mr Bennett says, will you wait out here? He's got somebody with him.'

Gorse is surprised. 'Really? Ah, well.' He takes out his gold cigarette case and lights a Player's with his gold lighter. 'Ciggy?'

Both men look at him. They don't like him much. They think he's a snob. They also suspect he had more to do with the fire than has yet come out. They are ordinary working men and know Gorse is no gent, whatever he says he is.

'No. Working,' declares the man.

'As you wish.' Gorse walks back to the Railton and sits in it, smoking. He glances at his watch. He does not seem overly worried by anything at all, on that sunny autumn morning.

Gorse might have been worried if he had known what was happening at that moment in Harold Bennett's office. Mr Sawyer, a sharply funereal figure, is standing and shaking hands with Mr Stimpson. Behind him stands Harold Bennett and Mr Smith.

'Thank you, Mr Stimpson,' Mr Sawyer is saying. 'Most interesting. All of it. *Most* interesting . . . eh, Mr Smith?'

'Yes, sir. Very,' nods Mr Smith.

'I'll show you out, Mr Stimpson,' says Harold Bennett.

'Thank you, gentlemen.' Mr Stimpson nods good-bye to Mr Sawyer.

After Mr Stimpson and Bennett go out, Sawyer and Smith sit silently for a moment. Smith waits for his superior to speak. At last he does, and his words are accompanied by a wintry smile. 'Hope, Mr Smith. Hope.'

Harold Bennett and Mr Stimpson come out of the office, Mr Stimpson looking very satisfied and Harold Bennett not as gloomy, perhaps, as of late. In fact, there is an air of grim satisfaction about Harold Bennett. Gorse in the Railton notices that, just as he notices Mr Stimpson. Mr Stimpson just looks at him, a long moment. They exchange no greeting. Gorse feels a tremor of foreboding, but does not show it. Harold Bennett crosses to the Railton. 'The gentlemen are ready for you inside,' he tells Gorse, curtly.

'*Are* they really?' asks Gorse, airily.

Harold Bennett does not reply. He turns and walks with Mr Stimpson to his parked Rover. Gorse watches them all the way, trying to take in the situation. Mr Stimpson and Harold Bennett get in the car and watch him. The Rover is not driven away. Gorse looks very thoughtful. He gets out of the Railton and walks into the office, where he finds Mr Sawyer sitting in Harold Bennett's chair. He looks benign but somehow relentless. Behind him stands his assistant, Mr Smith, blinking through his glasses. Sawyer begins by talking to Gorse, who sits down opposite across the desk, as if he is on trial. Which, in a way, he is.

Mr Sawyer gets immediately to the point. 'Mr Gorse, you told the Coroner that you stayed, on the night of the fire, at the Royal Commercial Hotel, in Paddington.'

Gorse nods. 'So I did. I produced the bill. The reception clerk gave written evidence I stayed there.'

Sawyer smiled. 'It was highly fortunate he remembered you.'

'Most people do,' says Gorse.

'So I understand,' replies Sawyer. 'If he had been in any way indecisive about remembering you, I think you might have had trouble, not from Mr Smith and myself . . . but from another quarter.'

Gorse looks at him coolly. 'Are you saying that I lit that fire? That I drove all the way from London and back to do it?'

Sawyer looks at him a very long moment. 'I have not said that, Mr Gorse. You have said it. But it is a most interesting hypothesis. Mr Smith?'

'Yes. It is,' says Mr Smith. Gorse curses himself but says no more. He is wary. These people are not the usual fools he deals with.

Mr Sawyer is talking. 'Mr Smith and I see a lot of fires

and we hear a lot of people say things, both to the . . . police . . . and to coroners and to our good selves, that contradict each other, or are not well remembered, or sometimes, regrettably, are short of being the whole truth.'

Gorse is quick with an answer. 'Are you saying I told the Coroner a pack of lies?'

'Did I say that, Mr Smith?' Mr Smith shakes his head. 'I didn't say that . . . Not exactly.'

Gorse is very irritated and showing it, for once. 'Then what did you say?'

'I said that you . . . may not have, in your very understandably upset state of mind, told us – quite – the whole truth.' Sawyer smiles, then: '*Is* it a fact that you and your wife have been in a state of domestic unhappiness for some time?'

Gorse is taken aback by the abruptness of the question. 'No. It isn't.'

'If you say so. That, Mr Gorse, does not really concern us. It may concern others. It may even concern the police.' Again, the smile. '*How* the fire started? That concerns us a very great deal, Mr Gorse.'

Gorse is now cooler. 'I thought that had been disposed of by the Coroner.'

'The Coroner returned an open verdict. Death by . . . misadventure. We were surprised, were we not, Mr Smith, that he did not ask for more detailed forensic evidence?'

'We were very surprised,' says Mr Smith, on cue.

'Of course, there is a war on. Things are slacker, perhaps,' says Mr Sawyer silkily.

Gorse asks, 'Just what did you expect this . . . further forensic work to . . . find?'

Sawyer muses, 'Evidence of how the fire *really* started?

Was it by accident?' He looks at his file. 'You'd left, by your evidence, newspapers adjacent to the stove, from time to time?' Gorse nods. '. . . Mr Gorse, how often do you think Mr Smith and I have investigated a fire started from that particular make of stove?'

'I have no idea,' says Gorse.

There is a silence, then Sawyer says very softly, '*Never*, Mr Gorse. Not from that particular make of stove. They are considered very safe.' Gorse says nothing. 'Mr Gorse, you have this policy with us, solely in your name, very recently transferred to be *solely in your name*, should your wife die. And then you have this fire, of a kind Mr Smith and I have never seen before . . . And your wife dies.' He lets it sink in, then: 'Were there any firelighters near the stove?'

Gorse frowns. 'I . . . have no idea.'

'But there could have been?'

'Perhaps. I did not light the stove or tend to it, so I don't know.'

'Very well,' says Mr Sawyer. 'Let us leave that for just a moment and turn to a rather disturbing aspect of this case.' He looks long at Gorse. 'I have, from an independent source, a sworn statement that you threatened to kill your wife, less than a week before she died . . .'

Gorse is very shaken by this. 'A sworn statement from whom?'

'I regret I cannot tell you that. Only if it is put into evidence in a court of law. That is the only way you can learn who the person is.'

Gorse says, 'I think . . . I can guess.'

Sawyer elucidates. 'Other information was laid . . . That you have a less than . . . shall I say impeccable? . . . history of money dealings. I am referring to Mrs Joan Plumleigh-Bruce. Does that name mean anything to you?'

'Go on,' says Gorse, grimly.

Mr Sawyer goes on. 'There is little more for me to say . . . Except that Mr Smith and myself are not prepared to pay out to you, in full or in part, the sum insured – two thousand pounds in all – without a very great deal more investigation of this fire . . . both from the forensic point of view, and from the . . . shall I say . . . motivational point of view. In short, we are not satisfied. Not satisfied at all. Correct, Mr Smith?'

'Absolutely correct,' says Mr Smith.

Mr Sawyer resumes. 'Of course, you can sue us through the courts. If you wish to do that.' Mr Sawyer waits.

Gorse falters, thinking hard. 'I . . . will let you know what course of action I propose to take.'

'Naturally,' says Mr Sawyer. 'We will await your decision with interest.'

Gorse stares at them. There is no more to say. He gets to his feet. 'Good-day, gentlemen.'

Mr Sawyer allows himself a thin, sour smile. 'And to *you*, Mr Gorse.'

After Gorse closes the door behind him Mr Sawyer looks at Mr Smith. Mr Sawyer closes his file with a snap. 'I don't think we'll be seeing that young gentleman again, Mr Smith.'

Harold Bennett's Rover is still parked along the road, and Harold Bennett is still in the motor, along with Mr Stimpson. They watch as Gorse comes out of the office and, disgusted, stands there drawing on a cigarette. He throws it away in a gesture of defeat. Gorse walks over to the Railton, gets in, and drives furiously away.

Harold Bennett and Mr Stimpson smile, bitter and conspiratorial, at each other. There is, after all, some justice in the world.

Chapter Five

It is May, 1940.

In front of an army hut 'Somewhere in England' stands a sergeant-major of an infantry regiment, a tough-looking regular soldier, dressed in army battledress, forage cap and gaiters. He wears a ribbon for long service, and he is watching the approach of Private Gorse who, since he is newly joined, wears nothing in the way of decorations. Gorse marches smartly enough towards the hut. He comes to attention. 'Morning, Sar'Major.'

'On time but only just, Gorse, as usual! The Captain's waiting.'

'What's it about?' asks Gorse.

'He'll tell yer!'

Gorse nods. He looks somewhat apprehensive, but squares his shoulders and follows the sergeant-major into the hut.

The captain's office (which the hut basically is) has a table covered by an army blanket, behind which sits the captain, also a professional soldier, of about forty. On the wall are 'parade states' and 'sick rolls'. A company clerk sits at a desk in the background, making out leave chits. The captain, who is hatless, sits behind his desk, some official papers in front of him. Gorse stamps to the front of the table, and comes to attention. To the side, slightly behind, is the sergeant-major, also at attention.

'At ease, Gorse,' says the captain.

'Sir.' Gorse puts his left foot out and his hands behind his back.

'It's regarding your application for a commission.'

'Sir?'

The captain smiles to take the sting out. 'As you know, we've nothing against you here, in the company. Or, for that matter, the battalion . . . But, the Colonel feels that, since you've only been in the Army six months, and you have no special military or technical qualifications . . . that you'd be better advised to try again in six months or a year, when you've got some soldiering under your belt. All right?'

Gorse is bitterly disappointed but tries not to show it.

'Sir!'

The captain closes the file. 'Enjoy your leave, Gorse. It may be your last for a while.'

'Yessir. Thank you, sir.' Gorse comes to attention and turns to go out. Once outside the hut, the sergeant-major regards Gorse curiously. 'Fancy yourself as an officer, do you, Gorse?'

'Somebody has to do it,' says Gorse noncommittally.

The sergeant-major laughs at the idea. 'You? Givin' *me* orders? That'll be the bleedin' day!'

'Permission to go, Sar'Major?' asks Gorse. Nobody argues with sergeant-majors.

'Got yer leave-pass, 'ave yer?' asks the sergeant-major.

'Yes, Sar'Major.'

'Like the Captain said, enjoy it while yer can.' The sergeant-major looks round, and drops his voice. 'The buzz is, we're orf to France next week.'

Gorse takes this in, and thinks about it hard.

The sergeant-major adds, 'You'll get a bellyful of soldiering, *if* that's what you're after, unless I'm very much mistaken.' Gorse just nods.

'You goin' orf in yer motor, are yer?'

'Yes,' says Gorse.

'I dunno 'ow you get the petrol to run it, and I don't suppose you'll tell me.' Gorse says nothing, merely smiles. 'Where you goin' for yer forty-eight? To the ancestral 'ome?' asks the sergeant-major.

'Something like that,' replies Gorse. He comes to attention, turns, and walks away. The sergeant-major watches him go. To himself the sergeant-major adds, 'Officer material? Never, Private Gorse.'

Once Ralph Gorse has driven the Railton – which is full of black-market petrol – a few miles from the camp to a quiet country lane, he stops the car. He quickly changes into a civilian suit and puts his uniform into his army kitbag. Everything, boots, gaiters, small-pack, it all goes in. It is now a very heavy kitbag. Gorse looks at it, wondering how heavy it is. Then he decides it will do. He drives on. Ralph Ernest Gorse's destination is Brighton. Five hours later he is there.

We find him at the end of the deserted West Pier. It is night and there is a blackout. Gorse humps his army kitbag into the deep water, with an effort. It falls in with a distant splash. 'Good riddance to all *that*!' says Gorse, peering down into the dark. The kitbag is swirling away on the tide. Gorse smiles to himself.

An hour later, Gorse sits in a sleazy caff off the Brighton seafront. He sits behind an *Argus* wartime edition, cut down to four pages. The caff is a haunt of spivs, run by a fat man in a rather dirty apron presiding over a silver tea-urn. Some sugarless rock cakes are under glass. Lino is on the tables, and heavy blackout at the windows. There have, however, been no air-raids yet. The war is only just starting, in reality, which is why Gorse is where he is and has done what he has done. Joining the Army, after the 'trouble' with the Bennetts, now seemed, in retrospect, a silly thing to have done. But now, Gorse had taken the decision of his life. The Army was not for him. It wasn't for the poor devils of the British Expeditionary Force either. The headlines in the *Argus* that Gorse had in his hands read 'Germans Invade Holland. Heavy Allied Casualties.'

Gorse looked up as a man, flashily dressed in a suit and hat, came into the place. Gorse breathed a sigh of relief. Henry hadn't changed except that, in his wide-brimmed hat and sharp suit, he looked much more prosperous than Gorse recalled. Henry smiled, showing poor teeth, despite his twenty-five years. He sat down opposite Gorse. 'Well, well, well. *Mr* Gorse?'

'*You* look as if you're doing all right, Henry,' said Gorse.

Henry nodded. 'Better'n I was, workin' for old Bennett . . . You heard he's gone to live in Devon?'

'No,' said Gorse, 'and I don't much care.'

Henry nodded. 'Don't care much about nothing, do yer, Ralph, thass why I like yer.' He called to the proprietor. 'Cup o' rosy, guv, an' a cake, if you has it?' He looked at Gorse. 'I was a bit surprised to 'ear you was asking for me? Why was that?'

Gorse was a moment before he replied. 'Because you're a thief and I need your help.' As Henry began, 'Hey, leave it out, old mate,' Gorse carried on. 'I knew you were nicking stuff when you were working for Bennett but I kept my mouth shut, didn't I?'

Henry had to admit it. 'That's true. Well, 'ow can I help *you*, then?'

Gorse looked round, lowered his voice. 'I'm in the Army. Or was till today.'

Henry thinks, takes a long, shrewd look at Gorse. 'You've gone on the trot?' As Gorse doesn't reply, 'You'll be wantin' papers, then. Discharge from the Army on medical grounds is best, but they cost money. A hundred, last I heard. Plus false identity card. Employment card. Gonna cost you two hundred quid, all told.'

'Two hundred?' This was a lot more than Gorse had expected.

Henry nods. 'Could be more. Ain't got it nor nothin' like it, 'ave yer?'

The fat man brought a cup of tea and a slab of grey cake and laid them silently in front of Henry, an obvious habitué of the caff.

Gorse presses, 'What about . . . an identity card on its own?'

'Fifty quid, but it ain't enough. You could get checked any time.'

'I see,' says Gorse thoughtfully. Henry lowers his voice. 'Them army detention prisons ain't civvy prisons. Got to be worse than the Front Line. Stands to reason.'

Gorse thinks, then nods. 'I'll see you here tomorrow evening. Same time.'

Henry shakes his head. 'Not unless you have the money, old love.'

'I'll have it,' says Gorse.

Henry laughs. 'You sound sure. You found a new woman, then?' He shuffles as Gorse just looks at him, in a very deadly fashion. 'No offence, Ralph. I'll be here.'

Gorse nods, gets up and goes. Henry picks up the *Argus*, sips his tea, shakes his head. Ralph Gorse makes him uneasy. He always has.

The Crown, in wartime, was about the poshest bar in Brighton. As Gorse enters it, later that same evening, it is full of uniformed officers of all three services, and attractive women, mostly in civilian dress, although a number are in uniform. There are a few well-dressed civilians who are, one way or another, doing well out of the war. At the bar, Gorse waits, looking round. He finds a young RAF pilot officer on his left. The boy (he's about twenty) has a hand in plaster. He wears a blue forage cap, tunic, and a pilot's wings. His name is Stokes. And what is most important, he is roughly Gorse's build. Gorse addresses the barmaid. 'You have any scotch?'

'Sorry, sir, only beer.'

Gorse, in reply, puts a ten-shilling note on the bar. 'Large scotch, my love. No change required.'

The barmaid smiles. 'I'll have a look, sir. There might be a drop left.'

Pilot Officer Stokes is watching all this. He is a bit tipsy, and sways gently from time to time. He turns to Gorse. 'Do they know you here?'

'No. They know ten-shilling notes here.'

Stokes smiles. 'Should *I* try?'

'Better let me.' Gorse takes out another ten-shilling note and calls to the barmaid. 'Any chance of making that two? My gallant friend here has just been shot up by Jerry.'

Stokes laughs. 'Caught it in a bloody door, actually.'

The barmaid puts two drinks down, and takes the money. Gorse picks up the glasses. 'Shall we get out of this crush?'

Stokes nods. 'That's a thought.' Gorse and Stokes find two seats unexpectedly vacant and sit down. Stokes holds up his glass. 'I looks towards yer.'

Says Gorse, 'I catches yer eye.'

'I bows according,' replies Stokes.

'Down the hatch!' They both drink and laugh together.

Gorse nods towards Stokes's injured hand. 'On sick leave?'

Stokes nods. 'A month. I'm going to miss all the action in France by the look of it. You a brown job?'

Gorse knew he meant Army. 'That's right. Go back tomorrow.'

'You're going to need a few more of those then.' He indicates the empty glasses.

Gorse winks, takes his silver flask from his inside jacket-pocket, and pours large measures into both their glasses.

'I say, is that whisky?'

'No idea. He said it was.'

'Who . . . who said it was?' asks Stokes, befogged.

'Fellow who sold it to me. Think it *is*?'

'No idea.' Stokes drinks it all, gasps and coughs. 'It's . . . certainly *something*, old boy!'

'In that case, let's have another.' Gorse pours, into Stokes's glass but not his own, another large measure. Stokes holds up his hand, blearily. 'Hey, go easy, old boy, I've been on this stuff all day, y'know . . . Terribly browned-off, y'see, mooning about in this place on my own. Actually, I'm just down from London for the day . . . Looking for a bit of feminine company . . . No luck . . . Must get the last train . . . eleven-fifteen . . .'

Gorse listens extremely carefully to that. 'Don't worry. I'll see you do.'

Stokes looks at him with the earnestness of the very drunk. 'Will you, old boy? Promise?'

'Promise,' replies Gorse. Then he pours another large slug of the whisky – or whatever it is – into Stokes's glass.

An hour later, in the deep dark of the blackout, Gorse and Stokes come out of a gentlemen's convenience just off the seafront. But something has happened. Gorse is now in Stokes's uniform, and Stokes is wearing Gorse's suit. Stokes is singing drunk, out of it all. His arms are draped around Gorse's neck. Gorse, on the other hand, is coolness personified. Stokes elects to sing. 'Bless 'Em All . . . Bless 'Em All . . . The Long and the Short and the Tall. Bless all the Sergeants and W.O. Ones, Bless all the Corporals and their Bleedin' Sons . . .' He stops, and swallows.

'Don't be sick, old boy. Please,' says Gorse.

Stokes isn't, but only just. He swallows again. 'Gotta get . . . train . . . old boy.'

'We'll get you to the train,' promises Gorse, as they stagger off towards the seafront.

'We're saying Farewell to them All, As Back to their Billets they Crawl . . .' Still singing, Gorse and Stokes, locked together, stagger down the steps leading to the beach. They reach the shingle and Gorse looks around. Nobody. Nothing, except the wash of the surf, far away. The tide, as he expected, is out. 'This way, old son . . .'

Stokes stands still, swaying. 'I say . . . Where . . . *are* we?'

'Nearly there . . . Nearly there, old chap.' Gorse looks around. He sees an old boat embedded in the shingle. Still singing, they stagger over to it. Gorse stops as they reach it. 'Here will do . . . Very nicely indeed.'

Stokes shakes his head. 'I . . . I . . . whass this? . . . Whaa?'

'Just a rest, old boy. Just a nap, what?' Slowly, with great difficulty, Gorse manoeuvres Stokes into the boat. Gorse sits down, and Stokes lies back, closing his eyes.

Gorse intones very softly, 'Beddy-byes, old chap . . . That's it. Go to sleep. You'll wake up in the morning with some . . . explaining . . . to do . . . That's all . . .' But Stokes does not reply. He is out cold. Gorse steps out of the boat, takes a deep breath and smiles wryly at the sleeping Stokes. 'Goodnight, old boy.' Gorse turns, and crunches away across the shingle.

Pilot Officer Stokes lies quite still in the boat. If he were conscious, all he would hear would be the far-off hum of the surf.

Early the following morning Gorse, in the RAF uniform and carrying an RAF raincoat and valise, both new, is being ushered out of a local tailor's shop. 'Thank you for all your help, Mr Collard,' Gorse is saying.

The tailor shakes his head. 'Don't know who made your uniform, sir, but it was a very poor fit . . . I've done what I can, but – '

Gorse reassures him. 'It's splendid. First rate. You sure a cheque's all right?'

'Of course, sir. Anything for Our Boys.'

'Then good-bye, and thank you.' Gorse goes out of the shop and, once in the street, he hefts the valise, and smiles. He walks off briskly, then stops abruptly as he sees two RAF Military Policemen stop an airman and check his papers. Gorse turns round and goes back the way he came, at an even brisker pace. His destination is the caff. He does not know what he will do if Henry doesn't show up.

Once in the caff, Gorse sits behind the *Argus* again, feeling conspicuous in the officer's uniform. This time the *Argus* headlines read 'Nazis Occupy Holland' and 'British Troops in Severe Fighting'. Gorse feels even more certain that he has done the right thing. He is profoundly reassured when Henry comes into the caff and sits at the table. All he can see is Gorse's head and face, for the newspaper covers the rest. Gorse now has an elastic bandage round his left hand.

'Well, yer here, anyway, Ralph,' says Henry, conversationally.

Slowly, Gorse lowers the *Argus*, and Henry sees the RAF uniform. 'Gawdblimey . . . How d'yer get *that*?'

'Never mind,' says Gorse. 'I want these documents fixed, with the photograph enclosed in *this* envelope. All instructions inside. Not a big job.' Gorse puts a brown envelope on the table.

Henry looks round, lowers his voice. 'In your own name?'

Gorse nods. 'Better be. Some people know me in this town.'

Henry is silent a moment. 'But impersonating an officer? That can get you a lotta grief, Ralph.'

Gorse taps the envelope. 'There's twenty-five pounds in cash. That's in there as well.'

'What did you do? Steal somebody's luggage?'

'Something like that. When do I get the documents?'

'In a coupla days . . . But I dunno about twenty-five quid . . . I mean, *military* documents, dear oh dear!'

'I can't do any better. It's all *he* . . . it's all *I* have.'

Henry looks at him. '. . . Okay. I'll try for you . . . What y'done to your hand?'

'It's nothing.'

Henry puts the envelope in his pocket. 'When you can, you'll be back for better cover than this lot? Medical discharge? Civvy ID card, the real gear?'

'We'll see,' replies Gorse. Henry looks at him, then, softly, 'Hey! Don't get to *like* that uniform, old mate, whatever you do.'

Gorse lights a cigarette from his gold case and basks in the admiring glance of a bold girl at a nearby table.

* * *

At four o'clock that afternoon Alison Warren arrives at the Carlton Hotel, in Brighton, by taxi from the station. She is solid English middle-class, thirty-six years old, recently widowed, good-looking in a quiet tweedy way. She pauses on the steps to take in the hotel, then enters the reception. A porter gathers up her luggage.

At that very moment, Gorse, in his RAF uniform, is sitting at a small table in the reception. He is writing a letter on the hotel's stationery. He seals the envelope and puts a stamp on it. He looks at it and sighs. It is addressed to 'Mrs Joan Plumleigh-Bruce, 27 Wilton Avenue, Reading, Berks'. Gorse crosses to the 'letter-box' on the reception counter and drops it in. As he does so, he catches sight of Alison Warren. He looks, and listens. The receptionist is instructing the porter. 'Mrs Warren is in Room 202.' He hands the porter the key, and the porter leads the way, carrying the two suitcases.

'Thank you.' Alison smiles – she is attractive, notes Gorse, and he very thoughtfully watches her go up the stairs.

The residents' lounge at the Carlton is busy after dinner, for this is a Saturday in wartime. Some music is playing. It is a contemporary hit, 'In the Mood', and obviously comes from a dance being held in the hotel. Alison Warren is sitting alone at a small table, being served with coffee by the old hotel waiter. 'Will that be all, madam?'

'Thank you, yes.' Alison looks up as Gorse slides into a chair at the table next to hers. He looks very good in his uniform, and she notes that.

Gorse leans over. 'I say . . . Excuse me.' He calls across to the waiter. 'Could I have the same?'

'Coffee for one, sir? Certainly, sir.'

'If you have a brandy, I'd like that.'

'I will enquire, sir.'

Gorse looks at Alison, 'Er . . . May I . . . er . . . I don't suppose you'd join me? In a brandy or anything?' It is wartime and such approaches are allowed.

Alison shakes her head. 'No, thank you.' But her manner is pleasant, notes Gorse.

'Just one, then,' Gorse tells the waiter. 'Large, if possible.'

'I will see what I can do, sir.' The waiter, who is old and magisterial, bows and, flat-footed, walks away across the lounge.

Gorse laughs. 'He looks just like my old headmaster.'

Alison laughs, too. 'Yes, I rather think he's been brought out of retirement.' Gorse allows a moment to go by in silence. 'Are you . . . a sort of regular here, then?'

Alison lays down her *Tatler*, as if she's bored by it anyway. 'Not at all. First time. People recommended it.'

Gorse nods. 'I knew it a bit in the old days. It's noisier now.'

'Yes, there seems to be a dance on, or something . . .'

'I might look in later,' says Gorse. 'Trouble is, one hates to go into these places alone.' He looks up. 'Oh, well done!' For the old waiter has brought him his large brandy.

'Room number, sir? You *are* staying, sir?'

'Good Lord, yes. I'm in 521.'

The waiter notes it. 'Very good, sir. I will bring your coffee, sir.' Alison smiles.

Gorse sips his brandy. 'All on your own . . . er? It is *Mrs*?' Alison looks down a moment at her wedding ring. 'Er . . . Yes, I'm Alison Warren.'

'Ralph Gorse . . . Is your husband in the Forces?'

Alison is a long time replying. 'Actually . . . I'm a widow . . . He *was* in the Navy. He was on convoy duty, destroyers. A U-Boat got them, so they told me.'

Gorse affects surprise. 'God . . . I'm *so* sorry.'

Alison is stone-faced. 'That's all right. It was almost six months ago. I should really be used to it by now.'

The old waiter arrives with Gorse's coffee. 'Your coffee, sir.'

'I say, d'you think you could find us two more brandies, large ones?' Gorse passes over a note and it goes with practised alacrity into the old waiter's palm.

'I will enquire, sir.'

'Thank you . . . It *is* George, isn't it?'

'It is, sir. Thank *you*, sir.' The waiter bows, very slightly, and walks away, in his penguin-like fashion.

Alison giggles. 'Really. I shouldn't. I hardly ever drink brandy.'

Gorse suddenly becomes the firm friend. 'Make tonight an exception. In fact, tonight is going to be given over to hilarity and mirth. Because, when we have had our brandy and our coffee, we are, Alison Warren, going to gatecrash that noisy Hop, and we are going, as the Bard has it, to Dance the Night Away . . . What do you say to *that*?' Alison, extremely surprised, looks at Gorse a long moment. Then she laughs out loud at his effrontery and charm. For after all, this is wartime and who knows what tomorrow may bring. Gorse smiles. He has a good idea what it will bring. Or he would not be Ralph Gorse.

He is, of course, right. For at ten o'clock the following morning in Gorse's room at the Carlton, Gorse and Alison Warren are in bed. Gorse is awake, but Alison is still sleeping. The room is in half-darkness. Alison's clothes hang neatly over a chair, but Gorse's uniform is thrown untidily across another chair. Gorse looks at his wristwatch and yawns. He gets out of bed and stumbles to the bathroom. He wears only silk pyjama-bottoms. While he is in the bathroom Alison wakens. She is, suddenly, aware of what she has done. Her eyes roam the room, in a startled fashion. Alison breathes softly, 'Oh . . . My God.' Slowly, Alison gets out of bed, and begins to collect her clothes. She wears only a slip. Furiously, she pulls on the evening dress she had worn the night before.

Gorse comes back into the room, behind her. She starts, and turns to him, and he folds her in his arms. 'It's all right.'

'No, it isn't. I shouldn't *be* here!'

'Don't. It does you credit – but don't – '

'But it's only been *six* months! Oh, I feel awful . . .'

'He's dead . . . I might be, soon. Who knows?'

'No, don't say that!' And she clings to him.

'It's true. We all might be.'

Alison says, very softly, 'Oh, Ralph,' and they kiss, then she draws away. 'Give me time . . . to get used to what I'm doing . . . Please.'

'All right,' says the ever-understanding Gorse.

Alison finishes her haphazard dressing. 'I'll go now.'

'Whatever you say.'

'Oh, my God – the maid!'

Gorse puts his hand on her arm. 'I put a "Don't Disturb" on your door, as well as this one. Take your time. No hurry.'

Alison is still, and looks at him. '. . . Is there anything you don't think of?'

'Not much,' admits Gorse. Alison laughs and suddenly kisses him. This time they stay in the embrace a long time. Then she breaks away, gathers the rest of her clothes and, holding her shoes, she is gone. Gorse sits on the bed. He sighs and lights a cigarette. It has been a long night.

•

Joan Plumleigh-Bruce's living room has been changed little by war, except for the strips of anti-glass that stretch across the windows. Joan, in her housecoat, is finishing her last slice of margarined toast, served by Mary, and reading a letter at the same time. She is so astonished by its contents that she can't contain herself. 'Mary! . . . You'll never guess who this letter is from?'

'No, mam?'

'Ralph Gorse . . . You remember Mr Gorse?'

Mary does indeed. 'Oh, yes, mam . . . He was a very nice young man, Mr Gorse, I always thought, mam.'

Joan muses, half to herself, 'He's nice but he's in trouble, as usual.'

'I'm sorry to hear that, mam.'

But Joan is still reading. '*Brighton?* He's in Brighton!'

'Wasn't he there before, mam?' enquires Mary.

'Yes, he was. Oh, and Mary! Not a word about him to anybody, particularly Mr Stimpson!'

'No, mam. Of course not, mam.'

At this moment, there is a 'chime' at the front door. Joan is irritated. 'Who can that be at this time of the morning? Go and answer it, girl!'

Joan is tucking the letter into her handbag as Mary ushers in Mr Stimpson, who looks brisk and morning-fresh. He greets Joan, jovially. 'Good morning, my dear. Sorry to call so early, but I was passing this way, and I . . .' He sees the letter. '*Do* read your post . . . It could be important . . . I don't mind.'

'Not at all!' Joan has the letter firmly tucked away by now. She smiles, with an effort. '*You* don't often call at *this* hour, do you?'

'Joan,' declares Mr Stimpson importantly, 'I have been closeted with my lawyers since eight-thirty and I felt I had to call round and tell you the outcome.'

'Of *what*, dear? And do sit down, please.'

Mr Stimpson sits. 'I have today received from the Air Ministry an order for as many small machine-parts as we can make!'

'Just like *that*?'

'Not exactly just like *that*! The fruit, my dear, of some very hard work! . . . We are going to make quite a bit of money, Joan.'

'Really?'

Mr Stimpson is no reader of atmospheres and does not see Joan's irritation. 'The way it works is this: if I spend a hundred pounds on making a part for an aircraft, I get one hundred and ten pounds from the Ministry . . . it's called ten-per-cent-plus, and it is an arrangement that is very advantageous to small firms like ours.'

'How interesting . . . So you *were* right, after all, Donald? Perhaps I should have put my little savings into your firm.'

'Well, I could only advise it. You said no.'

'Poor *me*!'

Mr Stimpson regards her a long moment. 'There is a way of ensuring that you share in my success, you know.'

'Oh yes, dear, and what is that?'

'Marriage.'

'Marriage?' echoes Joan.

'It's time we did, isn't it?' asks Mr Stimpson.

'I thought you said you'd never marry me while Ralph Gorse was alive.'

Mr Stimpson waves his hands, largely. '*Did* I say that? Well . . . who knows if he is? There *is* a war on, you know, and people are dying every day. After he left

Bennett's he might have done anything. He had no money. He could even have joined the Army.'

'Do you think so?'

'They'd have to make him a colonel at least. All that talk of his about the Frontier Scouts, all lies!'

'Well, all that's water under the bridge. Your proposal . . . It's a shock, Donald, I have to admit.'

Mr Stimpson smiles smugly. 'Yes, I can imagine it is.'

'You'll have to give me time . . . to think about it,' says Joan.

Mr Stimpson affects surprise. 'Really? Why?'

'It's such a big step. Since the dear Major died I've been all alone.'

'Hardly *alone*, I would have said.'

'Well, almost. So . . . let us see . . . shall we?'

'You'll let me know . . . your decision?' asks Mr Stimpson, drily.

'Of course I will, my dear . . . Oh, it's really got me all of a tizz!' Joan sees Mary gaping. 'Mary! Coffee for Mr Stimpson, girl! *Really!*'

Mary jumps to it, grabs the pot, spills the hot coffee all over the table in a large, spreading pool. Joan and Mr Stimpson look at each other. They actually laugh, to Mary's astonishment and relief. Joan wonders: will she ever see Ralph Gorse again?

In his room at the Carlton Hotel at that moment, Ralph Gorse – in RAF shirt and trousers – is on the telephone. 'Can I speak to Miss Clarice Mannors, please?'

'Hello, yes?'

'Guess who?' asks Gorse, softly.

'. . . It *isn't*?'

'It is, y'know!'

'Never! Where are you?'

'Brighton.'

'Brighton! Doing what?'

'Oh . . . on leave.'

'What are you *in*?'

'The RAF . . . But never mind that.'

'Where are you staying?'

'The Carlton. But I thought we might meet in London?'

Clarice is breathless. 'Darling, I'm in the Wrens myself, I'm not exactly my own mistress! . . . Look, I have a car waiting, I have to go *now*! How long will you be there?'

'I don't know . . . A week or so, at least.'

Clarice is suddenly decisive. 'I'll try to be in touch, but I'm on this hush-hush job at the Admiralty. I must go now, darling. Lovely to hear your voice. Take care. 'Bye!'

'Look, I'll ring you, we'll meet in London. Here's no good . . . Clarice . . . ? Clarice . . . ?' The 'phone is down and all Gorse hears is a buzz. He sits on the edge of the bed, thoroughly put out of sorts by all that.

The caff is as gloomy as ever. A few customers – flashy-looking girls and dubious men – sit around, drinking cups of weak tea and reading the four-page papers. Gorse wonders what they do for a living – something mildly criminal, he decides, and feels better. Gorse sits, as before, behind his *Argus*, a cup of weak tea in front of him. Opposite sits Henry, the spiv. 'You still in that uniform? You're asking for trouble, old son.'

'Never mind that, did you get my papers?' asks Gorse.

Henry nods. 'Sure. Here.' He passes the envelope over. Gorse puts it in his pocket. 'It took time, but it's a good job, done by a real craftsman, that is.'

'Right. Thanks, Henry.'

Henry looks shrewdly at him. 'What are you doin' for money, Ralph?'

'I'll be all right.'

'Where you livin'?'

'The Carlton. Where else would an officer stay?'

Henry looks at him and shakes his head admiringly. Then he frowns, leans forward. 'That's pricey. And very public. Look, old son. Take my tip. You never know when somebody's hand's gonna be on yer shoulder. Get rid of that uniform as soon as you can. Come to me with two hundred quid and I'll set you up, absolutely fireproof, medical discharge, the lot!'

Gorse is dubious. 'You're talking about a lot of money, Henry.'

Henry insists. 'I know I am. But it's the only way you're gonna be safe, Ralph. You're dicing, me old son, an' for one good reason.'

'And what's that?'

Henry sighs. 'Ralph, yer getting to *like* it, ain't-cher? The uniform. The women looking at yer, envy from the fellas, best attention at all times . . . But it's dangerous, Ralph.'

'Henry, I told you,' says Gorse. 'Don't worry about me.'

'Ah, but I do, Ralph. Because I didden used to like you when you worked for old Bennett, but now yer on the trot, I worry about yer.'

Gorse gets up to go, and puts his hand on Henry's shoulder as he does so. 'Nice to know one has a friend.'

Henry hisses, 'One last word. Careful with the women. They get curious. And they talk.' He looks at Gorse a long moment. 'Be lucky, old son.'

Gorse nods and goes out of the caff. Henry shakes his head. Gorse is one on his own. Henry has never met anybody like him. And he's met a few. By God, he has. He calls for another cup of tea.

* * *

In the residents' lounge of the Carlton Hotel Alison is sitting, afternoon tea in front of her. She holds a *Daily Mail* with the headlines: 'German Tanks in Breakthrough'. As Gorse comes towards her she smiles rather shyly at him, and puts down the paper. 'Things look bad in France.'

Gorse agrees. 'Yes . . . they do.'

Alison busies herself with tea things. 'I ordered for two. I'm afraid the sandwiches aren't very good, but they're eatable . . . How's the hand?'

'Oh. Fine.'

Alison smiles. 'I must say, it doesn't seem to restrict you all that much, does it?'

Gorse smiles back. 'Not really, no.'

Alison says, 'Poor darling. Why don't you change that bandage? It's getting a bit grubby. Let *me* . . .' Alison takes his hand, makes to look at the bandage more closely.

'Leave it *alone*!' Alison stares at Gorse, alarmed by his tone. Gorse pulls his hand away sharply, then with an effort, smiles. 'Sorry. It's rather tender.'

But Alison is now tight-lipped. 'I'm terribly sorry. I was simply trying to help.'

At once, Gorse switches on the charm. 'I know . . . Sorry, darling . . . I'm terribly grumpy these days.'

Alison relents but she is still a bit put out. 'Yes, well . . . If you're in pain you will be grumpy, won't you? What exactly is supposed to be the matter with the hand, anyway?'

'Supposed? What does that mean, supposed?' asks Gorse.

'Nothing . . . It's just a figure of speech. I mean, what is wrong with it? Is it a bullet wound, or what? You've never said.'

Gorse smiles wryly. '. . . I caught it in a door, actually.'

'You didn't!'

'Yes, I did!'

Alison laughs. 'No wonder you've never said! So . . . it's just bruising, is it? Or has it really damaged the hand?'

Gorse takes a deep breath. 'I don't *know* . . .'

'Did they take X-rays?'

'Yes. They took X-rays, Alison.'

'Well, what did the X-rays show? Any bones broken or cracked, or what?'

Gorse sips his tea. 'I don't know, they didn't tell me.'

'Really? . . . Most curious.'

Gorse lights a cigarette, irritably. 'Yes. *Isn't* it?' He sees her eyes on him, doubtful, perhaps even suspicious, and at once, being Gorse, he is off on a new tack. 'Alison, there's something I've been meaning to talk to you about.'

'Oh, yes, what?'

Gorse hesitates. '. . . I've been less than honest with you about something.'

'Oh? What?'

'I don't know quite how to say this, but here goes.' Gorse takes a deep breath. 'I have a wife . . . I mean, I had a wife . . . I'm on my own now . . . But my RAF money isn't much, and I have to pay allowances and all that. The result is, I can't take you around as I'd like to . . .'

Alison looks at him steadily. 'It's really over? Your marriage?'

Gorse is adamant. 'It's all . . . dead and buried . . . Absolutely dead and buried.'

Alison keeps her eyes on his. '. . . I wondered why you don't go out of the hotel much . . . You seem so very, I don't know . . . careful . . . Not a bit as I'd imagine a pilot to be.'

'And have you known many?' asks Gorse, playfully.

'One or two. Socially.'

'Well, maybe they were rich. I'm not.'

Alison looks surprised. '. . . Money? Is that the problem? I'd no idea . . .'

Gorse looks despondent. 'That's the problem . . . I do have my hotel bill to pay and, well, there it is, I am pretty strapped, I have to admit. This place can get to be rather expensive. That's why I'm rather . . . as you put it, careful.'

Alison looks at him, thoughtfully. 'Ralph, I'm not rich, but I'm not poor, either. I have a decent house in London and my Navy pension, and I do have some family money.'

Gorse takes all that in, with a thrill of discovery. 'I couldn't dream of taking anything from you, darling. As things stand, anyway . . .'

'Could things stand . . . otherwise?' asks Alison.

Gorse grimaces down at his hand. 'If the RAF throw me out on medical grounds, which I have a feeling they might . . . then I'd be Mr Unemployable with medical discharge papers . . . I'd be worse off than I am now.'

'It *could* be a blessing in disguise, Ralph! And there are lots of jobs going in industry.'

'Yes, I expect so,' agrees Gorse. 'Still, it's early days . . . They might send me back to duty. Expect they will, really.'

Alison frowns. '*Do* you? . . . I don't know if I could go through all the worry I had with Geoffrey . . . all over again. Wondering if you're dead or alive . . . I don't honestly think I could do it.'

'It may never come to that,' says Gorse hastily. 'I think I do have a very good chance of getting my ticket actually. A gammy hand's no good to anybody, especially a pilot, is it? . . . Not if you're trying to *kill* people.' Gorse moves his bandaged hand slowly, and as if painfully, and Alison's gaze shows sympathy.

A decent house, thinks Gorse. A Navy pension. Some family money, too. Gorse sighs, in pure pleasure. Once again, he had been right. Alison Warren was just what he needed. Carefully, he lit her cigarette.

It is evening in Joan Plumleigh-Bruce's living room. She is drinking a gin and It and listening to Ambrose and his Orchestra on the radio. She is thinking, as she usually does on the few occasions that she listens to 'romantic' music, of Ralph Ernest Gorse. Suddenly, the doorbell chimes, and before Joan can even be curious as to who it might be, Mary enters. 'It's Mr Stimpson, mam.'

Behind her, without ceremony, Mr Stimpson enters. He carries a large bunch of red roses, and he is, Joan notices, wearing his best suit. She rises to greet him. 'Donald, what a nice surprise! I didn't expect you this evening.'

'I know that.' Mr Stimpson nods. 'But I had something . . . I wanted to say, you see?' Joan notices Mary hovering. 'That will be all, *thank* you, Mary!'

'Yes, mam.'

Joan is in truth surprised to see Mr Stimpson and even more surprised at the roses. 'What *is* it you want to say, Donald? I rather thought you said it all before. Are these for me?' She takes the roses and sniffs them. 'Lovely! But it's hardly *you*, is it, Donald, bringing flowers to a lady?'

Mr Stimpson looks uneasy but determined. 'I have something else, another surprise, for you.'

'As *well* as flowers? I can't *believe* it!'

'I have booked a table at The Friar restaurant for two at eight-thirty,' states Mr Stimpson solemnly. 'I left the factory early, to change, as you see.'

Joan responds with delight but delight tinged with doubt. 'You didn't! Isn't that wonderful of you? You know, I've been sitting here, getting the glooms! You're so busy at that factory, I hardly ever see you nowadays, *do* I? And this awful blackout makes everything so *down*, doesn't it? But . . . this is so nice . . . I wonder what I'll wear?' She calls loudly, 'Mary!'

Mr Stimpson holds up his hand. 'There was one other thing, Joan.'

'What can that be?' asks Joan, totally mystified now.

'This . . .' Mr Stimpson takes out of his pocket a velvet-covered box. He opens it for her to see. 'It isn't exactly an engagement ring, because I didn't know if you'd want that . . . And you have one already, don't you . . . From . . . from the Major. This is, I'm told, quite a good little ring. It's emeralds and diamonds, I believe . . .' With that he slides the ring on to the third finger of Joan's right hand. Joan's first thought is: this is very large and ostentatious, and not very ladylike at all, qualified by the thought that it must have cost a lot of money. 'Oh, Donald! Really! It's wonderful!'

Mary, on call, appears and ogles at the ring as Joan flashes it on her hand. Joan is beginning to feel better about it already.

'Ooh, it's lovely, mam!' gasps the maid.

Joan looks fondly on Mr Stimpson. 'Well, I shall have to take you very seriously now, won't I, Donald, after a present like *this*?' And Joan acts the queenly part, and twirls her hand, with the roses and the ring. Mr Stimpson beams. He is, there can be no doubt, as happy as he can ever be.

In Gorse's room at the Carlton Hotel the telephone is ringing insistently. The room is empty, but Gorse comes in suddenly and goes across to it, picking up an unopened envelope left on a small table, as he does so. He throws off his RAF cap and loosens his tunic as he speaks into the telephone. '. . . Hello, yes?' While he speaks he opens the envelope and looks at it in astonishment. It contains a large number of white fifty-pound notes. Gorse goggles at them, and at the scrawled note: 'I Love You, Alison'. Into the telephone he echoes, 'Hello? . . . Hello . . . ?' An irritated female voice answers. 'It's me, Clarice.'

'Oh . . . Yes . . . Hello.'

'Ralph? Are you all right?' Clarice has divination.

'What? . . . Yes . . . Yes, of course . . . I'm fine . . . Where are you?'

'At the station.'

Gorse is alarmed. 'Here? In Brighton?'

'Yes, of course! I have a weekend pass, so I thought I'd just get on a train, and hey presto!'

But Gorse is still looking at the money and cannot think straight. 'Oh . . . I see . . . Yes . . .'

'Is something the matter?' asks Clarice.

Gorse recovers. 'No. No . . . Look, I'll meet you at the Crown. It's a pub near the station. Ask anybody. See you in twenty minutes, all right?'

'Yes . . . All right. Fine.' Clarice, who is in a public telephone box at the station, puts down the receiver hard. She had hoped to surprise Ralph and had expected, at the very least, enthusiasm. But Ralph Gorse hadn't sounded in the least enthusiastic. Well, to hell with him! Nonetheless, she stepped out into the blackout to look for the Crown Hotel.

Gorse, on the other hand, replaced the receiver very gently indeed. After a long moment he pushed the packet of notes into his inside tunic-pocket. Money, always a problem, was now no problem at all. Clarice was the problem. Gorse would have to do some juggling tonight. Two women and only one Ralph Gorse. He would have to step carefully, very carefully indeed. Gorse ran himself a hot bath and in it he sang to himself the song he had last sung with the young RAF pilot, Stokes. As he lay luxuriating in the soapy water, Ralph Gorse decided that things were certainly picking up. Very much so. But the word was still: careful.

In the residents' lounge at the Carlton Hotel half an hour later, Alison Warren sat, a glass of sherry in front of her, dressed for dinner in an expensive pre-war gown. She looked anxiously at her watch, as the old waiter approached her. 'May I book madam a table for dinner? It *is* getting a little late.'

'Er . . . Yes, please. For two, George.'

'For two, but of course, madam.' As he trudged off, Alison looked at her watch again. She was beginning to be annoyed with Ralph Gorse.

In the cocktail lounge at the Crown, Clarice, in her Wren Officer's uniform, is looking very fetching indeed. Gorse, too, is handsome in his uniform. A bottle of wine is in front of them. The bar is crowded, as it obviously is every night, thinks Gorse, full of people getting drunk and trying to forget there's a War on. Clarice is staring at him in amazement. 'A *pilot*? I can't *believe* it! I always thought . . .'

'What?' Gorse smiles.

Clarice shrugs. 'Oh, just all your stories, about the Army . . . I never believed them . . . I thought you were too smart to risk getting killed, or anything stupid like that.'

Gorse pours wine into her glass. 'You think being a pilot is . . . stupid?'

'Yes, but if it gives you a thrill, why not? Ralph, have you hurt your hand?'

Gorse closes his eyes. He's just been through all this with Alison Warren, for God's sake. 'Yes, I'm on sick leave, actually.'

'Oh, from which hospital?'

'What?'

'Which hospital are you on sick leave *from*?'

'Does it matter?' Gorse moves his bandaged hand freely, and picks up a drink with it.

This is not lost on Clarice. 'Why *are* you flying, Ralph? It's bloody dangerous, darling!'

'Somebody has to do it.'

'Nobody has to die. Unless they want to.'

'Let's *leave* it, shall we?'

Clarice shrugs. 'All right . . . Where *are* we staying tonight? The Carlton?'

'I don't know . . . Perhaps.'

'Well . . . You'll think of something, I expect.'

Gorse looks at her. She looks at him. As usual, there is a chemistry between them. 'Yes. I expect so,' says Gorse. 'Er, let me make a call . . . about that, will you?' Clarice watches Gorse rather curiously as he goes to the 'phone booth near the bar. Once inside, Gorse dials and waits. He smiles across at Clarice. Clarice smiles back. Into the telephone Gorse says, 'Hello, Carlton Hotel? Give me the residents' lounge, will you?' He turns away from Clarice's eyes. Clarice for her part takes out her compact and fixes her lipstick. She had rather a lot on already but in wartime everybody seemed to do too much of everything.

In the booth Gorse puts his hand half over the telephone. 'Hello? Residents' lounge? Is that George? Is Mrs Warren there? . . . No, don't disturb her if she's gone in to dinner. This is Pilot Officer Gorse. Will you apologize on my behalf and tell her I've been unavoidably detained. I'll see her tomorrow . . . Tomorrow, yes. Will you see she gets the message? Good. Thank you, George. 'Bye.'

Gorse replaces the receiver. Then he squares his shoulders and returns to Clarice. She puts her compact away and looks up at him. 'Are we all fixed up then?'

'Yes . . . We are all fixed up.' Gorse sits and expels his breath . . . He feels tired. He wonders if it is all worth it.

'I could do with another drink,' says Clarice, looking at the almost empty wine bottle.

'Yes. In a moment.'

Clarice looks at Gorse closely. His fingers shake as he takes a cigarette from his gold case and lights it. Clarice thinks she knows him as nobody else does. She is his sort. And now he is upset and worried, or she knows nothing about him at all. Clarice reaches out and pours her own drink. 'I don't know how you got this stuff. It's very decent.'

'Paid black-market rates.'

Clarice leans forward. 'There's something *wrong*, isn't there, Ralph?'

'No.'

'What is it?'

'Nothing.'

'There *is*!'

'No, there bloody well isn't!' Gorse's voice is loud enough to silence the chatter in the bar. People turn round and stare. Gorse avoids their eyes. 'Everything is all right . . . Everything is all right . . . There are no problems that can't be solved . . . one way or another . . . None at all. If someone is in the way, that's their bad luck! . . .' Such an outburst is unusual for Gorse and shows him – to himself – how near the line he must be. Then he sees how it all must look and sound. Gorse smiles, ruefully, the charmer again. 'What am I going on about, do *you* know? I must be a bit tanked. Drink up, darling, the night is young . . .' Gorse raises his glass, gallantly. So does Clarice, her eyes on his over the rim of her glass. I wonder, she thinks, what the trouble really is?

Two hours later Alison Warren, having had dinner alone, returns to her room at the Carlton Hotel. Alison turns on the light and closes the door behind her. She throws her evening bag on to the bed in total frustration. The bloody, bloody man. After all she's done. Given him the money. Slept with him. And he just sends a telephone message, doesn't even ask to speak to her personally. It was not to be borne. Alison Warren never cried, she had not cried even for Geoffrey, so she wasn't going to cry now. She threw herself down on the bed and lit a cigarette and stared at the ceiling, thinking of nothing at all. After lying like that for what seemed a very long time, almost an hour, she got up and went out of the room and along the corridor, then up the stairs to the next floor.

At Gorse's room she stopped and knocked, softly at first, and called 'Ralph?'

Inside Gorse's room Gorse and Clarice are in bed engaged in a complicated sexual act. They freeze at the tap on the door. Gorse's hand goes to Clarice's mouth to stifle her giggle. They stay perfectly still until whoever is outside elects to walk away. They hear the footfalls retreat along the corridor.

In Gorse's room Clarice whispers, 'Some tart you've picked up, Ralph?'

Gorse does not reply. He does not proceed with the

complicated sexual act either. He falls on to his back and reaches for his cigarettes.

'It's all right, darling,' says Clarice, 'I don't mind. I know you, darling.'

Gorse smiles. Clarice laughs, hoarsely. And suddenly they are in each other's arms and bodies again. For Gorse there is never to be anybody like Clarice Mannors. Nothing, to her, was wrong. Everything was right. Gorse had never found that in a woman before, except when he paid them for their services, and that didn't count. Clarice wanted *this*, that was the difference.

In a corner of the reception area at the Carlton Hotel early next morning, Gorse is talking to the middle-aged receptionist.

'. . . Thank you for fixing that for me. Naturally, on my bill. We were so late in last night I didn't bother.'

The receptionist is understanding. 'Perfectly all right, sir. Would you like a morning paper, sir? They're just in.'

Gorse shakes his head. 'No thanks. Nothing in 'em but bad news! Lovely morning. Think I'll have a breath of air.' And Gorse goes out of the front door of the Carlton.

Outside, on the seafront, nobody is about. Gorse, in his uniform, looks this way and that, and walks away along the promenade towards the pier. He feels a little better for being out. Clarice is asleep in his room but soon she must leave the hotel. Alison would be up and about early. He would take a short walk, he decided, and go back and wake Clarice, get her a taxi to the station, get her away. On reflection, it had been foolish to bring her back to the Carlton but no other hotel had any vacancies. It was weekend, it was wartime. Everybody was playing bed-games with their weekend leaves. Not a room in the town, he'd been told by the hotel receptionists he tried. So, what choice had he had?

Gorse walked on, musing thus, and came, after a few minutes, to the steps that led to the beach, the ones down which, what seemed an age ago, he had led the drunken pilot, Stokes. Gorse saw several people at the top of the steep steps to the beach, and a few hurrying down. Curious, he quickened his step and looked towards the end of the West Pier. He saw a small group of people – a policeman in waders, two soldiers, and a couple of ambulancemen – standing looking at something on the shingle, something under the West Pier, half-in, half-out of the water.

An elderly, military-looking man in civilian clothes has a pair of binoculars to his eyes. As he lowers them, not really believing what he has seen, Gorse asks him for a look. The old gentleman obliges, politely. Gorse puts the binoculars to his eyes. He knows what he will see before he sees it: the body of a man. The body of Pilot Officer Stokes.

The military gentleman is explaining. 'They found him an hour ago. He's been in the water a while, a few days, I s'pose.'

Gorse's hands begin to shake as he hands back the binoculars. 'Thank you, sir.'

'Welcome.'

Gorse turns and walks away. Once he is clear of the knot of people he stops, as if sick, and stands, swaying. Of all the rotten luck, he thinks, for that to happen. Of all the rotten lousy luck. He is, of course, not thinking of Pilot Officer Stokes. He is thinking of Ralph Ernest Gorse.

His legs shaking, Gorse walks back to the Carlton. In his room, he finds that Clarice has breakfasted. The remains of the meal are in front of her as she sits up in bed. She smiles as Gorse comes in and takes off his tunic. Clarice has borrowed his dressing gown and turned the cuffs back, and she looks very fetching, as she drinks her large breakfast cup of coffee and looks over the rim at Gorse. 'You been out?'

Gorse nods shakily. '. . . I had a short stroll.'

'There's coffee and toast, if you want it.' She pours him a cup of coffee. 'Everything all right?'

'Yes. Fine . . . Everything's fine.'

'You sure? You look a bit odd.' Gorse says nothing. 'Who did you tell the reception I was?'

But Gorse is hardly listening. 'My wife, of course.'

'Did they believe you?' laughs Clarice.

'Does it matter?' shouts Gorse suddenly.

'Not to *me*, darling!' Clarice puts down her cup and stretches. 'It's been lovely! Really, I'd forgotten just how right we are for each other . . . How our tastes . . . complement each other.'

Gorse's mind is in turmoil but he tries. 'So had I.'

Clarice smiles, then, 'You're absolutely free of everything, that awful marriage . . .'

'All over! I *told* you!'

'You've told me a *lot* . . . But not quite everything, have you?'

'What gives you that idea?'

Clarice looks at him a long moment. 'Darling, for one thing there's nothing the matter with that *hand*, is there?'

Gorse is tired of lying. 'Perhaps.' But Clarice presses. 'You're in some kind of trouble, aren't you?'

'Not really.'

'Ralph, I might be able to help.'

'I doubt it.'

Clarice is silent, then: 'Have you deserted from the Air Force?'

'Certainly *not*!' says Gorse. '. . . From the Army, actually!'

Clarice stares at him in alarm. Then suddenly, they both laugh, Clarice lightly, Gorse bitterly. '*No!* The *Army*? For God's sake *why*?'

Gorse shrugs. 'They were going to send me overseas as a private soldier. So I thought, not bloody likely! So I got out.'

Clarice is slowly taking it all in. 'So, that uniform *isn't* yours?' Gorse shakes his head. 'Did you just buy it?'

Gorse's voice is dull, for once, as he explains. 'No. I borrowed it from a young officer. He was completely cut, so I left him to sleep it off on the beach. That was two days ago. The awkward thing is, he's still there.'

'I don't understand,' says Clarice.

'He never woke up. His body went for a swim on the tide. He's dead. Drowned. In my clothes.'

'Oh, my God!'

'I didn't kill him, you know,' says Gorse.

'But Ralph,' says Clarice in reply, 'who's going to believe *that*?'

'You, I hope.'

Clarice gets up from the bed and throws her arms round Gorse. 'Of course I do!' Clarice pauses, thinking hard. 'For the moment, anyway, you're safe? . . . In this place? Nobody suspects anything?'

'I don't know how long for,' says Gorse moodily.

Clarice makes an instant decision. 'I'm going back to London!' She takes off the dressing gown. 'To talk to my uncle, the Admiral . . . I'm going with him to the United States, on a naval mission, sometime soon.'

Gorse is aghast. 'You're going to *America*? Then that's *it*, isn't it?'

Clarice pulls on her white Wren shirt, skirt and regulation jacket. 'Look, we have to straighten out this mess you're in somehow! That's priority number one, then we'll see . . .'

Gorse sits, defeated. 'This really is a pill, you going off like that!'

Clarice takes him by the shoulders. 'Ralph, do you realize the fix you're in? We have to bloody move! Now, whatever you do, don't go out of this hotel! Not out of this room, unless you have to! I'll call you from London, but whatever happens I'll be back tomorrow morning at the latest . . . Now, I want your army number, your unit, all that stuff.'

Gorse looks at her perplexed. 'Darling, I don't know what you think you can *do*?'

'Let's *see*, shall we?' And they suddenly kiss, very passionately. Everything with Gorse and Clarice Mannors is a thing of passion.

Half an hour later, in her Wren officer's uniform, Clarice gets into a taxi outside the Carlton Hotel. 'The station, please.' And the taxi drives off. Watching it go is Gorse in his RAF uniform. He waves, and turns back into the hotel to find Alison Warren looking at him.

'Who *is* she?' asks Alison, coolly.

Gorse recovers, puts his hand on her arm. 'Come inside and I'll tell you.' Alison half-shrugs him off. Gorse follows her into the hotel, with a sigh.

In the residents' lounge the old waiter is serving morning coffee. Gorse and Alison sit. Gorse knows that the social niceties demand that Alison won't make a scene, but he guesses she will be profoundly curious. He wonders how to begin. But the old waiter gives him a little more time. 'Will you require toast, madam? There are no biscuits, I'm afraid.'

'No, thank you,' says Alison, ever the lady. The old waiter moves away. Alison turns to Gorse. Her eyes are cold and Gorse guesses she is in no mood for lies. And lies are all he has. 'You haven't yet said *who* she was,' Alison remarks.

Gorse is brisk. 'She's an old friend, that's all, Alison.'

'I see? Leaving after a late breakfast, I suppose?' asks Alison Warren with a small, hurt laugh.

'Darling, don't be silly, please! I said she was an *old* friend . . . Alison, she's in trouble . . . I can't discuss details, gentleman's word, and all that.' It is the best Gorse can do and it sounds hollow even to his own ears.

'Pregnant, I suppose?' remarks Alison in her upper-class way. It reeks of contempt for everybody and everything, especially Gorse.

'Good Lord, *no*! Now, I said I can't talk about it, so I won't. But it's nothing to do with *us*,' insists Gorse.

Alison looks at him steadily. 'Is that *really* true, Ralph?'

Gorse makes an immense effort. 'Darling, of course it is!' He presses her hand. She is unresponsive. 'You *know* it is! Why on earth would I tell you such an unlikely story if it wasn't true?' Gorse smiles. The charm works, or anyway, to Gorse it *seems* to.

Alison relents a little. 'I waited an hour last evening, you know.'

'I know, I'm terribly sorry. You did get my telephone message?'

Alison admits, 'After an hour, yes.'

Gorse sees he is making headway, tries harder. 'I *am* terribly sorry. I feel so awful. Especially after you left me that money. Look . . .' Gorse feels in his pocket, brings out the envelope containing the money Alison left him. '. . . It's all there . . . Well, most of it. Take it. Keep it. Either you trust me, Alison, or you don't. If you don't, then let's not go on with any of this.' It is a massive risk, Gorse knows that, but he puts the envelope on the table. He watches her and reckons that Alison doesn't know what to believe. Finally, she believes what she wants to believe, as Gorse had hoped she would.

'I didn't *say* I didn't trust you, Ralph.'

'It sounded like that, to me.' Gorse feels he is winning now.

'Put the money away, darling. It isn't the money,' says Alison.

Gorse does not touch the money. 'I rather thought it was.'

'Put it away, please.'

Gorse sighs, takes the envelope and puts it back in his tunic pocket. Alison takes a deep breath, pours coffee for them both and tries for normality. 'Have you seen the morning paper yet?' Gorse shakes his head. 'We seem to be falling back all over the place, in France . . . Very bad news, that.'

'Yes . . . Yes, it is, rather,' says Gorse. Thank God that's over, he thinks, gratefully.

Says Alison, wonderingly, '. . . I've never taken it seriously before . . . the idea of the Germans *here* . . .'

Gorse has never thought of it seriously either and does not propose to do so now. 'We always lose the first battle or two, everybody knows *that*.'

'I'm worried for you too, Ralph,' says Alison, suddenly tender.

Women, thinks Ralph Gorse, contemptuously, it's so easy, so bloody easy. 'I've been thinking, about what I said, about trying to get out of the Raff,' says Gorse. 'I feel they'll be needing everybody.' Alison looks alarmed. The right note that, thinks Gorse with satisfaction.

'Ralph. Don't even think about it. Let them decide if you're fit to fly again, don't you volunteer to go on, or anything like that.'

Gorse nods. 'Well. Let's see, shall we? There's time yet.'

'Did they give you a definite date to go back to your Unit?' asks Alison.

'They're letting me know,' says Gorse. Suddenly, Alison looks at him, hard. Gorse smiles, uneasy. He keeps forgetting that Alison was a service wife, and knows how things are done. He will have to be careful, there. Gorse offers her a cigarette and lights it with the lighter he stole from Ronnie Shooter all those months ago and wonders how it will all end.

But the women are not finished with Ralph Ernest Gorse. That very evening, in his hotel room, Gorse receives a surprising telephone call.

'Is that you, Ralph?' asks a half-familiar female voice. Gorse cannot at once place it. There have been, after all, many women in his life, and there are few he would care to meet again. 'Yes, ' he admits warily. 'Who's this?'

'It's Joan . . . Joan Plumleigh-Bruce.'

Gorse is astonished, and not best pleased. 'Oh, Joan . . . Well, I'm damned . . . Hello. How are you?' Gorse is always polite to women. Until he has got their money.

'I'm calling . . . because I got your letter . . .' explains Joan. Gorse has almost forgotten he'd written to Joan Plumleigh-Bruce.

'My letter? . . . Oh, yes . . . My *begging* letter.'

Joan falters, then, brightly, 'I thought they said . . .

Pilot Officer Gorse at the reception? Are you in the Air Force, Ralph?'

Gorse is patriotic. 'We're all doing our bit, aren't we, Joan? How are you, I mean really?'

'I'm fine. Ralph . . . Your letter sounded . . . desperate.'

Gorse laughs dismissively. 'You know me Joan, up and down. Temporary embarrassment, that was all . . . But it was nice of you to call.' But Joan persists. 'Ralph, is there anything I can do, anything at all? I'll send the money, of course.'

'No, really. Not at all. Really, I *can* manage.' Gorse looks at the money in the envelope – he has taken it from his pocket – and grimaces.

'I want to help,' says Joan. 'You were in my mind, Ralph. I wondered what had happened to you.'

Replies Gorse glibly, 'And I've thought of you often, Joan.'

There is a pause at the other end of the line. '*Have* you, Ralph? Really? I felt so bad when I heard about your wife.'

'Please, Joan. I'd rather not talk about it,' says Gorse the loving husband.

'Yes, well . . . I'm sorry, that's all. And I suppose I wanted to say . . . Good-bye, in a nicer way than . . . we did, last time.' Joan hesitates, 'I always felt . . . Mr Stimpson was very . . . revengeful about you.'

'I suppose I gave him reason, didn't I?' asks Gorse, wondering how to end the conversation.

'. . . He's a good man, but he's so jealous and possessive. You wouldn't dream he could hate so much . . .'

'You mean *me*?' asks Gorse. 'Oh, he's forgotten all that, surely? You got your money back, didn't you?'

'It wasn't just the money, Ralph. It was us, you and me.'

'What?'

'Us. You and me.'

'He has no proof of anything.'

'No proof, no. Only his feelings.'

'You know the old rule in these matters. Deny. Deny. Deny.'

'Oh, I do! But he doesn't believe me.'

'You don't mean he's *still* on about it?' asks Gorse, in some irritation.

'Jealousy is an awful thing, Ralph,' says Joan Plumleigh-Bruce, rather miserably. But Gorse is a bit put out by all this. He hardly needs it, does he? 'Yes . . . I suppose it must be. Well, I'll say good-bye, then . . . Let's not lose touch . . . Good-bye . . . Oh, and thanks . . .' And Gorse puts the telephone down abruptly.

'. . . There was one thing I wanted to say, Ralph. Mr Stimpson and I are – ' But the telephone has gone dead. In her living room, very slowly, Joan replaces the receiver on the hook.

As Gorse comes down the stairs into the reception area of the Hotel some time later, he sees the old waiter crossing the foyer, carrying drinks on a tray. Gorse puts a ten-shilling note on the tray. 'George, do you by any chance have a bottle of good champagne tucked away in the cellars?'

'It is entirely possible, sir,' admits George. 'I will enquire.'

'I'll be in the lounge,' says Gorse.

'Certainly, sir . . . Shall I bring two glasses, sir?'

'What? . . . No . . . Just *one* glass, please.'

'As you say, sir.' As the old waiter moves off, Gorse

notices two men at the desk, talking to the male clerk. They are out of place here, with their trilby hats and raincoats, but Gorse suspects, at a glance, what they really are. Gorse moves over and takes an *Argus* from a pile of newspapers on the counter, and leaves a coin. He hears the senior detective (both men are in their forties) speak to the reception clerk in a low voice. 'We're checking to see if any hotel or boarding house has a guest missing . . . No . . . We haven't a name for him yet . . . But he's young, late twenties, slim build, grey worsted suit, single-breasted, white shirt . . . All guests accounted for, nobody reported anybody missing?'

The reception clerk shakes his head. 'No . . . Nothing like that . . . No.'

'If they do, ring us at once . . . We might be back, once we've found out some more about him.' The receptionist nods. The two detectives turn and go out into the street. Gorse watches them go. He is, suddenly, very shocked and afraid. He looks up as the old waiter swans into view, his tray empty now.

'I'll just go down to the cellars now, sir, and see what we have for you.'

'What . . . ? Oh . . . Don't bother, George . . .'

'But, sir . . . ?'

'Change of plan.'

'Very good, sir.'

Gorse turns and goes back up the stairs. The old waiter watches him go, curiously. He supposes that being hors-de-combat while the fighting in France is going on must be a very depressing business for the young gentleman.

In Alison Warren's room at the hotel, the blinds are drawn. Alison is on the bed, taking an afternoon nap. She comes out of a half-doze. She's troubled. She cannot think what by, and then she half-sits up on one elbow and recalls that Ralph Gorse is in her life. She smiles, wryly. Better than nobody. Is that, she wonders, all it is? Is she behaving foolishly? Very foolishly? She lies in wonderment for a few minutes, marvelling at the things she has done with Ralph Gorse, many of them, after all, sexual and strange. Then she shivers, and looks at the telephone. After a moment's hesitation, Alison picks it up. 'Room 521, please,' she asks the operator.

But the telephone is ringing in an empty room. A full minute after it has stopped, Gorse comes into the room. His telephone rings again. It is the receptionist to tell him that Miss Clarice Mannors is in the hotel and asking for him. 'Please ask her to come up to my room,' says Gorse. He sits and waits. To his surprise, he finds he is trembling.

In her room Alison reaches for her cigarettes and lights one, very thoughtfully. Then she makes a decision. She picks up the telephone once again. 'Operator,' she asks, 'would you get me a London number please . . . Whitehall 1634 . . . Yes, thank you . . . I'll wait . . .' Alison wishes she did not have to do this. But all her training says that she must.

In Gorse's room, Gorse and Clarice are in earnest conversation. She hasn't even taken off her uniform. Her tricorn hat and gas mask lie on the sofa. 'Darling, the Admiral has talked to somebody at the War Office already, and they're very sympathetic . . . about your nervous breakdown.'

'. . . My *what*?' asks Gorse.

Clarice passes him a white envelope with a name on it. '*He's* a doctor in Harley Street. He's also a very dear friend of mine. You've had a loss of memory but you feel better now. You can remember nothing . . . *nothing* . . . about the past weeks . . . All right?'

Gorse demurs. 'I haven't got much time, Clarice.'

Clarice takes a deep breath and explains. '*He'll* give you a letter to take round to an Army doctor at the War Office. He'll telephone him first . . . What you'll take will be, virtually, a medical certificate.' As Gorse begins to protest she holds up her hand. '*They'll* give you your ticket out of the Army, Ralph, with that medical report . . . Don't worry. It'll all be absolutely fine. It's the network operating. We look after our own. We'll get you out of this.'

Gorse asks, drily, 'And *I'm* one of *you*?'

Clarice grimaces and laughs. 'I've adopted you. I had a bit of a problem with the Admiral but the moment I said I was going to marry you, he had to help.'

'Are you serious?'

'Oh, absolutely,' says Clarice. 'It may not last, darling, but we'll have a hell of a time while it does!'

Gorse protests, 'But you're going to the States? On this – whatever it is?'

'Once you get out of the Army, the Admiral will move heaven and earth to get you to join us . . . As a business consultant, or something. Believe me, it can be done, and it will. You'll be in Washington this time next month.'

Gorse sits, puts his head in his hands. 'Washington . . . Is it *possible*?'

'Yes, it is, darling.' She kisses him. '. . . I must *go*! Do get *rid* of that uniform, won't you?' As Gorse nods, bemused, ''Bye for now.'

Clarice slings her gas mask, picks up her tricorn hat, smiles a shade mockingly, and goes.

Gorse shakes his head. He drains his glass of whisky. He has been drinking rather a lot lately, and why not? He smiles at himself in the mirror, with an effort at bravado. He breathes the words, 'Everything . . . Clarice . . . Washington . . . Money . . . The lot!' Gorse is awed by it all. It's all in his hands, at last.

Everything he's ever wanted.

In Joan Plumleigh-Bruce's hall Mary the maid opens the front door to Mr Stimpson. He stands there and looks very excited about something. A copy of the London *Evening News* is in his hand. 'Is Mrs Plumleigh-Bruce at home?' he asks, and enters without waiting for an answer. He brushes past the maid and into the living room. Joan looks up, removing her spectacles at once. 'Oh . . . ? Hello, Donald. I didn't think you'd be coming. I thought it was another of your late nights at the factory.' Then she sees his face. 'Donald, what's the matter?'

In reply, Mr Stimpson holds up the *Evening News*. He reads from it, slowly and pedantically.

'Joan . . . In the stop-press. It says here . . . "The body of a man in his thirties has been washed up on the South Coast. Initial investigations suggest it to be a Mr R. E. Gorse. No further details are known. The police ask friends or relatives to come forward if they have any knowledge of a missing person of that name" . . .'

'*What?*' asks Joan, dizzily.

'Gorse. R. E. Gorse. Ralph Ernest Gorse,' repeats Mr Stimpson.

'You mean *Ralph*?' cries Joan. 'It can't be Ralph . . . I only just . . . I can't *believe* it . . . Let me see that! I can't *believe* it, Donald!'

Joan takes the paper, reads the item, looks up at Mr Stimpson, her eyes wide with shock. Mr Stimpson is standing quite still in the middle of the room. 'Neither can I . . .' says Mr Stimpson, his voice only a whisper. 'Neither can I.'

Chapter Six

At the County of Sussex mortuary a taxi pulls up. Joan Plumleigh-Bruce and Mr Stimpson get out and look up at the grim stone building. Joan is anything but happy but Mr Stimpson has the air of a man who anticipates a pleasant event. Mr Stimpson pays off the taxi with a flourish, even behaving so far out of character as to tip the cabby a shilling. Then they go into the building, Mr Stimpson first, a spring in his step.

Joan Plumleigh-Bruce, dressed in her best tweed coat, sighs to herself as she sits in the waiting room of the mortuary. The decor is public-lavatory and there are hard bentwood chairs. Joan looks up as Mr Stimpson comes in. He seems irritated. 'We have to wait. Somebody from the police has arrived.'

Joan hesitates. 'Did they say if . . . he was in a uniform? The man who drowned?'

'What?'

'Oh, never mind . . .'

'Why do you suddenly ask about a uniform?'

'Stop being so pedantic, Donald,' says Joan, irritably. She is irritated by the whole thing, by even being in this horrible place. She takes a deep breath. 'They didn't say for sure it was Ralph?'

'They didn't say anything, that's what they want to hear from us. We're here to identify the body!'

Joan feels somewhat sick at this. 'You might be, but I'm not . . . Donald, you're not going to like this, but . . . I can't stay here . . .' Joan gets to her feet, clutching her handbag. Mr Stimpson is annoyed. 'Why ever not? They'll need you as well as me!'

'I don't care what they'll need. I've never seen a dead body before and I don't want to start by looking at poor Ralph.'

'So it's poor Ralph again, is it?' asks Mr Stimpson, nastily.

'Well, certainly it is, if he's dead! I mean, if it is him.'

'Well, if it isn't him, who else would it be?' He raises a newspaper. 'Last night's *Evening News* said – '

Joan interrupts, 'I know what last night's *Evening News* said, Donald. I'm not going to do it, and that's final. If Ralph is dead, I don't want to see him.' Before Mr Stimpson can say more, she adds, 'Please ask them to ring for a taxi for me. I simply must get away from this dreadful place, I must!'

'If you don't want to do it, I don't know why you came with me in the first place?' demands Mr Stimpson.

'Because you bullied me to come along, Donald, because you're so desperate to find out if that's poor Ralph in there, and to look at him and gloat – '

'Gloat? Did you say gloat?' asks Mr Stimpson, gratingly. But Joan will not reply to that.

'Now, will you please get them to ring for a taxi for me? I will wait for it outside in the good clean air!'

'But where will you go?'

Joan thinks, then: 'I'll be . . . at the Carlton Hotel. I'll see you in the lounge there . . . In an hour, or whenever you are through with this dreadful business you've taken upon yourself.' And she sweeps out of the gloomy, deathly place, and its persistent reek of formaldehyde.

Mr Stimpson wonders why she has just now decided she cannot go through with the identification of the dead man, who must, of course, be Ralph Gorse. Who else can it be?

* * *

At that moment, very much alive, Ralph Gorse is walking along the West Pier towards Henry the spiv, who is sitting on a bench in the sunshine. 'I got your message,' Gorse tells him.

Henry looks quickly around. 'Sorry, but it was important, old mate. Take a deep breath an' read that. In the stop press.'

Henry passes Gorse an *Argus*. He points his finger to the back page. Gorse reads the item swiftly and looks thoughtful. 'I see . . .'

'Put your own clobber on him, dincher? RAF Officer, wannee?' asks Henry.

Gorse nods slowly, looking up from the paper. 'Henry, it's no use trying to blackmail me.'

Henry protests, 'I'm trying to 'elp you, mate, not put the blag on yer.' He indicates the newspaper. 'You 'adn't seen it, 'ad yer?'

'No.'

Henry adds, 'It was in the London edition of the *Evening News* last night an' all.' As Gorse looks at him . . . 'Ralph, somebody's gonna put two an' two together, old mate, it's only a matter of when!'

Gorse says slowly, 'I didn't kill him, you know, Henry.'

'I believe yer, but who else will?' asks Henry.

'I just left him . . . On the beach . . . That's all.'

'Well . . . that was his hard luck . . . what do you do now?'

Gorse sighs. 'Not sure, actually.'

Henry is impatient. 'You got to get rid of that uniform! I told you!'

But Gorse is thinking very hard. 'No. It's a protection.'

Henry shakes his head. 'I must say you're taking this very cool. You got some kind of stroke going, 'ave yer? Somethink to get you out of all this?'

Gorse nods. 'I sincerely hope so, Henry.' He shakes Henry's hand. 'I don't think we'll be meeting again for a long time.'

Henry agrees. 'I ain't seen yer, I don't know yer, I never spoke to yer! Be lucky, old son.'

Gorse waves his hand and walks away, back along the pier to the promenade. Henry watches him go. He shakes his head admiringly. He, too, wonders if he'll ever see Gorse again.

Detective-Sergeant Hammond wears a somewhat crumpled dark tweed suit. He is a large, heavy, watchful man, a veteran of the local CID. He is local-voiced and nobody's fool, but imagination isn't his strong suit. He has a file in his hand.

'Excuse me, sir. Mr Stimpson, is it? Detective-Sergeant Hammond, CID. Sit down a minute, will you, sir?'

Irritated, Mr Stimpson sits. 'I don't have a lot of time, Sergeant. I'm engaged on work of National Importance.'

'Aren't we all these days, sir?' He opens his file. 'We haven't much to go on with this floater . . . er . . . beg pardon, sir, this particular body . . . Just as we put out in the newspapers. Seems the jacket the deceased man was wearing was made by a West End tailor three years ago. He had the name Gorse in his order book and the initials, R.E. No address given, but he remembers it because the customer paid him with a dud cheque.'

Mr Stimpson is very still. 'A dud cheque?'

'That's what the tailor said. I only spoke to him on the telephone.'

'How did he describe the man . . . This Gorse?'

Hammond looks at his notes. 'He said he was young, slim. Which certainly fits the dead man . . . Why, does that mean something to you, sir?'

Mr Stimpson looks deliberately doubtful. 'I think I have to see the er . . . body first, don't you?'

The Detective-Sergeant looks at Mr Stimpson a moment. 'Certainly, sir. They have him ready for us. If you'd like to step this way?'

'Very well.'

As they move out the Detective-Sergeant turns. 'You have seen a stiff . . . er . . . a dead man before, sir? . . . I mean, if this man Gorse is a particular friend of yours – ?'

'Anything but. Please lead on.' Hammond looks at Mr Stimpson again, but says nothing.

In the mortuary Detective-Sergeant Hammond waits, as a body under a white sheet is brought to them on a mobile stretcher. A mortuary assistant, in a white coat, is in attendance. At a nod from Hammond, he pulls the sheet back. Mr Stimpson stares down owlishly at the body. Detective-Sergeant Hammond asks softly, 'Is that your Mr R.E. Gorse?'

In the waiting room of the mortuary Detective-Sergeant Hammond is sitting gazing at Mr Stimpson with disappointment. He takes a Woodbine from a 'twenty' packet and offers Mr Stimpson one. Mr Stimpson declines. Hammond persists, 'You're sure he isn't the fellow you knew as – what do you call him? – Ralph Ernest Gorse?'

'Positive.'

Hammond closes the file. 'That's that, then. Thanks for coming, Mr Stimpson. You'll have to move if you want to get the London train, they're a bit erratic these days.'

Mr Stimpson is surprised. 'Is that all?'

'Well, as I say, sir . . . I'm sorry you've had such a long journey.' The detective is ironic. He thinks Mr Stimpson is an old bumbler. On top of a full day's toil on work of National Importance. 'But what I'm after is positive identification of the deceased, sir, and your Mr Gorse just isn't our Mr Gorse. So that's it, isn't it?'

'How many R.E. Gorses can there be?' asks Mr Stimpson.

Hammond shakes his head. 'I dunno, sir, but I'd settle for one, if somebody could identify him for sure . . . It's the war, people can't be traced, everything in a state of flux . . . We'll probably never know who he is . . .'

'You mean, you won't do any more?'

Hammond nods. 'Can't keep him on ice for ever. We'll put him on the general missing list, but if nobody claims him in a week or two then the Coroner will call it misadventure, and that's it.'

Mr Stimpson asks, 'Can you tell me the cause of death?'

'Well, I shouldn't, but it was drowning. The lungs were full of water.'

'No . . . marks on him? No suggestion of foul play? Or anything like that?'

Hammond shakes his head. 'None whatever. He choked on his own vomit. The pathologist says a lot of alcohol in his blood, obviously drunk when it happened. We get that sometimes here. They fall asleep on the beach. They forget the tide comes in.'

Mr Stimpson gets to his feet. 'Well, I'll bid you good-day, Sergeant Hammond.'

'Good-day to you, sir. And thank you for going to the trouble of coming all that way. Sorry it's been a wasted journey for you.'

Mr Stimpson straightens his glasses. 'Not necessarily, Sergeant Hammond.'

And Mr Stimpson is gone. The Detective-Sergeant ponders a moment. A funny bugger, he thinks. He shakes his head. He meets a lot of funny buggers in his job.

* * *

Joan Plumleigh-Bruce goes into the Carlton Hotel in a nervous but expectant mood. She walks into the lounge, and then sees Gorse at the desk, in RAF uniform. The room swims. She feels quite giddy. Joan turns and blindly studies a noticeboard giving details of a dance. Gorse does not see her. He goes back into the residents' lounge. As if sleep-walking, Joan follows him. At the door of the residents' lounge, she stops: for into her vision comes Gorse, now sitting and talking to Alison Warren. Gorse's back is to her, but Alison sits there as if by right, and Gorse's hand is on hers, on the table top. Joan turns away as if struck. She really does feel very giddy indeed. The receptionist sees her steady herself on his counter. '. . . May I help you, madam?'

Joan recovers. 'No . . . No . . . I'm just waiting for somebody.'

'If you would like to wait in the Foyer Bar, madam?'

'Er . . . Where is that?'

The receptionist points. 'That way, madam. I will send a waiter. Perhaps you would like coffee? Or a drink?'

'Thank you.' Joan goes into the Foyer Bar, away from the residents' lounge, hardly conscious of what she is doing or why.

The receptionist smacks a bell, and the old waiter takes Joan's order for a gin and Italian. She drinks it without tasting it.

In the residents' lounge Gorse and Alison are talking. Alison is quietly militant, Gorse smiling, as pleasant as ever. His hand still rests on hers. 'What have you been doing with yourself all day, Ralph? I tried your room several times,' says Alison in a chilly voice.

'Oh . . . This and that . . . I was hoping I could get a

few extra days' leave. I rang my Unit, but no such luck.' Gorse looks at his watch.

'Is the time so important?'

'Sorry, what?'

'You've looked at that watch every half-minute since you sat down!'

'Oh, sorry. I was just hoping to hear from an old pal. What my chances are . . . of getting my ticket out of the Air Force.'

'I see. You know people in high places, do you?'

Gorse is surprised at her tone. 'What? Oh no. Just an opinion. From an old friend. That sort of thing.'

'You seem to have an awful lot of old friends, Ralph. Most of them female?' says Alison.

Gorse recognizes the danger signs but ignores them. He has other things on his mind. 'What? . . . Look, I really must pop up and make this call. Only take a minute.' He gets to his feet.

'Oh, very well,' says Alison, dismissively. Gorse is up and gone at once. As he goes out of the place, Alison looks after him with a grim expression on her face. Then she picks up her *Tatler* and leafs through it.

Joan, from her seat in the Foyer Bar, sees Gorse hurry up the hotel stairs. She rises to her feet, cool and almost collected now, and goes into the residents' lounge, followed by the old waiter, carrying a second gin and It on a tray. 'Where shall I put it, madam?' asks the old waiter.

'Here will do . . .' The old waiter puts the drink onto the table where Alison sits. Joan sits, too. Secretively, she appraises Alison Warren. Her clothes, her manner, her social status, everything about her, then she speaks. 'Do you mind awfully?'

Alison looks annoyed. 'Well, I am expecting someone,

as a matter of fact.' Joan coughs, then asks in a pointed voice, 'May I speak to you for a moment?'

Alison Warren looks alarmed. 'What? . . . I don't think we've met, have we?'

'No, but we have something in common. Or rather, somebody.'

'Oh? Really? Who could that be, pray?'

'Ralph Gorse.'

When she has said that, Joan sits looking at Alison Warren, and waits.

Alison is silent a very long moment, just looking back at Joan. 'You *know* Ralph?'

Joan nods. 'Oh, yes. Very well.'

'I see. Were you expecting to meet him here?'

Joan smiles. 'Not really, no. I was . . . surprised to see him, actually.'

'Surprised?'

'Yes . . . My name is Joan Plumleigh-Bruce, by the way.' Alison wonders if this is all right; but Joan seems a lady; and she's very curious by now. 'Er . . . I'm Alison Warren . . . You've . . . known Ralph a long time, Mrs Plumleigh-Bruce?'

'Let us say it seems like a long time . . . We were quite close friends . . . for a while.'

'I see.'

Alison looks at Joan. Joan looks at Alison. Both elect to speak. Neither does. Then Joan finally breaks the silence. 'Ralph isn't the reliable sort but . . . I like him, I always have. He has such . . . charm, don't you find?'

'Oh yes, he has that all right,' answers Alison, a trifle bitterly.

'You sound a little . . . upset? Are you? Have I upset you? I'm sorry.'

'Not at all. I'm perfectly all right, thank you.'

Then Joan, who knows exactly what she's doing, adds, 'I know you are going to find this a very impertinent question, Mrs Warren, but have you lent Ralph any money?'

Alison is profoundly shocked. 'I think that is my business!'

'Yes, it was an impertinent question, I'm so sorry.'

Alison looks at her, very curious by now. '. . . I'm afraid I may have been very foolish.'

'Was it a lot of money?' asks Joan softly.

'Two hundred pounds.'

'That is not a lot of money to Ralph.'

'It is to me.'

'I suppose it could be called . . . payment in kind, really?'

Alison is suddenly very cold. 'I'm afraid I don't understand that remark!'

Joan smiles, woman-to-woman. 'You've slept with him, haven't you?'

Alison sits up very straight. 'Really! This is outrageous!'

'No, it isn't. I did the same thing myself.'

Says Alison sharply, 'I'm sure that is your own business and nobody else's!'

Joan is silent for a long moment, then she lowers her voice to a confidential tone . . . 'Don't tell me some small part of you didn't sound a warning note? Somewhere in your head? That he wasn't exactly what he seemed to be? Be honest with yourself, Mrs Warren, if not with me.'

Alison looks at her a long moment; then she's less than honest. 'Mrs Plumleigh-Bruce, I'm sure I have no idea what you are talking about.' And with that Alison gets to her feet. Somehow, she must end this.

Joan nods, smiling sadly. 'Then I'm wasting my time.'

'Excuse me.' And Alison Warren walks out of the residents' lounge.

'Goodbye, Mrs Warren,' says Joan Plumleigh-Bruce softly. Then she drinks her second gin and It with something like relish.

Alison Warren, very agitated by what she has just heard, hurries out of the hotel entrance. She simply wants to get away, to think things through clearly. Has she made a terrible mistake with Ralph Gorse? If she hasn't, what is the explanation of the events described by Joan Whatever-her-name-was? Alison made her way to the West Pier, paid her admission at the turnstile and found herself a seat in the sun amongst the suntanned holidaymakers who, at last, were beginning to realize that a war was, indeed, On. All around her they talked of the German advance in France in low, worried tones, looking in the sparse and fudged newspaper reports for some sign of hope. Alison neither heard the talk nor felt the worry. Her mind was entirely filled with the picture of Ralph Gorse in bed with that awful Plumleigh-what's-it-woman. Somehow the fact, if it was fact, that he had robbed her of money seemed unimportant. Yet, it was important. She wasn't rich. She'd behaved, possibly, like a fool. Alison sat in the hot sun, and felt increasingly furious and betrayed.

In Gorse's room at the Carlton Hotel, he sits, smoking nervously, on the bed, the telephone in his hand. A valise is open on the bed and on it are laid out a pre-war civilian suit, a shirt and a tie. Gorse is speaking into the telephone.

'Hello, yes . . . Can I speak to Clarice Mannors, please

. . . No, this is not a personal call . . . Pilot Officer Gorse.'

Gorse waits.

'Hello, yes? . . . Ralph?'

Gorse is flooded with relief. 'Thank God . . . Clarice! Listen! I have to get out of here! Now! The police have my name. My tailor's label must have given me away! It was on the suit. There's been a newspaper report – '

Clarice's voice is low but brisk. 'Nobody's . . . been to see you? From the police?'

'No, but they soon will be,' says Gorse, urgently.

Clarice talks in code, very carefully. 'I'm not sure my doctor friend will be at his surgery . . . But come up to London now! Go straight to my flat by taxi.'

'How will I get in?'

'I'll leave a key next door, at flat 27. Got that?'

'Got it.'

Clarice adds, 'Ralph? Keep calm. And get rid of that uniform!'

'Yes, of course. I've got a civvy suit, all is well.'

'Fine. Must go. See you later.'

'Right . . . And Clarice . . .'

'Yes?'

'Thanks . . .' Gorse puts the telephone down, and smiles. Everything was going to be all right, after all. The passport to the New Life, the end of all his troubles, was in sight. He would be safe. He would, just possibly, be rich. He would take his place at the top table, which had always been his due, with Clarice Mannors at his side. Everything was indeed going to be all right.

In the residents' lounge Joan Plumleigh-Bruce is drinking her third gin and It and looking rather pleased with herself. The episode with Alison Warren has cheered her.

The expression is wiped from her face by the sudden appearance of Mr Stimpson, behind her. '. . . Good Lord, Donald! You gave me a shock!'

Mr Stimpson sits, heavily. 'I have another shock for you. That body in the mortuary is not Ralph Gorse.'

'Really? It isn't?' asks Joan faintly.

'No, it isn't.' Mr Stimpson turns to the hovering old waiter. 'Waiter, do you have a pint of bitter?'

'We serve only half-pints in the lounge, sir.'

'Then bring me two half-pints!'

'Two half-pints, sir? Certainly, sir.'

Mr Stimpson turns back to Joan. 'The point is, if that body in the mortuary isn't him, where the hell is Ralph Gorse?'

Joan puts her hand on his. She has no alternative to the truth now. 'Donald, he's here . . . in this hotel . . .'

Mr Stimpson stares at her for a very long moment. 'Here! Did you know he was here? All the time?'

Joan says humbly, 'I couldn't be sure of it. He wrote to me from here . . . A begging letter . . . A couple of days ago . . .'

'Why didn't you tell me?'

'Donald, if you're going to be like this, I don't know why I'm telling you now!'

Mr Stimpson closes his eyes and counts to ten. 'Where is Gorse? This minute. Do you know?'

Joan feels she must say more. 'Well, if you must know, Ralph has a lady friend, a well-to-do woman I would say, and he seems to spend most of his time with her!'

'My God . . . you sound as if you're jealous!'

Joan is by now a bit tipsy. 'I don't give a damn how I sound, Donald.'

After a moment's silence Mr Stimpson asks, 'This woman. Well-to-do, you say?'

'For Heaven's sake, Donald, does it matter? He's nothing to do with us, any more. It was a mistake to come here . . . Please don't get all worked up about it. Ralph's a pilot in the Air Force. He has his Wings. He's a hero.'

Mr Stimpson is astonished to hear this. 'A hero? If I saw him given the Victoria Cross by the King himself I wouldn't believe it!'

'Two half-pints of bitter, sir.' The old waiter, with a faint air of disapproval, puts down two glasses. Mr Stimpson sips one in some bewilderment. Then, 'You asked about the dead man being in a uniform, at the mortuary?' Softly but inexorably he goes on, 'You guessed something even then, didn't you . . . And tried to protect him . . . Even then . . . ?' But Joan will not meet his gaze. 'What else are you hiding from me about Gorse?'

'I can tell you one thing. The woman he's picked up, in this hotel,' Joan pauses, then can't help herself. '. . . She's lent him money, you know?'

Mr Stimpson leans forward. 'How d'you know that?'

'She told me.'

Mr Stimpson almost spills his half-pint of bitter.

Gorse has booked out of the hotel. He has already paid his bill. Now he is packing, in a hurry. He has taken off his uniform tunic, and is putting on his civilian suit but decides not to change his shirt, in the interests of haste. He gets the trousers and jacket on, when there is a sudden knock at the door. He is still, wondering. Then he crosses the room and opens the door.

It is Alison. Gorse hesitates a moment, but she pushes her way inside. She is upset and also determined, Gorse sees that at once. She takes in the civilian suit and the half-packed valise and turns to Gorse. 'Going somewhere, Ralph?'

Gorse grimaces. 'Alison, I have to go. I'm sorry. I'm in rather a hurry . . . darling.'

Alison just looks at him. 'Who is it this time? The beautiful Wren?'

'What? Oh, her? I told you – she was just an old friend.'

'I know what you told me, Ralph.'

Gorse is thinking about time, about trains, about escape, but he asks, 'What's the matter, Alison?'

'I rather think . . . you are, Ralph.'

'Me? What have I done?'

Alison gestures. 'What's happened to your hand? Where's your bandage?'

Gorse shrugs. 'I took it off. It didn't seem to be helping. Anyway, I've got to turn up at the Medical Board tomorrow.'

Asks Alison disbelievingly, 'Tomorrow? Really?'

Gorse smiles brightly, shooting a glance at his watch. 'If I go in without the bandage and say it's improved a lot, there's always a chance they'll post me back to duty.'

Alison snorts, 'Ralph, I don't believe a single bloody word you say, I really don't!'

In reply, Gorse takes out his wallet and pulls out the money and gives it to her. 'Take it! I'll manage without it. Good-bye, Alison.' With that Gorse picks up the valise, snaps the straps together and walks to the door. Alison looks at the money. She is a moment or two making her decision. Then, with the money in her hand, she follows Gorse into the corridor.

Gorse is setting off along the corridor, bag in hand. Alison watches him go a few paces. She calls calmly, but with fury boiling under the calm, 'Ralph. I know you're a fake. In how many ways I can only guess.'

Gorse freezes. He stops and turns to her. 'What?'

'Do you want to talk about it?' asks Alison coolly, 'or do you want me to report it?'

Gorse is still. Then his shoulders droop. He is beaten, his demeanour signals. 'Let's talk about it, shall we, darling?'

'In my room, then,' says Alison briskly. 'I have something to show you.'

'Very well,' says Gorse.

Alison walks past him. After a moment, Gorse follows her along the corridor.

Mr Stimpson and Joan are near the reception desk. They are arguing, trying to keep their voices down. The receptionist is looking at his register.

'I must say, you are being utterly crass about this whole business, Donald,' says Joan.

'That dead man was in Gorse's suit,' says Mr Stimpson. 'If he was, how did he get into it?'

'If he was, if he was! It's all ifs and buts.'

'The man's dead, Joan. And Ralph Gorse, according to you, is still in this hotel, isn't he?'

The receptionist turns to Mr Stimpson. 'Mr Gorse has checked out, sir.'

'Checked out?'

'Yes, sir.'

'Room 521. He's probably left the key in the room . . .'

But Mr Stimpson is already heading up the stairs.

Alison Warren's room at the Carlton is similar to Gorse's, with a few additions, mostly feminine. There are flowers, dresses around the place, and small expensive items like a travelling alarm clock and scent bottles containing Chanel No 5. Gorse, carrying his valise, and Alison enter,

Alison using her key. She does not lock the door, but simply closes it. Gorse turns to Alison with an apologetic expression on his face. 'Alison, what *is* all this about?'

In reply, Alison gives him a telegram form. 'Look at that. I got it from my brother, who's at the Air Ministry in London. He checked with RAF records at Gloucester. Those are his words . . . "There's no such person as Pilot Officer Ralph Ernest Gorse in the Royal Air Force!"'

'Rubbish! He made a mistake,' declares Gorse, thoroughly shaken. But Alison is furious. 'No, he didn't. If you're impersonating an officer, who are you, for God's sake!'

Gorse shakes his head, sadly. 'Alison. It isn't what it seems.'

'An hotel crook? A confidence man? Oh, I know all about that, I had it at first hand from your ex-lady friend, Joan Plumleigh-whatever-her-name-is.'

Gorse thinks he is going mad. 'When did you talk to *her*?'

'Just now. In the lounge.'

'She's *here*?'

'Very much so. And still starry-eyed about you, I'd say. However, I'm not, not in the least, not any more.'

'Is she alone? Is anybody with her? A man?'

'Not as far as I know. Does it matter?'

Gorse takes a deep breath. He moves nearer to Alison. 'Darling. Let me tell you the truth. All this. You've got it all wrong. Once you hear what I have to say, you'll understand . . .'

'I doubt it,' says Alison Warren. But her legs feel suddenly weak. She is not used to emotional scenes, and she sits down abruptly.

Ralph Ernest Gorse smiles down at her.

* * *

Mr Stimpson is marching along the fifth floor of the Carlton Hotel. He reaches Gorse's room, No 521. The door is ajar and the room clearly has been vacated. Mr Stimpson enters and peers around, suspiciously. As he does so, the telephone rings. Mr Stimpson snatches up the receiver. He hears Joan's voice quite clearly. It speaks one single word. 'Ralph?'

Mr Stimpson asks, 'Is that you, Joan? Are you calling him from downstairs? Have you no shame?' There is a gasp at the other end of the line and it goes dead. Mr Stimpson jiggles the telephone cradle until he obtains the hotel operator. He asks for the room number of Mrs Alison Warren.

In Alison Warren's room the afternoon sun shines through the windows, throwing two shafts of light across the room. The net curtains blow in the breeze. Alison Warren, a woman scorned, stands behind Gorse halfway across the room. She is very much in two minds. She feels she hates Gorse . . . but a part of her feels the sexual pull towards him, and she hates him all the more for that. Gorse is talking softly. 'There's an explanation, Alison, if you'll only listen to it. I'm none of the things Joan told you I was . . . I'm quite simply . . . a deserter . . . I'm on the run. I need to go . . . To get away . . . Simple as that.'

'A deserter?' Alison is prepared to believe that.

'Darling, if I'm caught I go into a military prison. They aren't very nice. I'm sorry if I've lied to you but now you have the absolute truth. Now, can I go? I really must, darling . . .'

Alison is suddenly very angry and it erupts . . . 'You have a bloody nerve. You expect me – who lost a husband in the Atlantic – a better man dead than you are alive!'

'I'm sure of it,' murmurs Gorse. 'But – '

' – I'd respect you, at least that, if you'd give yourself up and take your medicine!' declares Alison in a sudden rage, something she has never experienced before in all her life.

Gorse is taken aback, then nods in pretended agreement. 'Perhaps you're right,' says Gorse, wishing himself out of the room, out of the hotel, away. 'If I promise to give myself up, would that be enough? If I gave you my word I'll go straight out of this hotel, round to the nearest military police unit and do it, will that satisfy you?'

'No,' says Alison, 'because you wouldn't do it, would you?'

Gorse, suddenly, smoothly, takes hold of her lightly by her elbows.

'No! Don't! You've made a complete bloody fool of me,' cries Alison, shrilly.

'Alison, I did you no harm. You're none the worse for having known me . . . What have you lost? It was just a nice interlude . . .' Still he holds her arms. 'Surely we can leave it there, let it be just that . . . Why make more of it than it is?'

But Alison is now beyond reason. 'Because you can't be allowed to get away with it! Because you've obviously been getting away with murder for a very long time. That poor Plumleigh-Bruce woman and then me, and God knows who else!'

'Alison . . . *please*!' pleads Gorse, thinking: the bloody woman, time's going, it's slipping away, all of it . . . 'Alison, let me go!'

But Alison is saying, 'No, this is the end of the story, Ralph, because I'm going to tell my brother just exactly who and what you are!'

Gorse stares at her. He sees at once that she means it.

He attempts to pull her to him and he tries to kiss her. Alison fights him off, tears in her eyes, but tears of fury. 'You are an absolute unmitigated bastard, Ralph Gorse, if that *is* your real name!'

'Please . . . Alison,' says Gorse the lover, gently trying to soften her. But she pulls back and slaps him, hard, across the face. Now Gorse is looking at her through a haze of pain and rage and is hardly listening at all to her words, which are almost as stinging – did he hear them – as the slap itself.

'You pretend to be a gentleman but you're just a *nobody*, and a military prison's the right place for you – and I mean to see that that is where you go and I hope you rot there!'

Now Alison is turning away to the door and Gorse knows that if she reaches it and gets to a telephone everything he has ever wanted, everything he has ever hoped for, is gone. There will be no Clarice, no Washington, no place at the top table of life for Ralph Gorse . . . Only the stink and shit of a military prison, disgrace, humiliation and rot. The red haze of rage has almost obliterated Alison's features now, as he reaches forward and, with arms of steely strength, pulls her to him, strains to kiss her lips.

'Let me go!' Alison breathes. 'Let me go!'

Slowly, slowly, Alison gives way to him. She tries to fight her feelings. Gorse brings his hand up her back, touches her neck and in that moment she sees something in his face: by then it is far, far too late . . . Gorse has taken her silk scarf in his hand and he is tightening and tightening it and her shout is stifled and she is struggling, but only for a moment. She is still . . . and then she goes limp. Slowly, he lowers her onto the sofa. He stands back and looks down at her staring eyes and still body.

Our Ralph Ernest Gorse, who has been so close to doing this, so close so often with so many different women, has done it at last, and he feels an awful despair and relief in the doing of it. And an even more awful finality and pain.

Outside in the corridor Mr Stimpson hurries along towards Alison Warren's room. Shortsightedly he peers up at the doors, looking for the number.

Inside Room 202 Ralph Gorse is still looking at the dead body of Alison Warren. He is wondering exactly what to do next.

Mr Stimpson arrives outside Alison's door. He looks, sees the number. Then after a moment's hesitation, he knocks.

Gorse starts at the knock. He freezes. He looks quickly at the unlocked door. Slowly, making no noise at all, he tiptoes across the room and gently, very gently, he turns the key on the inside. Then he leans against the door and, cold sweat pouring down his back, he listens.

In the corridor Mr Stimpson stands perplexed. He knocks again but there is still no reply. He stares at the door a long time. Then he knocks yet again. There is still no reply. He tries the door-handle and finds it firmly closed. He turns to see a middle-aged chambermaid coming along the corridor, holding a pile of sheets. She addresses him. 'Isn't anybody in, sir?'

'Seemingly not,' says Mr Stimpson.

The chambermaid hesitates. 'I think there was, sir . . . At least there was a few minutes ago.'

'Oh?' asks Mr Stimpson, alerted. He knocks again, but again no reply.

'They must have gone out, sir.' The chambermaid makes to go on. Mr Stimpson moves after her, and asks, very softly . . . 'How did you know there was somebody in the room?'

'Well, sir . . . I went to turn the bed down . . . And I heard voices . . . So I didn't go in.'

'But why? Don't you ever go into a room with people in it?'

'Well . . . sir . . . I shouldn't say, really, sir . . . They were having words I think, sir . . . A gentleman and a lady . . . sir.'

Mr Stimpson asks very slowly, 'Words? Did you hear what they were saying?'

'Oh, no, sir!'

Mr Stimpson nods his thanks and the chambermaid disappears into a room along the corridor, leaving Mr Stimpson on his own. He gazes at the door for a full minute. Then, slowly, thoughtfully, Mr Stimpson makes his way downstairs.

In Alison Warren's room, his back pressed against the door, and privy to every word of that conversation, Ralph Gorse slowly expels his breath.

Mr Stimpson comes down the stairs into the reception area and sees, to his irritation, Joan Plumleigh-Bruce waiting there. She does not seem at all ashamed of having tried to warn Ralph Gorse that he was on the way upstairs. Quite the contrary.

'Gorse isn't in his room and Mrs Warren's room was locked.'

'Oh . . . Well . . . She's out, then.'

'I checked the telephone from upstairs,' says Mr Stimpson. 'The clerk said she was in. Her key's not on the rack.'

Joan shrugs. 'Well, she took it out. People do, sometimes.'

'Just one minute.' Mr Stimpson crosses to the reception desk.

'Did Mr Gorse have a motorcar with him?' he asks the receptionist.

The receptionist looks surprised. 'Yes, I believe he did, sir.' He crosses to look out of the window. 'It's still in the car park, sir. The green Railton, sir.'

'Thank you.' Mr Stimpson walks back to Joan. 'Joan. Don't ask any questions. Just go and sit in Gorse's motorcar.'

'What?'

'You don't want to miss him, do you? You don't want to let dear Ralph go, possibly to his death, as a hero? Never to see him again? You wouldn't want that, would you?'

Joan just looks at him. '. . . Donald, you get odder the longer I know you.'

Huffily, she goes out of the front of the hotel, and walks towards the Railton. Mr Stimpson stations himself in the middle of the reception lobby and he waits.

Gorse, in a civilian suit and carrying the valise, is coming down the stairs towards reception, when he sees Mr Stimpson's back, and freezes. Then, before Mr Stimpson can turn round, Gorse sees a door marked 'Exit to Garage' at the bottom of the stairs. By the time Mr Stimpson turns around, Gorse is there no longer.

Instead, Gorse walks quickly along a passageway still

carrying his valise. He follows the signs marked 'Hotel Garage'.

In the reception area of the hotel Mr Stimpson waits impatiently. There has been no sign of Gorse. Possibly, he has things all wrong, although he thinks not. He turns away towards the stairs down which he supposes Gorse may yet come.

Joan sits in Gorse's Railton in the car park. She is bored. She tries to remember the very first day she rode in the car with Gorse, out to the stables. What a lovely day that had been, how attentive to her every need and whim dear, dear Ralph had been, and now, here she was, and Donald Stimpson too, chasing around Brighton in search of him, and for what? To confront him with what? Only Donald seemed to know, and he wasn't telling her . . . All she wanted was to get away from the place. If Ralph was sleeping with that silly widow-lady, Alison, well, why not, she was probably paying him, in one way or another, whereas *she* . . . well . . . But she hadn't actually *paid* him, had she? No indeed . . . Certainly not. There had been affection on his part, hadn't there? Of course there had. Nobody could doubt it. Certainly she didn't. Joan came out of her reverie to see, as if part of the dream, the form of Ralph Gorse hurrying towards her, in his civilian suit.

At that very moment, Gorse sees Joan. He turns abruptly and runs, very quickly, not looking back once, out of the car park.

Joan calls out of the car, 'Ralph? . . . Ralph?' She is puzzled, and shakes her head disbelievingly. Slowly, she gets out of the car and goes falteringly and somewhat flustered back into the hotel.

* * *

Mr Stimpson watches from his vantage point at the foot of the stairs as Joan comes in and walks towards him.

Joan calls out, in a curious, faint voice, 'Donald . . . I've just seen Ralph . . . But he's gone!'

'Gone? Where?'

'He was in the car park. I called to him but he ran off.'

'Ran off?'

'Simply disappeared!'

Mr Stimpson turns to the receptionist, who is watching the scene with interest.

'Can I,' asks Mr Stimpson, 'see the manager? At once, please.'

At Brighton railway station Gorse is still running. He sees a porter come out of the station. 'The London train?' he gasps. 'Goes in two minutes, sir.' Gorse runs into the station. The word hammers in his head. Safe, safe, safe.

Alison's room at the Carlton Hotel is shuttered and dark, and there is no sign of Alison Warren. The dark explodes into light as Mr Stimpson, Joan Plumleigh-Bruce and the manager enter, admitted by the manager's key. They stand, disappointed, with nothing to see. Then quite suddenly, Mr Stimpson wrenches open the wardrobe. Inside is the body of Alison Warren.

At the booking office at Brighton station, Gorse is buying a ticket. He is in a queue, and agitated. Sailors, airmen, soldiers, land girls, civilians, jostle around in a last-minute rush to buy tickets. Gorse finally gets to the window. 'First-class single to London, please.' Gorse takes his ticket and goes on towards the platform, at a run.

He is only just in time. The train is about to leave, and the engine-driver is making steam. The last soldiers and sailors have climbed on board. Doors slam. Whistles blow. Gorse runs hard and wrenches the last door of the last carriage open. He clambers aboard in a muck sweat. The guard slams the door. The train moves slowly, in a cloud of steam, out of the station. Safe, Gorse tells himself. Safe. Safe. Safe. The word still hammers in his head.

Gorse walks unsteadily along the train corridor, full of servicemen sitting on kitbags and standing against the doors. But Gorse elbows his way through to the first-class buffet. It is crowded with officers of all services. Gorse catches the barman's eye. 'Large scotch. No change.' He gives the barman a pound note. The scotch arrives deftly from under the counter, and the pound note disappears. Gorse drinks the alcohol in one gulp. He closes his eyes, puts down another pound note on the counter. Another whisky arrives. Gorse forces his way through the crush to a seat. He sits, the drink in front of him. He closes his eyes. Safe.

The Sussex countryside rolls by. It seems, to Gorse, untouched by the war. Only the train and the people on it belong to the present. The countryside will still be there, Gorse thinks, when all the present killing is forgotten. He smiles to himself. What, after all, is one life against the hundreds, thousands maybe, now dying in France or Belgium, under the tractors of tanks, by rifle and machine-gun bullet, by flame-thrower and artillery shrapnel, by aerial bombardment . . . What was one life, against all that?

Gorse sipped his whisky and slowly the trembling eased. Nobody seemed to be looking at him, which was good. They were all smiling and talking, the young men in uniform, living life to the full while they had it to live. Well, he would soon be out of it all, once he got to Clarice

Mannors' flat he was safe. After that, the network would look after him. One way or another. Hadn't Clarice said it would? Gorse breathed easier. Safe. He was safe.

Suddenly, the train ground to a halt. Gorse struggled to his feet and went to a window. He opened it and looked down the sleepy sunlit rural platform. Nobody. Behind him, a door slammed. Gorse looked back along the platform. Nothing. A porter waved a green flag. The train made steam and puffed away out of the rural halt. Gorse closed the window and returned to his seat.

Gorse, in a mood of celebration, returned to the bar for another drink. He was just raising his glass to his lips as he saw, coming towards him through the crush of people, the form of Mr Stimpson. Gorse is still, and very shocked, and does not move until Mr Stimpson stands opposite him. Then he sets down his drink, unsteadily, and makes to push blindly past Mr Stimpson; anywhere, away from that revengeful face, those icy glasses.

'I wouldn't try to run, Ralph. There's nowhere to go,' says Mr Stimpson, almost kindly.

Gorse just stares at him. '. . . What are *you* doing here?'

Mr Stimpson smiles. 'Me? I'm in at, what they call in hunting circles . . . the Death . . . Yes, I think I can say I'm in at the Death.'

Gorse recovers, fast. 'I haven't the faintest idea what you're talking about.'

Mr Stimpson regards Gorse, still almost kindly, as the train chugs on through the green Sussex countryside. 'Ralph, haven't you got the picture yet? This train is taking you straight to prison.'

Gorse shakes his head. 'What . . . why are you here?'

Mr Stimpson picks his words carefully. Almost as if he has rehearsed them many times. 'Because . . . Until you came into my life, Ralph, I was content . . . Until you violated . . . the woman I loved and respected above everything else in the world . . . That is why I am standing here now . . . that is why I will not rest content until I see you . . . gone from this earth.'

Even Gorse is awed by these words. 'What . . . the hell are you talking about?' Then Gorse looks over Mr Stimpson's shoulder. His heart almost stops at what he sees. For there, grimly unsmiling, stands Detective-Sergeant Hammond of the Sussex CID.

* * *

Three people are preparing for the trial for murder, at the Old Bailey, of Ralph Ernest Gorse.

Joan Plumleigh-Bruce is sitting in front of the mirror in her bedroom, still in her slip, making up her face. She is having difficulty steadying her hand as she applies her lipstick.

The crying jags (at night, alone in her bed) have stopped. The Sunday rags have stopped ringing on her telephone or knocking at her door – really, in wartime, you would think they had something better to do. But, as one of them, foot in the door, spectacles flashing, mackintosh and notebook open, told her, 'The public's fed up with Dunkirk stories. They're ready for a bit of smut, dear.'

Joan Plumleigh-Bruce had slammed the door on him and stood in the hallway trembling with shame.

Now, the day of reckoning had arrived for poor dear Ralph.

Joan tried again with the lipstick.

This, she thinks to herself, is going to be one of the most terrible days of her life.

* * *

Mr Stimpson, too, is in his bedroom, preparing for the great day. He is adjusting his tie in the mirror. As he does it, he hums a totally inappropriate tune, 'Run Rabbit Run', a favourite on the wireless until very recently, when the ones doing the running had turned out to be the British and the French. But somehow, most of the British Army had got off at Dunkirk and there was an astonishing optimism in the land. A terrible military defeat, facing Hitler and all his legions quite alone, and the British found it possible to be cheerful. Mr Stimpson certainly did. This day would prove to be the most satisfactory of his life. It was a day when the terrible, burning pain of jealousy and hate would be eased, and justice, at long, long last, would be done, in the case of Ralph Ernest Gorse.

Mr Stimpson continues to hum his tune, and put on his best jacket. He will need to look his best, on this fateful day.

Yes, indeed.

In his cell at the Old Bailey Gorse sits blankly, in this gloomy underground place. He is still in his civilian clothes, although they are somewhat crumpled by now. He takes a cigarette from his gold case, and lights it with Ronnie Shooter's gold lighter. He expels the smoke and looks at the door, which has a small grille, through which, from time to time, a warder peers, to make sure he is still there, a joke they make, down here. These tough, married men are pleasant to Gorse, as if he is somebody special, different from other men, marked out for a different fate, perhaps, from the common run of dubious humanity they see every day of their working lives. For Gorse is on a murder charge. And that makes him different.

Gorse swallows and tries not to think of the possibilities of doom. His solicitor and the defending barrister have talked to him for the last time, an hour before, and seem hopeful. A good case, they say. Every chance. Stick to his story, no matter what. Yes, indeed, they had said, staring at their polished shoes, a very good chance.

Then they had gone and the cell door had banged behind them, leaving Gorse alone. Gorse drew on the cigarette and shivered. Chin up, old boy, he told himself. Bags of style. Show them you're not one of the riff-raff, or the Great Unwashed. Let them see – the barrister, the judge, the jury (sure to be all male, all middle-class he'd been told) – let them all see that Ralph Ernest Gorse was a gentleman.

In the corridor at the Old Bailey Joan and Mr Stimpson, dressed in their best clothes, wait to be called as witnesses, for by now the case is on. Joan is still nervous and fidgety. Mr Stimpson is determined, and to Joan's eyes, smug, and actually enjoying this terrible business. She has been smoking incessantly all day. 'Donald . . . I wish I didn't have to do this . . . I'm dreading it.'

Mr Stimpson is reassuring. 'There's nothing to worry about. Just give your evidence in a clear voice.'

He is so fatherly, Joan can stand it no more. 'You're enjoying this! Your damn vendetta with Ralph! Nothing but dreadful, sordid publicity, the newspapers writing all that awful stuff!'

But Mr Stimpson is not listening. 'I tell you, Joan, Gorse is finished.'

Nor is Joan – 'I'll never be able to go into The Friar again! Or anywhere else for that matter! My life is *ruined*!'

Mr Stimpson is still not listening. 'The forensic evidence has linked him to the murder . . . Alison Warren's hair and finger-clipping samples all over him! The prosecution have established a motive . . .'

'I don't think I'm going into that witness box . . .' This remark brings Mr Stimpson back to reality. 'You have to, and so do I! We have no choice, we were witnesses to the whole business . . .' he declares.

Joan accuses him. 'You don't care about me, do you? All you care about is seeing Ralph convicted.'

'Well,' says Mr Stimpson, 'there's no doubt our evidence will be the final nail.'

'Who knows what they'll ask me, in that witness box?' wails Joan. But Mr Stimpson is remorseless. 'Why worry, you have nothing to hide, do you?'

But before Joan can reply, a court official calls, 'Donald Stimpson!'

Mr Stimpson hurries forward, smiling, Joan sees with disgust, actually smiling!

The first thing Mr Stimpson sees, in a blur of impressions – how small the court is, how near everybody is to everybody else – is Gorse in the dock. Mr Stimpson, who is nervous at this great moment, can only see and marvel at how imperturbable and somehow above all this Gorse seems to be, even in the dock, with a warder at his side. Mr Stimpson takes the Oath in a daze and then the prosecuting counsel is asking, but gently, 'Mr Stimpson, had you reason to believe that Ralph Gorse was the owner of the civilian suit, Exhibit Twelve?' The suit is held up for him to see, by the court usher.

'Yes, I did,' nods Mr Stimpson.

'Where did you see this suit?'

'It was at the mortuary. It had been found on the dead man, Pilot Officer Stokes.'

'Why did you think the suit belonged to Gorse?'

‘I guessed. Once I heard that he’d never paid for it.’ To Mr Stimpson’s pleasure there are some titters – quickly suppressed – in the court-room.

The prosecuting counsel presses on. ‘Mr Stimpson, tell the Court what happened when you went to Mrs Warren’s room in the Carlton Hotel?’

Mr Stimpson has rehearsed this, often. ‘She didn’t answer my knock. When I tried the door it was locked, although I had reason to believe that some person or persons were in the room.’

‘Why do you say that?’

‘A chambermaid told me she had heard raised voices there.’

‘Very well. What did you do next?’

‘I went down to find the hotel manager, and we both returned to Mrs Warren’s room.’

‘What did you find when you searched the room?’

‘The dead body of Alison Warren. In a wardrobe.’ At last, there is a hush in the court. Everybody is looking at Ralph Gorse in the dock. He shows no emotion. He simply regards his fingernails. Mr Stimpson marvels again at his coolness, and is almost unprepared for the defence counsel’s first question.

‘Mr Stimpson, would it be true to say that you have systematically hounded the accused since his . . . intimate relationship with your lady-friend, Joan Plumleigh-Bruce?’

Mr Stimpson trembles with sudden fright and fury as he answers. ‘No, it would not be true to say!’

The defence counsel asks, in the same low, but clear voice, ‘What would it be true to say? Were you not enraged with jealousy, when you discovered he had an intimate relationship with that lady?’

Mr Stimpson is hurt, but shows as little of it as he can.

'She . . . was swept away by his . . . charm . . . He later defrauded her of her savings.' Defence counsel thunders, 'I am not asking what he did or she did, Mr Stimpson, I am asking what *you* felt, and still do most probably feel towards the defendant! That is, I put it to you, sexual jealousy, hatred, and envy!'

Mr Stimpson by now is choking, but trying for calm . . . 'Hardly,' is the best answer he can manage and his voice sounds a croak in his ears.

'Why not? He was everything you were not,' the defence counsel says. 'Young, good-looking, as you say, *charming*? And, in addition, he stole your lady-friend, the woman you hoped to marry – is that true or is it not?'

Mr Stimpson tries for calm. 'There is . . . some truth in that. Perhaps.'

Defence counsel asks, coldly, 'I submit you are an extremely prejudiced witness, Mr Stimpson.' Mr Stimpson is rock-steady at this. 'Possibly. But my evidence is the truth.'

The defence counsel gestures contemptuously. 'Milord . . . I have quite finished with *this* witness.'

The judge intones, 'Mr Stimpson, you may step down.' Mr Stimpson hesitates. He stares at Ralph Gorse in the dock and knows that there are a million things he would like to say . . . but that he will never be allowed to say them, that this clinical, matter-of-fact procedure is all there is. With a sad sigh and a last look at Gorse he leaves the witness box.

In the same witness box, a little later, Joan Plumleigh-Bruce's feelings are very different. She can hardly bring herself to look at Ralph Gorse, or at anybody, for that matter. Her feelings are of shame and anger that she, the daughter of an army officer and the widow of another, should have to endure this public torture; it was beyond bearing. Joan, therefore, gave her evidence in a low, whispery voice and tried to pretend that none of this was actually happening to her. She stammered through the friendly questions of the prosecuting counsel as best she could . . . 'I was waiting in the motorcar,' she falters, 'when . . .'

The prosecuting counsel purrs gently. 'When? . . . What happened? Take your time.'

Joan swallows. 'I saw Ralph Gorse come into the car park . . .'

'What happened then?'

Joan closes her eyes. Then, in a very low voice, 'He saw *me* . . .'

'And then?'

'. . . He ran away . . .'

The prosecuting counsel asks, even more gently, 'You are sure it was the defendant? Just point to him, if you will, Mrs Plumleigh-Bruce?'

With a terrible effort, Joan raises her eyes and sees Ralph Gorse smiling, actually smiling, at her. Trembling, she raises her arm – it seems not to belong to her – and points her finger at him. 'Yes . . . It was Ralph.' The prosecuting counsel repeats her words, 'It was Ralph Ernest Gorse, the accused?'

'Yes . . . it was.' Joan feels she might break down into tears, or collapse, but amazingly she is still on her feet. The prosecuting counsel is saying, 'No more questions of this witness, milord.'

Then the defence counsel is on his feet. He is a young, ruthless man and Joan is profoundly unprepared for his first question. 'Do you still *love* Ralph Gorse?'

The court swims. 'What?'

'A perfectly straightforward question. Do you still love Ralph Gorse?' asks the defence counsel.

Joan demurs. 'I . . . I am . . . fond of him . . . I mean, I was . . . fond of him.'

The defence counsel's voice is now rock-hard. '*Fond* of him? I submit you were much more than merely fond of him, Mrs Plumleigh-Bruce?' Joan says nothing, can think of nothing to say. 'I submit that you and he were intimate on a number of occasions and that you loved him. And that you, perhaps, still do?'

Again, the court swims. 'No. Please. That is not fair.'

'It is extremely fair because it is the truth, madam, and you know it! You and your present paramour, Mr Stimpson, pursued Ralph Gorse to Brighton, did you not?'

Joan wails, or so it sounds in her ears, 'We did not pursue him . . . *I* did not pursue him.'

The defence counsel shakes his head. 'I submit you did, madam. In an attempt to get him back into your bed. When you found you could not, you invented this story of seeing him running away from the scene of the murder.'

'No!' whispers Joan.

'I further submit that in common with Donald Stimpson you were sexually jealous of Gorse. In Stimpson's case because he slept with you. In your case because he slept with Alison Warren.'

'No . . . that . . . isn't true . . .' Joan lowers her eyes. She is trembling violently. She feels sick. She has never felt so ashamed in her life.

Defence counsel sits with a flourish. 'No more questions of *this* witness, milord.'

The prosecuting counsel rises. 'May I put a supplementary, milord?'

'Do so,' says the judge.

The prosecuting counsel asks Joan, very softly, 'I'm

sorry to have to put these next questions to you, Mrs Plumleigh-Bruce, but it is in the interest of establishing the truth. You were once the lover of Ralph Gorse?'

Joan is a long time answering. Then, '. . . Yes . . .'

'Very well . . . Now, was there anything at all . . . strange . . . in the love-making of Ralph Gorse?'

'I . . . don't know what you mean.'

Prosecuting counsel is still smiling encouragingly at her. 'Let me put it another way. Did he ever frighten you or threaten you?'

Joan is unsure what he wants her to say . . . 'No.'

'Did he ever . . . tie anything around you . . . around your neck, for example?'

Joan is silent. Then, finally, in her lowest whisper yet, she answers, 'Only in play.'

There are titters – again quickly suppressed – around the court room. But Joan does not hear them. She is listening, sick, to the prosecuting counsel's next question. 'And what was it? That Ralph Gorse tied around your neck?'

'. . . A scarf,' whispers Joan.

'He tied a scarf around your neck?' The prosecuting counsel's voice seems to fill the court room, the world itself.

'Once, yes,' corrects Joan.

'Did you like it?'

'No.'

'Then why did you allow him to do it?'

Joan speaks the simple truth. 'Because I loved him . . . then. I loved him then.'

Prosecuting counsel is nodding and smiling as if she is a very bright pupil. 'Thank you, Mrs Plumleigh-Bruce.'

The judge adds, 'You may stand down, Mrs Plumleigh-

Bruce.' He is looking at her, Joan notices, with some interest. Slowly, broken, Joan does so.

As witnesses and court officials pass briskly by, Joan, dazed and angry in equal measure, comes back into the corridor, from the court-room. Mr Stimpson is waiting there. He comes forward, eagerly. 'Joan . . . how did it go? . . . Joan?'

Joan sees him, and sees everything. Her words are clear and her voice sounds, to Mr Stimpson, quite dead. He has never heard Joan speak like that before. 'It was absolutely the worst thing I ever had to do in my life . . . It was shaming and degrading and horrible . . . And *you* made me do it, Donald.'

Mr Stimpson is taken aback, but not for long. '. . . No! It was Gorse, not me. Without him, none of this would have happened . . . Look . . . Joan!' He takes her arm . . . 'Let us go away from Reading, find a house somewhere else, put all this behind us. We'll be together . . . Just the two of us . . . Forget Ralph Gorse, forget and *forgive* . . .'

'You may forget and forgive, Donald, and good luck to you, but I have been branded a loose woman in that court room, for all the world to see, and *I* do not forget and forgive!' Joan wrenches Mr Stimpson's ring from her finger and hurls it to the floor. 'Good-bye, Donald!'

Mr Stimpson stares at her. But he is in no doubt it *is* good-bye. He makes to go after her, then restrains himself. He bends and fishes the ring from the floor and puts it in his pocket. After what has obviously been said in that court room, perhaps it is, after all, for the best. Alone, he might live it all down a lot more easily. No mud, after all, sticks to him. He was merely the agent of Justice. Yes, indeed.

* * *

Now, the jury is out and Gorse awaits his fate in his cell at the Old Bailey. Gorse is pacing four steps each way. He is agitated and cannot sit still, and his mouth is dry and his stomach made of water. Steady, old boy, he tells himself, things could have gone a lot worse, the jury seemed sympathetic, anyway not hostile, even in the worst stages of the cross-examination, even when the prosecuting counsel had asked him, his voice low and deadly, the court hushed, as if they knew this was the climax of the duel: 'Mr Gorse, I put it to you . . . You were in a desperate position! You were a deserter, carrying on a sexual relationship with the dead woman, Alison Warren, and you had, in the style of your previous liaisons with women, obtained money from Alison Warren . . .'

Gorse had answered, 'I borrowed some money, certainly.'

But the prosecuting counsel had waited, then: '. . . I put it to you, Mr Gorse, that this is what happened that night at Brighton. When Alison Warren told you she had been in touch with her brother in the RAF, and knew you to be an imposter, *and threatened to expose you*, you flew into a rage, there was a violent argument, and *you killed her*!'

Gorse could not get that exchange of words out of his mind. Those words had seemed frozen, his defence – that he had simply not been there, that somebody else had killed her, leaving it to the prosecution to prove *everything*, as his lawyers had advised – that defence had seemed, suddenly, in ruins . . . At that moment Gorse had realized that what it amounted to was: did the jury *believe* he was capable of killing Alison Warren or not?

Simple as that: My God, simple as bloody that.

There was a sudden blow on the cell door and it

opened. The grizzled warder looked in. He spoke gently, as if to an invalid. 'Jury's back. Up we go, son.'

Gorse nodded and followed him out. Four minutes later it was over. The voice of the clerk intoned, 'How do you find the defendant, guilty or not guilty?'

'Guilty.' The word echoed through the brain of Ralph Ernest Gorse . . . Guilty . . . Guilty . . . *Guilty*.

No, no, no, he wanted to scream. But he knew he could never do that. Not scream. A gentleman never screamed. So he stood quite still, and listened, as the judge, looking remarkably like his old headmaster when he had expelled him all those years ago, asked: 'Before I pass sentence on you, Ralph Ernest Gorse, do you have anything to say?'

Gorse knew that the eyes of . . . well, the *News of the World* were on him, and he straightened his striped tie and stood straight and still and looked back at the judge, and he said: 'I have never given . . . in my relationships with the ladies I've met . . . anything other than what they have wanted . . . They came to me with their eyes open . . . of their own free will . . . They didn't exactly run away from me, any of them, did they? . . . I always felt it my duty to give them a good time . . . and on the whole I think I succeeded . . . And I have at all times tried to behave like an English gentleman . . .'

All he remembered after that was the judge putting on the black cap.

Two weeks later, in a Wormwood Scrubs cell, Gorse sits, wearing a rough, collarless prison shirt and trousers. He has on no tie or shoelaces. He is at a plain table, in this grim, whitewashed room with the small, barred window. An empty chair is in front of the table. There is a dim noise coming from the main prison but in here it is like the noise of a distant sea. A middle-aged uniformed warder stands in the room but he is at the back, behind Gorse. Suddenly, the door opens and Clarice Mannors, in her Wren officer's uniform, carrying her hat, slowly walks in, and sits on the chair opposite Gorse.

Clarice tries to smile, but can't. 'Ralph. Oh God, Ralph.'

'Clarice . . .' Gorse, gallant to the last, offers her a cigarette. She declines. He takes one, lights it with Ronnie Shooter's lighter, and hands her the gold case.

'I'd like you to have that. It's all I have left.'

Slowly, Clarice takes it. She is near to tears, and does not know what to say. Dimly, she feels that somehow it is all her fault. 'Ralph . . . I'd have come before but I couldn't . . . I'm going to the States tomorrow.'

Gorse smiles wanly. To her, he seems very pale. 'Good. That way you'll miss . . . the Show.'

'Oh, my God,' Clarice whispers.

Gorse smiles, the awful wan smile. 'Just think about me. Not too often. Now and then will do.'

Clarice almost breaks down, at that, but doesn't quite. 'Don't be brave . . . Just for me . . .'

Gorse shakes his head. 'I'm not brave, really. Nobody feels much, in here. They have it all worked out so you don't. They've done it before.'

'Oh, my God,' whispers Clarice again.

'It's just the waiting. And there isn't much of that to do, now.'

But there is something that Clarice must know. 'Ralph?' She looks at him a very long moment, then asks, in a low voice, 'Why did you do it? Any of it? For God's sake, *why*?'

Gorse is a long time replying. When he does it is with the same slight, wan smile. 'Because . . . I wanted to be like you.'

Clarice stares at him, shocked. 'But darling . . . *I'm bloody awful!*' And then Clarice is stumbling to her feet and, clasping the gold cigarette case, she is stumbling out of the awful death-house, and out of the prison itself and into a taxi. She is to keep the gold cigarette case all her life.

In Joan's bedroom it is early morning on the fateful day set for the execution of Ralph Ernest Gorse. The curtains are half-pulled. Joan has not slept all night. She is half-sitting up in the bed, staring into space. Mary enters quietly, carrying a breakfast tray and the morning paper. She looks morbidly at Joan as she lays the tray on the bed.

'I'm not hungry.' Joan takes up the *Daily Mail* and pauses before slowly unfolding it. A headline catches her eye immediately. It reads: 'No reprieve for Gorse.' In smaller type she sees the words: 'Execution will be carried out at 8.00 A.M. this morning.' Joan whispers, 'Poor dear Ralph!' She looks around at the bedside clock. It reads five minutes to eight. The loud ticking of the small clock fills the room. Joan does not cry. She simply closes her eyes and whispers, 'Good-bye, dear, dear Ralph.'

Gorse is in the condemned cell at Wormwood Scrubs. He does not know that the hangman is studying him through a peephole in the false wall of his cell. Gorse is standing with his back to the peephole. As he turns, the hangman sees he is holding his last drink, a glass of champagne, a last request approved by the Governor. Anything for a quiet hanging.

Gorse takes a sip. It is, all things accepted, wartime and all that, quite good stuff. The drink – he has had most of the bottle – will numb him. The important thing is to go like a gentleman. 'Good-bye, dear Joan,' he says softly, putting down the tin mug and seeing the warder's eyes flicker to a point behind him. Hearing the noises behind him that mean they are coming for him, that he has only minutes to live now. 'Good-bye dear, dear Clarice . . .' He feels little as his hands are suddenly, roughly, pinioned behind him and a small restraining jacket slipped around his body, but he mutters, 'Not too tight, old boy . . .'

They are the last words of Ralph Ernest Gorse.